W9-BID-713

AT GUNPOINT

Lockhart was dozing on and off, but was aware the man next to him in the stage was not asleep, only faking. He heard Beezah tell the Swede that the fresh team was on the side of the building. At that moment came the sounds of harnessed horses, followed by a gruff "Settle down. We're comin'."

Hooves clattered on the hard ground. Leather creaked. Trace chains rattled. Horses snorted. From around the far corner came the harnessed team of horses.

"*Ja. Ja.* Hurry up. I am behind the schedule an' *du* know *vad* the boss think of that," Norborg said. He then laid the reins over the front edge of the driver's box and prepared to get down.

The two men eased the horses toward the coach, their faces mostly covered by their hats and growing shadows.

"*Vad* is this? Who are *du*? *Var* are..."

"Shuddup and don't move." Both men had rifles aimed at Norborg and Beezah.

Inside the coach, Lockhart awoke, pushed aside the pulled-down leather curtain enough to see what was happening. His hand slid inside his coat to the shoulder holster....

Other *Leisure* books by Cotton Smith:

BLOOD OF BASS TILLMAN
STANDS A RANGER
DEATH RIDES A RED HORSE
DARK TRAIL TO DODGE
PRAY FOR TEXAS
BEHOLD A RED HORSE
BROTHERS OF THE GUN
SPIRIT RIDER
SONS OF THUNDER
WINTER KILL

HIGH PRAISE FOR COTTON SMITH!

"Cotton Smith is one of the finest of a new breed of writers of the American West."

—Don Coldsmith

"Cotton Smith's is a significant voice in the development of the American Western."

—Loren D. Estleman

"In just a few years on the scene, Cotton Smith has made a strong mark as a Western writer of the new breed, telling it like it was."

—Elmer Kelton, Seven-time
Spur Award–winning author

"Cotton Smith is another modern writer with cinematic potential. Grand themes, moral conflicts and courage are characteristic of his fiction."

—*True West Magazine*

"These days, the traditional Western doesn't get much better than Cotton Smith."

—*Roundup Magazine*

"Hats off to Cotton Smith for keeping the spirit of the West alive in today's fiction. His plots are as twisted as a gnarled juniper, his prose as solid as granite, and his characters ring as true as jinglebobs on a cowboy's spurs."

—Johnny D. Boggs, Wrangler and
Spur Award–winning author

"When it came to literature, middle-age had only three good things to show me: Patrick O'Brian, Larry McMurtry and Cotton Smith."

—Jay Wolpert, screenwriter of *The Count Of Monte Cristo* and *Pirates Of The Caribbean*

"From his vivid descriptions of a prairie night to his hoof-pounding action scenes, Cotton Smith captures the look and feel of the real West."

—Mike Blakley, Spur Award–winning author

COTTON SMITH

RETURN OF THE SPIRIT RIDER

LEISURE BOOKS NEW YORK CITY

For my newest little treasure, Jesse Margaret.

A LEISURE BOOK®

July 2008

Published by

Dorchester Publishing Co., Inc.
200 Madison Avenue
New York, NY 10016

If you purchased this book without a cover you should be aware that this book is stolen property. It was reported as "unsold and destroyed" to the publisher and neither the author nor the publisher has received any payment for this "stripped book."

Copyright © 2008 by Cotton Smith

All rights reserved. No part of this book may be reproduced or transmitted in any form or by any electronic or mechanical means, including photocopying, recording or by any information storage and retrieval system, without the written permission of the publisher, except where permitted by law.

ISBN 10: 0-8439-5854-5
ISBN 13: 978-0-8439-5854-6

The name "Leisure Books" and the stylized "L" with design are trademarks of Dorchester Publishing Co., Inc.

Printed in the United States of America.

10 9 8 7 6 5 4 3 2 1

Visit us on the web at www.dorchesterpub.com.

RETURN OF THE SPIRIT RIDER

CHAPTER ONE

The well-dressed, Denver businessman slapped the folded newspaper in his fist against his thigh, unaware of dangerous shadows lurking in the alley ahead. As he stepped from his Black Horse Hotel into the sweet May evening, his mind was heavy with worry. Worry that wouldn't leave in spite of the prosperity that he and his partner were enjoying in this rich and raw town.

His nightly stroll along the boardwalk, from his hotel to his fine saloon three blocks away, would help free him from concerns seeking control of his thoughts. Usually he liked this time alone, away from the constant whirl of activity. This time, though, his mind wouldn't let go of the report that the U. S. Army had taken the field with a major force against the Sioux and Cheyenne. The tribes had not gone to their reservations in the Dakotas and Nebraska as ordered, after government negotiations to purchase the sacred Black Hills had failed last fall.

Why was he worrying? His old friends in Black Fire's band of Oglala Sioux may not have even survived the harsh winter. If they did, would they join Crazy Horse, Gaul and Sitting Bull in the coming holy war? Why should he care? It had been eight years since he left them for good. Another lifetime ago. They had forced him to leave their ways, or so he told himself. His visit to his old friends' village a year ago had felt good, but had also reinforced the rightness of his new life. Except for the lingering bittersweet memories of Morning Bird, the younger sister of his late wife.

None of that mattered. Not really. He was here and life was good. Very good.

Cool night air flirted with his dark hair covering his ears and tugged on his black swallowtail coat. A loose board squeaked under his polished boots. He tugged on the wide brim of his black, low-crowned hat and adjusted his silk cravat.

In the alley ahead, a shadow danced and disappeared.

"Alleys are a good place for trouble. Pay attention, Panther-Strikes," Vin Lockhart muttered to himself, using his Oglala warrior name.

Dark eyes studied the now innocent-appearing opening between buildings. The needed attention shoved his worry into a crouching position inside his head. How many waited? Denver was bubbling with new people, and the bulging settlement built on gold and silver was doing its best to keep up. That many strangers meant some weren't here to earn their wealth. Such activity wasn't new to him. It wasn't to be treated casually either. A cut throat could be the reward of anyone careless enough. Or unlucky enough.

He began to whistle as he walked toward the opening. Loudly. Custer's "Garryowen." He had heard it last fall from some passing soldiers. Whoever was waiting would be hiding now so their surprise would be complete.

As he eased next to the front wall of the general store, Lockhart drew the ivory-handled, short-barreled Smith & Wesson revolver from its shoulder holster under his tailored cutaway coat. Ten feet from the alley itself, he stopped walking, whistled a little longer and ended it abruptly. He waited. Not cocking the gun for fear its sound would alert his would-be attackers.

He waited, still holding the folded newspaper in his left hand. Ten seconds. Fifteen. Finally, curiosity led two shadows from the alley, wondering what had happened to their intended victim.

The first man was thick-bellied; a derby hat squatted on a

head too large for it. Long, stringy hair sprung from its small brim in all directions. In his fist was a long-barreled Colt .45. His too-small coat was slick in places with mud and muck, and torn at both sleeves. Beside him came a thinner shadow, several inches shorter. In his hand glimmered a knife. Both looked down the street first, in the opposite direction of where Lockhart stood.

"Swate Jaysus, where'd hisself go, Big Mike?"

"Dunno, boy. Look smart now. Fat for the takin' he be. Canna let hisself jus' disappear like some wee ghost now, can we?"

"He's right here, boys." Lockhart cocked his revolver and stepped away from the wall. "Drop the weapons."

"Jaysus, Mary an' Joseph, the bugger's got hisself a piece." The heavyset Irishman spun toward Lockhart's declaration and froze with his gun aimed in the businessman's direction.

From the deeper shadows came a third Irish voice, "Sure, an' Dooblin's a fine green this time o' year. Be returnin' the sentiment I am. Ye be droppin' that fancy piece now. 'Tis your gold we be seekin', not your lead, me lordship."

A third bandit! Lockhart cursed himself for not being more careful.

The three hoodlums expected him to meekly comply; their surprise complete, although not what they had originally planned. He counted on that satisfaction to make their initial responses slow. Slow enough.

"All right, don't shoot. Don't shoot." Lockhart lowered the gun as if to drop it, then dove to the ground, throwing the newspaper toward the alley as he moved and fired into its blackness.

The unexpected move startled the hidden bandit and his first shot split the night air above the prone Lockhart, catching the bottom edge of a newspaper sheet. The other sheets cascaded in the air as if trying to escape, before fluttering to the ground again. Second and third shots from Lockhart's revolver quickly went where orange flame in the blackness had been an instant before. An ugly thud followed. And a cry of pain.

Screaming an Irish curse, the heavyset Irishman fired at Lockhart, who had already rolled away toward the street.

The second bandit's bullet snarled its own declaration past Lockhart's ear.

His own pistol roared again into the night. Twice more.

Staggering backward, the gunman slammed into a water barrel shoved against the alley wall. His big gun wouldn't stay upright in his hand and drove its second bullet into the dirt. The robber's mouth sagged open and blood spread across yellowed teeth. He slumped to his knees and fell against the barrel. His eyes glazed and he was still.

Lean-faced with high cheekbones and a nose that hinted at being broken once, Lockhart stood slowly, swiping at his pants and coat to remove the just-acquired dirt.

"Drop the knife. Now," he commanded. "You, in the alley, get out here. I've got one bullet left. One'll take your head off."

Squatting in the middle of the alley, the third bandit held his stomach. Blood covered both his hands. A long-barreled, open-top Merwin & Hulbert revolver lay on the ground in front of him.

"Jaysus, donna shoot. Please. I-I canna. Me stomach's gone, it is. I canna walk. I canna . . ."

Stunned by the violence and its outcome, the shorter hoodlum hesitated, looked at his dead partner beside the barrel, then the third bandit, badly wounded, and let the knife slip from his hands. It clanked against the boardwalk, glistened briefly from a passing moonbeam, and was still.

"A-Ay, mister. Ye be takin' us to wrong. B-Be lookin' for a wee work 'tis all."

"Not much work in an alley. Especially at night." Lockhart walked over to the heavyset bandit and took the smoking pistol from his silent hand.

"S-Sure an' be true it is . . . w-well, 'twere a start, ye see.

On me mither's grave, we dinna mean ye no harm," the hoodlum said. "H-Hungry we . . . I-I be, 'tis all."

From across the street, a yell split the night air. "Over here. The shots came from over here. By the Black Horse!"

Lockhart took a step closer and realized the remaining assailant was a boy of fourteen or so. An Irish lad, barely in his teens, with worn-out brogans and a coat that was more of a rag than a garment. The boy's eyes were light blue with an army of freckles patrolling his cheeks and nose. His lip quivered and he studied the medium-sized man with the angular face of tanned stone, before him, unsure of what to expect.

His two older companions, battle savvy and worldly wise, were dead and dying. For the first time, the lad realized the businessman's tailored coat and vest hid arms and shoulders heavy with muscle. This businessman was more street fighter than either of his older friends. That now was obvious.

"What were these two—to you? Is one your father?" Lockhart motioned first toward the dead man with his gun, then the squatting Irishman.

"No, sir. No pa have I. No ma neither. Dead they be. Sickness. Back in Ohio," the boy said. "Big Mike, well, he just sorta took me along. Teachin' me, he was." He pointed at the dead man.

"Teaching you to steal."

"Well, sure an' it might look so. But hisself also be teachin' me the ways o' findin' silver. We was . . . prospectors." He motioned toward the dying third gunman. "That be Murphy. Lightnin' Murphy, he be called. The why o' it I not be knowin'. Lightnin', that is. He be thinkin' we woulda strike it rich out here. Ay, that he did."

"You have a claim?"

"Well, not so ye would call it such . . . sir."

Three men were running their way. In the front was a broad-shouldered man. A badge caught moonlight and signaled.

"Let me do the talking, son," Lockhart said and waved at the advancing men. "Over here! It's all over."

He returned his revolver to his shoulder holster, deciding to reload it later. He held the bandit's pistol at his side; a thin smoke trail ran up his sleeve from its nose. Walking over to the third Irishman, he took Murphy's pistol in his left hand. A circle of crimson had taken over the thug's midsection.

The Irishman's eyes fluttered open. "Ay, kilt meself ye did, me lordship."

"You didn't give me any choice."

"Ay, our thinkin' it be. Swate Jaysus."

The Irishman's eyes closed as the waves of agonizing pain charged his torn insides again and he started an Irish curse, but his waning strength wouldn't let him finish.

"It's Lockhart!" one of the townsmen declared. "Looks like somebody picked on the wrong fella to rob."

"If it's Lockhart, I'd say so. Almost feel sorry for any bastards who'd be that stupid." The comment came from the taller man in a dark double-breasted coat. In his hand was a short-barreled revolver.

City Marshal Joe Benson slowed his hurrying and came to a stop a few feet from the alley. His experienced gaze took in the situation immediately. Returning his gun to its holster at his hip and covering it with his coat, he asked what had happened.

Lockhart explained the dead man and the wounded one had tried to ambush him with the intent of killing and robbing him. He handed both of the would-be bandits' guns to the marshal as he described the encounter.

"What about this fella?" Marshal Benson asked, shoving one gun in his right-hand pocket and the other, into his waistband.

The other two men joined the lawman and silently assessed the situation. The taller man whispered a comment to the other.

"Oh, him. He's one of my new employees. At the Silver Queen. Dishwasher. Going to be a good one," Lockhart said and put his hand on the boy's thin shoulder. "He and I were headed there, when these fellows jumped us."

The lad stared at him, but said nothing, noticing for the first time that the surprising businessman had blue eyes like he did. Only Lockhart's were narrowed and intense.

Benson turned to the other two men. "Anybody know either of them?"

"Naw. Just more Irish riffraff."

"Good riddance, I'd say."

Lockhart felt the boy tense under his hand; his eyes warned him not to respond, then removed his grip. "Evening, Mr. Galloway. Mr. Hairston. Appreciate your promptness to . . . my situation."

The two businessmen returned the greeting.

Alvin Galloway, the taller man with long, thick sideburns, returned his pistol to his pocket and said, "Glad to oblige, Mr. Lockhart. Our city needs to get rid of this kind of scum."

"I didn't have a choice. They shot at me."

"Damn fools," Galloway said.

Trying to quell a shiver, Benjamin Hairston mumbled, "That could've been any one of us." He looked around to see if the others agreed.

Ignoring the remark, Lockhart cocked his head toward the alley. "The one back there needs a doctor. Gut shot, but he might make it."

"Why bother?" Galloway asked. "Just more trouble. And cost. Hanging's are expensive, you know."

"He needs a doctor, Marshal," Lockhart said. "Do you want me to get Doc Wright?"

"No need for that, Vin. I'll take care of it." Marshal Benson folded his arms. "I'll get Hawkens to send over a couple of Orientals to handle the body."

Lockhart nodded approval of the lawman's decision to

contact the city undertaker and declared, "Marshal . . . gentlemen . . . you are welcome to join us at the Queen, for a drink. On me. Along with my thanks."

Smiling, Benson responded that he would need to take care of the wounded man first, and the body; then he would enjoy a nightcap. The two businessmen readily agreed. They walked away, chatting to themselves about the fight. To the question of payment, Benson said the city would be paying for both expenses. In a whisper, Galloway asked why Lockhart shouldn't have to pay. The marshal's response was a snort.

Stepping away, the boy studied Lockhart and frowned. "What did you mean . . . your employee? I ain't your employee. I ain't nobody's."

"Said you were hungry. Awhile ago. Figured you'd be interested in working to pay for a meal," Lockhart said, redrawing his gun and adding fresh cartridges. "I'm headed to the Silver Queen Saloon. My partner and I own it—and the Black Horse Hotel. You can go with me—if you want. You don't have to." He reholstered the weapon and resumed his walk. "Either way, consider it a second chance."

"Swate Jaysus! That be it? Ye ain't gonna have meself arrested? Or shot? Or hanged?" the boy exclaimed, waving his arms in support of his surprise.

Lockhart turned back. "What's your name, son?"

Inhaling proudly, the boy proclaimed, "Sure an' Sean Augustus Kavanagh I be. Of the Ohio Kavanaghs." He studied the well-dressed businessman. Never had he met anyone like this. Vin Lockhart reminded him of an Indian warrior. Even in his fancy clothes and his blue eyes.

"Good to meet you, Sean," Lockhart said. "I'm Vin Lockhart. Of Denver City." He continued to use the original name of the town, even after it had formally been changed to just "Denver," when the city fathers sought to make it the territorial capital.

Looking down at the planked sidewalk, Sean Kavanagh

said softly, "Better it is that I stay with Lightnin' 'til he settles hisself." He bit his lower lip. "Ay, I shouldna leave Big Mike 'til they come. They, ah, they be . . . me friends." He squeezed his eyes shut and opened them quickly. "What will they be doin' . . . with the body?"

"He'll be buried in the cemetery. Just outside of town," Lockhart said.

"A proper headstone will there be?"

Lockhart shook his head. "Not unless someone pays for it. Just a wooden cross."

The boy hesitated, waiting for more, but the hard man facing him was through with the subject.

Lockhart nodded. "Wait here for Doc Wright—and Hammer Hawkens. He's the undertaker. Cabinetmaker, too. Might just be two Orientals that work for him from time to time, though." He studied the frightened boy. "If anybody asks, tell them I said for you to stay until things were taken care of. Your *friends* don't need to bring you into this. Anymore." His gaze sought the boy's eyes. "You understand?"

"A-Ay, that me does, sir," Sean Kavanagh said and licked his chapped lips again. "Ah, wonderin' I be. Woulda your offer still stand . . . after?"

"Of course it does, Sean, but I expect you to work for your meal."

"Ay, an' ye can be certain I be the best dishwasher ye'll ever see," Sean declared. "Enough for a fine headstone, too, I be hopin' to earn."

"Good. Come to the Silver Queen and ask for me." Lockhart pointed at the knife on the ground. "Don't forget your knife." He turned back and walked away.

The boy watched him. He had never met anyone like this before. Big Mike and Lightning Murphy had told him that all businessmen were weak and foolish. What else had they told him that wasn't true? He picked up the knife, shoved it into his belt and turned toward the dying Murphy.

"T'weren't it the good an' great Wild Bill Hickok hisself

ye just faced? Or were it that crazy New Mexico outlaw, Clay Allison, ye be talkin' of?" The boy stopped and took a deep breath.

No recognition of the boy or his words came from Murphy. Only the fingers on his right hand twitched, held against his bleeding stomach.

"May be there is another such pistol fighter. May be 'tis Vin Lockhart." Sean continued, "Sure, and a blessing it is that ye gave me no gun. Or meself be lyin' in me own blood as ye. Oh, I'm a proud one. Wrong it was to think himself to be weak—an' wrong me be to listen to ye." He paused again and his shoulders rose and fell. "But I forgive ye. Ay, revenge, I must be gettin' . . . for you . . . an' for Big Mike. I promise on me mither's grave."

CHAPTER TWO

Vin Lockhart walked into the night, his mind and body seeking their prefight state. During battle, a cold fire always seemed to fill his soul, driving him on and on. Always attacking. Always charging. Afterward, the roaring ice-flames vanished and his manner became subdued and reflective.

This internal force, whatever it was, had almost killed him in that near-mad attack on a Shoshoni war party years ago. Alone. They had killed his young wife and burned much of the village. His intensity made everything and everyone move in slow motion. It was so then, and only three Shoshoni escaped to raid another day. Stone-Dreamer said it was the Grandfathers grabbing his enemies and holding them in place.

Indeed, it was a remembered fight; the "spirit rain battle" they named it, and a song of the Grandfathers coming to aid him was sung. He knew it was just a foggy day. His fellow

Oglalas thought the awful battle had killed him. They began honoring him as a Grandfather. *Wanagi*. A spirit to be revered. *Wanagi Yanka*, they called him. Rides-With-Spirits. Spirit Rider.

As soon as he was well enough, Lockhart had left, rather than be treated so. He was a man. Merely a man. Not some ghost. He was Panther-Strikes. He knew part of the problem was what his adoptive father had told the village about the great remembered fight. He also knew Stone-Dreamer believed what he said.

"*Hoka hey*. It is a good day to die. I am Oglala. Only the earth and sky live forever. It is a good day to die." The Oglala battle cry tumbled from his lips, followed by the Kit Fox song, "I am a Fox . . . I am supposed to die." He and his one-time brother-in-law, Touches-Horses, had been members of that elite warrior soldier society.

He blinked and realized his thoughts were grinding back to the days when he rode as an honored warrior. He shook his head. Those days were long gone.

That was years ago. Years ago. Now he was a successful businessman. A rich businessman. Yet he continued to think of himself as an Oglala warrior.

Yet recollections of his brief time with Morning Bird were always close in his thoughts. Would Stone-Dreamer say this was another of the Grandfathers' tricks? Or was it love as his best friend and business partner, Desmond T. "Crawfish" Crawford, said? Lockhart and Morning Bird had spent many hours together, as his bullet wounds healed from saving Touches-Horses from an outlaw gang that prized his horse-training skills. That effort had precipitated the return to his old village.

Two couples strolled toward him, chatting and laughing. He stepped to the side, next to the corner lamppost, to let them pass. The coal-oil, yellow light from the street lamp cut across his chiseled face and magnetic blue eyes. A touch of his brim with his hand followed. Automatically. His partner had taught him well the ways of the white man. Very well. His mind was still riding elsewhere. The closest woman's eyes danced with his as she passed. He barely noticed the flirtation.

After they were safely beyond his hearing, the taller man in a top hat and wielding a silver-topped cane whispered, "That's Vin Lockhart. He's a man to avoid. He was a pistol fighter, they say. A dangerous man."

His female companion's expression definitely disagreed, but she said nothing, only glancing back to see if Lockhart was watching her. He wasn't and she was disappointed.

Withdrawing a cigar from his inside coat pocket, Lockhart tried to refocus. He studied the dark city with its glowing street lamps, spotting even now remnants of its boomtown birth. Among brick buildings and multistoried mansions nestled an occasional tent, or basic hut, or split-log cabin. But a city gasworks began operating five years ago, supplying fuel for streetlights, bringing a sense of civic pride and a team of lamplighters to tend them. A year later came city water mains, drawing from deep artesian wells.

In many ways, Denver's evolution mirrored his own, from adventurous warrior, to hardworking prospector, to polished businessman. The last two stages, thanks to his older partner and friend.

Railroads had changed the region. Forever. That and quartz mining. Over the last few years, loose gold had mostly disappeared, except in memory and taller tale. Oh, springtime would bring new optimism and renewed placer mining. But the mountain streams were no longer bountiful sources of wealth. Ore of the day was being ripped from deep within the land. The simple pan had been replaced by shafts and tunnels, as men and machines attacked the rich belt hidden from view. It was an industry involving considerable capital and producing much gain. The nicer weather meant the mines were working in double shifts again. Thousands of workers roamed the streets when not under the land.

His Oglala friends would never understand this raping of Mother Earth. *Aiiee, Panther-Strikes, how could one dare to treat her so?* Their beliefs were so deeply intertwined with nature and natural phenomenon. Sky. Earth. Winds. Lightning. Thunder. All sacred, all a part of *Wakantanka*, the Great Spirit. It made understanding Christianity and even Judaism difficult for him, although he wanted to learn, to understand. That driving curiosity had come from his partner, Desmond T. Crawford, who seemed to be interested in everything and anything.

Of course, Central City-Black Hawk was still richer than Denver. Far richer. The "little kingdom of Gilpin" also claimed a more elegant way of life, epitomized by their fine opera house. Opulence had shown itself dramatically three years ago. Silver ingots had been used to create a special pathway for the visiting President Ulysses S. Grant to walk upon.

And Golden had served as the early territorial capital, until Denver City's politicians finally got the prize in 1865 and immediately shortened the city's name from Denver City to just Denver. It was all about silver now in Denver, too. He smiled. His partner, Crawfish, as everyone called him, had wanted to change the name of the Black Horse Hotel, after they bought it, to the Silver Horse Hotel for that reason. That and the eccentric businessman liked having it match their saloon's name, the Silver Queen.

Lockhart had disagreed. He thought it would be confusing, so the hotel's name remained unchanged.

A passing freight wagon, loaded with timber, caught his attention.

"Evening, Jeremiah," he yelled warmly. It was good to see a familiar face. "Any news from the Dakota Territory?"

The fat-faced freighter cursed at his lead mules to keep them at a walk and yelled back, "Gettin' real scary up there, Mr. Lockhart. Ya heard General Crook's leadin' an army to get them red niggers all rounded up."

Wincing at the derogatory phrase, Lockhart lit his cigar as the freighter reined to a stop, cursing his mules again for their slower-than-he-wished reaction.

As white smoke curled around his face before fleeing into the night, the businessman with the haunting Oglala past said, "Yeah, heard that. Heard the Federals announced any Indian not on the reservation was going to be treated as a hostile, too. Wonder if anyone told the Indians." He watched a fancy carriage with matching sorrel horses prance past the heavy wagon. Both the uniformed carriage driver and the well-dressed female passenger responded to Lockhart's easy wave.

"More gold up thar . . . in them Black Hills . . . than even hyar in the ol' days, I hear tell," the freight driver announced and spat a brown stream of tobacco juice toward the back of his right-rear mule. "An' as many hostiles, all wantin' your scalp. Gold's a hard find I figger. Yah sur, a hard find." He spat again, watching the stream proudly. "Freightin' ain't far behin'."

"*Paha Sapa* is a holy place for them, Jeremiah. They wouldn't understand our fascination for tearing it up," Lockhart said and touched the small pebble hanging from his gold chain stretched across his vest. He had once worn it as a medicine earring when he lived with Black Fire's band.

Among his Denver friends and acquaintances, only Crawfish knew of the small stone's significance. It was Crawfish who had retrieved it after Lockhart had tried to leave the memory behind. The pebble and a choker necklace of white elk-bone and dark blue stones were the only physical things remaining of his wild Oglala past. The necklace had been a wedding gift from Young Evening, his murdered bride, and was kept in a drawer.

A curled family tintype, a small box containing a pale-blue-and-moss-green stone pin that had belonged to his mother, and a Bible were the only items left of his real family before that. Except for mental pieces of yesterday finding sunrise in his mind every now and then. The tintype, box and Bible were kept displayed on the top of his dresser.

He was only eight when they died of cholera and the Oglalas found him and took him with them. "Angry Dog" had been the name they gave him, until he earned a warrior's name, "Panther-Strikes."

"Pa ha . . . sappy, I'd say," Jeremiah Elston yanked on the reins to keep his team quiet. "Heard tell Custer and his Seventh are with Crook. That oughta do it. Custer'll cut them red niggers a new one. Yah sur." He spat a third time, frowning at the thinness of the released juice. "Bringin' in Gatlin' guns, I hear tell. Gonna be a real war up thar. Real soon, I reckon." He shook his head and the misshapen hat brim jiggled. "Glad I be hyar. Yah sur."

"Glad you are, too, Jeremiah," Lockhart said. "Maybe the Indians will move to the reservations peacefully." He had finally broken the habit of repeating a person's full name each time, a habit left over from his Oglala days.

He wondered if his old friends would be seeking their customary spring camping ground in the Black Hills, or would they seek safety farther northwest, perhaps along the Tongue River or at the base of the Bighorns? Or even Rosebud Creek. Stone-Dreamer, in particular, loved returning to that beautiful land of the Black Hills each spring. From a distance the isolated mountain range actually did look black. The sacred center of the world, his Oglala brethren considered it. A place where the spirits and their grandfathers rule. Morning Bird had told him that she loved the Black Hills in the spring as well; a land rich with wildlife and wildflowers.

"Hellfire, that'd be the day. Didn't ya hear Crazy Horse dun bin a'whippin' all them redskins into a lather? Tellin' 'em to leave the reservations." Jeremiah waved his arms. "Hellfire. Them Sioux kin fi't. Made ol' General Reynolds an' his troops go a'packin' from the Powder in March." He laughed and slapped his thigh. "Them redskins even stole back the horse herd them soldjur boys had run off."

"There's no way the Indians can win."

"Nope, reckon not. But nobody's tolt 'em that, I reckon," Jeremiah declared. "Say, ya still got any whiskey at your place?"

Lockhart chuckled, removed and rolled the cheroot in his fingers and returned it to his mouth. "I do. And I've got a tall one waiting for you. On me."

"Count on it, Mr. Lockhart."

Lockhart patted the wagon and stepped behind it as the driver's loud curse and companion snap of his whip started the heavy vehicle again. Lockhart's heart was heavy. He feared Black Fire, Touches-Horses, and the rest would finally decide to ride with Crazy Horse. What choice did they have? Would they be driven from *Paha Sapa*? Had they already? What would he have done, if he were still among them? Marry Morning Bird? Probably. The idea was rich in his mind.

All of the previous victories by the army in the last few years had followed the same strategy—surprise attacks on villages: Harney at Ash Hollow, Chivington at Sand Creek, Connor at Tongue Creek and Custer at Washita. What if they surprised Black Fire's village? Was their only real option to join with the magical war leader Crazy Horse?

He walked on, glimpsing a sign in the window of a gun shop. It was advertising fireworks for sale to celebrate the Colorado Territory becoming a state. July 1, 1876, would be the grand day and a festive parade was planned, along with picnics, contests and speeches, especially one by John Routt, the first governor. Around the city for miles and miles, "colony towns" created by the railroads would also be celebrating. It would truly be a grand time for the entire region. Of course, it would be nothing compared to the American Centennial celebration planned in Philadelphia.

Probably the holiday's events were made even bigger to get the nation's mind off of the scandals riddling the Grant administration. However, Crawfish seemed more fascinated with the destruction of the Tweed Ring political machine in New York. But, then, the eccentric former prospector and teacher was fascinated by many things: politics, science, medicine. Of course, among his keen interests right now was the creation of their hotel's grand restaurant and the upgrading of the hotel itself. His constant and voracious reading produced a stream of ideas. His dream for the hotel's restaurant was a glorious place of crystal glasses, good wines, crisp white tablecloths and napkins and necktied waiters. A mahogany bar would be a centerpiece of the two-story room.

Still, expectations for a memorable time in Colorado were running high and Crawfish was excited about the coming celebration, too. Lockhart was quietly looking forward to the Fourth of July as well. Celebrations like Independence Day and Christmas, especially Christmas, made him feel both happy and sad, at the same time.

"The state of Jefferson," he mumbled to himself. "The state of Jefferson." He had liked the sound of the initial proposed name for the territory, so had Crawfish. But "Colorado" had prevailed in powerful political circles.

Shaking his head, he recalled Crawfish badly wanting their hotel restaurant addition to be ready for this wonderful time. From what Lockhart had seen tonight, the restaurant wasn't going to happen. Too much carpentry and decorating were left to be done. Way too much. Besides that, none of the kitchen equipment had arrived, nor the tables and chairs from St. Louis, nor the chandelier—far larger than the one hanging in their saloon—being freighted from Chicago. However, the grand piano had arrived. It was still uncrated, but it was there, right in the middle of the main room.

He would share the bad news with his old friend, who would storm and yell, and then become philosophical. It was the first day in a long time Crawfish hadn't been at the hotel at all; his momentary attention was on the saloon's books. Lockhart halfway expected Crawfish to have another business idea to share with him. As long as it wasn't mining, he would listen with an open mind.

Certainly, Crawfish's idea to build their own icehouse to keep beer cool had paid off immensely. Miners didn't like warm beer and in the summer months the price of ice was unbelievable.

Two weeks ago, Crawfish had said, in passing, that they should open a bank. Lockhart thought it was a joke at the time. It probably wasn't. Originally, they were going to build on a casino at the hotel, but his friend had decided on fine dining, instead. Lockhart always let Crawfish make those kinds of decisions.

If the money was right.

The Silver Queen Saloon sat on the corner of Blake Street, the beginning of the city's sporting district. Saloons, dance halls, whorehouses and opium dens were gathered in a three-block area. Over on Holladay Street were the whorehouses, from cribs to the single block of more elegant parlor houses, referred to as "young ladies' boardinghouses."

From the scattered yellow lights of town, his gaze went to the spring sky. The Milky Way drew his attention with its spreading whiteness. *Wanagi tacanku*. The Ghost Road, as the Oglala knew it. A special place where the spirits of tribesmen went, after dwelling near their families for a year, to await passage to great hunting lands. His old tribesmen believed the lights were the campfires of the departed. He remembered Stone-Dreamer telling him an old woman guarded the end of the passageway and she assessed the deeds of all who would pass. The good did so; the bad were pushed off the Ghost Road. Those evil spirits returned to the earth to do mischief. He couldn't help wondering if many of his old friends would be walking that road soon.

Crawfish had told him long ago that all men have different views of what was the same God, but that science had long ago proven the existence of the star mass known as the

Milky Way. He also said white men enjoyed stories of creation and the afterlife that were no different in feeling than those of his Indian friends. Mankind was meant to believe because God had created men and women with the ability to think.

Puffing on his cigar, Lockhart tried to free his mind of such wandering. The soft glow from the glass windows of the Silver Queen were a welcoming sight. He wasn't as fond of saloons as Crawfish, but he liked their friendliness. They reminded him a little of an Oglala council fire.

He chuckled to himself that few white men ever thought of Indians as laughing and joking with each other. Some of his favorite tribal memories were of such wonderful times. Men and women gathered in a secluded encampment with bright tepees standing in a sacred circle to hold in the greatness of the universe and to honor it. Laughter ever reverberated from the circle as they worked and played together. Honored each other for bravery. Cared for their elderly. Revered their young. Prayed for their continued bounty.

Would their way of life soon be just a memory?

The fighting with the U. S. Army would not be about counting coup and showing how brave an individual warrior could be in battle.

It would be about death.

He shook his head to push away that idea and entered the saloon. Golden light from hardworking wall lamps tried their best to make everyone forget the day's harsh trials. Men of every manner of dress and station crowded around the gaming tables to try their luck at faro, twenty-one, Spanish monte, chuck-a-luck, poker or roulette. Others lined the grand bar, told lies about their strikes of ore and flirted with the town's fanciest waitresses.

News of gold in the Black Hills was never far from any conversation, taking over from gossip about President Grant's cabinet and their disgraceful actions. Nor were bloodthirsty tales of the Indians who waited there, or now, the U. S. Army tracking them with varying opinions about what would happen when they finally met. Most often, it was that Custer would once more prove his military merit over the savages.

"Where the hell have you been?" the red-bearded man hurried toward him, walking as fast as his stiffened leg and silver-topped walking stick would allow. He had started using the fancy piece a month ago, instead of his cane.

Still more hyperactive professor than serious businessman, "Crawfish" Crawford pushed his wire-rimmed glasses into place on his strawberry nose and waited for his younger friend's response. His full, reddish beard was laced with gray and sporting unruly, wiry hair of several colors. Crawfish's clothes were rumpled, but they usually were. Lockhart wondered if his friend deliberately rolled them into a ball before he put them on.

"Had a little trouble. Outside of the hotel." Lockhart's cigar slid from the left side of his mouth to the right, propelled by an unseen tongue.

"A little? Hop-a-bunny!" Crawfish spoke rapidly; the gap between his front teeth as prominent as always. He always did talk too much and too fast, often incorporating phrases that meant something only to him, or so Lockhart always assumed. Sometimes, Lockhart thought his friend's voice sounded like a bird chirping. Certainly, it was that high-pitched. Rarely, it seemed to Lockhart, did a thought pass through Crawfish's mind that didn't go expressed—and elaborated upon.

"Galloway and Hairston came in here, all blustery and full of themselves," Crawfish said and waved the walking stick. "Nothing new there, of course. Told me about the gunfight. Irish hoodlums. Right? Leprechauns-and-toadstools!" His eyebrows jumped in rhythm to the expression and the questions that followed like a Gatling gun. "Are both of them dead? Did you get hurt? Did you see them coming? Did they shoot first? How did you get your gun out without being shot yourself? Two gunmen! Two! Do we need a guard at the hotel? That kinda stuff's bad for business, ya know. Bedclothes and bullets, no siree."

Lockhart didn't think it was necessary to hire a guard, that he wasn't hurt even though they shot first, that one hoodlum was dead and the other seriously wounded. He looked around the crowded room, to end the discussion and to see if Sean Kavanagh had come. He didn't expect to see him, though, at least not this soon.

"A boy hasn't come in, has he? Looking for me?" Lockhart asked, continuing to look. "Maybe thirteen, fourteen years old? Irish lad. Poorly dressed."

"No. Nobody like that," Crawfish said, his left side twitching slightly and talking with considerable, and typical, speed. "Oh, I gave the two jaybirds, Galloway and Hairston, a free drink. Said you promised them." He studied his younger friend for a moment; there was more to the question about the boy.

"I did. Invited Marshal Benson, too. He was going to take care of the wounded man and the body first." Lockhart pushed back his hat to reveal damp curls. "Got any coffee?"

"Sure do. Just cooked, too."

"Say, I also promised Jeremiah Elston a free whiskey."

"Cock-a-doodle-do, you've been busy with our liquor."

"Right. Busy." Lockhart smiled.

Finally, the red-haired businessman couldn't hold back his curiosity and asked what the concern about the Irish boy was about. Lockhart explained and Crawfish nodded his understanding, but wondered to himself if the lad would appear. He also imagined the youngster would likely be holding a grudge against Lockhart for having killed the two men in his life. But it was clear Lockhart didn't want to talk more about the gunfight or the boy.

Crawfish had never killed a man and hoped he never would have to do so; he also knew from what his young friend had told him before, that killing ate at him, even when there was no choice, and the killed man was evil. Regardless of the circumstances, it was destroying something living and breathing, turning it into earth, taking away dreams and hopes and loves. This wasn't the time to ask more about the gunfight. Later, maybe. Much later.

"How about some ham and eggs? Got some fresh from a farmer." Crawfish waved his long stick toward the billiard room. "He's over there, somewhere."

"Sounds good." Lockhart drew on the cigar and let the smoke find its way into the busy saloon.

"You know that boy . . . he's not going to be your friend, Vin," Crawfish blurted. "He can't. Shoot-a-whistle, you killed his friend. Likely both. He's probably going to want to even the score. That gun-shot Irishman probably told the boy he's got to do it. Before he . . . passed, if he has." Realizing what he was saying, Crawfish looked around, but no one was close enough to hear.

Lockhart's frown came quicker than his response. "What do you think I should've done, Crawfish? Let them arrest him? He's a boy. Just a boy."

"No. No, you did right, son. Still, I wouldn't turn my back on the lad." Crawfish looked away. He wanted to ask Lockhart what he was doing when he was that age as a fledgling warrior, but didn't.

It was time to change the subject.

"Got more to tell about opening a bank." Crawfish pointed with his staff toward their intended table. "Can't wait for you to hear. Worked up a major sweat about it, I did. Goodness-and-Newton!"

Lockhart smiled. "Newton" was the imaginary friend that Crawfish liked talking to, when he first met the eccentric man prospecting for gold. Since their riches were secured, that name had rarely surfaced. It brought an instant rush of memories. Crawfish had taught Lockhart the ways of white civilization, exceptionally good English, superior mathematics, business principles, social etiquette and the like, in exchange for helping work the claim. Skill with weapons came from his time with the Oglalas. Instinct combined with practice and nerve. Crawfish had also taught him the art of boxing, having been the best in his weight class at Yale.

Eventually this interchange had evolved into a full partnership, true friendship and Vin Lockhart had become a gentleman. A very successful gentleman. Along the way, he had also saved his friend's life and recovered their gold from bandits.

Midway to their table, Lockhart saw an army captain at the bar and told Crawfish to go on, that he wanted to speak with the young officer. He walked over, taking his cigar from his mouth as he approached. Crawfish nodded and headed for the small kitchen in the back.

"Pardon me, Captain," Lockhart said to the goateed officer sipping whiskey. "I'm Vin Lockhart. Are you en route to Montana Territory?"

Looking at him with suspicious eyes, the officer laid his glass on the bar's shiny surface. "Why do you ask, Mr. Lockhart?"

Lockhart chuckled and crossed his arms, holding the cigar upright in his left hand. "Guess that didn't sound quite right. I'll try again. Got some family up north, Montana way. Wondered if you knew anything of the situation up there. With the Sioux and Cheyenne." He cocked his head to the side. "Not asking for any army secrets."

"I see." The young officer smiled slightly and said, "I'm Captain Ferguson Blake. Department of the Platte. Stationed in Omaha. I'm on leave, sir."

In a few sentences, it was clear to Lockhart the young officer didn't know as much about the army's surge as he did. The captain was en route to visit his parents in Longmont with an approved absence from departmental headquarters. It quickly became clear to Lockhart why the officer wasn't deemed necessary during this well-publicized push. After listening to Captain Blake's whining dissertation about the consistent lack of properly filled-out forms by field commanders, their foolish approach to handling the hostile Indians, the leadership inadequacies of Crook, Terry and Custer, Lockhart excused himself and headed to the table where Crawfish had just sat.

Two mugs of steaming coffee, an ashtray and a filled sugar bowl with a spoon sticking from it adorned the tabletop. Crawfish lifted his mug in greeting.

"Learn anything from the army boy?"

"Everything that's wrong with the army." Lockhart grimaced and sat.

Studying his friend, Crawfish blew on the mug's surface, sipped it gingerly, and said, "I know you're worried, son. About your . . . friends."

"Well, it's a little silly to worry about something you can't do anything about." Lockhart removed his cigar and laid it in the ashtray, then poured a teaspoon of sugar into his coffee, then another.

"Maybe they're already on the reservation." Crawfish ignored his friend's remark. "Heard a bunch are."

Lockhart was silent, drinking from the sweetened mug and returning it to the table.

"You told me Black Fire was a savvy leader. And Touches-Horses, he was, too." Crawfish looked away at the wall. "What about Stone-Dreamer? Wouldn't that ol' boy preach . . . peace?" He grinned impishly. "And what about that little gal you were so smitten with? In the village. Morning Bird, wasn't that her name? What about her? Or is she just another forgotten love, like Mattie Bacon?"

Lockhart's face cracked into a wide smile that didn't reach his eyes. "Crawfish, you rascal. You really want to talk about this, don't you?"

"No. I want you to."

Lockhart shook his head and ran his forefinger around the lip of his mug. "What you call peace, they see as something far worse than death."

Crawfish nodded, hoping for more.

"How can men who lived free, with honor and courage, with the buffalo and the wolf as their friends," Lockhart said softly, "how can they stand behind some damn fence and be treated like children? Or dogs?"

"They don't have a choice, Vin."

"Yes, they do. They can fight."

As a refutation of that argument, Crawfish immediately began a recitation of what the Indians were facing. Newspapers had been blaring the details for weeks. Three full columns, under the overall command of General Alfred Terry, were on the march with two objectives: find hostiles and kill them. Their three-directional pincer was to slam through the Indians' hunting lands and meet in its center, close to the mouth of the Little Bighorn River. A steamship, the *Far West*, was accompanying the massive pursuit, navigating up the Missouri, then the Yellowstone, up the Powder, the Tongue, the Rosebud, and the Bighorn rivers. Its objective was to establish a supply base for the army up-river.

General John Gibbons was leading his column down from Montana Territory; General George Crook was coming from Wyoming; Terry was marching from North Dakota. Actually, Lt. Colonel George Custer had the field command of this group. The regiment itself was supported by three Gatling guns, 150 supply wagons, a herd of cattle, 175 pack mules, and 34 Indian scouts, most of them Arikara.

When he finished, Crawfish's left cheek twitched and his eyes found Lockhart's gaze. The answer he sought was easily read; Lockhart knew his old Oglala band would not go willingly to the reservation. No way.

"Then they will choose death. As warriors."

"Death's not much of an answer, Vin. That's a mighty big territory up there." Crawfish's voice was soft. "Ever think they might keep out of sight? Ya know, just keep moving. Keep away from those army boys." He inhaled deeply before continuing. "Shoot-in-the-air, all those wagons and stuff. They'll make a lot of noise. Won't move that fast either. Might be they're over Deadwood way—an' not straight north at all."

"Hotel restaurant won't be ready for the celebration." Lockhart's comment meant further discussion of his Indian friends would not be coming from him. "Maybe a month out."

"Yeah, figured as much. Three-of-a-kind-beats-two."

Lockhart shook his head again at the expression, surprised at his friend's understanding. Obviously, Crawfish had been to the hotel today, before he did.

After the two men drank their coffee in silence for a minute, Crawfish started in again. This time on the idea he had brought up earlier: a bank. Three local businessmen had approached him about Lockhart and Crawfish investing in the creation of a new financial institution in Denver. Their share would require selling one of their lesser properties, but not the saloon or hotel. The other businessmen also wanted Crawfish to serve as the bank's president. The last element of the offer was delivered with a giggle and the exclamation, "Hogwash-and-belly-beans!"

"That what you want to do?"

"Ya know, I think I do." Crawfish wiggled the tip of his forefinger in his coffee. "Been looking for a new challenge. After the hotel restaurant's up and running." He looked up. "And I like making money. Didn't have any for a long time."

"Me neither."

Crawfish chuckled. Turning slightly red with enthusiasm, he outlined how a bank would be set up, how J. R. Parks, their head of gambling, could take over full management of the saloon, and the hotel itself was already being run well by C. W. Damian. They would need someone good to run the restaurant, however.

Lockhart listened without commenting. He was considering moving from the Denver House where he had a room to one in their hotel when the redecorating was finished; Crawfish owned his own home, but Lockhart hadn't yet decided it was something he wanted. In the back of his mind, not yet spoken of, was the thought of starting a horse ranch somewhere outside of town. Good horses were needed everywhere. Maybe he could convince his former brother-in-law, Touches-Horses, to join him. Maybe Stone-Dreamer would come and live out his last years there.

Maybe Morning Bird. The thought startled him. What made him think she would be interested? Could an Indian woman live among whites? Would she want to? He couldn't bear the idea of his friends being cooped up on a reservation, but the idea of their dying was worse.

The dream of a horse ranch—and all of its possibilities—grew daily in his mind. It was never far from taking over his thoughts. Now, though, it triggered an uneasiness in his stomach. The concept was intricately connected to his Indian friends and he was certain they were in trouble. Or would be soon. But it wasn't practical, bringing Indians to the white man's world. It would only produce pain. For them. But how could such a situation be more painful than rotting on a reservation?

"Hey, you know that new minister, the yellow-haired fella?" Crawfish said, returning his attention to his coffee and changing subjects.

Lockhart nodded. He had met Dr. Hugo Milens on the street last week. The preacher's appearance reminded Lockhart of a coyote. Not the wolf. The Oglala knew the wolf to be a highly intelligent being. A friend. A bringer of messages from the spirits.

Dr. Milens gave him the sense of something at home watching others from the shadows. Waiting for the right opportunity.

"Well, he's a mesmerist, a doctor of Egyptology," Crawfish said. "You know, a spiritualist." He rubbed his nose energetically. "You know, one of those fellas who calls up . . . ghosts. Ah, spirits."

"Interesting."

"Yeah. Maybe we should sit in on one of his sessions. Wouldn't that be a kick! Betsy-bell-and-locomotion!"

CHAPTER THREE

Taking another long swallow of hot liquid, Lockhart was drawn from his conversation with his best friend by a voice beyond the normal cacophony of bar talk. At the bar, a muscular young miner, quite proud of his frame, was loudly critical of his perceived slow response of Jimmy Helt, the Silver Queen's oldest bartender. The miner's comments were increasing in repetition and intensity.

Helt was patient and cheery, as usual, but the customer was on the edge of surly and definitely looking for someone to challenge him.

Slamming his empty glass on the bar, the miner growled, "Come on, you old fart, I said I wanted another goddamn bottle. You so damn old, you can't hear?"

A middle-aged, slump-shouldered businessman, sitting on the adjacent stool, told him to be patient and the younger man shoved him off the stool.

Lockhart put down his coffee mug and was on his feet.

Behind him, Crawford urged gentleness. "It's all right, Vin. Let Jimmy handle it. It's nothing. He was just foolin'. Come on now. You've already had one fight tonight. Isn't that enough?"

Lockhart didn't acknowledge his friend's observation. Calmly, he helped the disheveled customer to his feet, then sat down at the vacant stool on the opposite side of the puffed-up young miner.

In his late twenties, the man's dress was a mixture of clothes, all filthy; a once-red flannel shirt was pulled mercilessly by his enlarged biceps and thickened chest, signs of consistent hard work. His was a harsh face with a nose like a potato stuck in the middle of pockmarked cheeks. His scarred knuckles bore the signs of fistfights.

The frightened businessman brushed himself off and went hurriedly toward the door. Crawford met him there and urged him to stay with a drink on the house. The man glanced back at the miner and saw Lockhart engage him, paused and accepted the offer, moving to the far end of the bar.

"You're kinda hard on that old man, aren't you?" Lockhart said in a low, friendly voice.

His eyes blazing, the young miner swung in the stool toward Lockhart. Heavy eyebrows with a life of their own arched defiantly. His mouth became a snarl readying itself to spout more defiance.

The blur of Lockhart's hand was missed by everyone, except Crawford. Lockhart's right fist grabbed the combative miner's testicles and squeezed hard.

The younger man's whiskey-laden eyes widened and his face shattered into white fear. "I-I d-didn't . . ."

"My friend's worried that I might get violent. You know, slap you silly in front of everyone here. But that's not going to be necessary, is it?" Lockhart's voice was a razor through the saloon's thick air. "I've already had to kill two men tonight. I'm not in the mood for bad manners, like yours."

The obnoxious man nodded negatively. Sweat lines raced down his frozen face. He tried not to move, but his half-raised arms flapped slowly like a giant bird. The only sound from him was a teeth-locked groan.

"I can tell you need a fight—and I always want to help my fellow man when I can," Lockhart said. "Kinda like the idea myself. Might help clear my head. I'm a lot older than you.

Smaller, too. That ought to fit your needs about right. How about you and me stepping outside? It's nice outside. Real nice. Spring and all."

"I-I d-didn't mean nothin'. H-Honest, I'm sorry. R-Really, I'm sorry . . ."

"Too late for that, partner. I don't think you mean it anyway," Lockhart said. "Pay your bill, add a nice tip, then walk out. I'll be right behind you."

As Lockhart released his hold, the miner looked like he was going to vomit. He scrambled for coins in his pocket and left most of them. Sliding from the stool, the stunned bully took two steps toward the door and spun toward Lockhart with a vicious haymaker aimed at his head.

Lockhart's left forearm met the oncoming blow and deflected it past himself, ducking with the strike. Lockhart's right fist disappeared into the bigger man's stomach with a fury that drove away most of the breath there, leaving a painful fire in its place. Lockhart's left fist followed to the same spot an eyeblink behind and extracted any remaining air. Another thundering right followed like a cavalry charge into the stunned miner's gut.

The icy fury swelling within Lockhart translated into the beginning of an unneeded, finishing kick. But a scream that found no sound stopped him as the miner held his midsection and retched. Lockhart stepped aside to avoid the projectile vomit. The bent-over man grabbed at his stomach and wobbled sideways. The rage within Lockhart disappeared almost as swiftly as it arose.

Somewhere in the back of the room came a long gasp, followed by: "Did you see that?" "That bastard's been asking for it ever since he came in." "Looks like he picked on the wrong guy." "Yeah, looks that way. Who'd want to mess with Lockhart anyway." "Is that Lockhart?" "Yeah, that's Lockhart."

Lockhart put his hand on the man's heaving back and said, "You sit over here, until the pain goes away." His voice was comforting.

With that, he guided his groaning adversary to a bentwood chair. It didn't match the other three pushed around one of the eight square tables in the open area of the saloon all filled with customers. No other table had an empty chair; the rest sported patrons in various stages of curiosity, relief and amazement. Immediately, the half-dazed miner sank into the chair and put his head on the table, both hands remained grasped tightly to his midsection.

"When you've caught your breath, you're going to clean up that mess, right?" Lockhart asked, standing over the young man who looked up at him with glazed, fearful eyes and whitish spittle in the corner of his mouth.

"Y-Yes, sir, I-I will."

"Good. I'll bring over a bucket and a mop," Lockhart said. "After that you're gone. I don't ever want to catch you here again. Understand?"

"Y-Yes, sir."

Nervous chatter rushed into the entire saloon as Jimmy Helt hurried to Lockhart's side, looked first at the miner, then at the calm saloonkeeper.

"Goodness, Vin, I'm sorry you had to step in."

"I'm the one that's sorry. I was trying to get him outside."

"Shall I go get the marshal?"

"No, he's busy . . . with something else," Lockhart said. "He'll be along later, I think."

"I know." Helt chuckled as Lockhart moved toward his table in the corner. "Vin?"

"Yeah, Jimmy?"

"Thank you. That was getting bad. He was in here yesterday and roughed up two of our regulars. They haven't been back."

"He won't be back either. But he'll clean up his mess first."

"Oh, that's okay. I'll take care of it," the bartender said, touching Lockhart's right arm.

"No, it's a good way to learn some manners. You got a mop and a bucket?"

"Sure, Vin, sure." Helt shook his head in agreement and scurried to the kitchen, returning quickly with a damp, gray mop and a tin bucket full of soapy water. Crawfish was hurrying behind him.

Lockhart motioned and Helt handed them to the miner. Taking both without hesitation or looking at either man, the young miner bit his lower lip and wobbled to the area where his retching occupied a prominent place.

First, hesitating, then slowly dipping the mop into the bucket and out again, he began to wipe up the forced-out remains. He looked up once to see Lockhart's hard stare and resumed his task vigorously. Two well-dressed men stepped beside Lockhart, patted him on the shoulder, and walked on toward a beckoning poker table.

As they left, an attractive waitress with long blond-streaked hair and a tightly fitted skirt came up to thank Lockhart for getting rid of the miner. She said the young man had been annoying her and the other waitresses earlier, and she wanted to thank him for stepping in. Her angular face invited Lockhart for a more personal show of gratitude.

"Thank you, Beula," Lockhart said and smiled easily. "But I was trying to get him to leave."

"I'm sure he wishes he did," she said, her eyes seeking his attention. Her examination of Lockhart stopped at his belt buckle, then returned to his dark eyes. She touched his forearm and held it. "Did he—"

"No, no, he was too busy with other things," Lockhart interrupted.

"Sure. I understand. Guess I'd better get back to work." A smile again filled her face.

Lockhart returned the smile as she gave an exaggerated curtsy and walked away. Returning to her assigned area, she glanced back and was disappointed to see Lockhart wasn't watching. He was talking with another patron at the bar and slapped him on the back in a warm exchange. The Silver Queen resumed its conquest of the night.

Meanwhile, Lockhart said something quietly to the young miner no one else could hear. The pale man shook his head in exaggerated agreement and rose to leave, apologizing over and over as he did.

In the far corner of the saloon, sitting quietly with several others, a rough-looking stranger watched. Mostly, he watched Vin Lockhart. Chewing on an unlit cigar, the tall man stood slowly and headed directly toward Lockhart, who was now talking with an agitated Crawfish at the corner of the bar.

"Lockhart, my name's Fisher. I'm the manager of the Rocky Mountain Freight Company. Like a word with you."

At the bar, Crawfish eyed his friend with concern. Cooking was forgotten for the moment. Surely, this stranger wasn't related to the trouble with the miner, or the earlier violence in the street. Surely. His younger partner seemed undisturbed by such violence. Or he hid it well. Was it just his warrior upbringing or was there something else that made Vin Lockhart so ferocious when threatened? He had heard the stories about Hickok and his fearless eyes. Was his friend of the same cut? Truly dangerous. Truly fearless.

Stepping toward the stranger, Lockhart held out his hand. "Heard about you, Mr. Fisher. Good to meet you. Please call me Vin."

Crawfish couldn't help smiling. Lockhart's manners made most people think he had been educated at some exclusive eastern school. His friend had, indeed, been his best pupil.

"Vin, it is. Make mine just Bill." Fisher took Lockhart's hand and shook it. "I'd like to hire you to ride guard on our freight wagons. We're hauling out some serious ore. Got twenty or so rigs goin' all the time. Supplies in and ore out. I need a man of your reputation to see that we get to the mint. One of my rigs was hit last week."

A thin smile began to creep across Lockhart's face. He glanced at Crawfish, then back to Fisher. "That's mighty flattering, Bill, but no thanks."

"You haven't heard my offer yet."

"No, I haven't. But my gun isn't for hire," Lockhart said. "Don't know what you might have heard about me, but I defend myself when necessary. That's all." He waved his arm toward the main part of the saloon. "I'm sure there are many good men who'll be glad to oblige you."

Shaking his head, Fisher chomped down on his cigar, before responding. "Yeah, there are. I need somebody special. Even thought about tracking down Hickok and seeing if he'd be interested." He removed the cigar. "See, I don't want trouble. I want somebody who nobody'll want to try. That's what I want." He placed a heavy hand on Lockhart's shoulder. "I want you."

Lockhart's eyes followed the movement, then returned to Fisher's face. "Sometimes, we don't get what we want."

"A thousand dollars a month—and you can hire whoever you want to help you—and I'll pay them three hundred apiece."

Reaching over to remove Fisher's hand, Lockhart smiled again. "I'm sure you'll get somebody real good for that kind of money. Bill." His attention was drawn to the saloon door where Sean Kavanagh stood, looking wide-eyed. "Excuse me, Bill, I see a friend I've been expecting. Good luck to you."

With that, Lockhart spun away and headed toward the boy.

Crawfish chuckled and said, "Well, sir, I'd tell you to try again, but I know Vin. He's not going to take that kind of job. No offense, but he's just not going to do that."

Jamming his cigar back into his mouth, Fisher glowered at the red-haired man. "I didn't get where I am takin' no for an answer."

Folding his arms, Crawfish chuckled. "Hickok, huh?"

"Yeah, him or Lockhart. Or Jean-Jacques Beezah, that black gun from Orleans."

"I read where Hickok is with Cody and, eh, Texas Jack Omohundro, in some play," Crawfish said. "Back East. Somethin' Colonel Judson put together. You know, he goes by Ned Buntline—in his writing."

Fisher's face became a smirk. "Well, if you really wanna know, Hickok's headed this way. Left the show. Didn't like all that silly crap. Tried putting together an expedition to the Black Hills. Miners, you know. He'll be in Cheyenne soon. So's Cody, I hear. Scouting for the Fifth." His lower lip protruded and stayed there. "That's where Beezah is, too."

"Did I hear Hickok got married?" Crawfish asked.

"Yeah. March. In Cheyenne." Fisher chuckled. "Wild Bill broke a lot of ladies' hearts."

"I see. Wonder if his new bride will join him? In Deadwood?"

"Naw. Heard she was staying in Cincinnati. 'Til he makes enough to buy them a house." The hard man shook his head to emphasize the point.

Crawfish glanced around the crowded room. "You seem to know a lot about Mr. Hickok."

Fisher inhaled and his chest extended. "It's my business to know people who can help me—or hurt me."

Crawfish nodded and returned his gaze to the freighter. "Well, you don't know Vin Lockhart very well, if you think he'd be interested."

Fisher's right eyebrow popped upward in anticipation of responding.

Crawfish decided it was time to change the subject. "How would somebody get away with a bunch of twenty-mule team wagons loaded with silver anyway? Wouldn't that be easy enough to track?"

This time Fisher frowned and his eyebrow arched defiantly. "Yeah, probably so. I just don't want anybody trying. There's a gang that's hit a bunch of stagecoaches. Don't want them getting greedy and lookin' my way."

Pushing his eyeglasses back on his nose, Crawfish blinked, muttered "Good luck" and headed to the front door, where Lockhart and the boy were talking. He didn't hear Fisher say, "I want Lockhart."

"Sean, I was just going to have some eggs and ham.

Would you join me?" Lockhart said to the wide-eyed youngster.

The boy's eyes were all the answer needed.

"What say, we eat and, if you're interested, we can check out a job in the kitchen." Lockhart nodded toward their table in the back.

Sean bit his lower lip and stared at his worn boots. "M-me not be havin' any . . . coin."

"You don't need any. Right now. I invited you to join me. Besides, I don't like eating alone." Lockhart pointed at the advancing Crawfish, leaning on his walking stick, and proclaimed, "Sean, this is my good friend and business partner—and soon-to-be bank president, Desmond Crawford."

"Crawfish, boy. Crawfish to my friends," the red-haired entrepreneur bellowed. "Welcome to the Silver Queen." He held out his hand.

Hesitating, the gawky lad took his hand and shook it slowly at first, then hardily. "Honored to meet ye. Sean Kavanagh, me be."

"Hop-a-bunny, Vin. With all that commotion, I forgot all about the eggs and ham. Still want them?"

"You bet. Over easy."

"Sean, you can help me," Crawfish said. "I want to hear all about you. Then we'll eat."

"Be careful, Sean," Lockhart teased, "he'll have you working for his new bank before you can say 'silver.'"

CHAPTER FOUR

From his boardinghouse window, Vin Lockhart saw the sun bring a new morning to a quiet Denver. He didn't want to; it was his mind's idea. He grabbed his watch lying on the bedside table, along with his Smith & Wesson revolver. It was 5:20.

He lay on the wood-framed bed in his sparsely decorated room and stared at the pink halo brightening against the dark mountains. Stone-Dreamer's stories about *Wi*, the Sun, filled his half-awake thoughts. He let them come and saw again the intense shaman in a full-length, white elkskin cape worn over his customary white buckskin shirt and leggings. On his head was a winter wolf's head with owl and eagle feathers dangling from the side of the whitish hide. Across his shoulder was a large white pouch with long straps. In it were many sacred stones.

The holy man, his adoptive Oglala father, had told him often of the mysteries of the universe. How *Wakantanka* represented all sixteen supernatural beings and powers. In the sacred language, this was known as *Tobtob*. Four-four. He held up four fingers and told the young Lockhart, then known as Angry Dog, that there were four groups of powers; each with four beings. The superior group was *Wakan akanta*. In this foursome were *Wi*, the Sun; *Skan*, the Sky; *Maka*, the Earth; and *Inyan*, the Rock. Each power had an associated power. The moon was the sun's associated power. Wind was the sky's; Falling Star, the earth's; and the Winged-Being, the Thunder-Being was the rock's.

In Lakota creation myths, the Sun's wife was the Moon. When they separated, night and day was created. Falling Star was their daughter who eventually took up with South Wind. Tributes must always be given in the order in which the directions were born—west was first born, then north, followed by east, and lastly by south.

He blinked and Stone-Dreamer was gone. In his place was the smiling face of Morning Bird. He bit his lower lip and blinked her away. Yet his mind wandered to the Sun Dance where selected warriors were honored by being chosen to dance for the tribe's well-being for the coming year. The scars on his chest were a reminder of that ordeal for him. A time of great honor.

He was again riding beside his best friend, his *kola*, and

former brother-in-law, Touches-Horses, the warrior with the gift of training great horses. He heard Touches-Horses tell him again that they were true brothers in deed, in friendship. Brother-friends. Touches-Horses was Young Evening's brother.

"You honor him every day, Panther-Strikes," Touches-Horses said. "The *wasicun* firestick is magic in your hands. You have already led three successful war parties. Only Bear-Heart and Thunder Lance are seen as greater warriors—and they are much older. You are also *skaiela*, a white speaker. And you can talk the words with our *wasicun* brothers. And you were chosen for the Sun Dance at the gathering of all Lakota. Any father would be proud of such a son."

"But I do not hear the stones sing."

He sat up in bed and let his bare legs slide over the side. It was Sunday. The Lord's Day, so the town proclaimed. His Oglala friends believed every day, every hour, was to honor *Wakantanka*. Every step was, therefore, sacred; every action, a prayer.

From the beginning of their relationship, Crawfish had shared Bible stories and the white man's various religions with him. Lockhart hadn't embraced any of them, however, although he vaguely remembered his white parents reading the Bible often and praying. Mostly, though, it was because he couldn't imagine an all-powerful God being locked up in a small building. Deeply engrained in him was the belief that God, whatever His name, was everywhere and watched over all creatures and all things. That was Stone-Dreamer's teaching.

So was the idea that certain stones sang to certain men and women worthy to hear them. And the concept of spirit helpers that came to a warrior in a vision, helpers that would come to the warrior's aid or help make him battle worthy. Or the understanding that a man's words reached God while smoking a special pipe. Or that the eagle alone could fly to *Wakantanka*. Or that the wolf would act as a messenger with the underground people. Or that the meadowlark spoke the Oglala language.

When he prayed, it was definitely a mixture of Indian and white ways and words. Always though, he ended with a sprinkle of tobacco as a tribute to the spirits. Always.

Lockhart lifted his legs and wiggled his toes. He would feel better after washing and shaving. Sleep was out of the question. He stood and watched a timid shadow flinch as sunlight crept closer to the windowsill. He rolled his shoulders and remembered that Sean Kavanagh had gone home with Crawfish to sleep; his partner had insisted since he had an extra bedroom. Three to be exact.

Maybe he would join them for breakfast at Crawfish's house. It was a fine, gabled home in one of the better residential areas of the town. His home and a silver-adorned carriage with matching black horses were the older man's early purchases after they struck it rich. A fancy stove and bathtub soon followed.

Lockhart hadn't purchased a permanent residence. Yet. It wasn't something he wanted. Crawfish had invited him to live at his house—or certainly he could stay at the hotel. Lockhart liked time alone. Silence was holy, to his old Indian friends. That's when a man was closest to the Great Spirit. He felt the same way. The boardinghouse suited his needs. So would the hotel. However, living there would place him in a position of managing it, even without the title or the responsibility. He didn't want that. He would be bored quickly by the repetition. In his heart, he was an Oglala warrior, even if he didn't want to admit it.

A look outside told him the day was going to be a handsome one. He decided to walk to his friend's house. As he stepped to the cracked mirror above his dresser, he let his mind return to last summer. He had returned to the tribe briefly, riding with Touches-Horses after rescuing him from Virgil "Vinegar" Farrell. The man and his gang had captured

Indians and were forcing them to train horses for sale to the army. Warriors from Black Fire's band had come to the Silver Queen to ask him to save his friend. It had been a shock to see his past again. His first reaction had been angry denial.

Five other warriors were saved as well; none from Black Fire's tribe however. Afterward, he had told his adoptive father, Stone-Dreamer, that he had heard the stones sing. At least, he thought he had. There had been a faint murmur in his pocket, where he kept the small pebble earring that now hung from his watch chain. When he reached for it, the pebble slipped from his grasp and he bent over to catch it. A bullet missed him. In the ensuing gunfight, he shot Farrell and his right-hand killer, Valentine. His own wounds were treated by Touches-Horses and, later, healed by Stone-Dreamer. The old holy man had been visibly pleased to hear his story of the stone.

His thoughts immediately fled to an even earlier time, just after he had received his spirit-guide vision of the fearless mountain lion.

"Father, I have seen beyond. Will you teach me the songs of the stone?"

"My son, I cannot teach you this. They are powerful songs."

"I know, my father. I know the *inyan* are the most ancient of people. I know they are very wise. I am ready to hear the songs of the stones."

"The stones will decide when you are ready. If ever. The songs of the stones come only to a few. The stones choose. Not the man."

The memory splintered and faded. He wandered across the room to the cracked mirror above his ornately carved dresser. On its top were an old family Bible, a daguerreotype of his parents on their wedding day, and a small box containing his mother's pin, which he wore only on special occasions. They were the only things remaining from his early childhood, before the Indians found him beside a sod hut; his parents and sister were dead from cholera.

Resting among the earlier mementos were two small cardinal feathers. One was male and crimson; the other, female and cinnamon. Morning Bird gave them to him when he left the village. It was "remembrance magic," she said with a tearful smile. She called the cardinals "spirits of the morning" because she often saw them on morning walks alone, and with Lockhart. She was drawn to their mating for life—and the male cardinal's fierce protection of his mate and his territory from other cardinals—and the female cardinal's caring ways, singing in her nest. She was named after them, by her parents.

He didn't need feathers though, or anything, to remind him of her love, but there was something about them that fascinated him. Every time he saw them, their last moment together came to him, more intense than the last.

After pouring water into a white basin from a matching pitcher, he washed and shaved. Today, he chose a herringbone suit, made for him by Louis Knowles, the tailor. A maroon vest contrasted with the gray of the suit; his silk cravat was striped in shades of gray and black. For a moment he thought about not carrying a gun, but last night's violence was a grim reminder that Denver was a long way from being safe. He buckled the shoulder holster in place, and walked over to the bedside table where his revolver still lay.

A check of the loads satisfied him and he shoved the weapon into the leather. His suit coat covered the weapon nicely. He retrieved his watch from the bedside table, checked the time once more, closed the lid and slid the timepiece into his vest pocket and attached the chain to the inside of the other pocket.

"Wonder if Crawfish will have coffee on?" he asked himself. "Probably. And he'll have young Sean reading the newspaper. Or working in his garden." He chuckled.

As he left the room, he grabbed a wide-brimmed Stetson.

It was gray. After a stop at the outhouse in the back, he walked back into the Denver House. The sun was still playing hide-and-seek with the land.

"Well, good morning, Mr. Lockhart. You're certainly about at an early hour," Mrs. Arbuckle called as he entered the back door, adjacent to the kitchen where she was working.

Touching his hand to his hat brim, he paused in the doorway. "How are you, Mrs. Arbuckle? You're up early yourself—and working hard I see."

Turning from the large bowl on the counter, her smile invited him to come into the small kitchen. "I've got to, if I'm going to get yo'all fed—before church. That new spiritualist, Dr. Hugo Milens, is preaching this morning. You know, a doctor of Egyptology. At the Methodist church, he will be." Her wide face was slightly reddened from the heat of the stove.

"I won't be at the breakfast table this morning, Mrs. Arbuckle," he volunteered. "I have a meeting across town. With my partner. You know . . . Mr. Crawford." He almost said Crawfish and he knew the woman was quite formal in ways and wouldn't appreciate a nickname like that. Any nickname, for that manner.

She stiffened and the smile left her face for an instant, before reappearing in a more stilted manner. "We will miss you, of course." She swallowed and added, "I . . . We . . . always enjoy your observations about our fair city. Will you be joining us for Sunday dinner? Chicken and dumplings, I plan. One of your favorites, I believe."

"That sounds good, but I'd better say no. I have business outside of town." He continued out the door, before she could ask him about the story she had heard from another boarder about trouble outside of the Black Horse Hotel last night.

Outside, he walked along the cobblestoned walkway that led to the street. It was a good day to stroll over to Crawfish's, he told himself once more. Lockhart hoped the older man would be up and have coffee made. At least that. Then he remembered Crawfish had bought a cow and was keeping the animal in his backyard. Along with a small chicken coop. His neighbors weren't too happy about the gathering, but the former prospector, now businessman, didn't care. He could have fresh milk and fresh eggs whenever he wanted. The eccentric ex-professor was always fascinated with new things, new ideas, new adventures. That's why the bank was high on his mind right now. That and the chandelier coming from Chicago. And a wine cellar at the restaurant. In another year, it would be something else.

In a way, Lockhart envied Crawfish's enthusiasm for life. It was a wonderful trait, one that his former brother-in-law also shared. That thought returned him to an idea that had been nurturing itself in his mind. A horse ranch. Especially if Touches-Horses would join him in the venture. It would keep him from the awfulness of the reservation. Maybe Stone-Dreamer would join them. Would the army leave them alone? Why would the army have to know? Morning Bird . . .

When he was honest with himself, the daily chores of owning a saloon and a hotel, as well as their other properties, didn't grab him in the way it did Crawfish. Oh, he liked the wealth they brought, but something was missing. Maybe he could find it in raising horses. Good horses. The market for them was strong and growing. Why not? What would Crawfish say? He would be welcome to join him in the enterprise. Of course.

Would he? Or maybe Lockhart should sell his share of their other businesses back to him. To raise the money needed for the ranch.

He chuckled. "Maybe I'll be the first man to borrow money from the new bank." He shook his head and walked on.

Then he stopped.

At his feet, a spider crept across the walk. Slowly. Purposefully.

"Well, well, my little friend. Are you related to the great *Inktomi*?" He leaned over to watch the spider and was surprised at his own words.

Inktomi, the Spider, was the subject of many Oglala creation myths. He was the son of Rock and the Winged, and the older brother of *Iya*, the Giant who carried the cold from the north. Stone-Dreamer enjoyed telling the stories as much as he had enjoyed hearing them as a boy.

Inktomi, the trickster, playing tricks on man and animals, while often the prank ended up on himself. *Inktomi*, the transformer, responsible for giving shape to animals and naming them, as well as transforming himself into any shape. However, he preferred becoming a coyote or a handsome warrior. *Inktomi*, the creator, who gave man culture, time, space and language. *Inktomi*, the enticer, who led man out of his subterranean world and onto the earth, then made it so man couldn't find his way back. *Inktomi*, the depriver, who deprived the *wasicun* from having any form, after they had asked for and been granted invisibility. He made it so they had to assume the shape of something else whenever they wanted to communicate—with anything.

Lockhart stood, transfixed on the tiny object below him, lost again in yesterday. He grinned and mumbled, "I remember a story—from Bear-Heart—about *Inktomi* carrying his huge penis around in a box!" He laughed out loud. "Oh, and the time *Inktomi* roasted his own butt!" He leaned over again and slapped both hands on his thighs, seeing the brawny Bear-Heart telling Spider stories and laughing so hard at them himself that tears ran from his eyes. "Oh yes, *Inktomi* juggled his own eyes—and threw them up so high, they got hung up in a tree branch—and he was blind."

He shook his head, amazed at the continuing stream of Indian memories that had engulfed his mind. A walk with Morning Bird one early evening when they had come across a spider and she had sung to it. Her words haunted his soul.

He walked on, being careful not to disturb the spider. He

wondered, though, if the tribe still held Spider sings and, if they would continue doing so on the reservation. Would they even be allowed to do so? Did Morning Bird sing such songs? Did she ever think of him as he did her?

His easy journey took him along the edge of the commercial district. None of the merchants were open for business. Too early, he surmised, then remembered it was Sunday. In the distance, he could see the city hall, a proud structure of only a few years. He walked past the closed Overland Stage Line office and soon strolled past the *Rocky Mountain News* office. He could barely hear the muted celebrations in the sporting district and wondered if the Silver Queen was busy.

Rounding the corner, he saw Mattie Bacon and her father, leaving his store, Bacon's General Store. Lockhart froze. He and Mattie had been very close, maybe in love, for several months. Even making love just before he left town to find his Indian brother-in-law. That was a year ago. Things had not been the same when he returned. It was his feelings that had changed. Not hers.

He had not been able to bring himself to tell her that seeing his dead wife's younger sister had triggered something inside him that wasn't supposed to be there.

Three years younger than her sister, Morning Bird was beautiful.

She looked so much like Young Evening, he had been startled by her appearance when he and Touches-Horses entered the village. Their time together was brief, so brief, as everyone in the village wanted to see him. Yet her countenance lingered in his mind like a spring mist.

When he finally returned to Denver, he avoided seeing Mattie for several days and when she finally cornered him at the Black Horse Hotel, he told her that they shouldn't see each other anymore, that her initial concerns were right: he was a gunfighter, a killer of men, and that they would never be able to have a normal life together. It wasn't a lie; it was just an exaggeration. He didn't think of himself as a gunfighter; he was a businessman who chooses to defend himself if attacked. He could do nothing about the rumors that floated around from saloon to saloon. Crawfish told him that those rumors kept the riffraff from their saloon—and troublemaking to a minimum.

He took a deep breath and continued walking down the boardwalk. He knew she had seen him almost immediately.

"Good morning, Ms. Bacon. Mr. Bacon." He removed his hat as he advanced.

Albert Bacon's face couldn't hide his emotions any better than his daughter's eyes could avoid their instant look of longing before blinking it away. Albert, on the other hand, was afraid; his every expression and movement telegraphed that fear. He mumbled a greeting and took his daughter's arm to keep her moving.

Mattie Bacon didn't move. Her cinnamon hair was rolled into its usual tight bun and her dress was soft and simple. Her blue eyes gave away her conflicted thoughts before she spoke.

"Good morning to you . . . Mr. Lockhart. I'm surprised to see you up and out so early—and on a Sunday morning. Are you headed for worship services?" Her smile was a half one, more taunting than friendly, as her mind brought back Lockhart's rejection.

Lockhart slowed, gazed at Albert Bacon and couldn't resist saying, "There's no need to be fearful, Mr. Bacon. I've given up hurting store owners and their beautiful daughters." He glanced at Mattie. "Mattie, you make the morning even brighter. I'm sure every man in church will feel better. Just seeing you."

"Your flattery is excessive, Mr. Lockhart," she said, "but thank you for the kindness intended." She studied his face for answers to her own confused emotions.

It was a handsome face. Rough-hewned, perhaps, with unreadable eyes that cut apart everything they viewed. A warm tingling passed through her body. She was drawn to him in a disturbing way she couldn't explain, except possibly to another woman. In spite of what he was, of what he had said. It just made him more dangerous, more inviting.

"I only speak the truth." With that, he returned his hat to his head, pulled on the brim and continued walking past them.

Father and daughter stopped after a few steps and turned to watch Lockhart, both drawn to him in a different way. Whistling sounds of "Garryowen" reached them.

"That's terrible. Whistling a drinking song—in public. On Sunday," Albert Bacon declared.

"Be careful, Father. He might hear you," Mattie said. "Come on. I told Mrs. Hostal I would meet with her before church. She wants me to sing at her daughter's wedding."

"Oh, how nice." Albert Bacon glanced one last time in Lockhart's direction and gladly hurried down the street with her hand on his arm.

As they reached the alley and the end of one sidewalk section, she glanced back. Lockhart was barely in sight. Her sigh was mistaken by her father as an indication that she was displeased with the composition of the space between the sidewalks.

Quickly assuring her there was no mud, he added, "I'm so glad you broke up with Lockhart. He's a bad man, Matilda. A very bad man."

He didn't see her grimace.

CHAPTER FIVE

Strolling down the street past a double row of buildings, Lockhart tried to concentrate on his surroundings; he wasn't going to let seeing Mattie Bacon add to his clouded thoughts. He just wasn't. It was better this way, he assured himself. She needed to find a respectable man, someone gentle.

Morning Bird again flooded his mind.

"And what do you need, Panther-Strikes?" he muttered aloud and answered, "That's the problem. You don't know. Or do you?"

He was two steps past the alley and onto the boardwalk again when his mind registered on a huddled shape there. An old woman! Yes, it was. An elderly Indian woman.

He spun on his heels and retreated to the opening between the buildings.

She was asleep. Her long, gray hair spread about her shoulders and partly covered her wrinkled face. Held tightly in her hands was an apparently empty buckskin pipe bag with half the beading torn free. Moving closer, he saw the butt of a revolver clearing the top of the bag. He hadn't seen the woman before, of that he was certain. Her filthy dress was definitely Sioux, although the beadwork was of an old style and was hanging loose in several places. A trade blanket lay at her feet, tightly rolled and unused. At her neck was a wide choker of beads and stone.

He wasn't sure what Sioux tribe she was from, but thought it was Hunkpapa. At least, the design of the beadwork and choker reminded him of their styling. Seeing her, curled into a miserable sleep, jolted him back to the agonizing days of his recovery from the great battle with the Crow raiding party. On the way to a stream near their encampment to clean his healing body, he had come upon an elderly woman. She had been sleeping, too.

That elderly woman had been startled by his approaching, then frightened by what she thought she saw with him. Ghosts. Of her family. She had thought he was a spirit, too, and had come to hasten her death. The experience had been very unsettling to Lockhart and had helped convince him that it was time to leave the tribe, that they would never view him as just a warrior again, but only as one of the *Tunkasila*, one of the Grandfathers. A spirit helper. *Wakan*.

For a moment, he thought about leaving her and walking on.

Two couples passed the alley, without a glance in their direction. He hesitated, but felt compelled to see if she was all right. As he neared, she sensed his closeness and straightened herself, watching him come closer. She held out her right hand and pointed toward him. Her bony finger shook.

"Have you come to take me to my ancestors?"

The dialect was definitely Sioux, but not Oglala. Hunkpapa, he was certain now. The Lakotan language was the same among all the Sioux, as the white men called them; the Oglala, Hunkpapa, Miniconjou, Brule, and Sans Arc were all part of the same great family. Their speaking, though, had different accents, like listening to a Minnesotan talking to an Alabaman.

"The Grandfathers are with you," she whispered as her hand shook.

Gently, he took her hand and tried to reassure her. "*Unci*, I come to help you."

His Lakotan was simple and he hoped she understood it. *Unci* was the word for "grandmother," a term of endearment.

"Aiiee, South Wind sings this day. You have come. From the south. *Hokay hey*. It is a good day to die." Fat tears rolled from her weary eyes and down her bony cheeks.

He swallowed to push back the bile that wanted to be freed. The old woman in the Oglala camp had said she saw spirits with him. She, too, had said something about the wind from the south being strong. South was regarded as the direction of death, and spirits traveled along the Ghost Road to the south. But the Oglala also believed ghosts could appear whenever they wanted and talk with the living; they could heal or they could harm.

It didn't matter what she thought she saw, he told himself. She needed help.

Kneeling beside her, Lockhart put his arms around her and began to sing. It was a cradle song he had heard long ago in the Indian camp. The words and melody slipped easily from his mouth as if he had been rehearsing it.

She nestled against his chest and shut her eyes. Her crying ceased.

After singing the song four times, he asked, in Lakotan, if she was hungry or thirsty, if she had a place to sleep.

Without looking up, she said, "You are the one who rides with the Grandfathers. I have heard of you. You are Oglala. A great warrior of many coups. One against many. They sing songs about the spirits riding with you in battle. At the summer gatherings, they sing these songs. I have heard them." She stopped and turned her eyes toward him. "Have you come to hear my death song?"

He couldn't think of anything to say. It appeared she was not sick, only weak from hunger and a lack of sleep.

Finally, he repeated what he had told the old woman in camp. "No. I come because you are my mother, my sister, my grandmother."

She whimpered, bit her cracked, lower lip and said her name was Falling Leaf. A garbled story of unbelievable hardship followed. She and several others had slipped away from the reservation months ago. Soldiers had followed and had finally caught up with them, killing all of the escaping band, except her. She had played dead until they had ridden away. After they were gone, she had found the revolver next to a dead warrior and taken it with her. A handful of cartridges, too. A wounded horse left behind took her for miles and miles, before giving out. She walked the rest of the way and thought she had been in Denver for three days. Her empty parfleche had carried what food she had—and had gathered from the other dead Indians after the massacre. When it was empty, she had placed the gun and bullets there. She said two of the dead were her brother and his wife.

Without being asked, she opened the parfleche for him to see her gun. It was a French Le Faucheux pinfire revolver, a wheelgun, one of the first to take metallic cartridges. He wondered if it would even fire, how old the bullets were, and thanked her for showing him.

She must eat—and be given a place to rest. His only real option was the Black Horse Hotel. It was a block away, in the other direction. He told her what he was going to do, then lifted her into his arms and stood. She began to weep once more and squeezed the parfleche with both hands, holding the gun in the bag as if it were a small child.

He walked through the front doors of the hotel, holding her in his arms, and told the assistant manager in charge for the day that he wanted a room.

Aaron Whitaker cocked his heads sideways, unbelieving. "What'll my boss say? She's an Injun squaw. She can't be here." He raked a hand through dark, greasy hair. "Besides, half the rooms are being redecorated."

Holding his anger in check, Lockhart explained the woman was important to him personally, and that the hotel would be taking her on as a boarder for awhile.

"Well, I guess it's your hotel, Mr. Lockhart. Reckon ya can do what ya want with it," Whitaker continued, "but ya know thar'll be folks . . . ah, who won't wanna stay hyar . . . on account o' her. No offense, Mr. Lockhart."

The last statement was carefully framed and took courage to say, Lockhart realized, and nodded his agreement.

The assistant manager seemed more surprised at his gentleness with the old woman than the Indian's presence itself. Lockhart spoke soothingly to her in a language the young man didn't know, some kind of Indian words he assumed. His face was wrapped in bewilderment; he alternated between looking at the old woman and looking at Lockhart.

"Ah . . . Room 24's empty," Whitaker said and swallowed. "An' . . . ah, the rooms on either side are closed—for fixin'."

"Good. Let's go."

With a sudden sense of urgency, Whitaker led the way to

an unused room on the second floor. He hoped no guest would see them. His mind was whirring with questions and concerns. What would the hotel manager say? Would he be fired for this? What about Mr. Crawford? What would he think?

Lockhart carefully laid the old woman in a large, planked bed with a quilted spread and blankets. When he tried to take away the parfleche, she cried out and he stopped. With the bag and its gun laying against her body, she grabbed for his hand and held it. Realizing her fear, he sat down on the edge of the bed, holding the wrinkled hand, patting her shoulder and talking softly to her.

"Go get her some warm broth. Cool water, too. And a glass of whiskey." Lockhart motioned with his head for Whitaker to leave. "Oh, and some vinegar, if you can find some."

As the hotel employee turned, the unexpected sounds of a lullaby, or something like that, in words foreign to him, reached him. They came from this strange businessman with the gunfighter reputation. Lockhart's voice was low; the song, sweet and relaxing. Whitaker wanted to stay and listen, but knew he needed to act quickly.

Minutes later, the businessman was holding a water glass for her to drink; it was laced with two spoonfuls of vinegar. Crawfish thought apple cider vinegar was a wonderful medicine, drinking a small amount daily in water; he said it was good for the heart and gave him energy. Of course, he also used it to keep away dandruff, for aching muscles, to heal sores and sunburn, and even under his arms to stop the smell of sweat. Lockhart figured it wouldn't hurt to give some to Falling Leaf.

After alternating sips of water and giving her spoonfuls of broth, he let her hold the bowl and gave her a taste of the whiskey. She grunted and took another; her smile revealed many missing teeth. He laid the whiskey glass on the bedside table, next to the unlit lamp and the water glass, then handed her a piece of fresh cornbread. She took small bites and began to spoon the broth by herself.

Finally satisfied, she held out the nearly emptied bowl for Lockhart to take. He accepted it and handed her the glass of water, laced with a tablespoon of vinegar, which she finished at his urging; then she finished the glass of whiskey. With a deep sigh, she laid back in the bed and was asleep in seconds.

Lockhart backed away, glancing at the drawn window curtains to see that they would keep the light from disturbing her. He stepped into the hall and closed the door behind him. Whitaker stood, waiting, his hands clasped together at his waist.

"I'll be back to check on her," Lockhart said.

"What if someone asks about her?"

"Why would they? Unless you say something."

Whitaker's eyes widened. "W-why, why, I wouldn't say anything . . . but . . ."

"I'll tell Craw . . . Mr. Crawford—and Mr. Damian."

"Of course . . . ah, Mr. Lockhart, sir?"

Lockhart turned, half-expecting more resistance.

"What if she dun wake up—while you're a'gone—an' gits all upset?" Whitaker asked, swallowing his concern. "What'll I do . . . sir?"

"Don't worry about it. She won't. I told her I was leaving and would be back—and to wait in the room. For me."

"Is thar a word . . . or somethin' . . . I could say to, ah, to make her know she were safe, ya know, hyar?" Whitaker asked seriously.

"Sure. That's smart. Ah, say to her . . . *ko-LAH. Ko-LAH.* That means 'friend.' *Ko-LAH,*" Lockhart said and added, "You can also say . . . *blo-KAH glee.* He will come back. *Blo-KAH glee.*"

Whitaker repeated both phrases over and over to himself.

"If you think she's hungry, bring her some more broth, or cornbread. You might try coffee with lots of sugar, too."

CHAPTER SIX

Crawfish was standing in his front doorway as Lockhart rounded the far corner of the upscale neighborhood. Lockhart guessed his old friend was simply welcoming the morning as he often did. Or he was tending to the freshly planted row of lilies of the valley and honeysuckle that adorned most of the front of the house.

Seeing him approach, Crawfish waved his walking stick enthusiastically and yelled, "Good Morning, Vin! A glorious day, eh!"

"Got any coffee?" Lockhart yelled back. "I came for a good hot cup of coffee."

Crawfish laughed and bit his lower lip. "Coffee? You bet. The best you've ever tasted. Just starting breakfast, too. Sean's in the kitchen. Cracking eggs." Crawfish motioned with his hand toward the unseen Irish lad.

Lockhart pushed his hat back on his head and walked faster. "So, you've already got him working, I see."

Crawfish laughed again and turned his head toward the inside of the house. "Hey, Sean, we've got one more for breakfast. What did I tell you? Vin's here."

"Ay, an' a grand meal he be havin'," came the cheery reply.

Lockhart and Crawfish shook hands on the older man's doorstep and Crawfish advised him that Sean Kavanagh seemed smart and eager to learn, that he didn't think the boy could read or write, however. He said the boy had told him that he had spent the last four years with the two hoodlums who tried to kill Lockhart last night. Shoving his glasses back into place on his nose, the red-haired entrepreneur said he thought the boy was confused and understandably so.

"You know, his world got torn up real bad last night," Crawfish said. "The two men he had depended upon for everything, who were supposedly taking care of him . . . well, one you killed and the other's not likely to make it either."

Lockhart pulled his hat brim, returning it to a lowered position. "They didn't give me much choice."

"I know that. So does he," Crawfish said, talking faster now. "Doesn't really help though. If you get my meaning. I think the boy is trying to figure out if he should hate you—or embrace you as his savior."

"Sounds like you're trying to tell me that the boy might try to kill me, too."

"Well, if someone killed Stone-Dreamer—when you were a lad that age—how would you have felt?"

"What do you mean, a lad that age? If someone hurts that old man, I'm going after him. Wherever he goes."

"Including the U. S. Army?"

"Including Grant. Sheridan. Sherman. Custer. The whole damn bunch." Lockhart's eyes flashed his irritation at the thought.

Crawfish put one hand on Lockhart's shoulder and leaned on his staff with the other. "Well, now, you understand what Sean's going through. Just give the boy some time. Some room."

"He can have all of both that he wants."

As the two men entered the house, Lockhart told Crawfish about Falling Leaf.

"Mercy-taters, are you certain she isn't hurt?" Crawfish's hands flew up with the question as they stepped into the living room. "Maybe we'd better go get the doc."

"Do you really think Doc Wright'd treat an Indian?" Lockhart said, dodging his friend's hands. "Nobody in town would ever let him forget it."

"Well, I . . . I'll look at her," Crawfish said. "I know a thing or two about medicine. Of course, that's it." He spun around as if intending to go to the hotel.

"Right now, she's sleeping, Crawfish," Lockhart said. "That'll do her more good than anything. She's eaten and had some water—and a little whiskey."

"Good. Good. After breakfast, we'll go. Before church," Crawfish declared, studied his friend and asked, "There's more. Something's bothering you . . . more than her health. Isn't there." It wasn't a question.

Half-grinning, half-grimacing, Lockhart explained the old woman said she saw spirits around him and identified him as the "one who rides with the Grandfathers." She had heard him sung about at summer gatherings and thought he had come to quicken her death.

"I'm sorry, Vin." Crawfish crossed his arms and looked down. "You know, people. Especially folks in bad shape . . . they'll see things. Things that aren't there. She didn't expect to see you, or anyone, to come and help her. It would be natural, I think, to see you as something special."

"I understand that, old friend," Lockhart said, "but she reminded me . . . of another time. A time I want to forget."

Crawfish shook his head in agreement. "Understand that, Vin. Sometimes, we can't run away from the past. Just have to deal with it." He tried to smile. "Candles-and-catechism! You know, there'd be a lot of folks who'd like the idea of being, well, resurrected. That's what Jesus did, remember?"

Lockhart's expression sank into a tight mouth line. "That is not a thing to say, my friend."

"Come into the kitchen—and let's get you some of Sean's great coffee," Crawfish said, deciding his friend didn't want to discuss the matter further. He headed across the living room toward the kitchen.

Nodding agreement, Lockhart followed him through the living room cluttered with papers of all kinds. Yesterday's newspaper was spread upon the heavy oak table. Under it was a copy of *Harper's New Monthly* magazine and on the floor next to one of the chairs was a crumpled copy of a *DeWitt Ten Cent Romance* booklet, barely covering several medical journals, a historical pamphlet of some kind and a Chicago magazine featuring fine restaurants. Last year's important book, *Science and Health with Key to the Scriptures*, by Mary Baker Eddy, lay nearby with a sock for a bookmark.

Lockhart tossed his hat on the dark green, overstuffed chair as they passed. It was the only piece of furniture not covered with newspapers, magazines, pamphlets or other papers. He guessed most of the reading materials were related to Crawfish's current interest in establishing a new bank or the completion of the hotel restaurant. The man's day always started with coffee and the newspaper, and usually anything else worthy of reading that he had gathered the day before.

"Good morning, Sean. How are you doing?" Lockhart said as they entered the small kitchen, making no attempt to shake his hand.

The Irish teenager was wearing a clean shirt and pants; they looked familiar and were likely clothes Crawfish had given him from his closet. They were a bit large for him in the shoulders and waist, but not bad. Certainly far better than the dirty rags he had been wearing. His footwear was also new—to him. A pair of black boots that Crawfish rarely wore. From the looks of his scrubbed face, the businessman had encouraged the boy to take a bath as well. A huge porcelain bathtub was one of Crawfish's early purchases; it had been shipped all the way from Chicago.

Another was the fancy, wrought-iron stove that was occupying the boy at the moment.

"Fine I be, sir. An' thank ye for askin'." Sean Kavanagh nodded his head and returned to tending to the bacon now sizzling in the large, black frying pan.

A few minutes later, the three sat at a round table with plates heaped with fried eggs, fat slices of bacon, and wedges of pan-fried potatoes. A separate plate held a half-dozen warm biscuits. At Crawfish's plate was also a glass of water, mixed with some vinegar. His customary morning ritual.

Lockhart added two spoonfuls of sugar to his coffee while Crawfish praised the boy for his cooking skills. Sean blushed and eyed Lockhart out of the corner of his eyes.

"Before we eat, Sean, it is our custom—Vin and mine—to say thanks to the good Lord," Crawfish said. "Are you familiar . . . with saying grace?" He didn't wait for a response, but folded his hands and recited, "'God is great. God is good. Him we thank for daily food. By his hand we all are fed, by his love, we all are led.' Amen."

Lockhart's voice mirrored Crawfish's; his hands grasped together; his eyes, closed.

Sean watched them both. Surprised.

As soon as the prayer was finished, Lockhart cut away a small piece of bacon, rose and took it in his fingers and went to the back door. The Irish lad watched him as the well-dressed businessman whispered something, motioned in seven directions and tossed the meat into the yard, and returned.

"First food to *Wakantanka*," Crawfish explained and shifted the walking stick leaning against his chair to a different position. "Like I told you, Vin was raised by Indians. Oglala Sioux to be exact. They believe in honoring God by giving him the first bite of each meal." He scratched his unshaven chin. "He motions in seven directions, that's also to . . . ah, recognize the four Winds, Mother Earth, Father Sky—and the Eagle who soars to the Great Spirit, taking messages to him. Well, that's pretty close, I think. Right, Vin?"

Lockhart nodded agreement as he returned to the table and sat.

"Now, Sean, you may be wondering about these plates—and utensils," Crawfish continued. "I keep 'em to remind me of how poor we once were. These old tin plates and such were what we had in our gold camp. Yessir, the very same ones."

"They be lookin' jus' fine, I be thinkin'."

"Well, thank you, son. Thank you." Crawfish downed a glass of water and vinegar and placed a forkful of eggs into his mouth and began to chew them vigorously.

Sean ate with gusto, shoving food into his mouth so fast that even Lockhart stopped to watch him.

"Slow down, boy," Lockhart cautioned. "It's not going anywhere." He took a sip of coffee and decided it needed more sugar.

With a mouthful of eggs and bacon, Sean apologized. "Ay, 'tis sorry I be. 'Tis fine food."

"Try some of this jam. Gooseberry. Made it myself. Mighty good on that biscuit." Crawfish pointed at the half-filled jar.

Immediately, the boy took the jar, spooned out a large swarm of sweetness and plopped it on the half biscuit he held in his other hand.

Both men watched him for a moment; then Crawfish asked Lockhart if he remembered what they had to eat at their first meal together. Lockhart smiled and recounted that there were beans, steak and sourdough bread dipped in sorghum molasses. He nodded his head to emphasize his liking for the latter.

Crawfish laughed. "Say, Newton, is that right? Did we eat that good?" He winced. "Holy catfish! That's the first time ol' Newton's been . . . around for a long time, isn't it? Kinda missed the old boy." He laughed again and the left side of his mouth twitched slightly and was still.

Lockhart chuckled and added some jam to his own biscuit.

"Tell Sean . . . about Falling Leaf."

"Not much to tell," Lockhart replied as he finished spreading the jam.

Without waiting, Crawfish explained the situation with the Indian woman at the hotel without mentioning her initial reaction about ghosts being around him.

Sean glanced at Lockhart, then at Crawfish, finally getting up the nerve to ask, "Do ye be knowin' her?"

"I took the liberty of telling Sean about your days with the Oglala," Crawfish quickly added. "Some of it, anyway."

Lockhart nodded. "No. I've never seen her before." He took a bite of his biscuit.

"Does the red man be carin' of his elders . . . like . . . like ye be doin'?" Sean asked.

"More than that really," Lockart answered as he swallowed. "The older man, or woman, was considered to be, uh, all wise. They are the ones listened to at councils."

"Indian women, be they . . . looked to . . . for decisions?"

"They were in our village. One was even a shirtwearer. I heard of other women honored in that way, too. A few were warriors, although I only saw one. At a summer gathering."

"What be a shirtwearer?"

Lockhart thought for a second, then explained that a "shirtwearer" was like being on the town council, one of the camp's chosen leaders. Only nobody gave anyone orders. Most things were known because of tradition, passed down among families. He explained that it was tradition that a husband never spoke directly to his mother-in-law, and that relatives of a boy were responsible for most of his actual raising, not his parents. However, shirtwearers were expected to do one duty particularly well, that of praying for the tribe's well-being.

"Does not be soundin' much like the red devils I be hearin' about."

"Well, I'm afraid most of those stories are true—or close to it." Lockhart stared at the remaining biscuit in his hand. "White men have been taking away their land almost since the day the two races met." He took a deep breath. "It isn't going to end good . . . for the Indian."

Crawfish quickly asked, "What could we bring to Falling Leaf to eat? What would she like?"

Cocking his head to the side, Lockhart said, "She'd really favor buffalo fat—and we don't have any of that, so we'll just offer her whatever's available. She'll tend toward greasier things, I suppose. She had soup earlier—and some cornbread. Most anything will be fine, when you come right down to it. She'll have a real hankering for sweet stuff. Coffee with lots of sugar." He smiled. "Like me." He took another bite of the biscuit and washed it down with coffee.

"Say, we've still got some venison. Out in the cooling shed. How about that?" Crawfish asked.

"Sure. We could roast it and add some tallow grease. And some sugar," Lockhart replied. "You know what would be good—with that?"

Crawfish looked at Sean, smiled and leaned forward.

"Apples. We can add some apples to the venison."

"That's easy enough. Sean and I can get working on that later today."

"That's mighty nice of you, Crawfish," Lockhart said. "But she's my concern, not yours. Or Sean's."

Crawfish grinned and scratched his chin with his fork. "Well, let's see. Half that hotel is mine, so I reckon she's half my concern, too. Don't you think?"

Lockhart chuckled and drank the rest of his coffee. "Don't ever get in an argument with Crawfish, Sean. You aren't going to win it."

The boy looked like he wanted to say something, but decided it wasn't the time or place.

"Say, what if she gets upset when you're not there?" Crawfish asked and reached for his own coffee mug.

Lockhart explained what he had told the assistant manager and soon the conversation wound down with Sean spellbound by the two men who had just entered his life.

After breakfast, the threesome carried their dishes into the kitchen and Crawfish showed Sean how he wanted them cleaned and washed. First, the boy went outside to pump water into a large basin. A stone well and pump were in excellent condition. Crawfish had taken the pump completely apart, cleaned and oiled each piece and reconstructed it. That was a month after he bought the residence.

As Lockhart and Crawfish watched the boy, the eccentric older man said he was planning on going to hear Dr. Hugo Milens preach at the Methodist church this morning and asked Lockhart if he wanted to go, too.

"I don't understand your fascination for this man, Crawfish," Lockhart said, frowning. "Do you believe he can talk to the spirits, bring them to you?" He cocked his head to the side. "You didn't believe me when I told you that Stone-Dreamer could do such things."

Crawfish pointed at the counter with his walking stick for Sean to set the filled basin and began placing the used plates into the water. He took a large bar of soap, and with a knife, removed a small handful of crumbles and flakes, then swished them around in the water to create a base of suds.

"Well, you know me, Vin," the red-faced man replied, pushing his glasses back on his nose, and reciting quickly as he usually did when excited about something. "I like learning new things. Books-and-bookmarks! I liked learning about your Indian ways, didn't I? Just figure it would be fun to hear him. Like to sit in on one of his seances, too. Now that would be something!" The side of his face twitched as it did on occasion. He wanted to mention Lockhart and the ghost story, but didn't think his friend would like bringing it up.

"Anything in the *Rocky Mountain News* about the army? Up north?" Lockhart changed the subject and headed for the parlor where one entire wall was lined with books, magazines and newspapers. Crawfish rarely threw anything away, especially reading material.

Most parlors in finer homes were used exclusively to entertain guests and little else. In Crawfish's house, it was a combination study and project area. In one corner, three large canning jars each contained a singular green plant. Lockhart didn't know what they were; Crawfish was constantly growing things and transplanting them in his vast backyard. His huge garden supplied many of the vegetables for the hotel restaurant.

In another corner were several glasses of beer, each mixed with something. Orange juice. Berry juice. Even tobacco juice. Crawfish was trying various combinations of beer.

Next to it was a wooden frame that eventually would become a hitching rack for outside the saloon. It was his intent to construct a rack that would hold more horses; this one had three long poles set vertically a few inches apart on support posts. Work had not proceeded further since Lockhart observed that the problem with getting more horses at a rack wouldn't be solved by tying them at different levels.

A rolltop desk in the corner was also crammed with papers of various kinds. Above the desk was a framed daguerreotype of a young man and woman in traditional wedding pose. Crawfish and his late Almina. Even the wooden armchair in front of the desk held a stack of documents. In the other corner, a potbellied stove rested from its labors.

"Naw. Just a rehash of what we've been reading." Crawfish knew his friend had no intention of either going to church or talking more about the mesmerist. "They're supposedly closing in on the Indians from three directions. I'm betting they don't even find any." He patted the top of the chair with his staff.

Lockhart stopped and thought for a moment. "They might. The Greasy Grass is a good hunting ground. Ah, around the Little Bighorn. Or Rosebud Creek."

"Naw, you know it's all just politics. A big show to look like the army's doing something," Crawfish replied and added, "Maybe no Indians will even go there. If they did, they'd hear that bunch coming for miles—and skedaddle." His statement wasn't as positive as he wanted it to be.

Lockhart stared at Crawfish, but didn't respond. The older man's face twitched again.

"You know what they're saying about Custer, though," Crawfish offered, wincing slightly.

"They say a lot of things about him." Lockhart knew his friend was continuing to refer to politics; it was another of

Crawfish's interests. So far, though, his only direct involvement had been taking an active role in the election of the mayor.

"Well, politics and pickles, they're saying Custer's going to be nominated for president. Democrat," Crawfish said, studying his friend for reaction. "The Democratic convention's going to be in St. Louis, you know. End of June. Starts on the twenty-seventh."

Lockhart nodded. The corner of his mouth indicated he had no idea of when such a gathering was taking place, or where, or who was running. Nor did he care.

Crawfish wasn't finished with the subject, adding that the key to Custer's ascension would be a major, and timely, victory up north against the Sioux and Cheyenne. The news would be relayed by telegraph to St. Louis and dramatically announced on the convention floor. He thought it was a definite possibility since the three contenders weren't all that popular. Samuel Tilden from New York, Thomas Hendricks from Indiana, and former Union general Winfield Scott Hancock from Pennsylvania were the candidates.

Lockhart picked up the nearest newspaper, then put it down again almost as quickly. His thoughts were visible only in the thinness of his mouth. "That all assumes he has a victory," he said, tapping the returned sheets with his fist. "He's got to find them first."

"True. True. Of course, that's only a rumor," Crawfish volunteered. "Politics and rumors are always bedfellows."

"Yeah, guess so."

"People like to vote for war heroes, you know. Like ol' General Grant. Custer's that, too."

Lockhart shoved both hands into his pockets, as if to hide them from the anger that wanted to make them fists again. "Do you get to be a war hero by wiping out a peaceful Indian village with a sneak attack in the middle of winter?"

Crawfish knew his friend was referring to Custer's "Battle

of the Washita" eight years ago. The army announced it was a major victory against "bloodthirsty savages." Sort of like the difference of opinion about Chivington's "Battle of Sand Creek" years earlier. Lockhart and a few others thought it was an unprovoked attack on a peaceful Cheyenne and Arapaho encampment; the news media hailed it as a major victory for progress. Some called it "Chivington's massacre," for the white leader, John Chivington.

Glancing back at Sean, who was nearly finished with drying the dishes, Crawfish stepped into the main room. "Sean's going with me. To church." He tilted his head back and forth. "Then we'll check in on Falling Leaf; then I told him that we'd look in on his friend. The gut-shot one."

Lockhart pursed his lips, then licked them. "All right."

"He's at Doc's place. Remember? I can ask him about Falling Leaf."

"We already talked about that," Lockhart said. "I would like you to see if she needs any doctoring."

"I'm thinking a good dose of cod-liver oil wouldn't hurt. Or, maybe, some of that what-ails-you tonic I bought from Hoag's Drug Store."

Lockhart shook his head. "Better wait until I'm there to do something like that. She might not understand."

"Oh, pickles-and-beets, of course I wouldn't do that without you, Vin."

Lockhart's eyes narrowed. "On the other subject. You know if that Irishman makes it, he'll be tried for attempted robbery and murder."

"I know that."

"Does Sean?"

Crawfish glanced toward the kitchen again. "Don't know. I'll ask him."

"No. I'll do it. I'm the one who shot his . . . friends." Lockhart crossed his arms. "Then I'm going back to check on Falling Leaf." He glanced away, then looked back at

Crawfish. "Then I'm going for a ride. Been thinking about getting into . . . the horse business."

"Horses, eh?" Crawfish's mouth crawled into a wide grin. "You looking for a partner?"

"Know of a good one?" Lockhart matched his friend's smile.

For once, Lockhart was the talkative one, explaining the idea that had been forming in his mind. It was as if the concept had just been waiting to pounce when his mouth was open. Lockhart thought he would buy an existing ranch operation and begin focusing entirely on horses. He wanted one or two really fine stallions to build a strong bloodline. He didn't care if the ranch had been used for cattle or even if it was a farm. He wanted good water, good grass, and an iron-clad deed. He acknowledged the latter had been learned from Crawfish.

"You know that Indian relative of yours, what's his name? Yeah, Touches-Horses," Crawfish said, looking away. "He'd be a good one to have join you, being so good at training horseflesh." The eccentric businessman grinned. "Wonder if that little Indian gal would want to come?"

Lockhart studied his friend's face as the crow's-feet around Crawfish's eyes jumped and fattened in the aftermath of his observation.

"You old crow bait," Lockhart snapped. "You said that with a straight face!"

Waving his arms in reaction to his remark, Crawfish yelled and waved the silver-topped staff. "Jumping pothooks! How was I supposed to know you planned on doing that all along? Huh? Tell me."

Their conversation continued a little longer with Crawfish suggesting three small ranches he thought worth checking into. Lockhart had already planned on visiting two of them, but appreciated hearing about a third. The Broken R was nestled in a fat basin not far from town. An older couple worked the land and used it for raising milk cows and a little farming. Mostly hay, Crawfish thought. He knew there was a nice pond on the land, but didn't know how many acres they actually owned.

Sean's appearance stopped the exchange. "Mr. Crawford, sir, the dishes they be done. Sparklin' clean, I'd say. What chores do ye be having next?"

"Well, Sean, no more chores today." Crawfish grinned. "You an' me, we'll try a little churchin', like I said earlier. Do you sing, Sean?"

"Sing?" Sean wasn't sure if he was being teased or not. "A bird I not be, Mr. Crawford, sir."

"Oh, I see." Crawfish shook his head. "Well, there's singing in church and I thought you might like that. No matter, though, we can just listen. My Almina used to sing real fine. Never got the hang of it myself."

Sean glanced at Lockhart, who shifted his weight from his right to left leg, obviously impatient to leave. The boy's gaze settled momentarily on the slight bulge in Lockhart's coat. An indication of his shoulder-holstered gun. Sean was certain he had never been around anyone so good with a gun, so calm in the middle of a fight, so difficult to read. How did this man feel about him?

Finally, his attention returned to Crawfish as he outlined the rest of their day. After church, they would visit Sean's wounded friend, Lightning Murphy, then make sure Falling Leaf hadn't been disturbed, and ultimately end up at the Silver Queen and relieve J. R. Parks. Sunday was a big day with the miners especially, trying to make the most of it before returning to the backbreaking drudgery of a new workweek.

Shaking his head, Crawfish realized his friend was going to make certain the boy understood the situation with the wounded Irish hoodlum.

"Eh, Vin, will you be joining us at the Queen later?" Crawfish asked quickly, trying to catch Lockhart's eyes by waving his walking stick. "Or will you be with Falling Leaf?"

"Depends," Lockhart said and looked at the boy. "Sean, you understand if this Murphy fellow survives—and that isn't likely—he's going to be tried for attempted robbery and murder. You understand that, don't you?"

"Me be believin' Big Mike an' Lightnin' not be intendin' to hurt ye. Just be want'un to scare ye." Sean's gaze found Crawfish first and could go no further. "Just be want'un to scare ye . . . sir."

"I see. Let's look at the facts. Three of you hide in the dark. You wait there. Your friends think they have an easy mark, a businessman walking alone. They tell you to get ready with your knife. Your friend Murphy tries to shoot me." Lockhart's face was tanned granite and his blue eyes burned the boy's face. "And the only reason he doesn't hit me is because I don't do what he expects. Neither does your other friend who also tries to shoot me." His chin lowered and his voice became deep. "Scare me, Sean? Come on. They intended to leave me dead or dying. Relieved of my wallet. And my dreams." He cocked his head to the side as he often did. It was a mannerism learned from Stone-Dreamer.

"Easy, Vin. Goodness gracious me! The boy's been through an awful lot in just a few short hours," Crawfish exclaimed.

Lockhart shook his head.

"Sean, you've been traveling with two no-good, murdering thieves," Lockhart said, almost softly. "The kind of thugs that good men don't want around. At all. The kind that want to take from good men because they're too lazy to work. The kind who tell themselves that they've gotten a bad break—and hard work is for suckers."

Sean's forehead rolled into a frown and stepped back.

Crawfish put his hand on the boy's shoulder, fearing what his friend was going to say next, yet not daring to stop it.

"You have a choice, young man," Lockhart continued. "A real choice. You can take advantage of this opportunity to learn something worthwhile. Something worth doing. Crawfish here is an amazing teacher. He turned an Indian warrior into a successful businessman. Me." He paused and leaned his hand against the back edge of the desk chair. "Or you can decide your friends are worth your loyalty—and try to kill me. For revenge. You probably promised Murphy that—or he asked for it."

Crawfish's eyes widened and his mouth popped open as his hand recoiled from Sean's shoulder.

"Here. This will help you make up your mind." Lockhart let go of the chair back, reached inside his coat, and pulled free his Smith & Wesson revolver. He spun it in his hand to leave the butt toward Sean. "Take it. Come on, take it. It's what you want, isn't it? Revenge?"

Sean's eyes blinked and matched Crawfish's in surprise. His hand twitched at his side for an instant and then was still.

Lockhart took a step closer and pushed the gun butt into Sean's stomach. "Take it, boy. It's a lot better than that knife. This is your chance. To honor Big Mike and Lightnin' Murphy."

Crawfish stammered and dropped his walking stick. "Q-quit that, Vin. P-put that damn thing away. P-please."

Lockhart spun the gun butt back into his hand and holstered it. "I'll see you boys later." He wheeled and walked out of the parlor.

Crawfish and Sean heard the front door open and slam shut.

"Sean . . . Vin Lockhart is a good man, but he's a hard one," Crawfish said, picking up his stick without looking at the boy. "He likes you. He wants you to succeed. Like he did. I can tell."

"A funny way o' showing it, he has."

"Maybe so. He wants you to make sure. Make sure . . . ah, you're sure."

"What would've happened if I took it?" Sean asked, looking at his feet, then at Crawfish.

The red-haired entrepreneur rubbed his chin. "Don't even think about that."

"Would me be right in sayin' he wonna be goin' to service—with ourselves?" Sean changed the subject quickly.

Crawfish smiled. "Vin has a powerful feeling for . . . ah, God. Not much patience, though, for . . . church."

"Seems they kinda be goin' together."

Making a circle with his hands, Crawfish explained what Lockhart believed and why. Then he told the boy about Lockhart's intention to look over some land for a possible horse ranch.

Sean's eyes widened and his jaw dropped open. "By the saints and all that be holy, me dun forgot all about 'em. Ay, that I did."

"Forgot what, Sean?"

"Big Mike's buckboard an' hosses, they be outside o' town. South o' here. A short ways. Near a sweet pond, they be," Sean declared. "An' . . . an' there be an' Injun pony, too."

"An Indian pony?"

"Ay. A fine he-hoss he be. Got paint an' feathers on his-self."

Crawfish asked where they got the horse and Sean explained they had just come across the animal on the way from Longmont. It was standing quietly by the road. He also admitted the wagon and horses had been stolen. They had driven it away while the owners were in the general store. No one had even noticed, he added proudly.

"We'll go to this pond later today and bring them in. I know where you're talking," Crawfish said and hit his walking stick forcefully against the floor. "I'll wire the marshal in Longmont and advise him of the wagon and horses."

"But—"

"No 'but's,' Sean. We don't steal and we don't lie around here. Understand?" Crawfish hit the floor again with the end of his staff.

"Ay, that I do. But what about the Injun pony?"

"Well, he should go back to his owner, too. But I don't know how to do that," Crawfish said. "We'll see what Vin thinks."

CHAPTER SEVEN

Dr. Hugo Milens's piercing green eyes had a glow to them that reminded of a summer day. Or was it eternity? The newspaper had spoken of him as "a mesmerist of note, someone that Denver was most fortunate to have in their midst for a short time" and "an accomplished professor of the ancient secrets of Egypt." Both were phrases used by Milens to describe himself.

The self-proclaimed mesmerist caught himself starting to smile at the full congregation. The beginning grin transformed into a scowl. There was much to be done—and quickly. Acquiring money from desperate believers must be done with a swiftness. He didn't plan on staying long in Denver. He never did anywhere. His long prayers—and longer sermons—would build an image of himself that would allow for certain opportunities to take place.

He decided on coming to Denver, after leaving Wichita. Things had gone well there. Very well. One wealthy widow had given him half her riches just to listen to her dead husband. He had been happy to oblige. So far, Mayor McCormick and Marshal Benson had been easy to get close to and aid, unwittingly, in the development of choice victims. Others would be similarly sought out and brought under his hypnotic spells. What a gift, this ability.

He was also curious about this Vin Lockhart. His interest had come initially from the man's reputation with a gun and had been whetted a few days ago when he ran into an old mountain man at a restaurant. The buckskin-clad trapper said Lockhart had lived with Indians for a long time and had actually stopped breathing once. Stopped breathing! Stone dead, the mountain man said, before an Indian holy man brought him back to life.

With relish, the grizzled man related that the Indians believed Lockhart was blessed so he couldn't be killed unless their ancestors decided so. Some, he said, thought Lockhart was a ghost, a spirit. When Dr. Milens asked the old-timer how he knew this, the mountain man said he had visited the same Oglala camp a week after Lockhart had left for good. He said the Indian holy man was a friend of his. A fine man, he had added, warming to his storytelling.

Dr. Milens knew he could use this to his advantage in courting the wealthy Lockhart. He thanked the old man and paid him to leave town immediately. A man like Lockhart might prove to be an easier prey than most would suspect. He had already placed Desmond Crawford on his list to solicit.

Not an empty seat on the wooden pews could be found in the Methodist church. Crawfish and Sean managed to squeeze into the next-to-the-last row. Behind the last pew was an ever-growing group of people standing. Waiting.

Clearly nervous, Pastor Jeffrey Tiemann, the regular minister, stepped to the front of the crowded church. His eyes sought approval from Dr. Milens before beginning. The crowd-attractor sat in a special chair to the side of the pulpit. He nodded his agreement and settled himself more comfortably.

"Good morning and welcome to the Lord's house of worship," Pastor Tiemann said, his voice gaining strength as he proceeded. "Let us begin by singing Hymn 308, 'Lift Up Your Heads, Ye Gates of Brass.'"

Crawfish looked at Sean, then opened the hymnal and began to point at each word as it was sung by the congregation. The Irish boy frowned and tried to concentrate on the gathered marks, comparing them to the sounds he heard.

Two rows in front of them were Mattie Bacon and her father. Crawfish was certain she had noticed them when he and Sean entered the church. He didn't really know why the relationship between her and Lockhart had cooled. His friend's only statement on the matter was that he wasn't ready to get married and she was. That had come shortly after he returned from freeing Touches-Horses and a visit to his old Indian tribe.

Mattie's soprano was clear and bright, cutting through the clutter of other voices. When the hymn ended, Mattie turned slightly in the pew, then a little more, so she could see Crawfish. Their eyes met briefly and he nodded. She smiled stiffly and turned back.

The rest of the service couldn't go fast enough for most. They sat on the edge of their pews or shifted their feet while standing. Waiting to hear Dr. Hugo Milens. All except an old man in the fourth row, who was asleep. His low snoring was a giveaway. Several small boys also fidgeted in the back. Their mother, standing beside them, was too interested in the service to be stern with them, or even aware of their disruptive behavior.

At last his sermon came.

With a nod of his head, Dr. Milens stood slowly in response to Paster Tiemann's introduction and headed to the pulpit. He stood behind it for a long moment, as if studying each and every person in the room.

"Good morning to you. I bring you news from your beloved brethren who have gone on before you. They gather close to watch and listen. They are heartened by your love—and your prayers."

A few sobs and several gasps rattled through the church, followed by almost absolute silence. His sermon was a mixture of heroic phrasing about the area . . . fearful deliverances of the ungodliness of the city's vices . . . earnest pleadings to let the riches of the area be handled by godly men . . . direct references to his special ability to help people talk to the spirits of departed loved ones, complete with three dramatic examples . . . all wrapped around verse four of the Twenty-Third Psalm: "Even though I walk through the valley of the shadow of death, I will fear no evil; for thou art with me; thy rod and thy staff, they comfort me."

He loved the look on parishioners' faces as he twisted this sentence from one of their favorite passages into something that suggested the spirit world—and let its unstated mystery seek their already timid souls. As he expected, the eyes of most of the women reflected their belief in his special calling. He couldn't help smiling as he spoke.

To cap off the sermon, he used a magnificent soliloquy from *King Richard II*, where Shakespeare had King Richard making a long-winded threat: " 'Draw near and list what with our council we have done . . . For that our kingdom's earth should not be soiled . . . With that dear blood which it hath fostered; . . . And for our eyes to hate this dire aspect . . . Of civil wounds ploughed up with neighbours; award, . . . And for we think the eagle-wing'd cradle . . . Draws the sweet infant breath of gentle sleep; . . . Which so roused up with boist'rous untuned drums, With harsh-resounding trumpets' dreadful bray, And grating shock of wrathful iron arms, Might from our quiet confines fright fair peace, And make us wade even in our kindred's blood; Therefore we banish you our territories . . . ' "

At least half the audience wouldn't even realize his long recital hadn't come from the Bible—and most wouldn't understand what this brilliantly written monologue even meant. But they would get the alarming words and phrases like "dear blood," "wake our peace," "fright," "kindred's blood," "wounds," and "dreadful." He delivered this segment of the sermon as his closing, envisioning himself in the role of King Richard as he performed the words. His face was rich with practiced emotion.

The last sentence dropped upon the crowd like an ax in a quiet wood. A woman in the fifth row was so overcome with emotion, she applauded. After a few unfettered, but solitary, handclaps, she realized where she was and looked around sheepishly, her red face ripening. Her smile was somewhat akin to the expression of someone tasting a sour persimmon.

Crawfish listened, appreciating the incorporation of the Shakespearean soliloquy and reminded himself to share more of the great writer's work with Sean some time.

Dr. Milens caught the movement of Marshal Benson entering from the back. The lawman was beaming. He nodded greetings to people who turned to see who it was. He was in a good mood from earlier praise about the way he had handled the Irish holdup men last night. The second hoodlum had passed away, early this morning.

After the passing of the collection plate, which resulted in a far-above-average return, Dr. Milens stood beside Pastor Tiemann and closed with a prayer: "O Lord, you have been our protector in times of danger, in times of need, in times of sorrow. From the tall mountains around us . . . your mountains . . . has come a vicious menace tearing into our families, our homes, our commerce. Ah yes, Lord, we understand that the lifting of ore from your mountains is not good in your precious sight. Deliver us from this . . . this evil of greed . . . and give us peace as we work together to build our valley . . . your beautiful valley . . . into a place of happiness and goodwill. Grant us the ability to hear those who have gone before us—and learn from them. Amen."

Pastor Tiemann seemed stunned by the words, but managed to mumble, "Go in peace."

People began to put on their coats, to speak with neighbors. Mingled conversation became a sort of garbled song.

"Reverend, may I speak to the group for a moment?" The voice was that of Alexander McCormick, mayor and town banker. The interaction was planned.

"Of course, Mr. McCormick. My friends, will you please give our mayor your attention. Please!" Pastor Tiemann glanced at Dr. Milens as he finished.

A fairly good speaker himself, McCormick had an unfortunate tendency to make arm motions only with his right hand and only in a stiff outward motion that never seemed to be timed with any phrasing. Like a loose driving rod on a steam engine. Still, he looked and sounded authoritative.

"Folks, I just wanted to tell you that our fine peace officer, Marshal Benson, has fully brought to justice the two Irish hoodlums who attempted to kill and rob one of our citizens last night."

A slight murmur followed this statement. Crawfish stopped halfway toward the aisle and looked back at Sean. The Irish lad's face was white and his eyes were wide.

"It's all right, Sean," Crawfish said. "This is just politics. I'll explain later."

McCormick continued his presentation. "In our midst right now is our brave officer. Marshal Benson, please . . . step forward and receive the recognition of a grateful community."

He began to clap and most of the congregation followed his lead.

Waving his hands in an exaggerated attempt to stop the applause, Benson announced, "One of the hoodlums was killed last night, trying to kill and rob Mr. Vin Lockhart." He paused for emphasis. "I should tell you that the second Irish outlaw met his maker this morning. From wounds received in the same attempt. Obviously, the Irish scum didn't know who they were tangling with!" He made no attempt to explain that his role was simply to show up and take away the bodies.

Laughter flitted for attention and whispered observations joined in, filling the church with a nervous clatter.

"Thank you, Mayor, and you, Pastor Tiemann, for the opportunity to inform our town that it is, indeed, safe—and me and my men will ever strive to keep it so." He made a quick bow, more of an extended nod.

McCormick turned to the minister, thanked him and returned to his family.

"Sounds like this Vin Lockhart fellow is no one to mess with," Dr. Milens said.

Nodding agreement, Pastor Tiemann explained that Lockhart and Crawford owned one of the larger saloons and one of the better hotels in town, as well as some other property. Dr. Milens already knew that, but expressed interest and asked if either man was in attendance today. He had already seen Crawfish in the back.

"Ah, I'm certain Mr. Lockhart isn't here, but I believe I saw Mr. Crawford. Yes . . . there he is."

"Oh good, would you introduce me?" Dr. Milens asked.

Pastor Tiemann seemed puzzled by the request.

"I find it useful to get to know all manner of people in a town, Pastor Tiemann." Dr. Milens motioned with his hand for the minister to lead the way to the businessman.

Nearing the far aisle, Crawfish was trying to calm Sean, who was upset about the news of Lightning Murphy's death and the marshal calling them "scum."

Crawfish's words weren't comforting and only served to rile the boy more.

"You're no different than the rest. Leave me alone!" Sean finally blurted. He pushed the old businessman and hurried in the other direction. He scooted along the pew into the center aisle, brushed through the exiting crowd and disappeared outside.

"Wait, Sean!" Crawfish said and cleared the narrow pew on the far aisle. He looked up and saw the Bacons standing there.

Albert Bacon spoke first; his voice, haughty and condescending. "Well, I see Vin Lockhart has found another reason to use his fancy gun."

Crawfish pursed his lips and pushed back the glasses on his nose. "Yeah, I reckon so. If it had been you they had jumped, Bacon, we'd be praying over your puny, bullet-riddled body right now." He looked around, but Sean was nowhere in sight.

Bacon scoffed. "Come now, Mr. Crawford. Surely you don't believe every encounter has to be handled with bullets."

"You're a fool, Bacon," Crawfish snarled. "Get out of my sight. I've got a young fellow to find. Before he does something stupid."

"What?"

"You heard me," Crawfish growled. "Take your beautiful daughter for a walk and explain to her just what you would've done if two men had come at you. From a dark alley. Shooting at you. Trying to kill you." He looked at the church entrance, was relieved to see Marshal Benson still there, talking to two couples, then brought his attention back to Bacon. "Maybe you could've told them you had a special sale on cooking pots. Or asked them if they would like to see some cloth."

"Well, I . . ."

"Don't." Crawfish waved his hand. "Tell Ms. Bacon. I don't care for nursery rhymes. Or cowards who let others keep them safe."

Mattie frowned and took her father's arm. "Come on, Father. Please. Good day to you, Mr. Crawford."

"Sure, miss."

"Mr. Crawford, may I bother you a moment, sir?" Pastor Tiemann announced as he lumbered up the far aisle with Dr. Milens behind him.

Crawfish turned. "Ah, what?" Behind him, the Bacons continued up the aisle with Albert Bacon speaking loudly and Mattie attempting to quiet him.

Without waiting for further comment from Pastor Tiemann, Dr. Milens strode past him and held out his hand. "Mr. Crawford, it is a pleasure to meet you, sir. Heard a great deal about you. Quite the businessman I understand."

Frowning, Crawfish took his hand and shook it. "Glad to meet you, Dr. Milens." He decided there was no hurry in pursuing Sean and was thrilled to meet the noted mesmerist. "I enjoyed your sermon, Dr. Milens. Especially liked your use of Shakespeare. *King Richard II*, I believe."

Smiling uncomfortably and nodding, Dr. Milens acknowledged the correctness of his assumption. "Very good, sir. A savvy businessman—and a learned one. A rare combination, I would say."

Crawfish felt the redness crawling up from his collar. "I have read about your, ah, seances. Fascinating experiences, it would seem."

"You must come tonight, Mr. Crawford," Dr. Milens said. "I'm having Mr. McCormick and his wife . . . and Earnest Wilcox and his fair lady. Six would be a perfect number. Are you married?"

"No sir. Was. She passed. Some time ago."

Dr. Milens tilted his head slightly to the left. "Perhaps, we can find her tonight. Perhaps, you can talk with her again." He paused for effect. "What about your . . . business friend, ah, Vin Lockhart. Would you like to bring him?"

"Of course."

"Wonderful. Let's say, eight o' clock. At my place. I'm staying in the home that was once that of the Swansons. Mayor McCormick owns it now. His rental fee was most generous."

CHAPTER EIGHT

It didn't take long for Crawfish to find the upset boy. Dr. Wright told the red-haired businessman that Sean had been there and had been advised the second Irishman's body had been picked up and taken to the undertaker's.

Crawfish knocked on the door of Joseph "Hammer" Hawkens's office. The adjacent sign read: CABINETMAKER/UNDERTAKER. On the second floor was an occulist, Jacob Mosely, who had just moved in. He had fitted Crawfish with new eye-glasses two weeks ago.

Finally, Hawkens came to the door and opened it a few inches.

"I'm closed on Sunday, Mr. Crawford. This is the Lord's day. Come back tomorrow."

"I appreciate that, Mr. Hawkens, but I'm looking for a boy. Thought he might be here."

"Irish kid?"

"Yes."

With a sigh, Hawkens opened the door wider. "Sure. Anything to get him out of here. He doesn't want to understand nothing's going to happen to either of those dead Micks today. Not tomorrow either. Not until I'm sure who's paying."

"The city . . . ah, the marshal's office. Of course, man." Crawfish studied the slimly built man with the slightly drooped shoulders and protruding belly standing before him.

The enterprising undertaker—cabinet and coffin maker—was mostly bald. What hair he had surrounded large ears like wispy worms. His clothes showed the signs of his multiple professions with stains of various kinds and reasons decorating a worn frock coat, an old brown vest, shabby morning coat, soiled collar and baggy-kneed pants. None of three main garments matched. Hawkens's red and puffy nose was a constant source of snorts and sneezing.

Crawfish figured it was due to exposure to turpentine, varnish, burial fluids and sawdust on a regular basis.

While not the most talented carpenter in town, he was certainly the most enterprising. Few coffin makers were actually undertakers, preferring to concentrate on wood instead of death. His close relationship with both the mayor and the marshal had secured the city's funeral business.

Shaking his head, Hawkens walked past the empty funeral parlor with its heavy draperies and two matching overstuffed chairs. In the center of the room, a long table waited the presentation of a casket. With his bowler in his hand, Crawfish wanted to ask how long a body could go uncared for, but decided he didn't really want to know. He hurried to catch up.

Hawkens paused beside a table containing a small stack of religious pamphlets, an ashtray filled with old cigars, and a lamp with a glass chimney lined with gray, greasy soot. He lit the lamp and the oil burned with a dull, filmy light, but it did help brighten the overall darkness of the area. Carrying it with him, Hawkens stepped through a smaller door and into a good-sized room. It served a dual purpose as his carpentry shop and his burial preparation area.

Two bodies laid on twin long tables; neither had apparently been touched since being delivered. The earlier body was covered with a sheet that had once been white, now a dull ivory. The second body of Lightning Murphy had only been delivered an hour ago. The man's blood-soaked shirt was torn open and lay against the table; his stomach was wrapped with a bandage that had given up trying to hold back the bleeding before death.

The hard smells of burial fluids and turpentine slithered about the gray enclosure, mixed with the scent of fresh pine. A varnished, hand-rubbed, wood casket rested on two sawhorses in the corner; its beveled lid was propped open. Surplus boards, a hammer, several chisels, a saw and T square, plus clumps of sawdust, surrounded the finished work. A large can of varnish sat nearby with fingers of dried liquid stringing down its sides.

Crawfish's eyes adjusted to the dim light and saw Sean standing ten feet beyond the tables. His arms were crossed and he was staring at the wall. In his folded right hand was a silver watch with a chain dangling through his fingers. It looked to Crawfish like he was holding something in the other hand as well.

Crawfish glanced at Hawkens, realized he was about to say something harsh to the boy and spoke first, motioning toward Sean with the hat in his hand. "Sean . . . there is nothing here for you. I'm sorry, but we have to leave. We can come back tomorrow, if you want."

At first, it didn't appear Sean heard him. Then he looked up, his eyes, glazed.

"What's going to happen to them?"

"Nothing until I—"

"They will be properly buried. Pastor Tiemann will do the service." Crawfish interrupted the annoyed undertaker, then turned to him. "I guarantee you will be paid."

Rubbing his cheek with his free hand, Hawkens said, "I will hold you to that."

"Of course you will," Crawfish responded.

Hawkens nodded.

"So, what is involved with a burial?" Crawfish asked, partly out of good business sense, but mostly out of curiosity.

In between nasal interruptions, Hawkens explained that the family usually cleaned the body with aromatic soap. A long watch followed to make certain the person had truly passed. He assured Crawfish and Sean that both thugs were, indeed, dead; his assessment came with a cocky relish and was followed by a blowing of his nose. He said the cleaning, using a strong and sweet-smelling soap would be done for a half-dollar each.

It would take two days for the coffins to be made; hand rubbing the varnish was extra. He pointed at the handsome coffin on the sawhorses and indicated it had been constructed for Charlie Izard who had just passed. His body was at the family home.

"Two days? Holy wishwash, what about the . . . ah, odor?" Crawfish asked without thinking about what it suggested to Sean.

"Well, I sprinkle sprigs of lavender all over the bodies. Keep them on hand. All the time. And the soap I mentioned, that helps. And cooling boards," Hawkens said, motioning toward a long board with holes in it, standing upright in the corner. "I lay one of them on a big block of ice, then put the body on it. Works pretty good." He wiped his nose with his handkerchief. "Except on real hot summer days. Ah, all that is another dollar. Each."

"What about embalming? I read where they put some kind of solution into an artery? Replaces the blood. Been experimenting with it, the whole idea, since the War between the States," Crawfish asked, pursed his lips and added, "Isn't it zinc chloride mixed with mercury chloride? All kinds of chemicals as I recall. Bichloride of mercury is another. Even an arsenic solution. Lead, too. Yes, just read about it. In a British medical journal. Yeah, I think that was it. Or was it from Ohio?"

Hawkens nodded. "Oh yeah, since the war, some folks been trying all kinds of chemicals and the like. All seems kinda unnatural to me." He dabbed his nose again.

"Hmmm, well, it seems to be gaining ground." Crawfish was talking fast now. He usually did when a subject interested him and he knew something about it.

"Wouldn't know." Hawkens was eager to change the subject.

"There's an organization of embalmers now. Around the country. Been reading about Professor Rhodes' Electro Bal Embalming Fluid. You might want to look into that." He whistled through the gap in his two front teeth and pushed back the spectacles on his nose.

"One of these days. Not right now."

Crawfish blinked and realized this wasn't the time or place to pursue the subject further. He glanced at Sean, but the boy was lost in his own thoughts.

"Sure. Sure," Crawfish said. "We're going to need headstones, too. Granite."

"Well, the marshal isn't going to pay for that." Hawkens raised the lamp to bring the yellow light closer to Crawfish's face. "You know that. A wood cross. Paint on the name, if it's known." He rubbed his nose with the handkerchief in his other hand.

"I will pay for the granite headstones."

"They come all the way from Cheyenne. Takes six weeks."

"That's just fine." Crawfish turned back to the grieving boy. "Sean, do you know . . . their names? To put on the headstones?"

Sean looked at Crawfish terrified, opened his mouth and closed it without speaking. He swallowed and muttered, "Lightnin' Murphy . . . an' Big Mike be all me be knowin'."

Hawkens stared at him as Crawfish took a few steps toward Sean. "Come on, Sean. We need to go—and see the pastor."

"Why be ye doin' this kind thing?" Sean asked, his eyes searching Crawfish's bespectacled face. "Nothin' but Irish thugs they be. Tryin' to kill your best friend, they did. They be scum nobody wants around. Good riddance."

"Because you are my friend—and they were important to you." Crawfish pushed the glasses back on his nose and waved his hand holding the hat toward the boy.

Sean squinted, holding back the anguish that wanted out. He swallowed and finally blurted, "I-I d-did not get to talk w-with . . . Lightnin' . . . again."

"I'm sorry. I . . ."

"A-A promise me did give him. To kill Vin L-Lockhart it was."

Crawfish glanced at the stunned undertaker, then walked over to the sobbing boy. Gently, he took the boy and held him.

His cheeks covered with wetness, Sean said, "I-I be goin' to tell . . . Lightin' that . . . that me canna . . ."

Crawfish patted the boy on the back. "I know you couldn't."

Sean stepped away; his mouth was a thin line of purpose.

"W-What . . . what should . . . me word I gave. 'Tis me word."

Rubbing his chin, Crawfish was uncharacteristically quiet. Should he remind the boy of the character of these men? Why did he think Sean himself was worth this time and money? What should he tell him? He heard himself saying, "Sean, what you said . . . to Lightning . . . was not a promise. Not really. It was . . . saying good-bye."

"Nay, 'twas me promise."

Crawfish studied the shaken boy. "These two men were important to you. Right?"

"Ay. They be good to meself. Swate Jaysus, they be."

"Do you think they wanted the best for you?"

"Sayin' so, they did."

Crawfish pointed toward the door. "Good. That means your real promise to them was to become your best. Right?"

Sean looked at Crawfish. "How does me do that?"

"Well, let's go an' see Pastor Tiemann about the funeral service and we can talk about your future on the way," Crawfish answered and took a step toward the door.

"Ye know me canna be readin' or writin'."

"Ah, that's going to change, lad. That's going to change."

Sean smiled and wiped a stray tear from his cheek. "The things in their pockets, me have." Sean held out both hands to reveal the watch and a few coins. "Mr. Hawkens be sayin' the constable has their guns."

"That sounds right, Sean," Crawfish said.

"Sounds right? Of course, it sounds right. Do you think I'd steal from a dead man?" Hawkens waved both hands with the lamp flame struggling to stay lit and the wet handkerchief flopping in rhythm.

"Ay, ye might. Findin' out, me be doin'," Sean said in his most threatening voice.

Hawkens lowered both the lamp and cloth. "Don't take that tone with me, you Irish whelp." He punctuated his statement by blowing his nose and the lamp flame jumped again.

"You know, a careful man like yourself should be aware that Vin Lockhart thinks highly of the boy." Crawfish's voice was firmer than the undertaker's. Yet softer.

Raising the lamp again, the cabinetmaker-undertaker studied the red-haired businessman, searching for a sign that he was kidding. Didn't he just hear the boy say he promised to kill Lockhart? What was that all about? Satisfied Crawfish was telling the truth, Hawkens decided not to press the question about the earlier statement.

He lowered the light, wiped his nose with his handkerchief and said gently, "There's not going to be any trial, so the marshal won't need the guns for evidence." He paused, sneezed and added, "Are you . . . related . . . to these . . . gentlemen? *Ach-ooo!*"

Staring at the watch in his opened palm, Sean closed his hand around it. "Nay. They only be me friends."

"Friends?" Hawkens forgot himself for a moment. "You're friends with these two no-good thugs?"

"Not every man's friends turn out the way he wants them to be, you know, Hawkens." Crawfish popped the bowler back on his head and patted it. "Let's be going, Sean. We need to see an old lady."

CHAPTER NINE

After passing under a lodgepole gateway, Lockhart reined up in front of a low-roofed house with a porch that crept across its front. A well-tended flower bed peeked at him from the east side. He had already seen the other two ranches on his short mental list, as he had several rides before. Now it was time to look over Crawfish's suggestion. The Broken R.

Late morning sun lay easy on two smaller buildings and a small, well-built corral to the south of a weathered barn with some missing boards. Next to it was a much larger corral in need of repair in several places. Poking its head above and behind the house was a windmill. On the rolling hillside, a dozen cows and three horses grazed on long grass.

"Hello, the house! I'm Vin Lockhart of Denver City," he called loudly from astride his bay. "I would like to talk with you . . . please."

The horse whinnied as if adding its own salutation.

He waited and was about to yell again when the front door wobbled and swung open. He couldn't make out whoever stood in the doorway. Only the gray silhouette was definitive. It was a man. An older man.

"Yes suh, Mr. Lockhart. Believe I've heard o' ya." The voice reaffirmed it was an older man. "The way I heard it, ya ain't a fella to cross."

Lockhart smiled and held his arms away from his body. "I don't take well to someone trying to steal what's mine, if that's what you mean."

"Neithur do I."

"May I get down?"

"Ya kin do whatever ya wants, I reckon." The voice had a bit of a smile to it.

Lockhart dismounted, but kept his horse between himself and the doorway. There was no reason to be careless.

"Are you the owner of the Broken R?" he asked, holding the reins so the horse continued to stand in front of him.

"I sure 'nuff is. Me an' the missus." Then the man laughed, realizing the significance of Lockhart's movement. "I like a fella with sand—an' savvy." He chuckled again. "But ya got no reason to fear me." He stepped through the doorway and onto the porch. "I'm Harry Rhymer. Me an' my missus own the place. Such as it is. Used to be a place whar a fella could buy hisself a fine hoss. But that were a while back. What kin I do fer ya?" Bright blue eyes flashed with interest. "Ain't got no hoss as good as the one yur a'ridin'."

The older man was quite bowlegged, but there was pride in

his movements. His head was covered in snow-white hair that curled around his fresh collar. It appeared he was wearing his Sunday best; a gray, pinstripe vest and pants with a crooked string tie. He wore no coat. When he moved, his bowlegged walk made him look like a toy figure in need of a play horse.

Tugging on his hat brim and stepping away from his horse, Lockhart explained what he was looking for and why. He asked how much of the surrounding land they actually owned.

Rhymer listened without comment. Nodding, he motioned toward the house. "We was 'bout to set our noon table. Sunday dinner 'n all. Be ri't proud to have ya join us." He chuckled and added, "The missus does a ri't smart baked chicken. Dumplin's, too."

"I wouldn't want to intrude on your day. I can come back if you're interested in talking about it."

"Naw, nuthin' could be further from the truth o' it," Rhymer said. "Sunday meetin' this morn left us a'wantin' more comp'ny, I reckon. Martha, that's my wife, she was a'sayin' jes'that when ya rode up."

"Well, you don't have to invite me twice," Lockhart said and led his horse toward the house and flipped the reins over the hitching rack.

"Good 'nuff. We kin talk 'bout your idea ov'r some eatin'. I like talkin' hoss."

Removing his hat as he entered, Lockhart followed Rhymer inside.

A hardy, rolltop desk with a matching chair was actually the central attraction of the main room in the three-room house. Even from where he stood, Lockhart could see scratch marks on the lower sides of the desk where, most likely, Rhymer's spurs had repeatedly passed. Above the desk was a framed, hand-drawn map of the Broken R ranch land. Resting on the desktop was a Bible. It appeared to have been well read judging by its many dog-eared pages.

A table and chairs filled the far side; Lockhart noticed it was already set for three.

The lone treasure representing a sense of elegance was a purple vase with gold trim waiting discovery on a scratched end table. It stood next to a threadbare settee that had been the height of fashion years ago. A cheaply framed Currier & Ives print of a mountain scene dominated the north wall. In the corner set a pair of worn mule-eared boots with strapped-on spurs.

On the adjoining wall was a daguerreotype of a young man and a woman in traditional wedding pose. The wedding day of Marsha and Harry Rhymer. A flicker of Morning Bird and him in such a pose passed through his mind.

"That's a mighty handsome couple," Lockhart said, motioning toward the picture.

Rhymer smiled and turned up the closest oil lamp to its fullest, letting the yellow light swagger through the room.

Without their noticing, Martha Rhymer entered from the kitchen. She brought cups of hot coffee for her husband and their guest.

Turning in reaction to something sensed, Lockhart saw her and said, "I'm Vin Lockhart, ma'am. And you must be the beautiful lady in that picture."

"Oh my, that was a long time ago," she proclaimed breathlessly. She recovered quickly from the surprising compliment and walked forward with the cups.

Lockhart took the offering, thanked her and said, "If I may say so, ma'am, you haven't changed much at all. I'd know you anywhere."

She looked at him without speaking; but with interest in her eyes. The light from the room's lone lamp didn't quite reach her face. Her pulled-back hair was mostly gray now with only hints of an earlier day's auburn coloring. Around her face, laugh lines and crow's-feet had taken control. She wore a prim gray dress that had never known fashion.

Harry Rhymer thanked her for his coffee with a wink. He

asked when dinner would be ready and she said it was. She curtseyed slightly to Lockhart and retreated to the kitchen. Rhymer motioned for Lockhart to join him at the oilcloth-covered table in the other part of the room.

After sitting down, the Rhymers quickly said grace in union. Lockhart folded his hands and was silent.

When they were finished, he turned to her. "Mrs. Rhymer, there is a custom . . . in my family . . . before eating. It goes way back."

She nodded with curiosity filling her face.

"My family . . . ah, gives the first bite of food to . . . ah, God . . . as a thank you," he continued. "Would you mind if I took a small bite of meat outside—and left it?"

"What kinda religion be that?" Harry blurted.

"Where are your manners, Harry," she said and laid her hand on the table. "Of course, Mr. Lockhart. You do your . . . grace . . . your way. We will wait."

Nodding his head, Lockhart cut a small piece of meat from the platter with his knife. Taking it in his hand, he rose and left, walking through the front door.

"Never hear-tell the likes o' that a'fer." Harry watched him leave.

"Oh, I believe that is an old Methodist tradition, Harry," she explained. "I remember my momma telling me about it. Back in Pennsylvania."

"Kind of a waste o' good food, seems to me."

"Some might think our ways are strange."

"Well, maybe. Leastwise, we don't go 'round throwin' out food."

"Hush. He's coming back," Martha said and added loudly, "Did it go well, Mr. Lockhart?"

"Yes, ma'am. Thank you for understanding."

She smiled. "Religion is important to all of us. Whether it's being a Methodist or a Presbyterian."

"Yes, ma'am." Lockhart sat and she handed him a bowl of mashed potatoes.

During dinner, Martha's eyes began to study Lockhart with a careful curiosity. He was uncomfortable, but polite. There was no conversation as they ate as most Western men and women did, in silence. Lockhart was eager to discuss the idea of purchasing the ranch, but felt it would be improper for him to bring up the subject.

After cleaning his plate with relish, Harry stood and sought a decanter of whiskey, hidden behind the coal shuttle propped against the wrought-iron stove. He declared it was all right to drink on Sunday because they had a guest as he disappeared into the kitchen and returned with two glasses. Quickly, he poured the brown liquid into them without waiting for Martha's response.

Harry's whiskey began to open up memories as they sat at the table. "Ya should'a seed this hyar valley the fust y'ars me an' the missus t'war hyar." He took another swig of whiskey. "We'uns got hit by a winter. Lawdy. Jes' wouldn't quit, that winter. Snow kept a'pilin' up." He cocked his head toward Lockhart and continued, "Our hosses was a'dyin' left an' ri't. Didn't haff room in the barn for most. No 'mount o' pawin' an' bellerin' could bust down through that ice an' snow nohow. Me an' the missus, we dun dug holes in that thar snow fer 'em whar we could, ya know. Down to the grass. Wouldn't stay dug longer'n a few minutes. Then we dun grabbed heaps o' hay . . . an' drug it out to 'em. Busted ice in that thar stream back yonder fer waterin'. Chopped trees with leaves still a'hangin' . . . fer 'em to ait."

Lockhart listened, assuming this story was to tell him why they wouldn't sell at any price.

"Hellfire, 'cuse me, Martha . . . snowed sumthin' awful. Night was godalmighty white sometimes . . . One blizzard on top o' nuther'n. Herd kept a'driftin'. Won't stop in no blizzard, ya know. Had to keep a'follerin' 'em. Could only save fifty head. That t'were it. Fifty head. 'Cludin' the wild stuff even."

"That must've been an awful time," Lockhart said and sipped his drink.

"Dun lost my furstest herd dawg in that thar winter hell. Didna' find 'im 'til spring-up. Froze stiff, he were. A'side some dead hosses. He was a good-un. Died a'tryin' to herd 'em, he did. Yessir."

Awkwardly, Lockhart tried to find a subject of interest to Martha. He didn't feel he could bring up the possibility of buying the ranch until Harry said something about it. He asked about her favorite mountain flower. It was the only thing he could think of.

She blushed and said, "Wild roses. I've been trying to grow them myself."

"Oh yes, I saw them. On the side of the house. Very pretty," he said. "I like Indian paintbrush, too."

She did, too. "And those pretty blue mountain poppies. I want to try them sometime, too, do you like them?"

He liked them as well, but then he remembered Young Evening was partial to the tiny blossoms and felt guilty. He blinked his eyes several times rapidly to clear that whisper away.

Harry's new declaration did it for him.

"Ya wasn't 'round hyar in '68, were ya?" He painted a zigzag with his finger on the table. "Rain came like the Bible story. Hey, Cherry Creek itself, down in town, dun flooded. Way ov'r. The ol' *Rocky Mountain News* building got washed away. Yessir, it did." He drew another zigzag line. "An' ya know what? Ol' William Byers, he owns the *News*, ya know. Wal, he ups an' buys the damn rival sheet . . . ah, *The Commonwealth* . . . an' took its building." He chuckled.

Lockhart shook his head in response, wondering if the old man would ever get to the subject of buying the ranch. Or was this the way Harry Rhymer dealt with a subject he wasn't interested in pursuing? Why did he invite him to eat? Just for the company? That was possible.

Another swig brought yet another tale from the old man.

"Seems like jes' yestiday, me an' the missus was a'takin' on Crow . . . an' them Sioux. Painted red devils. Ri't hyar, mind ya. Lost'd me a son to the Cheyenne."

"I'm sorry to hear that. You know I should be going." Lockhart pushed his glass aside. "Dinner was wonderful, Mrs. Rhymer. Thank you." He stood.

"Oh . . . that t'weren't whar I were a'trackin', Vin. Jes' that ya said ya was interested in buyin' our place—an' I was tryin' to get back to that subject." Harry waved his hands to demonstrate his maneuvering, saw his glass and drained it.

Martha looked like she had been burned. Her eyes shot open and her jaw flopped open. "W-What did you say? B-Buy our place? Oh my . . . oh my . . ."

Lockhart wasn't certain what he should say, but tried anyway. "Mrs. Rhymer, I told your husband that I hoped to start a horse ranch. Raise really good mounts, like you two used to do. I've been looking at several ranches in this area. Hadn't visited yours before."

"We wouldn't have anywhere to live." Her declaration stopped his presentation.

"We only raise milk cows now. And some hay. No more horses. No more. Those in the pasture are old. Nobody wants them. Except Harry and me." She tabbed her eye with the corner of her apron. "I have my flowers."

Harry watched her without speaking, then turned to Lockhart. "Guess that settles it, Vin. Me an' the missus will be stayin' put."

Lockhart studied the half-empty glass of whiskey before responding. "I understand. There are a lot of memories here, I'm sure." He looked at Martha, who was examining something on her apron in her lap. "But I wouldn't want you to leave. I could buy the place—and you would stay on. As partners. You would live here, just like you do now. Together, we can make this the best horse ranch around." He glanced at Harry. "I'm going to need good help. An' from what I hear, you were the best."

Martha was the first to respond. "But where would you stay?"

"I'd stay in town. Where I am," Lockhart said quietly. "Until I could build something for myself. Out here. You would stay in your beautiful house. Here. Forever."

"Wal, I'll be!" Harry blurted and looked around for the whiskey decanter. "Did I e'vr tell ya 'bout the time I broke a mustang stallion? He sired us a handful o' fine mounts, yessuh he did. Jericho were his name. Jericho. From the Bible. It were Martha's idée."

CHAPTER TEN

Lockhart was still smiling as he reined up at the hitching rack in front of the Black Horse Hotel. Nothing was settled, of course, but the Rhymers seemed excited about selling to him and staying on to help build a horse ranch. The price he offered was more than fair, and would give them a good return on their longtime effort, while relieving them of the ongoing burden of making the land work for them. They promised to let him know for certain by the end of the week.

"It's a good fit. For both of us, Panther-Strikes," Lockhart mumbled to himself as he entered the hotel lobby. "I think Harry's a horseman at heart." He chuckled and remembered the older man's comments about milk cows not being his favorite thing.

Talking with the Rhymers had helped crystallize the idea of a horse ranch for him. He would first make a swing north to find his former in-laws. Then together they would round up some wild mustangs and drive them back. He would purchase several good mares—and a stallion—to complete his initial stock. The Rhymers would remain on the ranch, living there and watching over the place. He would pay Harry foreman's wages. His biggest concern would be talking Crawfish out of renaming it the "Silver R." He chuckled to himself at the thought.

"I hope Touches-Horses likes the idea," he muttered and turned his head to the side. "Stone Dreamer, too." Unspoken was the thought of Morning Bird.

To be fair with the Rhymers, he had shared even this part of his dream, that of bringing three Indians to the ranch. Martha had reacted first and said, as Christians, they should not object. Harry said he was glad they weren't Jews—or Irish—and she had chastised him for the observation.

Inside the hotel, several men loitered in the dark crimson-curtained lobby, reading newspapers, relaxing in leather club and overstuffed chairs, smoking and talking among themselves. Lockhart paid little attention to any of them as he moved across the floor toward the stairs.

At the registration counter, Aaron Whitaker tried to get his attention. The young man's pale face was gripped with concern. Lockhart noticed him at the same time as a voice hailed him from the closest chair.

"Mr. Lockhart, I presume? May I have a word with you, sir?" An overweight gentleman in a too-tight, three-piece suit jumped from the overstuffed chair, dropping the newspaper in its seat. A large, leather valise remained beside the chair.

The man hurried toward Lockhart, who paused at the bottom of the staircase. Waiting.

With a nervous nod, the man introduced himself. "I'm Titus R. Kane, special representative of the Ives Linen Company." He paused and held out his hand. "I sell luxury linens and towels to several of your town's finest stores."

"Good for you." Lockhart shook his hand.

"Ah, I have a concern, sir," Kane said, dropping his voice to little more than a whisper. "A grave concern, I fear."

Lockhart turned slightly toward the man. "I'm sorry to hear that. How may I be of help?"

"It's about one of your . . . ah, guests, sir." Kane's face was flushed. "It's come to my attention, sir . . . and I'm certain it is an oversight only . . . that the hotel has a . . . person here . . . who is . . . ah, not an American."

"Really?" Lockhart knew where this was headed and clenched his teeth to hold back the anger rising.

Kane's shoulders rose and fell and his massive belly wiggled in response to the movement. "Ah, yes, I'm afraid so." He leaned toward Lockhart and whispered, "There is a savage . . . in one of your rooms."

"Only one?" Lockhart replied. "I would've sworn there were several. Some Texas boys, I believe. Here on business. They were in rare form Friday night." He chuckled.

It helped to curb his annoyance at the man's ignorant intolerance. He recalled Crawfish telling him that all intolerance was based on ignorance.

"Well, I'm sure they were . . . a little rowdy. That's fine. We all enjoy an occasional night of . . . pleasure." Kane shook his head and continued, "No sir, the guest I'm talking about . . . is an . . . Indian savage."

Lockhart's countenance shifted from being amused to being agitated. "An Indian savage, huh?"

"Yes sir. As I said, I'm sure you didn't know it. I'm sure it was done without your knowledge—or the manager's. I am, of course, concerned . . . about safety and . . ."

"Mr. Kane. The only thing you really need to be concerned about—is me," Lockhart snarled. "I am an Oglala Sioux warrior. I am one of the Kit Foxes. We never run from a fight." He folded his arms and was silent.

Swallowing to keep bile from entering his throat, Kane didn't know how to react. Was this man with the dangerous reputation kidding him? What did he mean by saying that he was some kind of Indian warrior? He stared at Lockhart, trying to decide how to respond.

"Ah, sir . . . I am really serious . . . about this matter," Kane finally blurted. "No hotel can . . . allow such, as you know."

Lockhart's eyes flashed heat and he turned to Aaron

Whitaker, who jumped, startled by the sudden attention. He couldn't pretend he wasn't watching and didn't try.

"Mr. Kane is checking out. Now. Help him with his luggage, please," Lockhart declared and spun back to the stunned salesman. "Don't ever come back here, Mr. Kane." His voice became low and coiled. "I don't want to hear you told somebody about this. Any of it."

Sweat exploded across Kane's forehead. He gulped something that sounded like he would never do that, but couldn't help glancing at the others in the lobby.

Lockhart started back up the stairs, hesitated and looked over at the quiet men seated there. It was obvious they had been discussing the same concern and were waiting for Kane's report.

"Excuse me, Mr. Kane," Lockhart said and stepped past the heavyset salesman to the open area.

"Gentlemen, if I may have your attention a moment, please." He waited for their response.

"Thank you. Some of you may have heard there is an elderly Indian woman staying here." His gaze caught the surprise in several eyes at the word, "elderly."

"Yes sir, Mr. Lockhart, I did hear that," one gray-haired businessman stated. "From Mr. Kane there."

"And?"

"Oh, I figured he had it wrong. This is a very fine hotel." He straightened his back, then touched his navy blue silk cravat. His wild eyebrows saluted.

Lockhart folded his arms. "No, Mr. Kane is right. There is an elderly Indian woman here. She's tired and hungry."

The businessman jumped to his feet. "My God, man! How could you have a red savage? Here?"

Seated next to him, a well-dressed man with long sideburns and thick glasses muttered, "Next thing you know they'll be letting Jews, Irish—and coloreds—in here."

The gray-haired businessman looked down at him and agreed. "Yeah, an' the damn Italians."

Lockhart's eyes narrowed. "She needed help—and we are giving it."

"B-But for how long?" another salesman asked. He was seated in the far southeast corner, wearing a brown suit and holding a matching bowler in his hand. His pronounced forehead was layered in a frown that sparkled with new perspiration.

"'Til she's well."

"B-But they're . . . they're not civilized!"

Lockhart smiled, but it didn't reach his eyes. "Not civilized, huh? Let's see, what makes a group of people civilized?" His mind raced to Crawfish's explanations. "They need a division of labor. Well-defined. Ah, they need a religion. A noble one. A true philosophy of life that honors others, respects truth, and the land around them. They must be willing to care for those in need." He cocked his head to the side. "What else? Oh yeah, art. They need art. You know, original art. They need music. They must have a rich legend to share. Stories of honor. Courage. Their children must be loved—and taught worthy values. Guess what that describes, Kane? Or do you disagree with my definition?"

The salesman wiped his forehead with his coat sleeve, glanced at the others for help, then finally stuttered, "I-It isn't the same. T-They just aren't the same . . . as us. Yeah, that's it. They just aren't the same as us."

"Thank God they aren't." Lockhart turned back toward the stairs.

Kane was already gone.

Lockhart looked back at the group murmuring among themselves. "Oh, you are most welcome to check out." His voice was ominous, rich with disgust. He took three steps, paused once more and added, "Just don't come back."

"Come on, men, this is ridiculous," the first businessman said, waving his arms to encourage support. "I'm not staying where people who aren't real Americans are allowed. My

God! I wouldn't let 'em in my house—and I sure as hell don't want 'em around me."

Only the brown-suited salesman and the gentleman with the long sideburns agreed. They stood and joined the gray-haired businessman in a supporting, animated conversation. Another gentleman, seated beside the long-sideburned man, returned to his newspaper and cigar. A businessman in the far opposite corner stood for a moment, then sat down again and began looking at his *Harper's* magazine as if nothing had occurred.

Seated across the lobby, against the northwest's drapes, a tall man turned to his friend sitting beside him in an over-stuffed chair. "I'm ready for a drink. How about you, Robert? Maybe some cards."

"Sounds good."

The two men stood without looking at the standing gentlemen who were reinforcing each other's decision to check out. Lockhart was halfway up the steps, no longer paying attention to the lobby.

"Mr. Lockhart, my friend, Robert, and I are heading out for a drink—and some poker," the taller man hollered. "We'll be back." He paused and yelled again, "You know a good place to get both?" His smile was wide.

Nodding, Lockhart stopped and turned toward them. "Glad to have you in our hotel, gentlemen." He cocked his head to the side. "You might want to try the Silver Queen. Tell the bartender there that I said the first round's on me." He continued up the stairs.

As he approached Room 24, he heard talking inside. The voice was Crawfish's. Gentle. Almost birdlike. He turned the brass doorknob, opened the door and stepped inside.

His gaze absorbed the entire room and he was both pleased and surprised. The disgusting exchange in the lobby was momentarily forgotten.

Sitting in a chair, shoved next to the bed, was Crawfish. He was holding a dark bottle in one hand; a tablespoon in the other. Standing behind him was Sean, holding a tray of food. In the bed, sitting up, was Falling Leaf with a smile on her face. On her right, resting on the quilted spread, was a piece of bluish gray galena, containing both gold and silver. Near it was the empty parfleche with her gun lying on top of it. Lockhart was surprised, and pleased, to see she had relinquished the weapon to them.

Lockhart recognized the rock from a bookshelf in Crawfish's library. It was an early discovery in their prospecting days. He had held on to it for luck.

Folding his arms, Lockhart spoke first to the Indian woman in his best Lakotan, hoping she would understand him. Her immediate response was forceful, almost shrill.

"Cinks', le niho' kin hwo?"

The question, "Son, is that your voice," made him wonder if she thought he was truly a relative, or if it was merely a term of endearment.

In her language, he said his name, both his Oglala warrior's name and his Christian name.

"Nitu'wa kin slolwa'ys," she responded.

To himself, he muttered her statement in English, "I know who you are," and expected her to say he was the one who rides with the Grandfathers. He braced himself.

"Tase' wanagi wan canpi' na hohu' iko'yake ka."

He laughed at her statement that surely a ghost has neither flesh nor bones. He asked her how she felt and she replied that she felt much better, thanks to him—and to the red-haired shaman and his *tunkan*.

Nodding, Lockhart stepped closer to the bed. "Well, Crawfish, you old goat, she thinks you're a wise shaman—with a holy stone. Thanks for coming." He looked over at Sean. "You, too, Sean."

"From the house, we be bringing some fine venison. Roasted brown an' fine, it be," Sean said and held the tray higher. "Crawfish hisself be the cook o' it. Tasty, she be. A sweet taste, it has." He examined the tray's several bowls.

"And a baked apple with brown sugar. Lots o' it. Cut up into small slices, it be. Aye, an' coffee with lots of sugar, too."

Lockhart smiled. "I'm sure she'll like it, Sean."

"Sean helped me, ~~Vin,~~" Crawfish said and held up the bottle. "Gave her a tablespoon of Dr. Kilmer's Female Remedy. It's a good tonic, I think. Supposed to purify the blood. Can't hurt her, that's for sure." He grinned. "Gave her a few swallows of whiskey, too. She liked that." He motioned toward the whiskey bottle on the nightstand, then glanced at the rock in her hand. "I remembered what your Indian friends say about stones. Thought it might be comforting to her. Remember it?"

"Yes, I sure do."

"Lordy be, that was like another lifetime ago, wasn't it?"

Lockhart walked to the side of the bed opposite Crawfish, took Falling Leaf's extended hand in his own, patted it and felt her forehead with his free left hand.

"You have no fever. You look much better," he said in her native language.

"Mawa' ni oa'hihi."

"Yes, I'm sure you can walk, but you need to rest here. Get strong. Eat much. Drink much."

She laughed and asked, *"Nitu'wa he'ci?"*

"Who *ever* are you?" he repeated in English and answered in Lakotan, "I am your friend, your son, your brother. You know that."

She thanked him and held up the rock for him to examine. He took it in both hands and turned it over several times, letting the window light reflect from its tiny indications of richness.

"Falling Leaf was awake when we came. About a half hour ago." Crawfish stood and retreated to a nightstand, where he placed the medicine bottle and the spoon beside the whiskey bottle.

"Should me be giving herself the tray now?" Sean asked.

"Sure," Crawfish and Lockhart replied in unison.

Lockhart explained what she was receiving to eat in her own tongue. Crawfish nodded, recognizing some of the words from their previous learning sessions.

Sean carefully laid the tray beside her on the bed and started to leave. Her feeble hand reached out and took hold of his wrist and held it. She looked at his face and said something he didn't understand.

Sean shrugged; his eyes were a question.

"She said you remind her of her grandson. He is strong, brave and caring," Lockhart said.

"Oh." Sean leaned over and held his hand over hers. "Thank ye, ma'am. That be the nicest thing said about meself. In all me life."

She studied the plate of meat and apple slices and tore a small piece from a wedge of venison. Words barely escaping from her slightly trembling mouth, she presented the morsel in all four directions, awkwardly leaned over to point it at the floor, then lifted the meat offering above her head, toward the ceiling. She paused and handed the dedicated meat piece toward Sean.

He stared at the offering, uncertain of what to do.

"She wants you to take it and offer it to God," Lockhart said. "Remember what I did at breakfast?"

"Aye, that me do, but where should me be takin' this meat?" Sean asked as he accepted the morsel, nodding at her and trying to smile.

"Go over to the window and toss it."

"Aye."

Lockhart, Crawfish and Falling Leaf watched the Irish boy move to the window, shove it open wider and toss the meat.

"Say thanks . . . to God," Crawfish suggested. "Ah, *Wakantanka*." He glanced at Lockhart. "She'll know that word, right?"

Lockhart smiled and nodded.

"'Tis a thank you from Falling Leaf to Ye . . . *Wakan-*

tanka." Sean threw the morsel with a backhanded flip into the air and surveyed its downward spin. He stood beside the window for a moment before turning back to the room.

"Ah-man," Falling Leaf said clearly.

"Aye, amen it be," Sean repeated and looked at Lockhart. "That's probably the only English she knows."

"Aye, Crawfish can be teachin' her the words," Sean said brightly.

Falling Leaf thanked him with her eyes as she began to eat. While she enjoyed the meal, the three shared their day, ending with Crawfish explaining they had been invited to Dr. Milens's house for a seance tonight. The strawberry-haired businessman was more excited about that than the news about Lockhart possibly finding a place to begin his horse ranch. Lockhart tried to hide his disappointment in that, but was outspoken in his lack of interest in attending the evening's gathering.

"Why don't you attend that—without me," Lockhart said. "I've heard enough about ghosts to last me a long time."

Crawfish's eyebrows jumped in response. "You have to go, Vin. Dr. Milens said he wants six. It's the perfect number." He pushed on Lockhart's arm. "Come on, man, you'll get a kick out of it."

Pursing his lips, Lockhart started to suggest that he take Sean instead, but realized that would be insensitive to say with the boy just losing two friends, and changed the subject. He shared that he thought Falling Leaf was Hunkpapa, one of the Sioux divisions, and told them about the confrontation in the lobby.

"I know Kane," Crawfish declared, waving his hands. "Linens-and-lice, he's a foolish one. He's a talker, though. Everybody in town'll know about this come nightfall."

Lockhart rubbed his nose with the back of his thumb. "I warned him about that." His lean face was dark and troubled. "I'll pay for the empty rooms."

"Sakes alive, don't be silly, Vin," Crawfish declared. "We're in this together. All of it. I want you involved in the new bank—and, I hope, you'll have me as your partner in this horse ranch."

Mesmerized, Sean watched the two men discuss their business situation. Crawfish was interested in having an orchestra at the restaurant. The Irish boy didn't know anyone with such wealth; they didn't act like his two Irish friends said all rich men acted. Crawfish and Lockhart were nothing like they said, although people certainly deferred to them. Especially Lockhart. But Sean thought that was because of his reputation with a gun. The boy was coming to the conclusion that Lightning Murphy and Big Mike had lied to him. It was hard to accept. They were family. Sort of. At least the only family he could remember. And now, it was becoming clear they were no good. The two men standing in front of him were that. Good men.

He had been taught that it was all right to steal because others had more than they needed. Or deserved. He had been taught to watch out for himself, because no one really cared about anybody else. He had been taught to lie when he had to, because no one wanted to hear the truth. Without realizing it, he shook his head and glanced at the old woman who was now sipping her coffee.

She saw his gaze and said something he didn't understand. He bit his lower lip and wanted to say something back. Something nice. All that came out was: "Me be hopin' ye feel better, Falling Leaf."

A smile was her answer.

He barely heard Crawfish ask Lockhart about the Irish thugs' guns and if he thought they could be secured from the sheriff's office. Lockhart said he would ask, but Sean shouldn't since the authorities would be suspicious of his interest and start asking questions.

"Hay-for-the-taking, I almost forgot. We need to get the boy's horses, Vin," Crawfish said and explained the situation about the wagon and the Indian horse, ending with a question about keeping it.

"An Indian pony? Really?" Lockhart said and turned to the boy. "Assuming that's where you found it, I think it belongs to you, Sean. You might have a good animal there. Worth something more than a stable mount."

"Na, 'tis not likely. Not wantin' anyone to ride it, it were. Mike, he be tyin' it to the wagon back. It didna want to go with us."

Lockhart walked over to the bed and talked quietly with Falling Leaf, telling her that they were leaving, but would be back later, and she was to stay in bed. With approval from him, Crawfish and Sean stepped closer and said their good-byes.

"Wica'sa wan lila ksa'pa kin he'ca," she said, reaching out with her hand to touch Crawfish's face.

Lockhart smiled. "She says you are a very wise man."

Crawfish beamed. "Thank you, Falling Leaf."

He wasn't familiar with this Lakotan dialect, even though he knew some of Lockhart's Indian language. He also learned a few words in Ute from their visit to a mining camp years before.

She nodded and reached over to Sean's face. *"Eda'a' u ye."*

He looked over at Lockhart.

"She said, 'Be sure to come,'" Lockhart interpreted.

Sean broke into a wide grin. "Aye, mum. Ye can be countin' on it."

As they left the room, Crawfish suggested it might be wise to move her to his house. It would be safer for her—and definitely less conspicuous. Surprising to him, Lockhart agreed and said they should move her after they returned with Sean's horses. Crawfish reminded him that they had an appointment with Dr. Milens later. Lockhart's frown was his only response.

At the bottom of the stairway, they stopped to talk with the young hotel clerk. Aaron Whitaker was clearly agitated and reported that Kane had checked out as well as three other men.

"Room 24 is locked," Crawfish said quietly. "I want you to check on her in an hour or so. See that she is comfortable."

"We'll be back a little later, to move her out of the hotel," Lockhart said. His gaze took in the lobby where only three men remained from earlier.

Whitaker's face glistened with relief at the statement. "Oh . . . w-where?"

"Doesn't matter," Lockhart responded. "She'll be well cared for. That's all you need to know."

"Of course, Mr. Lockhart. I was just . . ."

"I appreciate your concern."

CHAPTER ELEVEN

Behind the treeline was a shallow pond. Nearby was a squatty bowl of land where buffalo once rolled. Sean stared at it and remembered thinking it looked like a grave when he and the two Irishmen first saw it. A brisk, spring wind had intimidated any clouds from the sky, making the moment seem more desolate than it was. The day had definitely turned cool. Sean shivered, then glanced at Crawfish and Lockhart beside him in Crawfish's carriage, but neither seemed to notice that he was cold. Yet white frost-smoke encircled their faces.

Around them was mostly open and flat land, as far as a man could see, except for the long line of cottonwoods, blackjack and brush. From a narrow ravine on the far side of the pond, a skinny jackrabbit darted across the rock spoon that held the pond in place, narrowly missed the water, then scrambled away. They watched the small interruption as if it were the most important sight in the world.

"Aye, this be the place," Sean said.

Neither man responded.

Their limited field of vision took in the closest part of a shallow sleeve of water cut into the flat rock. The glistening small pool was barely twenty yards ahead. A brownish green jewel for an instant, then just flat brown water. Sounds of animals drinking came softly to their ears as Lockhart jumped from the carriage, followed by Sean.

"You might as well wait here, Crawfish," Lockhart said, walking farther to his left to take in the entire pond.

All breath was sucked from him as he saw a distinctive bay horse, a stallion, drinking, along with two wagon horses. He recognized the beautiful animal as a Cheyenne war horse. Paint medicine and battle records decorated its legs, chest and flanks. A small beaded pouch with a dangling eagle feather lay on its broad chest.

A rawhide thong was tied to the horse's lower jaw and acted as the reins and the bit—and were the only guides for the rider to control the animal. A long rope was tied around its neck; the other end was tied to the back of the buckboard. Lockhart knew the rope's original function: this was for a falling warrior to grab as he fell and the horse would stop. A doubled-over buffalo hide with its hair remaining was the saddle base. Over it was a doubled robe upon which the warrior sat. Twisted sinew straps became the stirrups. It was a simple rig but a traditional Cheyenne saddle.

Lockhart watched in admiration. There was something about the horse. A certain arrogance. The animal knew it was special. Lockhart smiled.

The two other horses had been left harnessed to the wagon and their long reins tied to a nearby tree branch. At least the Irish thugs had left the horses in a position to graze and drink.

The stallion's head came up, its ears perking to locate some sound that the horse didn't think should be there. Birds exploded from the tree as the great horse reared in defiance of the unseen enemy. The two other horses stutter-stepped and backed away from the water, bumping against each other.

"Easy now, boy. Easy," Lockhart called to the stallion as he worked his way down to the animal. "You're going to be fine. You're coming with us."

From the other side of the boulder, Sean's syrupy reinforcement was equally reassuring to the agitated animal.

As if understanding, the horse became as suddenly quiet as it had been fiercely struggling. The great animal was alert and ready to explode. The horse's head dropped slowly as its body shivered. The wagon horses' ears stood at attention.

"It's going to be fine, boy. Going to be fine." Lockhart reached the horse and stroked its neck and back.

Sean stayed where he was, watching wide-eyed.

"Quite a horse, Sean," Lockhart said, patting the horse's neck and rubbing its ears.

"Aye, that's what Big Mike hisself dun said."

"Well, he knew his horseflesh, I'll give him that."

"There are the makin's of a good bloodline here," Lockhart added. "He'd make a lot of stallions mighty jealous."

"Do ye want him for your ranch?"

"That would be real nice, Sean." Lockhart looked up. "We'll have to figure out a fair value. Crawfish can help us."

"Na. Me want ye to have it. A gift, it be."

Lockhart pushed his hat back on his forehead. "That is very generous of you, son, but it wouldn't be right. That stallion could be worth a lot."

Sean's face was a sunrise. He couldn't think of anything to say and finally blurted out a question about what the painted designs on the stallion meant.

"They tell the story of the warrior. Sorta like a soldier wearing his medals. See this handprint? That means the rider killed an enemy in hand-to-hand fighting."

"Gosh, four times he be doin' that, huh?"

"Looks that way. This square means he was a war leader.

And all these lines are coup marks, times when he touched an armed enemy and rode away. Takes a lot of courage to do that," Lockhart continued.

"Like horseshoes, those be lookin." Sean pointed to a cluster of painted marks.

Lockhart explained they indicated the number of horses he had stolen or the number of horse raids he'd been on.

"Hop-a-bunny!" Sean exclaimed, using Crawfish's favorite expression.

Lockhart grinned and continued the explanation.

Three circles meant the war leader had fought from behind rocks or some kind of protection three times. Another cluster of large dots and a lightning bolt represented the man's medicine and Lockhart guessed some other strange marks were similarly related. He said the same marks were presented on both sides of the horse and they weren't to be totaled.

The stallion was quiet; its ears followed Lockhart's words.

"What be that? It looks like, well, jus' two blotches, aye, that it does." Sean stared at two odd-shaped marks.

Lockhart nodded. "That's a sign he was in mourning."

A war chief's horse wouldn't necessarily be a fit for any ranch horses. Lockhart had realized that from the moment he saw the animal. The big bay had been trained to hunt buffalo, to swerve away from the beast when he heard the release of the arrow so he would not get hurt if the buffalo turned and charged. It had been trained for war, to rush at his master's enemies and to run until there was nothing left in him to run—and, then, to run more. Trained to stand silently beside the war chief's lodge at night, he was ready to challenge intruders in an instant, if needed. The great horse had been brought up with the power of paint markings and war medicine adorning his body.

Could this stallion learn to be a part of a herd—or would he be too cantankerous? If he wasn't trainable, it would be better to let him go now, Lockhart told himself. Stallions were generally regarded as too unstable and fierce to use as working horses. Mares were too sensitive. There were exceptions, of course, but most working horses were geldings. He didn't think it would be wise to put this great stallion with any herd when another stallion was there as well. That would only encourage a battle for control of the mares.

"Go back to the carriage and get my canteen, will you, Sean? It's in the back. On the floor."

"Aye." The boy spun and ran for the carriage.

When he returned, Crawfish was with him. The red-haired businessman was moving as fast as he could using his cane for balance.

When Crawfish saw the stallion, he pushed the bowler back on his head. "You sure this is what you want to be doing? Right now? That horse isn't going to take to a white man, you know." He crossed his arms. "Wouldn't a nice smoke be a bit more like it? A mite o' whiskey to boot? It's been a long day."

"Later, Crawfish, but you go ahead."

The stallion's ears perked up.

"Just you and my friend, big horse," Crawfish said. "You be good, you hear? Holy stirrups."

"What ye be sayin'?" Sean asked.

"Nothing. Just mumbling."

Sean studied his face, then saw Lockhart waving at him to bring the canteen.

Without looking at the boy, Crawfish's attention remained on the big bay and how it might react to his friend.

"Here ye be." Sean met Lockhart halfway, holding out the canteen. "Not much water in it, though." His rapid breath produced bursts of white in the cool air.

Lockhart took the canteen in his left hand and shook it. "That'll be plenty. Thanks." He draped the canteen straps over his shoulder and returned to the bay, who was now snorting a warning at the advancing man.

He took a few steps and the canteen straps slid down his arm. He grumbled at their disobedience.

"Let me be a'carryin' such," Sean volunteered.

"Thank you, son, I've got it. You stay with . . . Crawfish. Please."

Rebalancing the canteen, he faced the big bay who pawed the ground and snorted again.

Sean walked back to Crawfish, who motioned for him. Reluctantly, the boy scooted to his side and, immediately, was captivated by the challenge at the pond.

Ears flat against his head, the stallion kept pawing the ground and snorting; white puffs of frost-smoke bursting from his widened nostrils. An occasional buck, followed by a fierce kick, was a warning to stay away.

The tall man knew this and smiled. This was a lot of horse.

"Careful, Vin," Crawfish called out. "He doesn't like being tied up."

Lockhart nodded and untied the rope holding the horse and wrapped it around his fist.

"Oh my God! No, Vin, no!"

Holding the rope, Lockhart ran fifteen feet to his right, stopped in the adjoining clearing and dug his heels into the earth. The stallion's head jerked up and he reared, fighting the air with his powerful front hooves. Whinnying, the great horse bolted, but Lockhart was ready and began to guide the fierce animal in a wide circle around the clearing, held there by the now-taut rope.

The stallion continued his race for freedom, circling again and again. Running easily now, it was not quite a gallop, but more than a fast lope. Gradually, it slowed to canter, then to a trot. Still Lockhart made no attempt to move closer to the powerful mustang. Finally, the animal skidded to a complete stop and snorted. White frost-smoke engulfed its face momentarily and the stallion shook his head as if to rid himself of the strange surroundings and the strange thing in front of him.

Lockhart made no attempt to advance.

Slowly, the stallion turned to face the businessman and took a hesitant step toward him, then another. And another. When the animal was ten feet away, Lockhart stepped back several strides, retreating from its advance. He stopped and faced the horse.

The stallion's ears stood up and he whinnied.

Lockhart took another step backward.

The war horse stepped forward, closing the gap to five feet.

Smiling to himself, Lockhart retreated again, now only a few feet from the back of the wagon, and waited.

With a snort and shake of his head, the stallion took a step toward him. Lockhart took a corresponding step back and away from the horse and the wagon. The great horse's ears snapped to alertness and he took two steps toward Lockhart. The businessman matched the response with an equal retreat.

Lowering his head, the stallion walked toward him and, this time, Lockhart didn't move. The horse nuzzled Lockhart's chest.

Moving slowly so he would not frighten the stallion, Lockhart reached out his left hand and patted the horse's neck. Gradually, his hand worked its way across the animal's face and finally stroked the stallion's nose. The animal stepped even closer to receive the attention.

Horse and man stood together like that for several minutes. Lockhart didn't even hear his friend say something to Sean or respond to the boy's question about what Lockhart was doing and why.

After patting the horse's shoulders and withers, Lockhart dropped the rope and walked back to the center of the open area. The stallion followed, stride for stride. Lockhart glimpsed Crawfish and Sean at the boulder and nodded. Crawfish held up both hands clasped together, to indicate victory. Sean imitated the motion and asked if they should be praying.

"Well, you sure can, if you want," Crawfish said. "Reckon it's always a good idea."

"Were ye?"

Crawfish bit his lip, trying to decide how to respond. "Well, no, not then. I was telling Vin that he was doing good." He paused. "I, ah, I prayed earlier."

"What did ye be prayin' for?"

Shaking his head, Crawfish grinned. "For apples an' pears an' stick candy trees."

Sean laughed.

Lockhart's voice was soft and soothing. The horse didn't move.

"You are a good one, boy. You know I won't hurt you," Lockhart said. "I know the words sound different, but I don't know any Cheyenne. I'm betting you don't know any Lakota either."

He patted the stallion's head. The great horse pawed the earth once and was calm. With its head raised and ears erect, the stallion shifted its hooves and reexamined the strange man beside it. After a minute of evaluation, its head lowered and his ears righted themselves.

"Easy, Vin," Crawfish said, more to himself than to his friend.

Shaking his head, the red-haired businessman watched in amazement as Lockhart opened his canteen, poured water on his fingers and drew lines and circles with his fingers on the horse's neck, back and upper legs, replicating the dried markings.

Of course, Crawfish thought, tugged his bowler and grinned.

"What be hisself doin'?" Sean watched, his mouth remained open.

Crawfish explained, "Well, Vin wants the horse to feel real comfortable, The horse is used to having a warrior paint on it—before riding. Kinda like puttin' on old clothes, I reckon. Something comfortable."

Once more, Lockhart stepped away to let the stallion absorb all the new things that were happening to him. The lead rope remained loose, dragging on the ground.

Sean asked what he was doing now and Crawfish said, "I believe he's making the horse . . . ah, feel safe."

"Aye, safe."

"Did either of your, ah, friends ride that pony?"

"Na. Big Mike, he be sayin' it were a devil hoss." Sean shook his head. "Sellin' it to a rancher soon as we could. That was his plan."

Lockhart had mounted with the lead rope in his hand and the stallion was walking uneasily around the open area. The stallion crowhopped once, then again. He assumed it was nothing more than the horse greeting the day as many horses did. He smiled and told the stallion again that everything was fine. The horse's head dropped and his walk became smooth. A nudge of Lockhart's boots produced a trot.

"Well, it looks like we'll be heading back to town soon. I'm hungry. How about you?" Crawfish pointed at the wagon. "Can you handle the buckboard? I think Vin wants to ride the stallion back."

"Aye. Better'n Big Mike an' Lightnin', me could."

"Hey, Vin, can we head back now?" Crawfish yelled. "Sean can take the buckboard."

Lockhart waved and hollered back, "You've got quite a horse here, Sean."

"Aye, that we do."

CHAPTER TWELVE

They left the Cheyenne war horse and the wagon and its horses in McNair's livery. Henry McNair wasn't happy about stabling a stallion, let alone one painted with strange Indian symbols, but agreed to do so for a few days.

Lockhart went alone to the marshal's office while Sean

and Crawfish went to the Silver Queen Saloon to make certain things were all right there.

"Afternoon, Marshal." Lockhart stepped inside the combined office and jail.

Only one of the five cells was occupied; a drunken miner was asleep in the farthest cell. A coffeepot was chugging its boiling brew atop a cast-iron stove that was casting off as much smoke as it was warmth. Marshal Benson looked up from his desk and the fistful of papers resting there.

"Well, afternoon, Mr. Lockhart. What can I do for you?" Marshal Benson's smile was forced.

"Two things. First, if you're through with them, I'd like to have the guns of those two Irishmen."

Marshal Benson frowned, trying to let the request sink into his mind. What did Lockhart want with them? He tried to bring the weapons to his mind once more. A long-barreled Colt .45 and an open-top Merwin & Hulbert revolver. Neither one special in any way; both in need of cleaning. Did he dare ask?

Rubbing his chin, Lockhart saved him the trouble. "Mr. Crawford's been talking about having a handgun. For home protection, you know. Thought I'd save him a few bucks. Figure I have as much right of ownership as anyone. Right?"

"Well, sure. There's not gonna be any trial, so there's no need for 'em." Marshal Benson leaned over and pulled on the handle of a low, right-hand drawer. "Here, ya go. They need cleanin'." He held out both guns to Lockhart, holding them by their barrels in his right hand.

"Thanks. My partner will be pleased." Lockhart accepted the weapons, taking one in each hand and pushing them into his coat pockets.

"You said there was a second thing?"

"Oh, yeah. Out riding today, I came by a buckboard with two horses. Just outside of town. Looked like it had been there for a day or two. Judging by the tracks." He explained the location and his thought that the wagon belonged to the Irishmen, based on some clothes and supplies in the wagon. He said the rig was now at the livery and he thought the marshal's office would want to do some checking around to see if it was stolen.

"What makes you think it was stolen?" Marshal Benson glanced down, saw that the drawer was still open and leaned over to slam it shut.

"Nothing, really. Might not be. I shouldn't be trying to tell you how to do your job," Lockhart said. "Might belong to somebody in town and I just don't recognize it. Don't think so. Mr. McNair, he didn't know it either."

"I see." Marshal Benson licked his lower lip. He was always uncomfortable around Lockhart. The man seemed to see right into people. "I'll check it out. Tomorrow." He glanced at Lockhart, but let his eyes find the coffeepot in the corner. "If I can't find an owner, we'll put it up for sale. Or do you want it?"

"No. Just the guns. Any money should go to Mr. McNair to help pay for the stabling, don't you think?"

"Sure."

"You have a good day, Marshal," Lockhart said, turned and left.

The lawman watched him through the barred window, feeling a strange sense of relief.

After a quick meal at the Silver Queen, they moved Falling Leaf to Crawfish's house and Sean seemed pleased to stay with her. He agreed with Lockhart that the two guns should be cleaned and put away. Lockhart promised to teach him how to shoot, but only after he learned to read and write.

It was a few minutes after eight when Crawfish and a reluctant, and tired, Lockhart arrived at the small, wood-framed house Dr. Hugo Milens was renting from the mayor.

"Mr. Crawford. Mr. Lockhart. How good to see you." Dr. Milens greeted them warmly at the door. "Come in. Come in. Everyone else is here."

They entered the formally decorated house and were led to

a small room in the back. A lone lamp sat on a French-made table with ornate legs; the lamp was wrapped in a blue cloth that gave the room an otherworldly appearance. Lockhart thought it had once been a parlor, but now it looked like a forbidden cave.

Crawfish had shared what he knew about seances, mesmerists and spiritualists earlier. The idea was popular in various parts of the country. He said it was basically magicians and charlatans, usually interested in taking money from their guillible audiences. Fascinated by anything new, he was eager to participate, however. Magic itself had always been a curiosity. He assured his friend that his interest this evening lay in learning the techniques of the spiritualist, not in seeing or hearing spirits.

The air was alive with a strange smell.

"What is that . . . I smell? It's sort of sweet. Sort of musty," Crawfish said as he entered the room. "I'm sorry, I didn't mean . . ."

"No need to apologize." Dr. Milens turned toward him, smiling. "The odor has been growing all day." He inhaled dramatically. "It is the presence of spirits." He looked past the red-haired businessman to a stone-faced Lockhart. "There is one spirit who especially wants to talk with you, Mr. Lockhart. It is a young woman, I believe."

Lockhart's response was clearly one of annoyance. At being there. At being addressed in this way. He should have stayed with Sean and Falling Leaf.

Seven chairs were huddled around a black table; four were already occupied by Mayor McCormick and his wife, and Earnest Wilcox, a wealthy merchant, and his wife.

"Well, gentlemen and ladies, I believe you know each other—and no introductions are necessary." Dr. Milens made a wide sweep with his arm toward the table and back to Lockhart and Crawfish.

Both McCormick and Wilcox stood and held out their hands for a proper greeting.

"I'm sure you heard the second Irish thug departed this world earlier today," McCormick said as he shook Lockhart's hand. "You did our town a great favor in relieving such a threat. Yes, indeed, a great favor."

Lockhart nodded and turned to Wilcox as Crawfish greeted the mayor.

"Hope that Mick's ghost don't show up here," Wilcox said and laughed.

With a trace of hostility, Dr. Milens advised that such a ghost would not be present tonight. He made no attempt to explain why.

Cleta Wilcox, heavy-faced and wearing similarly applied makeup, looked up at Lockhart. A woolen wrap about her shoulders magnified her large face. Her long eyelashes flitted interest.

"Oh, I'm so excited, Mr. Lockhart. I'm hoping to hear from my dead departed sister. She passed three years ago, you know." She held out her hand, like a man, for him to shake.

"I hope you do, too." Lockhart took her hand and she pumped the handclasp vigorously, still trying to catch his eyes.

Across from her, Bertha McCormick sat stoically. She merely nodded at both Crawfish and Lockhart, keeping her hands in her lap. An ivory brooch adorned her thin neck; a dark green crepe dress hung on her frame.

Dr. Milens took a seat with his back to a black curtain that hung the length of the room. He motioned for Crawfish and Lockhart to take the two remaining open chairs. Lockhart's was directly across from Dr. Milens.

From the floor beside him, the Great Spiritualist took a lone candle well set in a silver bowl, lit it ceremoniously, and placed the flickering flame in the center of the table.

"Let us begin with a word of prayer," he said and folded his hands upon the table and shut his eyes. "O Heavenly Father, this night grant us the special connection to those who have gone on before us to the next world. Open the veil of eternity—for this precious moment—and let the spirits come close. Let us give ourselves to this night of all nights. Let us open our minds and hear. Humbly we beseech Thee in Thy name. Amen."

"Amen," repeated everyone around the table. Even Lockhart.

"Now, please announce the spirit you most wish to contact," Dr. Milens said in a low, soothing voice. "Remember, such contact can often take numerous sessions, because the spirit may not be close, or may have reasons for not wishing to communicate." He looked to his right. "Mrs. Wilcox?"

"Oh yes! Abigail Swanson. My sister. Oh yes, please, spirits, please."

Earnest Wilcox wanted to speak to his father; Crawfish, to his late wife, Almina.

Lockhart thought for a moment. "I hope the spirits find all of you tonight. If they want to find me, I am here."

Dr. Milens smiled. "Already a spirit is close wishing to talk with you, Mr. Lockhart. She made her presence known while I was praying. A Sioux princess, I believe."

Eagerly, McCormick selected "Abraham Lincoln," adding he wanted advice on the best way to lead the city as statehood neared.

Mrs. McCormick glanced at Dr. Milens, then at Lockhart, and whispered she would like to speak with her mother.

With that, Dr. Milens began to slowly wave his hands across his eyes and down his face, around the candle flame as if his hands were waltzing with it. Again and again, he repeated the sequence, holding his fingers together. Rhythmically, he moved. Enchantingly. Slowly. Gradually, ever so gradually, the hand motion tightened until his fingers circled only his vacant eyes. The room would soon be his, and his, alone.

Lockhart looked around the table. Everyone's eyes were

closed. He frowned to hold back the light-headed sensation that rocked him, as if he were on a ship in a gently swaying ocean. A soft moan came to Lockhart's ears. Barely audible.

Just behind the black curtain, a pale shape appeared and disappeared.

Lockhart closed his eyes. It wouldn't be right to ruin this for the others. He was tired from the long day. So very tired. Drowsy. Drowsy. He opened his eyes with some effort and Dr. Milens's gaze was upon him. A sense of sweetness filled him, flowed through him. He watched himself pass into darkness.

"She is coming now. Abigail. Yes. Yes. I hear you. Let your sister hear." Dr. Milens's voice was strained, barely a whisper.

A woman's voice slinked into the room; its thin vibration was like that of someone speaking through a long pipe.

"Cleta, my dear Cleta . . ."

Mrs. Wilcox shrieked and began to giggle hysterically.

"I am well, Cleta. Happy. Your son, Abraham, was here. Earlier. He is very happy, too. He left to be with his grand-parents. Our momma and poppa."

Her eyes closed, Mrs. Wilcox gurgled, "Oh, Abigail, what is it like? Heaven?"

"Like your most sweet dre—" Crackling crowded out the rest of the words.

"She is gone. She is gone." Dr. Milens choked out the words.

Mrs. Wilcox started to cry, but Dr. Milens hushed her like a mother quiets a baby. "Shhhh. Look at me now. Look at me. Shhhhh." His hands swirled around his eyes; then he slowly lowered them to the table.

Mrs. Wilcox was quiet again.

"I believe I can reach her again. Another time," Dr. Milens intoned.

Moans surfaced from the northwest corner of the curtain. Deeper. Raspy.

"Yes, he is here," Dr. Milens said in a hushed voice. "Earnest Wilcox is here." He stared at Mrs. Wilcox. "It is your mother, Eleanor."

A woman's voice, more throaty than the other, began to talk, but the crackling came again. A long extended sigh, then nothing.

"She, too, could not stay. Ah, but another spirit is close. She is patient. She is here to speak with Vin Lockhart."

Dizzy. So dizzy. He was peaceful. So peaceful. Over there, see? Young Evening was smiling at him. Now she was coming toward him. Oh, how he missed her. He would join her now. It would be good again. But she disappeared in the growing mist. Knots of thick fog emerged from the silent ground beneath the floor. The walls held the billows close. He tried to peer into their hazy whiteness but could see nothing.

Wait! A flicker of light! Then another, and another, and another! Tiny campfires. Hundreds of them in a big circle, all around him! All around the opening where he watched. Hundreds of fires! No, thousands! The campfires looked endless. As far as he could see into the haze, there were twinkles of campfire light. He closed his eyes and rubbed them. This couldn't be. He was surrounded by an army! A huge army! How could they have sneaked up on him so quietly in this small room?

He hurried to take out his pistol. But no shots came at him. Only silence whispered at his ears. He took a deep breath and studied the campfires more closely. Around each one were gathered warriors and women. Sioux! Oglalas! He began to recognize a few. There! There was Five Deer. And Star Arm. And look, it's Swift Hawk. And Black Bull. And, oh God! They are dead. Dead! He could recall the death of each one he recognized among the nearest campfires. Why were they here?

He stood unevenly, intending to go to them and discuss the strange situation. Upon rising and nearly stumbling, he realized their campfires were not on the ground anymore. Below them was the dark endless sky. The clearing where he once lay wasn't visible, even as a speck. My God! He was on the Ghost Road! The Ghost Road? *Wagaci Tacanku?* Here all the dead waited after a year of special ceremonies by their families. Here their campfires caused the aura of what the white man called the Milky Way.

Solemnly, each dead person waited at this, the end of the *wagaci tacanku,* for the Old Woman. Methodically, she would stop at each fire and assess each person's earthly deeds. The good people would be passed along to the other world that mirrored the first in many ways. To the north it was. A land of sweetgrass, pine, breath and forever life. The bad people would be pushed over a cliff; their spirits would return to roam the earth and always be a threat to the living.

Lockhart desperately tried to recall what Stone-Dreamer had told him about Oglala beliefs of the hereafter. They were now mixed with the *wasicun* Heaven in his mind. He did remember that the *wanagi* of humans and animals lived on buttes far to the west prior to coming here. Of course, all of them would have stayed close to their families for a year or so before that. Some would have tried to entice other loved ones into joining them in death. Once the ceremonies were over, though, the spirits would have begun their trail to the other world. Of course, some Oglalas believed spirits of the dead lived forever near where they died.

But why was he here? He wasn't dead, or was he? Even if he were, he hadn't been dead for the required time. Perhaps the Old Woman would help him. She would understand his problem and realize he shouldn't be here, at least not yet. In the distance, he could barely make out her walking through the campfires, pausing and talking. When she was finished at each gathering of spirits, the seated *wanagi* rose and departed. Some did so joyously, arm in arm singing loudly. Some were dragged away, crying insanely.

Ten campfires back, he caught a glimpse of Young Evening once more; she was talking with others, a man and a woman he did not know. She had not seen him yet. She would be happy to see him here. The gold glow from the small fire made her face clear to him for an instant; then it disappeared into the bleak mist. He began to run toward where she had been.

"Young Evening! Young Evening!" he called out but his voice had no sound.

A voice like thunder cracked through the murky black and stopped him with its fierce intensity. Even the Old Woman turned to the northernmost point of the *hanowakan*, sacred night, to see the menacing North Wind approaching angrily. As he passed, campfires hissed into icy ashes, food vanished from hands and pouches—and some *wanagi* froze in their blankets. Lockhart frantically looked for Young Evening, but could not see her anywhere.

Before the North Wind reached the Old Woman, two of his brothers—the East Wind and the West Wind—came forward to quiet him. Neither could slow him, even though he was as cowardly as he was cruel. East Wind was too lazy, anyway. West Wind, loud and boisterous himself, brought along Thunder-Beings to help. Although he was the first to be given a direction, the West Wind could not control the North Wind. He laughed at the Thunder-Beings and made them rain ice and sleet upon the waiting spirits.

Large and swarthy, the red-clad North Wind talked with the Old Woman briefly, then turned and pointed at Lockhart. The face was Vinegar Farrell's! Lockhart felt the chill enter his bones. The North Wind's eyes caught and held Lockhart's eyes like lightning momentarily freezes the night sky. From *Wakan Akanta's* shoulder flew his messenger, the magpie, who in turn swooped into Lockhart's face and screeched its hatred. He swung and missed the bird, and its head turned into the half-breed killer Valentine's leering face, then flew away, cackling loudly.

Lockhart was suddenly aware of someone tall standing

next to him, someone dressed in white. The South Wind! Warmth of his presence pushed back the terrifying cold. An aroma of sweetgrass filled Lockhart with renewed hope. Lockhart tried to gaze into the South Wind's face but it kept changing. Eveywhere the South Wind looked and smiled, the campfires glowed again, the clothes became decorated in bright colors and the food returned; and when eaten, re-plenished itself endlessly.

Where was Young Evening? There! She was farther away than he first remembered. She was waving at him though; she had seen him at last. Wait! It wasn't her. It was her sister. Morning Bird was waving at him. Smiling.

The South Wind put his hand on Lockhart's shoulder. "My brother, it is well."

"*Aiiee!*" Lockhart shouted and jumped up, making the table go sideways.

Startled, Crawfish grabbed his arm. "Vin, are you all right?"

Lockhart's arms dropped to his side. He was disoriented; his mind struggling to leave a world that didn't exist outside of his head.

"Uh, sorry, folks, I was . . . dreaming." He looked around at the others at the table, now in varying stages of alertness.

Dr. Milens coughed and jerked. "Give them time to leave . . . the spirits. Time. They must have time. Stay quiet. Please."

Minutes passed and the group sat quietly, yet impatiently. Finally, the spiritualist announced, "The circle is broken. The spirits have returned to their world. The spirit world." He stared at Lockhart, still standing. "I'm sorry, but this happens. It is a very fragile connection. Always." He shook his head as if very weary. "Some nights they shun me. Some nights, they become frightened. Some, angry. Those are the nights I fear the most."

"Oh, it was magnificent! I heard my sister. My sister!" Mrs. Wilcox gushed.

Smirking, Mrs. McCormick turned in her chair toward

Lockhart. "And you, Mr. Lockhart, did you hear from someone . . . dear?"

Breathing deeply, Lockhart looked at her. Hadn't she heard Young Evening's voice? Seen her run away? Hadn't she seen the same images from the spirit world as he had?

"It has been a long day for both of us," Crawfish said and stood beside his friend. "I think we should call it an evening."

Quickly, the evening ended in a disjointed manner with Dr. Milens inviting them back whenever convenient. Conversation among the participants was scattered as the couples headed for waiting carriages.

Within Crawfish's carriage, the red-haired businessman clicked the black horses into an easy trot and waited for his friend to speak. Even at night, the silver studs lining the clean lines of the carriage top snapped in the moonlight as the black fringe swished their private dance. Polished walnut and silver accents gleamed against black, padded leather. Red and silver spoked wheels clattered against the uneven dirt road.

"What happened, Crawfish?"

"Well, I doubt we experienced the same thing."

"What do you mean?"

"Well, he's good. Some wonderful parlor tricks, you know. Hoax-and-haircuts!" Crawfish said, watching the dark road. "Some woman talking through a pipe. Behind the curtain. A silver cloth pulled across back there. Noises."

"But I heard Young Evening. I saw her. She was . . ."

"You were mesmerized. That came later. You heard yourself. In your mind," Crawfish explained and adjusted the reins in his hands. "Like a dream. Nobody heard anything like that."

"What do you mean mesmerized?" Lockhart's eyes narrowed.

"It's a way of making people do and say things they might not otherwise. Magic-and-muscle! It's sort of like sleepwalking." Crawfish studied his friend for a moment, then returned his concentration to the horses. "Gidyap, Blackie. You, too, Ace."

"You mean he was able to make me do that?"

"Yes, and everybody else in the room."

Gazing out at the darkened houses as they passed, Lockhart asked, "So, you think he could've made me do something . . . anything?"

"Others, yes. Not you."

"Why not me?"

Crawfish snapped the reins again. "Well, first thing, you were tired—or it wouldn't have worked at all. I think your mind's too strong otherwise. Horns-and-cowhide, you popped out of the trance awfully fast. He didn't bring you out."

For a minute, Lockhart was silent, watching the fringe along the carriage roof wiggle in time with the moving horses. "My . . . people believe the real world is behind this one, and everything we see here is something like a shadow from that world. Crazy Horse travels back and forth to that world where there is nothing but the spirits of all things."

He folded his arms and leaned back against the carriage seat, feeling its leather softness. "So, were you mesmerized?"

"Yes, I heard Almina's voice, but I snapped out of it." Crawfish frowned.

"What are you supposed to say to a ghost?"

"Who knows? Never talked to one myself."

Lockhart permitted himself a thin smile. "Guess you can't count Newton."

CHAPTER THIRTEEN

By the early days of the Moon of Ripening Berries, hundreds of lodges of northern Indians had slipped away from their respective agencies and joined together once again in the sacred Black Hills. Oglalas. Brules. Miniconjous. Hunkpapas. Cheyennes and Sans Arcs. All bent on rejoining their still wild brethren, led by Sitting Bull and Crazy Horse. Gathered along the Little Missouri in the eastern lip of the sacred Black Hills, the tribes rejoiced in seeing old friends and separated relatives.

Six thousand strong converged on the bottomland with a thousand lodges. Their singular goal was the annual Sun Dance. *Wi wanyang wacipi.* The ceremonial and social high point of the entire year. A time of spiritual renewal and special prayer for the welfare of the tribes so gathered. A time to assure the buffalo would be plentiful once more. A time of dancing and gift giving and gratitude.

Men of honor pledged to give themselves to the Sun Dance and pray for their people. To participate in the Sun Dance was an act of courage and selflessness, seeking spiritual knowledge directly from the Great Spirit through personal sacrifice and asking for blessings on the tribes.

Some would be fulfilling vows made during the year that kept their individual tribes safe from cholera, measles, small pox, drought, prairie fires or enemy attacks. At the heart of each chosen dancer's requests from the Great Spirit would be the power to stop the white man from taking the Black Hills.

This year was especially urgent as all warriors were aware of the dangers inherent in leaving their reservations, made more apparent by the constant updating by scouts of Sheridan's pincer movement trying to find them.

Yet, it was like old times.

The putrifying ways of reservation life forgotten for the moment.

Black Fire's tribe was among the honored bands of Oglala who had not submitted to agency life. The steadfast leader had chosen to keep their village out of the way of the expanding *wasicun*, warning his warriors of the consequences of their raids upon the white settlements. So far they had listened to him. Much of his political strength came from the support of Stone-Dreamer. In quiet counsel with the holy man, however, Black Fire expressed his growing inclination to lead his people to reservation life.

Agreeing to the eventuality, the holy man walked about the busy circle of Oglala lodges—*Cangleska wakan*, the sacred hoop—within the greater circle of the other encampment circles of other tribes. A magnificent gathering of the Northern Nation. His shoulders were slightly stooped and his hair, more gray now, than black. Across his shoulders was the ever-present strap of his white elkskin bag containing the *sicum* from dead warriors and animals. Each *sicum* was held in a special stone for healing.

He paused at the edge of a Lodge of Isolation, *Isna Ti Ca Lowan*, where a girl celebrated her first menstruation, becoming a woman in a special ritual, guided by her mother and a favorite aunt. It felt right that such a celebration was occurring. Here. Now. He continued his walk, focusing on the advance of two men from his left.

Coming directly through the camp were Sitting Bull and Crazy Horse. They were clearly in charge of the Northern Nation and this gathering. Both were dressed simply with no visible signs of their singular leadership responsibility. In contrast to Stone-Dreamer's dramatic white buckskin shirt and leggings, beaded cape of white elkskin and winter wolf headdress. The holy man's attention was briefly interrupted by a passing warrior with vermillion circles surrounding his Sun Dance scars. His mind went to Vin Lockhart who had performed the dance years ago and then to the late Sun Wolf's son and Lockhart's former brother-in-law, Touches-Horses, who had been selected to perform it this year.

Heavy moccasined feet broke into Stone-Dreamer's memories and he turned his head to see a sweating scout rush up to the two leaders, reporting on the status of the various advancing columns of soldiers and cavalry. As usual, only Sitting Bull talked. His words calmed the scout; Crazy Horse finally spoke and the scout straightened himself and left as energetically as he had come.

Although Sitting Bull was the Northern Nation's recognized leader, Stone-Dreamer's attention was drawn to Crazy Horse, second in command. Not just because he was an Oglala Sioux and Sitting Bull was Hunkpapa. Perhaps, a little of his focus was due to jealousy of seeing another holy man so honored. Although Sitting Bull's oratory was more persuasive than any he had ever heard, even Red Cloud's. Mostly, though, it was the resemblance in Stone-Dreamer's mind, of Crazy Horse to his adopted son. Vin Lockhart. Panther-Strikes. Rides-With-Spirits.

Both had brown hair, lighter than their fellow tribesmen. And lighter skin. Both were lithe of build, of medium height and deceptive strength. Both contained the natural power of daring. Swift. Fierce. Enduring energy. Unstoppable when angered. And stories surrounded the two men of being protected by the spirit world. Crazy Horse could not be killed by a bullet; Rides-With-Spirits had been brought back to this life.

Silent once more, Crazy Horse left Sitting Bull's side and headed for the pony string. He was naked except for a breechclout and moccasins. Long braids, wrapped in fur, hung below his belt. They would be loosened and his hair free when fighting. In his hair were strung three long straws of prairie water grass; a spotted eagle's feather dangled from his scalp lock. A powder-darkened scar on the side of his nose made his skin seem even lighter.

"They both carry a sacred stone," Stone-Dreamer mumbled to himself, as he glimpsed the small stone nearly hidden behind his ear, and continued his assessment of their similarities, seeing a contingent of young warriors waiting for the fiery war chief. "Both, drawn to mystical ways."

He guessed the group were members of Crazy Horse's created warrior society, *Hoksi Hakakta*, the Last-Born Child Society. So typical of Crazy Horse's leadership, he had selected only the young sons of important families. The ones most likely to follow him without question, the most likely to fight without seeking quarter, the most likely to stand against any more treaties.

"I wish he were here." The words tumbled from his mouth.

"You wish who was here?" The voice behind him was a song, light and easy on the ears.

He smiled as he turned toward Morning Bird. She was beautiful of face and soul and much like her late father, Sun Wolf, in her energetic embrace of each new day. He knew he couldn't lie to her.

"I wish Panther-Strikes . . . Rides-With-Spirits . . . was here. I think he and Crazy Horse would have been friends," Stone-Dreamer said and repeated, "They both carry a sacred stone."

"Rides-With-Spirits is a *wasicun*," she chided gently. She loved being near the old holy man, primarily because he reminded her of Vin Lockhart.

"He fought for us. He hunted for us. He did the Sun Dance . . . for us."

"I know that, but he lives in another world now. Remember how the four warriors who went to see him described it? I doubt that he thinks of . . . us now."

Distracted, Stone-Dreamer glanced in the direction of Crazy Horse's leaving. He was no longer in sight. The intensity of true focus, of speed. Like the swift swoop of the red-tailed hawk from his first vision. Or the sudden appearance from the lake of the mysterious rider in his second and most powerful vision.

Or the strike of the panther in Panther-Strikes's vision.

Oh, how he missed Lockhart. His great son! He never thought of him as being adopted. Never as a *wasicun*. Only that he had chosen to live elsewhere. Even now guilt lay upon Stone-Dreamer's troubled mind; the holy man knew his presentations to the tribe about the young warrior's battle alone against the Shoshonis and the near-death result of his wounds from that awful conflict had helped drive him away. Seeing him once more last year—wounded again—had been both wonderful and terribly sad. He recalled the gleam in Lockhart's eyes when he said that the stones had finally talked to him, warning of an attack.

The old man smiled again at the memory. He straightened himself and looked down upon Morning Bird, remembering something. There had been a great attraction between her and Lockhart. He had sensed it immediately. Would this feeling be enough to bring him back? Was her statement about his not thinking of the village actually a more personal one? A question to him? He started to ask, but commotion in the camp took his attention.

Tribesmen from every direction were clustering around Sitting Bull. Women were trilling their joy. He seemed to enjoy the attention, talking and responding to their questions and comments. Comfortable in the honor place within the council tepee, his reassuring steadiness was a perfect companion to Crazy Horse's edgy magnetism. Yet, he was a boulder in the road against any more negotiations with the white man, any more giving in to encroachments on Indian lands. Even the steadfast Black Fire had avoided expressing his feelings about going to the agency for fear of it getting back to Crazy Horse.

"I hear Sitting Bull himself has agreed to do the Sun Dance. Is that so?"

"Yes, I have heard so." He glanced at her again, proud of her beauty, of her manner, of her mind. "It makes the honor for your brother even greater."

He smiled and continued, "Sitting Bull has chosen Good Weasel to cut the Sun Dance tree. A considerable honor." He patted her shoulder. "That assured Crazy Horse would be here. A wise move, indeed." He nodded, withdrew his hand and noted the great war chief was notably absent from last year's great gathering. The mystical warrior had chosen, instead, to guard the Black Hills from more white encroachment. Since Good Weasel was Crazy Horse's right-hand man in battle, the leader would feel it was important for him to attend the festivities.

"Are you going to speak to him, to Sitting Bull?" Morning Bird motioned toward the great leader still talking with animated arms.

"Later, perhaps," Stone-Dreamer said and guided her with his arm toward the south. "Let us watch the preparations."

They walked together without speaking; his question about her feelings for Lockhart forgotten for the moment. The creation of the Sun Dance arena took several days, including dancing, singing and ceremony. In the area where the Sun Dance would be held, a Cheyenne warrior society danced; another group of warriors from the Sans Arc lodges waited their turn to pound the sacred earth into a smooth, flat surface for the ritual. A sun lodge—basically a wide, circular arbor without sides—was nearly complete; its roof was made of pine boughs, to offer shade to the drummers, dance helpers and spectators.

Off to the side, holy men painted the Sun Dance pole, carried by a selected group that included virgins, mothers of babies and the old. The tree was chosen by Good Weasel earlier and cut down with an old ceremonial stone ax under his direction. The pole had been cleared of its branches except for the very top.

Warriors hung sprouts of chokeberry from its cut-off branch forks, along with banners and rawhide cutouts of buffalo and man shapes. These symbols would provide all tribesmen with power over the animals during the hunt and over their enemies during battle as well as encourage fertility. As they watched, a *heyoka*, a Contrary, walked backward to the pole and tied a fetish near the peak. The Ceremonial Decider, Nape of Neck, yelled orders and encouragement, enjoying his singular honor as chosen by Sitting Bull. Tomorrow, the pole would be erected into place by old ropes of rawhide and dedicated.

"Why aren't you painting the pole?" Morning Bird asked, watching the ceremonial painting.

Stone-Dreamer folded his arms. "The stones told me not to touch the pole. With Touches-Horses doing the dance." He paused and looked away. "They told me the same when Panther-Strikes did so."

She stared into his tired face and wanted to ask if he really thought Lockhart would return to them. To her. But dared not; her eyes would give away her feelings. It was best this way; the great *wasicun* was only someone she could dream about.

A tall warrior in a dyed-blue warshirt decorated with scalp locks, porcupine quills and beadwork passed them and stared at her. She averted her eyes.

Recalling her earlier question, Stone-Dreamer said softly, "Warriors come to your mother's lodge, asking for you. They offer many gifts. Many horses. Yet you do not speak with any one of them. Or walk out with any of them. Why is that so?"

She blushed and felt a rush of emotion, mostly anger.

"Do you wait for him to return?"

She began to walk away.

"Morning Bird, it is wrong for me to question. There are only two hearts that know the answer," Stone-Dreamer said. "And only two that need to know."

She stopped, but dared not face him for her face would answer that question. Yes, she waited—and dreamed—and prayed—for Lockhart's return, no matter how foolish that was.

"Go and find your brother. Please. See if he needs anything. I go to find a place where the stones might talk with me," he continued. "I am uneasy about our tribe. Our ways. I fear change is coming that we cannot stop. I must pray for seeing ahead."

With that he strode from the Sun Dance area. She watched him go, glad that she hadn't responded to his questions about Lockhart. It was too foolish to express or even consider. Lockhart was not coming back. Seeing her brother would be good to do; he loved Lockhart as much as she did. A rumble of thunder turned her gaze skyward. Rain was definitely coming.

Finally, dawn of the first day of the Sun Dance arrived and with it came the dance pledgers into the arbor, filled with tribesmen. Stone-Dreamer stood with the other holy men as Touches-Horses entered.

From the assembled crowd, Morning Bird watched both Stone-Dreamer and her brother. Earlier, the great holy man had shared with her that he had received a vision, from the stones, of a coming great darkness, that this would be the last great Sun Dance of the Plains. It had left him depressed and he did not want to tell others. She had remained silent after his telling, unsure of what to say or ask or think. Now she could only watch and wonder.

There was no sign of Sitting Bull among the pledgers. She had heard that he remained in the sweat lodge, seeking purity and guidance. Her gaze took in the assembled leaders, sitting together. A silent Crazy Horse was among them. It was hard not to stare at the mysterious war chief. She wondered about Stone-Dreamer's comparison of Crazy Horse and Lockhart. It only made her want to be with Lockhart more. She had prayed often to *Wakantanka* for such a union. Her mother had told her to dismiss such foolish thoughts and reminded her that Lockhart was actually a spirit, a Grandfather. Finally, her attention was drawn to the center of the ring where the holy men held up skewers, praying and letting the sun's ray bless them.

Stone-Dreamer walked solemnly over to where Touches-Horses stood. Beside the warrior with the gift for training horses was Swift Eagle who was his mentor for the Sun Dance. Old scars adorned the lanky warrior's chest and hints of gray hid among his black hair. Stone-Dreamer muttered a prayer and handed the skewers to Tall Wolf, looked into Touches-Horse's eyes and let his gaze tell him of his pride.

Tall Wolf turned to Touches-Horses and pushed the prongs of the skewers into his chest. Both men's gazes connected as first blood began to slide down the warrior's chest. Rawhide ropes, hanging from the pole, were looped through the skewers. Two other pledgers were similarly attached to the pole. The others had chosen to pull buffalo skulls by thongs tied to skewers thrust through their backs.

As the other mentors prepared their men, Tall Wolf stepped behind Touches-Horses, held him around the waist and yanked him backward four times. Blood popped from his wounds and Touches-Horses kept his gaze focused on the sun. Each pull brought loud wailing from the women in the crowd.

Satisfied with the preparations, Nape of Neck strode into the ring and held up a crystal as he spoke directly to the sun, asking that all of the pledgers' wishes be granted. Each pledger was then told to look through the crystal at the sun as the Ceremonial Decider walked among them. Most had committed to the sun-gazing ritual, never taking their gaze from the sun itself.

Almost in unison, the pledgers threw themselves backward, trying to tear away the skewers. They began to dance and jerk to break free. Pain was apparent on their faces as they moved around the pole. Straining and jerking. Staring at the sun.

To himself, Stone-Dreamer observed, "All good things in this world must come through suffering. All good things." He watched with a mixture of pride, awe and fear as if it were his own son.

He glanced skyward and saw the advancing dark cloud. Had his vision only meant a coming rain? He knew better. The end of their freedom was near, as near as the slowly advancing columns of soldiers. Blue chargers. He knew. Would he live to see Lockhart again? Was there a place for

Lockhart and Morning Bird? Where? He closed his eyes and saw nothing.

On the second day of dancing—and rain—Sitting Bull emerged from the sweat lodge and entered the arbor. The dancing continued, but all eyes were on the great leader as he offered a pipe in the seven directions, then presented it to the assembled leaders. Crazy Horse was the first.

Turning around, he sat against the pole as pledgers drudged around him, some barely standing. His adopted brother, Black Moon, performed the *hanblake oloan*, the special prayer for advance knowledge. He cut a hundred small pieces of skin from Sitting Bull's outstretched arms and gave them to *Wakantanka*. Sitting Bull stood, naked except for a breechclout. His arms, two red blankets. The crowd was still. Absolutely still. He began to dance; his eyes focused on the blossoming sun.

Even Stone-Dreamer watched the great man slowly bob and weave to the sound of the drum, to the heartbeat of Mother Earth. Touches-Horses wobbled against the taut rawhide; his entire body trembled and he staggered, caught himself and danced on.

Hours went by. In midstride, Sitting Bull froze, as if held by an unseen force. His gaze was locked against the sun. The crowd was again hushed, almost annoyed by the continued shuffling of the other pledgers. None of them was aware of anything happening. Beyond pain. Beyond reason. Beyond the arbor. Absorbed by the sun. One step. Another step.

Sitting Bull staggered and fell. Unconscious.

Black Moon was the first to reach him as holy men hurried forward. Stone-Dreamer was close enough to see Sitting Bull flutter into consciousness and whisper to Black Moon and collapse once more. Solemnly, Black Moon stood and announced that Sitting Bull had received a bright vision of a great many soldiers falling into the Indians' camp.

Somewhere in the crowd came a single cry of surprise and joy that instantly became a roar as the entire assembly reacted. The leaders stood and cheered. Crazy Horse raised his fist in triumph. A great victory was at hand.

Unseen by all, but Stone-Dreamer and Morning Bird, Touches-Horses tore free of his skewers and stumbled to the ground. Stone-Dreamer ran to him and held him close.

"Your son, my brother . . . Rides-With-Spirits . . . is coming. I have seen him." His face fell against the holy man's arm.

The Sun Dance continued, but the drama had evaporated with the powerful message from Sitting Bull. Two days later, the massive village moved up the creek, toward the Rosebud.

CHAPTER FOURTEEN

Lockhart and Sean slowly drove eight, newly purchased horses toward the Rhymer farm. After Harry and Martha had agreed to become partners in the venture, he immediately moved the war horse there and started work on building a worthy stable of good working mounts. It was the most excited the businessman had been in a long time. The only thing that would make it better would be having his Indian relatives with him.

Harry's sturdy corral had proved itself a solid retainer for the fiery mustang and the big horse had settled well into his new home. With Sean's enthusiastic help, and Harry's good intentions, Lockhart had fixed the larger corral to hold an initial group of horses. Rebuilding the barn would come later. Grazing land could handle a large herd. That would also come later.

For now, he was content to select horses a few at a time

from area ranchers. Mostly mares and colts, but some good geldings, too. They would be among the first to be trained and sold. He preferred horses not yet broken so he could create the mounts desired. His training skills had come entirely from his Indian brother-in-law. They didn't come up to Touches-Horses' exceptional ways, but they were better than most.

A week had passed since Lockhart and Crawfish had visited Dr. Milens's house. The mesmerism experience still clung like the aftertaste of bad milk. Crawfish's thorough explanations of the mesmerist's trick were both assuring and disturbing. His redheaded friend was fascinated by magic as well as many other subjects. However, when Crawfish suggested that Lockhart's Indian father had probably used magic as well, Lockhart had become upset. That had ended discussion of the subject, other than Crawfish's observation that Dr. Milens had secured a sizable amount of money from the Wilcoxes, who were seeking further contact with their dead relatives.

To keep his mind off of Morning Bird—or his Indian friends—Lockhart threw himself into work, spreading his time between the Silver Queen, Black Horse and now their horse ranch. It kept him too tired to think. Or worry.

"Will these hosses be stayin' in the big corral?" Sean asked, studying the group of horses moving easily ahead of them.

"Yes. We'll watch them for a few days," Lockhart said, "then we'll see about letting them out on the grazing land. You up to standing nighthawk?"

"What be a nighthawk?"

Lockhart explained it was a term used originally by drovers on a cattle drive to describe the guards watching the herd at night. He was using it to describe watching the horses during the night.

"Ye kin count on me." He repeated "nighthawk" to himself and looked again at the five mares and three young colts meandering in front of them.

They were all chestnuts or bays, except for one strawberry roan colt and one dun mare. The roan colt's mother was definitely a chestnut and Sean wondered what the foal's father looked like, until Lockhart pointed out a handsome roan stallion on the far side of the rancher's pasture.

Each horse purchased was a well-formed animal with a short straight back and good ribs. Lockhart had told Sean that most cowmen preferred "close-coupled" horses like that. He had pointed out a horse whose back end tapered too severely from its hip to its tail; that was called "goose-rumped" and was to be avoided. No staying power.

The back muscles of the selected horses were short and heavy. Their chests were full, but none were barrel-chested, as Lockhart said this was an indication that the horse might not give a comfortable ride. He favored horses with large nostrils because it meant they would run well and long. Sean had listened in awe.

The colts were spring foals, something Lockhart told Sean to look for. A spring birth meant the youngster had the advantages of warm sunshine and good grass. A winter foal always needed more handling—and, likely, a long stay in the barn.

Lockhart's observations about picking horses swirled in Sean's head. Stay away from blue-eyed horses; they would be weak. Always dark brown eyes. "Hazel" was the word Lockhart liked to use. Hazel. Avoid buying a foal with a small head because it meant the animal wouldn't have the size and strength needed. Like children, their heads should be larger in proportion to their small bodies, and grown into. Watch out for front legs that were too far apart; the horse would be slow. Nobody liked a horse with a long, thin head or a short, heavy one. He couldn't remember all that Lockhart had shared, only knew he wanted to learn more—and stay close to this strange man so many seemed to fear.

Lockhart's advice about selecting horses filled the

young Irishman's thoughts. The older man's zeal had been contagious and Sean could think of nothing greater than being in the horse business. Nothing. Always pick a horse with a straight head, one with good distance between the eyes. The back should also be straight, not "roached" or "sway-backed."

He watched a bay mare nibbling on an interesting clump of grass. The shoulder blades should be long and slope smoothly to bring long and powerful strides. His gaze moved to the mare's hind legs. Straight. Again that word. They weren't "cow-hocked" with bent-in knees. Not "sickle-hocked" either with back legs bent outward. He examined the mare, then the chestnut a few feet away. Withers. Fetlock joints. Pasterns. Words he had never heard just a few days ago—and now they seemed comfortable to evaluate and discuss.

The withers, according to Lockhart, should be prominent. That was the area just behind the crest of a horse's neck. If they were thick and not as visible, it would mean the horse wouldn't have free motion and wouldn't naturally take long strides. He smiled and muttered "hands." That was the measurement used with horses. So many hands high. A hand was four inches. About the width of a man's hand. The point of measurement was the tallest part of the withers.

His gaze took in both horses' rear legs again. That's where the two pasterns were. One long; one short. They shouldn't look low, close to the hoof, when a horse was still. Here was a place where "straight" wasn't good. Real straight pasterns meant the ride would be hard. Of course, if the pasterns curved too much, the animal was said to be "coon-footed" and it would be slow.

These horses had been bought from three different ranches Lockhart had visited during the last year, as his idea had taken shape in his mind. Now it was turning into reality.

Sean had been drawn to the idea of a horse ranch immediately, finally getting up the nerve to ask if he could help there, instead of washing dishes and glasses at the saloon.

He had been surprised when Lockhart told him that he was going to be a partner in the effort, along with Crawfish and the Rhymers. Sean's initial contribution was the great war horse. The rest would be helping Lockhart. That night—at Crawfish's house—Sean wouldn't sleep; he was too excited to get back to work. At breakfast, Crawfish had told him that he hoped Lockhart would change the name from "The Broken R" to "The Silver R." Sean liked that idea, too. Neither brought it up to him, though.

Lockhart eased his horse to the left, encouraging the dun mare to keep up with the others. "We'll let them get settled first, then we'll try putting Magic with the mares. Easy does it, as Crawfish likes to say."

"Me thinks he likes to say, 'Hop-a-bunny'."

Lockhart laughed. "True. True. Or name everything 'silver' something."

"Magic would like being with the mares, me be thinkin'."

The boy had called the stallion "Magic" once and the name had stuck; even Lockhart referred to the stallion as Magic now. Sean had ridden the stallion twice—once inside the corral and once outside—with Lockhart nearby. It had gone well both times; the boy was a natural, Lockhart thought, and told him so. He didn't say that the boy could learn much from Touches-Horses, but he felt it.

Conversation drifted into thoughts about what they would eat for dinner. Sean hoped Martha Rhymer would ask them to stay; her cooking was better than Crawfish's. They moved through a narrow draw with a trickle of water that became a definite stream. About forty yards from its opening, a scruffy sentinel of stubby post-oak, blackjack and redbud shouldered its way against the growing stream that had formed the land crease long ago.

Lockhart was drawn to a pair of cardinals, male and female, resting on a redbud branch. Their colors were reinforced by the dark, magenta leaves. Without hesitation, he greeted the birds in Lakotan, referring to them as "spirits of the morning," then caught himself. His mind found Morning Bird where he had seen her first, upon returning to the village with Touches-Horses last year. He first thought it was Young Evening herself, but he soon learned they were very different women. They spent many sweet hours together. Just as quickly, his thoughts whirled to his dream at Dr. Milens's house. He shook in the saddle.

"What's the matter? You see something? A ghost?" Sean asked, his head on a swivel to see what had bothered the intense businessman. He didn't dare ask about the strange words he had used. Guessed they were Indian.

"Oh, I'm sorry, Sean. Seeing the cardinals made me think of my old Indian friends. Didn't mean to scare you," Lockhart said and pointed toward the clearing. "Just on the other side of this thicket is Broken R land."

Sean's face tightened with growing courage as he asked, "Are you going to go an' be gettin' . . . Touches-Horses?"

They rode in silence for awhile. The only sounds came from the grunts and squeals of the horses, mixed with the padding and squishing of their hooves on the soft earth and the shallow water.

"This is a horse he trained. Touches-Horses gave it to me. Last year," Lockhart finally said. "You've ridden it. What do you think?"

"'T'would be a good thing, me be thinkin'." Sean straightened in the saddle, proud to be asked such an important question. "We will be needin' such a fine hossman as he."

They rode on a little farther in silence, stopping while the horses drank from the deeper part of the stream, where it gathered itself. Lockhart looked over at the boy and smiled.

"We're going to have to get you some chaps and spurs, if you're going to become a horseman."

"Aye, me be wishin' hard for that. To become a hossman," Sean said and then pointed, "Look! That colt, isn't he somethin'?"

"He is yours, Sean."

"Mine? He be mine? Really?"

Lockhart grinned and nodded. "But you will have to take good care of him. I think he just might grow to be a stallion."

"Like Magic be?"

"Yes, like Magic."

"May I be namin' him?" Sean asked excitedly.

"Well, unless you want to call him 'Six,'" Lockhart laughed.

"Aye," Sean laughed. "Me be givin' it some thinkin'."

After the horses finished drinking, they cleared the draw and left the scrub trees behind as the stream hurried toward a pond on their land and the ground flattened into open grassland. Eight cows watched them pass, mildly curious, before returning to their grazing. From that distance, they could see the windmill, and the top of the farmhouse and barn.

"Study the horses' ears, Sean." Lockhart pointed at the closest bay mare. "They'll tell you a lot about the horse. If its ears are always moving, always flickering, you've got a nervous horse. Or you've got one with bad eyesight." He motioned toward the strawberry roan colt. "If it never moves its ears, most likely you've got a slow horse on your hands. Or a lazy one."

"What do ye be thinkin' of . . . Strawberry there?"

"Strawberry, huh? That's a good name," Lockhart said. "I think ol' Strawberry is going to be a good one. Strong and tall. Kinda like you."

Sean beamed.

"Remember a horse may be strong and fast, but he isn't smart," Lockhart said, clucking to the horses to keep them moving. "Has a long memory though. You train him by repeating things. You build habits. Most horsemen do it by hurting them. Touches-Horses does it by rewarding them." He pushed his horse closer to the dun mare to give it an extra sense of urgency. "Now, if he saw something scary behind a certain rock, it'll be a long time before he decides it still isn't there. He'll jump every time he passes that rock. That's why they'll jump sideways sometimes at nothing. They survived by being quick."

"Me can see that."

As they crossed the open land, they could see Magic with his ears up, pressed against the poles of the corral. The stallion whinnied.

"Looks like we've got a welcoming committee," Lockhart said and pointed toward the big horse.

"Aye. An' a fine one he be." Sean waved and yelled, "Hiya, Magic. Be bringin'ye some lady friends."

Lockhart shielded his eyes with his hand. "Looks like Crawfish has joined us. Isn't that him standing next to Harry?"

"Aye, 'tis," Sean replied. "That's his fancy rig. Next to the house."

"Good eyes."

"Thank ye."

"A smart man sees what he's riding into."

"Aye." Sean's eyes widened. "Vin, I know what I wanna be namin' the colt."

"Already? What?" Lockhart leaned forward in the saddle, his arms resting on the saddle horn.

"*Kola*. I be namin' him *Kola*, if that be fittin' with ye," Sean asked, staring at the businessman.

"Hey, I like it. *Kola*." Lockhart looked over at the frisky colt. "All right, *Kola*, you've got a lot to live up to." He grinned.

As soon as the new horses were introduced to their new corral home, Lockhart swung down from his horse and flipped the reins over a corral pole. Sean did the same and immediately sought the new colt to watch. Lockhart patted his horse on the neck and wondered if his thoughts about going after his Indian relatives were motivated by caring—or by his desire to build up the horse ranch—or by wanting Morning Bird to be at his side. Was there something wrong with feeling some of all three?

Lockhart and Sean stood by the corral, watching his new colt, as Harry Rhymer hurried over to them, as fast as his bowed legs would carry him. The new arrangement had brought new life to him and he was quite excited about their progress and their plans. Right now, though, his face carried serious worry.

"Vin, thar's bad news from up north. Injun trouble. Crawfish dun come to tell ya." It was like the old man not to be able to keep a secret or wait for Crawfish to tell.

"Indian trouble?" Lockhart stared past him at Crawfish.

"I knew you'd want to know. Word just came over the telegraph office. Everybody in town is talking about it." Crawfish walked toward him, waving his walking stick as he moved. "Battle of the Rosebud, they're calling it. Crazy Horse and his warriors whipped General Crook. He had to retreat. Sounds like his troops were shot up some. All Crook's Injun scouts dun quit on 'im. Word is it'll be awhile before Crook can go at it again."

Lockhart swallowed. "At the Rosebud? How many were in this?"

"Crook had about a thousand troopers and, maybe, two hundred and fifty Indian scouts, and a bunch of miners," Crawfish related. "Crazy Horse attacked somewhere along Rosebud Creek."

"Do you know how many warriors were with him?"

"No. Hundreds, I suppose. Some folks in town are scared the Sioux will come riding down our way," Crawfish said. "Can you believe such stupid stuff?"

Sean watched Lockhart who looked like he was watching something in the horizon, toward the north. Sean glanced that way, but could only see rolling hills.

The news of the fight hit Lockhart in a way he hadn't expected. He should've been proud of his adopted people, fighting and winning against terrible odds, fighting when there was no chance of winning in the end. One fight they might win. Maybe two. Ultimately, they will lose. Even

Crazy Horse knows that. Has to. Overriding dread crowded his mind and turned it black. Were his friends at the Rosebud? With Crazy Horse?

Crawfish studied his friend and knew the anguish within him. It may have been a victory for the Sioux, but the whites were now screaming for blood. Indian blood.

Indians everywhere would be hunted and killed in the name of revenge. What would Lockhart do? Finally Crawfish could hold back no longer.

"You're going to find your friends, aren't you?"

Lockhart's eyes seared the red-haired businessman's face.

"You can't save them all, Vin. They've got to get to the reservation. Fast. It might already be too late."

Lockhart's shoulders rose and fell. He looked at the horses milling in the corral, then at Magic now prancing in his own space, and his arm slowly rose and formed a fist.

"No damned bunch of soldiers better bother them." The words snarled from his tightened mouth.

Crawfish shook his head, glanced at the frowning Harry Rhymer, then at the quiet Sean. "You don't know where they are. Your friends. Not for sure." He paused, unsure if he should say more, then decided he must. "They might be nowhere near there. The Rosebud. Your friends. Your tribe." He licked his lips and waved his arms. "They might be clear on the other side of the Black Hills, you know. Maybe they're already on the reservation. Might be." His face betrayed his real feelings.

"What were they supposed to do? They've been lied to. Over and over. That's their land. Theirs." Lockhart gritted his teeth to hold back the anger.

"They were supposed to go to the reservations." Crawfish knew he had gone too far the moment the words popped out. "Red Cloud has already gone there. The great Sioux leader."

The fury that had controlled Lockhart's gaze vanished. In its place was disappointment. "I thought you would understand, Crawfish. But you're just another white man." He spun toward his horse.

"I didn't deserve that, Vin," Crawfish said, without moving. "I do understand. You know I do. It isn't good, but this land is changing—and it won't change back."

With his hand on the saddle, Lockhart stopped and spoke into the leather. "I shouldn't have said that. I am sorry." He turned toward his friend. "What do you think I should do?" His face was laden with worry.

Surprising himself, Crawfish answered succinctly that Lockhart should leave as soon as possible and try to find his old tribe and convince them to go to the reservation, to leave Crazy Horse and the certain terrible ending that would ultimately occur.

"You should invite Touches-Horses . . . and Stone-Dreamer . . . and Morning Bird . . . to return with you. Here," Crawfish added and put his hand on Harry's shoulder. "Harry and Sean . . . and me . . . we'll keep everything in order around here until you get back." His face jerked slightly. "Crystal-and-brandy, the restaurant's coming along just fine—and so are the hotel rooms. All of the four-poster beds are in. Only a few rooms left to be all fancied up."

Biting his lower lip, Harry blurted, "Ya know'd they's welcome, Vin. Martha an' me, we tolt ya that. A'fer." He folded his arms. "An' when ya gits back, it'll be the Silver R. How's that sound?" He looked at Crawfish, who grimaced. This wasn't the time.

Lockhart tried to grin, and glanced at Crawfish. "Should've seen that coming. What's wrong with the Broken R? It's a name with honor."

Harry's face brightened with pride.

Crawfish nodded. "The Broken R is a good name."

"Will ye be back in time for Independence Day?" Sean asked, wide-eyed. "It'll be on July fourth."

Crawfish responded first. "That's not likely, Sean. Vin has to find his friends first and they won't be leaving any forwarding addresses. He'll be gone . . . a few months, I suppose."

"But that be such a grand day o' it," Sean said, his voice

pleading. "Crawfish be tellin' me o' it all. There be a rodeo, an' fireworks all over the sky, aye, an' a big parade, an' picnics . . . an' speeches all long an' grand . . . an' ice cream. Lots o' stuff, there be."

Lockhart nodded and swung into the saddle. "All of you will just have to celebrate extra hard to make up for my not being there. I'll take the stage tomorrow as far as Cheyenne." He turned to Crawfish. "I'm leaving you with a lot of work. It's not fair. Finishing the hotel. Getting things going here. What about your bank idea?"

Pushing his eyeglasses back in place and running his fingers through wild strawberry hair, Crawfish smiled. "Work-and-wishes, Vin. You know I like doing lots of things at the same time. I'm having second thoughts about the bank anyway. Could be boring. The idea of an orchestra in the hotel restaurant's growing on me, though. Fiddles-and-firecrackers! There would be room. Plenty of room." He held out his hand. "Besides, this ranching stuff gets in your blood. Doesn't it, Harry? Sean?"

"Thank you, my good friend."

"Be sure to pack that old sawed-off shotgun of mine— and take your medicine rock." Crawfish smiled. "For luck." He glanced away and added, "Better pack those pretty cardinal feathers. She'll ask about them."

Lockhart tried to smile, but couldn't.

CHAPTER FIFTEEN

The next day, Lockhart was aboard the northbound stage. He would buy two horses and supplies in Cheyenne and continue his quest from there. Crawfish had reminded him to use the telegraph office where he could to keep them informed.

He was surprised to find himself sitting across from Dr. Hugo Milens and two women he hadn't seen before. He guessed they were the mesmerist's assistants. The voices from the spirit world. One was thin-faced with light brown hair in a bun; the other was heavily made-up with long, auburn hair bouncing on her shoulders.

The mesmerist wasn't too happy to be riding with Lockhart, but had already decided he had secured all that he was likely to get from Denver and if things went as planned, it would be small potatoes anyway. He didn't like surprises and Lockhart being on board was certainly one. At the right time, he would have to make certain his presence was known to his men.

Jammed together, Dr. Milens and his ladies sat on the back, leather-upholstered row with the wall of the carriage to lean against. Equally pressed together, hip to hip, Lockhart and two other men sat in the center bench with leather loops suspended from the ceiling to steady them. Three other passengers sat in the front row, all men. Nine in all inside. All jammed together for the long, discomforting trip. The Concord coach's front and rear boots, and some of the top, were loaded with express freight, luggage and mail. Only five other passengers were allowed on top, instead of up to twelve. They looked like miners bound for Deadwood. Lockhart had boarded too late to select any of those seats, or either of the preferred front or back benches.

Six stout Morgan horses pulled the coach at a steady trot as the more-than-a-ton, sturdy vehicle jostled and bounced in response to the chewed-up road, rocking the passengers like a ship at sea. The carriage itself was suspended on two thoroughbraces; three-inch-thick strips of leather did their best as shock absorbers. Above the noise of the road, the driver's shrill cries to his team—and the crack of the nine-foot whip—were a constant reminder of the stage line's emphasis on speed.

Next to Lockhart was a hard-looking man in a herringbone

suit too big for him and a boiled shirt with a soiled paper collar and a black ribbon tie that needed retying. His slouch hat was pushed up in the back and had seen better days. The bulge in his coat indicated a shoulder-holstered gun. To this man's right was a short, stocky man in thick glasses trying to read a book while holding the strap with his right hand extended. Lockhart thought he might be a college professor or an accountant.

Lockhart took a deep breath and closed his eyes, but made no attempt to grasp the leather loop. He hadn't slept much last night, going over details about the ranch with Sean and Crawfish. The Silver Queen Saloon and the Black Horse Hotel were barely discussed. Falling Leaf would stay with Crawfish until he returned. It was too dangerous for her to go venturing north right now—and Lockhart didn't think it would be wise for her to accompany him either.

His energetic friend had insisted Lockhart take along his sawed-off shotgun and special quiver, for added firepower. The double-barreled shotgun had been shortened in both barrels and stock for use in one hand, like a pistol; Crawfish had used it in his prospecting days. It was with his other gear, packed with the other passenger luggage in the back coach boot. So were Morning Bird's remembrance feathers wrapped carefully in a white handkerchief and resting among his extra clothes.

Into his thoughts wandered the recollection of Stone-Dreamer telling him that Crazy Horse wore a special pebble into battle, behind his ear. He was carrying a pebble, too; his fingers went to the small stone hanging from his watch chain. The sacred *tunkan* carried the power of Eyes-Of-The-Wind, an ancient shaman Stone-Dreamer had revered as a young man.

A part of him wanted to repeat the vision quest so many years ago. He frowned, but the thought remained, as did concerns about Crazy Horse. The charismatic leader was a Thunder Dreamer and was committed to the old life. The old Sioux life. Would his friends be drawn to Crazy Horse? He knew he would have been if he were still among them. Will the unbending leader take them to their deaths?

"Business taking you to Cheyenne, Mr. Lockhart?" Dr. Milens asked, ignoring Lockhart's attempt at resting.

From under his pushed-down hat, Lockhart opened his eyes, nodded and closed them again.

The closest woman assistant flitted her eyelashes at him. "Did yo-all see that colored fella riding guard? He looks dangerous. Do yo-all know him? Why does he have a cat with him? Do they expect Indian trouble? We're not going close . . . to where that awful fight was . . . are we? Why aren't there troops with us?"

Her voice was syrupy and Southern with none of the airy, gentle quality he remembered from the seance. Lockhart started to comment on that fact, but decided it would be impolite. Maybe the other woman, the one with long hair and thick eyeglasses, had such a voice. From the looks of her, she hadn't smiled in a long time and that didn't match the angelic voice he remembered. He didn't really care, one way or the other; just wanted to get his body adjusted to the constant rocking.

Beside him, the hard-looking man in the slouch hat grunted, "That's Beezah. Jean-Jacques Beezah. He's from Orleans. Supposed to be good with a gun. Stage line hired him for awhile. Don't know about his cat. Likes them, I guess."

The man with the book looked up, frowned, then returned to his reading.

She acknowledged the statement, but continued to look at Lockhart waiting for his comment.

"I don't know him, ma'am. Sometimes, men who look dangerous, aren't. And ones that don't look dangerous, are." Lockhart's smile curled along his tightened mouth. "Like your magic tricks. You and the doctor here."

Dr. Milens's eyebrows jumped in defense and his bowler tilted backward. The man next to Lockhart chuckled cruelly.

"A-Are you calling me a f-fake?" Dr. Milens's words were laced with condescension.

"No. I was calling you a crook." Lockhart's stare was more than the mesmerist could handle.

The closest woman's eyes blinked once, twice. She huffed, started to say something, thought better of it and looked out the window. The long-haired assistant, next to her, whispered something and pushed on the leather curtain to make certain it was fully rolled up. In the distance, the Rocky Mountains looked like an oil painting.

"Sir, I'll have you know . . . you are angering the spirits with such talk. They are always near. To me. They trust me." Dr. Milens sat with his arms folded and wore his most serious expression. His eyes flashed anger, but couldn't quite hide the fear in them. The man across from him was not what he had expected. Even at the seance, his sudden reaction was a disappointment, a setback of sorts.

Lockhart leaned forward, resting his arms on his knees. "Maybe you should ask some of those ghosts to leave, so we'd have more room."

This time, even the bookish passenger laughed as well as the man beside Lockhart.

Dr. Milens drew himself up and tried to look indignant as the coach rocked and snapped back and forth.

"How much did you take from Mr. and Mrs. Wilcox?"

Eyes widening, Dr. Milens was surprised at Lockhart's question. He glanced at the men beside Lockhart who were still amused.

"I'm sorry the ways of Egyptology are beyond you, Mr. Lockhart," Dr. Milens declared. "Only a few are gifted with this insight. It is a rare and precious thing."

Lockhart leaned closer toward the upset spiritualist. "When we get to Cheyenne, you can send the money back. To them."

"What? I'll do no such thing. They gave me that. Out of appreciation."

Lockhart straightened his back and reached up for the support strap. His narrowed eyes never left Dr. Milens's face.

The mesmerist fidgeted in his seat, looked over at his lady friends, but both were engaged in the passing scenery.

Bump! The coach hit a rut in the road and jerked sideways, then straightened itself like a cracking bullwhip. All nine passengers groaned. Above, a miner cursed loudly, followed by swearing in Swedish from the driver, Big Nose Anton Norborg, a transplanted Swede with a tendency to swirl his native tongue into his speech.

"Perhaps, I could refund some of their money," Dr. Milens purred. "After all, they were most generous with my bringing their loved ones to them. Yes, I could do that."

Lockhart sat without speaking; his stare forcing the mesmerist to look at his own trembling hands.

Bump! The coach hit another rut and the passengers rose as one and banged down against their seats. Only the man next to Lockhart grunted his displeasure. The bespectacled man lost his page and muttered to himself as he sought its return.

"I don't know if you can trust money of that kind to the postal services," Dr. Milens sputtered. "Perhaps, you could return it for me."

"The driver's a good man. You give it to him. All of it. I guarantee it will get to the Wilcoxes." Lockhart's voice was harder now.

"Oh."

"When we stop to eat. At a home station. Be in a few hours. You give it to him then."

"If I refuse?" Dr. Milens's lower lip trembled slightly.

"If he doesn't shoot you, I will," the man beside Lockhart snarled. "I don't believe in spooks—an' I don't like cheats neither."

Pulling on his coat lapels to smooth them, Dr. Milens attempted to smile, but it was more like someone with an upset stomach. Nothing more was said until they reached the dusty-looking stable, granary and a corral, the swing station. Two stock tenders brought out the new team, six mules.

Regaining her poise, the closest woman asked, "Mr. Lockhart, you said we would eat . . . at a home station, was that it?"

"Yes. They'll change horses about every twelve miles. But we'll stop for dinner there," Lockhart answered. "It's bigger than here. Might even have a telegraph office. We can tell the Wilcoxes their money is coming back."

"Will we sleep . . . there?"

Lockhart shook his head. "No, ma'am. The stage doesn't stop."

"But, Dr. Milens, didn't you say there were beds there? Bunks?" Her eyes flashed at the mesmerist.

Lockhart shifted his weight. "They do have bunks, ma'am, for the stage-line employees."

"You mean we have to sleep . . . here in this?" Her eyebrows leapt upward.

The long-haired assistant turned away from the window; her sloe-eyed gaze studied Lockhart for the first time.

"You can sleep on my lap," the middle man said and grinned.

She snorted her disgust and said something to the other woman, who giggled and looked at Lockhart.

Arriving at a home station, Anton Norborg, the roly-poly Swedish driver, was mildly amused when the well-dressed mesmerist came to him with the request that he give a brown envelope to Mr. Earnest Wilcox on his return trip. Lockhart stood next to the main building where the passengers would eat before continuing. Watching silently.

Norborg agreed, unbuttoned his shirt, shoved the envelope inside his once-blue shirt and rebuttoned it, then said Dr. Milens should join the others inside. The stage would be moving again in fifteen minutes.

Climbing down from the lofty driver's seat, Beezah watched the exchange with mild curiosity, leaned his .44 Henry against the front wagon wheel and stretched himself.

Remaining in the box seat was a shotgun; its twin barrels staring upward. Next to it was a black cat. The ebony-skinned man wore a gray Prince Albert frock coat and a matching bowler. A black-handled .44 Remington revolver was carried in a black, form-fitting holster and silver-accented gunbelt strapped over his vest. Shoved into his belt was a second Remington revolver, matching the holstered gun.

The black man spoke with a soft French accent. Almost rhymthic. Definitely not New Orleans Cajun. "Excuse me, Governor, where am I to eat?"

Norborg hadn't thought about that before; his face showed it.

"*Ja*, well, I check wit' *Herr* Howell," Norborg said and hurried away, checking his shirt to make certain it remained buttoned.

"Just bring it out. I shall eat here."

The thick-waisted Swede waved over his shoulder.

"*Bonjour*. You are the one who talks with the spirits," Beezah said. "How are you doing with this trip?"

Dr. Milens bowed slightly. "I am Hugo Milens, doctor of Egyptology. At your service."

"Those are ladies of yours?"

"Ah, no sir. They are my assistants." Dr. Milens glanced around, but both women had already gone inside.

"I want one of them. Tonight when we hit the next home station. I will pay what she asks."

Frowning, Dr. Milens swallowed. "Ah, you misunderstand, sir. They are my assistants . . . ah, employees. They are . . . not whores."

Beezah looked beyond the mesmerist to Lockhart. "Has he already paid for them?"

Dr. Milens knew who was there, but he turned around to gain time to think. His gaze brushed past Lockhart who was watching a coyote amble through a nearby wash, searching for supper. The mesmerist wasn't sure who scared him the most, this strange black man or Lockhart. Nothing came to him of significance to say, or any courage either, so he reluctantly returned his attention to the tall black man.

"No, no, please, sir. I must go now."

"Have her come to me at the next main stop. Dark it will be."

Shaking his head, Dr. Milens spun around and shuffled away. The day was turning worse and worse. What would Elsie and Geraldine say? What would they do? He glanced at Lockhart as he passed.

The black man stood beside the stage, lit a hand-carved, ivory-bowled pipe. His manner was catlike. Haughty and confident of himself, his skills.

Meowing, the black cat jumped to the base of the brake, then to the front left wheel, to the spoke, and, finally, the ground, where it sought Beezah's leg to rub against.

Lockhart was the first to speak. "Hard to believe, the stage would hire a man like you to ride herd on some luggage."

"I do not understand, Governor. Do you believe I am not capable because of my blackness?"

Stepping away from the building, Lockhart smiled. "Hardly. I meant it as a compliment. I have heard of you. You are way above the standard express guard."

"Thank you, Governor."

"You are welcome." Lockhart walked toward him. "I'm guessing we're carrying gold."

Beezah met him midway and held out his hand. "*Bonjour.* You are Vin Lockhart, yes?"

"I am. And you are Jean-Jacques Beezah."

"And you are a good guesser." Beezah grinned. "The strongbox is full. And heavy. Very heavy."

They talked easily for a few minutes with Beezah explaining the obvious, that the stage was carrying a strongbox filled with gold being transferred to a Cheyenne bank. The black man asked if Dr. Milens was a *boko*, a certain kind of voodoo shaman feared for his magical powers, who also made protective amulets and communicated with the dead. Sometimes, he made zombies, forcing the dead to do what he wanted. Immediately, Beezah said that most voodoo priests and priestesses did only good, helping ordinary people to deal with the natural and supernatural forces of the universe, adding that he had grown up in Haiti, leaving it for America and New Orleans when he was eighteen.

Lockhart tried to explain what the mesmerist did and Beezah's only reaction was one word: spirits. Then Beezah reached into his coat pocket and slowly withdrew a small black stone. Nearly round and decorated with small red markings. Smiling broadly, he said a *boko* had blessed it for him when he decided to leave his homeland. Haiti had gotten too small, he said with an easy grin. It was an amulet made from a pebble he had found on the floor of an *ounfo*, a voodoo temple. He said the marking was a *ve´re´*, a ritual drawing—in miniature—that marked the four winds and created a crossroads to invite the spirits to come.

"Good luck," he said and added that he had asked *Iwa*, the intermediaries between people and the spirit world if it would be all right before he took it.

Smiling, Lockhart said he had something similar, held up the pebble carried on his watch chain, and explained it was from an Oglala holy man and that stone was considered sacred by his adopted tribe, that it was the oldest of living beings and, therefore, the wisest. He decided not to share the story of spirits riding with him into battle. Protecting him. It was only a myth started by his adoptive father. It had no basis in truth. None, he told himself.

Instead, he explained that the Oglala Great Spirit, *Wakantanka*, was seen in the sun, moon, sky, earth, winds, lightning, thunder and other natural forces. All were sacred elements of the whole. Somewhat like the voodoo religion. Spirits lived in the land, the trees, the streams, and most were dangerous.

"*Tunkan*, a sacred stone, like this, is named after the dead person whose spirit lives within it," Lockhart said. "I was raised in an Oglala village, mostly by a holy man." He smiled; it wasn't something he shared often and it felt good. "Sort of a guardian spirit within the rock. It is immortal, living forever. My tribe called it *sicun*. They believe that, sometimes, it is reincarnated."

"Ah, fascinating!" Beezah exclaimed. "Could it be the same magic, Governor? May I ask the name of your . . . stone?"

"It is named after an ancient holy man, Eyes-of-the-Wind. He was quite famous among my old tribe. I think my adopted father knew him—and respected him greatly."

"Do you think this Eyes-of-the-Wind will come back . . . some time?"

"Good question." Lockhart looked at the cat, still massaging Beezah's leg, and changed the subject. "That's quite a cat. Yours, I take it."

"Yes, she is a spirit, I think. I call her *Mawhu*, the name of the goddess of the moon in my religion."

Lockhart knelt and held out a hand.

"Be careful, Governor. *Mawhu* does not take well to . . . strangers . . ." Beezah's caution ended as the cat approached Lockhart, meowed an introduction and enjoyed the businessman's strokes along its back.

As he patted the cat, Lockhart said softly, "Yes, I know. You are a cousin to the panther." He stood and said, "Tell me more about your religion. It reminds me of others, yet it sounds quite different." His interest was genuine and it showed in his eyes.

"Of course. I am surprised at your interest, Governor. And pleased."

In a few sentences, Beezah explained his religion was voodoo, learned as a boy in Haiti. He had grown up there, coming to New Orleans as a young man. The religion was largely focused on ancestors with each family of spirits having its own priesthood, usually related to the spirits. The word, *voodoo*, itself meant spirit. His religion, as he was taught, was built around a double-divine concept with the God-Creator, *Nana Buluku*, as the supreme force, and a group of voduns, or God-Actors, who looked over things on earth.

He shrugged his shoulders and said it was a very complex religion. He reminded Lockhart of *Iwa*, supernatural beings who represented the great forces of nature. They were in the trees, the streams, the mountains, wind, plants and fire. They also represented human sentiments and values, like love, courage, truth, justice, fidelity. In certain voodoo ceremonies, they would enter the human body.

"Voodoo has many pieces, for it is built from African religions and is tightly connected to all that has happened in Haiti over the centures," Beezah said, motioning in a large circle. "It even has Catholic—and Freemason—tributes within it. I guess you would say it ties the unknown to the known, connecting those of us who are living with the dead and to those not yet born. It is quite complicated." He sighed.

"Aren't they all?" Lockhart replied. "It has taken me a long time to understand the different religions of the white man."

Beezah chuckled. "Ah yes, and each is the only true one."

Proudly, he added that Haiti was the world's first independent black republic, created by a revolution led by slaves at the turn of the century. Several of his slave ancestors had been in this struggle and he himself was named after Jean-Jacques Dessalines, the legendary founding father of the republic.

Holding his arms, Lockhart shared the fact that his interest in religions had mostly come from his partner and good friend, who had taught him much. Beezah said that his knowledge of voodoo was limited to his own temple and his own priest there, that he didn't really know the great picture of the African-based belief system.

Their discussion was interrupted by Norborg returning with a tin plate of food and a cup of coffee. The driver asked Lockhart if he intended to come inside to eat. Puzzled by what he had overheard, the big Swede wondered to himself why two men of the gun were talking about religion and decided it was none of his business.

Lockhart examined the plate; it was some kind of stew. "How about some dinner company, Beezah?"

"I would like that, Governor."

"Be right back," Lockhart said and headed for the station.

Norborg nodded and headed for the new team to check on the harness.

Walking away, Lockhart stopped and turned back to Beezah. "No offense, but have you checked out the men riding on top? Gold is a tough secret to keep."

Beezah's smile was glistening white against his dark skin. "Two have guns, but trouble they are not." He cocked his head to the side. "And inside?"

"The man next to me is carrying a shoulder holster—and he's got a small gun in his boot," Lockhart said. "Two of the men behind me are also armed. Guns are in their coat pockets."

"What about the spirit man?"

"No, he's not armed," Lockhart said and then added, "At least, I don't think he is."

"His ladies?"

"Don't know. Haven't looked."

Beezah laughed. "Do you want to share them, Governor?"

It was Lockhart's turn to laugh.

"Will you give me a hand—if there is need?" Beezah asked and took a small bite of the stew, balancing the plate in his right hand.

"Of course," Lockhart said and grinned.

"What if it is Indians?"

"I'll help you stop them. They won't be any of my friends."

Beezah laughed and it was deep and guttural as Lockhart disappeared into the building.

CHAPTER SIXTEEN

Heavy dusk found the stage pulling into a gray-looking station for a fresh team of animals. Anton Norborg brought the tired mules in at a full run as he liked to do. His reins gave a special command to his off-leader and the right-front mule responded as he wanted.

No stock tenders were in sight. Neither was the fresh team.

"Hey, Roberts! Dusty! *Var* are my horses?" Norborg yelled.

Lockhart was dozing on and off, but was aware the man next to him was not asleep, only faking. He heard Beezah tell the Swede that the fresh team was on the side of the building. At that moment came the sounds of the harnessed horses, followed by a gruff "Settle down. We're comin'."

Hooves clattered on the hard ground. Leather creaked. Trace chains rattled. Horses snorted. From around the far corner came the harnessed team of horses.

"*Ja. Ja.* Hurry up. I am behind the schedule an' *du* know *vad* the boss think of that," Norborg said, laid the reins over the front edge of the driver's box and prepared to get down.

The two men eased the horses toward the coach; their faces mostly covered by their hats and growing shadows.

"*Vad* is this? Who are *du*? *Var* are . . ."

"Shuddup and don't move." Both men had rifles aimed at Norborg and Beezah.

Inside the coach, Lockhart awoke, pushed aside the

pulled-down, leather curtain enough to see what was happening. His hand slid inside his coat to his shoulder holster.

"Don't do that." His leering face fat with victory, Dr. Milens leaned forward; a two-shot derringer cocked in his right hand. "Sorry it had to end this way for you, Lockhart. You should've stayed in Denver with your idiot friend."

Above, Jean-Jacques Beezah's response was to swing his gun toward them and fire twice. The closest outlaw winced and spun to the right. A shot from the other outlaw drove into Beezah's right leg. As the guard levered his rifle for another shot, a blast from behind Beezah straightened him. Dropping the gun, he pitched forward, crashed into the front boot and fell to the ground, narrowly missing the coach tongue, and lay still. His rifle bounced off the left-rear mule's back and clattered on the hard earth. Both of the closest two mules jumped at the intrusions and the right-rear mule stutter-stepped away from the sudden addition to its space.

Snarling, the black cat jumped from the driver's box and sprang at Beezah's attacker behind him. A curse, followed by a fierce swing of his arm, sent the small black shape hurling from the stage.

From the ground, the second outlaw tugged on his bell crown hat and yelled, "Ya got the nigra, Billy Joe! Good work."

The wounded outlaw, wearing a faded, woolen poncho, grimaced and held his side. "I'm shot, dammit, Gleason. I'm shot! Did you kill that black sonvabitch?"

"Me an' Billy Joe did." The second outlaw, named Nolan Gleason, waved his rifle in the direction of the coach roof. Thick-mustached and square-faced, he wore two belted-on handguns; one holstered with the butt forward, the other with the butt to the back.

"Get the box, Billy Joe, and throw it down," Gleason demanded.

"I have only a mail pouch." Norborg held up a filled leather bag.

"Don't play games. We know you're carryin' gold," Gleason responded. "It's under your seat."

From the stagecoach roof, a silhouette stood. The miners there were flattened against the coach, heads down. "If one of you bastards moves, I'll blast the lot of you." Billy Joe Thornton motioned with his gun.

"Give him a hand, driver—and be quick about it," Gleason yelled, pointing his rifle for emphasis

"How do you know about this? No one was . . ." Norborg mumbled and shook his head, then leaned over and yanked on the unseen strongbox. A moment later, he turned toward the outlaw behind him. "*Ja*. I need some help. It is heavy. Jean-Jacques helped me with it. Please, I cannot."

"Yeah. Yeah. Just wait. I'm coming." Thornton stepped closer.

The outlaw's corduroy coat was filthy and wrinkled, matching his woolen shirt; a misshapen, narrow-brimmed hat was yanked low on his lanky, unshaven face. Except for the shiny revolver, he looked just like the other miners on top.

As he passed, one miner looked up. "Thought ya was gonna look for gold with us."

"Found mine early," Thornton snapped and climbed into the driver's box. "Stand easy, Nolan. I'm gonna check on that nigger first." He leaned over to look at the downed coach guard lying on the ground at the base of the coach. Thornton's long-barreled Colt was cocked in his right fist.

On the ground, a grasping Beezah turned on his side and fired both of his Remington revolvers into Thornton's peering head. The outlaw's face disappeared in blood. His Colt fired in death's reaction, slamming its lead into the dirt beside Beezah. Thornton jerked and pitched forward, tumbling out of the seat and crashing into the coach tongue, then sliding to the dirt nearly on top of Beezah. The outlaw's

Colt clattered against the tongue and thudded to the ground. The closest two mules jumped again and, this time, the right-rear mule kicked Thornton's unmoving shoulder.

The badly wounded Beezah collapsed with his guns still in his fists.

"What the hell?" Gleason blurted and fired rapidly in Beezah's direction; one bullet splintered a wedge from the front part of the coach itself; another pounded into Beezah's left arm; a third thumped into Thornton's back. Beezah was again motionless; the gun in his left hand spun free, a foot from the dead Billy Joe Thornton.

"Driver, toss that box down here, before I put a bullet in you," Gleason yelled and swung his rifle in Norton's direction.

"Ja, I be doing that. Ja."

With the adrenaline of sheer fear, Norborg managed to push the heavy box against the side and shove it over the side. The green trunk, with the white lettering "Wells Fargo & Co.," on its side, landed with a dull sound. The lock and hinges rattled, but held.

"Do you want the mail, too?" Norborg again held up the pouch.

"Hell no," Gleason barked.

A fourth outlaw, pig-faced and long-haired, in duckin trousers and canvas suspenders, came from the station, brandishing a shotgun and leading a horse strapped with readied canvas bags. He paused beside the first outlaw, kneeling, holding his side.

"Are ya going to be able to ride, Diede, or are we gonna have to leave ya?"

"I can ride," the poncho-wearing Frank Diede grunted through clenched teeth. "It j-just h-hurts. Just cut along the side of my belly, that's all."

Jerking on the reins of the pack horse, the pig-faced outlaw grinned and walked over to Gleason standing beside the strongbox. "Thornton's dead, I take it."

"Guess so, Solak. He guessed wrong. But I took care of the black bastard."

"Thornton's tough luck. One less to split with," the pig-faced man named Solak said. "Anything inside the coach worth taking?"

"Don't know. The boss's two good-looking ladies are there." Gleason grinned.

"We're in no hurry. Let's get 'em out of there. Might be somethin'good on them other passengers, too."

"He won't like it, if'n ya mess with his ladies," Gleason warned. "He said they-all were plannin' on goin' with us."

"What's he gonna do about it? We're not gonna hurt 'em any, jes' poke 'em a little."

Both men laughed and Diede joined them, holding his side and trying to act like he wasn't hurt badly. His rifle remained in the dirt beside the waiting horse team.

Pushing aside the curtain in the coach window, Dr. Milens yelled, "I heard that crap. Hurry up and get the gold loaded. The good mayor said it was full." He snickered. "He didn't think anyone would suspect." A cackle followed. "I'll bring the passengers out."

As he finished, Dr. Milens heard the unmistakable cocking sound of a revolver.

"Drop the gun," the hard-looking man next to Lockhart growled.

Dr. Milens swung the derringer in his direction.

Lockhart's left hand was a blur, grabbing the mesmerist's gun hand and slamming it against the door. The hideaway gun sprang from his opened fingers and clunked against the stagecoach floor. A fraction behind, Lockhart's right fist rammed into Dr. Milens's jaw, driving his head backward.

"Hey, what's goin' on in there?" Gleason yelled, but made no attempt to move.

"You all right, boss?" Solak asked, dropping the pack horse reins to put both hands on his shotgun.

Shoving the unconscious mesmerist toward the assistants,

Lockhart slid into Dr. Milens's seat and stuck his hand out of the window, beside the curtain. His face remained in the dark as he pointed emphatically at the strongbox.

"Sure. Sure. We'll get it packed," Solak responded. "Blow off that lock, Gleason."

Gleason fired and the lock burst apart, and the two men began removing the tied pouches of gold dust and placing them in the canvas bags on the pack horse.

Inside, the hard-looking man said quietly, "Smart move. Name's Hogan. John Hogan. I'm a Deputy United States Marshal. Looks like we can count on you. Wasn't sure." He picked up Dr. Milens's derringer and shoved it into his pocket.

Lockhart said in a low voice. "Lockhart. Vin Lockhart. Wasn't sure about you either." He moved back to his seat, straightened the out-cold Dr. Milens and drew his Smith & Wesson revolver.

"Yes, I know who you are." Hogan glanced at the middle assistant. "Lady, you'd better be coming out of that bag with a powder puff."

The closest woman cursed and eased her empty hand from her purse in her lap. The bespectacled assistant folded her arms in disgust and looked out the window again.

"Who's 'we'? What about the men behind you? Two are armed." Lockhart motioned with his head.

What passed for a smile preceded the marshal's statement. "Roger'll handle them."

"Roger?"

"Next to me. Pinkerton Field Agent Roger Buenstahl. On assignment from Wells Fargo and Company."

Lockhart wanted to ask if the professorial-appearing man would hit them with a book, but decided it proved his earlier point about not looking dangerous and being so.

As he discarded the thought, the bespectacled man spun toward the men behind him; in his fist was a short-barreled pistol. His voice was thick with grit. "We'll sort this out later. Right now, I want your guns on the floor. Don't do anything I don't like." Satisfied with the passengers' immediate compliance, Roger Buenstahl looked back at the two women. "You neither, ladies. I haven't put lead in a woman. Yet. But I will if I need to. Real fast."

Hogan glanced back at Lockhart. "Consider yourself deputized, Lockhart."

"All right. How do you want to play this?" Lockhart studied the outlaws outside, filling the canvas bags. "They're expecting us to come out."

"That's what they're going to get. Milens goes first. You and I'll be right behind him," Hogan declared. "Roger, you cover us."

Shoving another stack into the bag, Solak squinted at the moving shadows within the dark interior of the coach. "Nolan, go take a look. Something's wrong in there. The boss said the passengers were coming out."

"Frank, you go," Gleason pushed the wounded outlaw, Frank Diede, toward the coach.

"Me? Why me? You do it. I'm hurt."

"They're going to kill us all," one of the passengers muttered from the back.

Buenstahl frowned and glanced in his direction. "Watch and see."

"You ready?" Lockhart pulled the unconscious mesmerist next to the door.

Behind him, Hogan said, "I'll take the long-haired one. Before he can use that scattergun. Be careful, there might be somebody else in the station."

"I'll slide over as soon as you leave," Buenstahl said.

"Let's go." Lockhart opened the coach door and shoved Dr. Milens out.

The mesmerist's limp arms and legs fluttered like some giant, ungainly bird and he flopped against the ground.

"What the hell?" Solak blurted and swung his shotgun toward the motion.

Marshal Hogan fired twice from the opened coach door as Lockhart jumped. Like it was a red-hot branding iron, Solak dropped the shotgun and grabbed his stomach.

Lockhart demanded their surrender. Solak groaned and begged him not to shoot. He grabbed his shirt, trying to hold back the seeping crimson. Already wounded, Diede cried out his submission and held up his arms to reinforce it, wincing as he did.

Gleason hesitated, squeezing his rifle with both hands.

"Drop the gun, mister, or you're next," Lockhart barked, pointing his revolver at the outlaw.

Behind him, Marshal Hogan cleared the coach. "The gun. Drop it. Now. Then those pistols. Unbuckle the belts and let them drop."

Gleason started to jerk his arm upward, thought better of it, and raised his hands. The rifle thudded on the ground, sending a puff of dust spinning away. The pistol belts followed.

Lying prone on the ground, Dr. Milens was jabbering to himself, not yet aware of where he was, or what was happening. "The spirits are . . . waiting. Waiting. They will . . . come. For . . . money . . . they will come."

Lockhart moved toward the three outlaws, to complete their surrender and make sure none were carrying a hidden weapon. Sensing movement at the station window, Lockhart dove to his left, rolled and came up firing. It was instinctive.

A rifle shot from there cracked the earth where he had just been.

Without waiting for the hidden shooter to find him in the shadows of the coach, Lockhart came up from his roll in a fierce run to his left. Hogan guessed his strategy and fired two shots at the window; Buenstahl did the same from the coach. Lockhart looped wide, then dashed for the station and came to a stop beside the front wall. The window from where the shot came was ten feet away. It was the only window on this side of the building. There was no sign of the shooter.

Lockhart guessed there was more than one door and eased himself backward to the corner and around it. The shallow building had no windows on this short side and he raced to the back. Mounting one of the seven waiting horses was the last outlaw.

"I wouldn't do that," Lockhart said, motioning with his revolver.

Midway into the saddle, the gray-haired outlaw held his rifle in one hand and the reins and a fistful of mane in the other. He was older than the others. By far. Too old for this kind of work, Lockhart thought. But probably as mean as an old bull.

"Toss the gun—and climb down. Or do you want to gamble I can't put three bullets in you before you can fire it."

"None of them boys has ever taken a bullet. Just a bunch of posies. I have. You point a gun at 'em and they'll fall down. Not me. Think I'm too old to be game, mister?" the older man with a weathered face and whip-lean body growled. What passed for a smile was stopped at the right corner of his mouth by a long scar.

"No, I think you're too smart."

The rifle flew in the air and the aging outlaw swung down. A minute later, Lockhart brought him to the assembled group of would-be holdup men, including the mesmerist and his assistants.

All of the passengers were huddled in another cluster; Buenstahl had satisfied himself that none were a part of the attempted holdup. Marshal Hogan had already informed the passengers that the gang intended to kill them so there would be no witnesses. The reaction was a range of anger, dismay and utter fear. The gang's weapons had been placed inside on the stagecoach floor, except for the shotgun. It was in Buenstahl's hands.

One businessman, wearing a black broadcloth suit sprinkled with trail dust and a plantation-styled straw hat, said he appreciated what had been done, but wanted to know when they would be going; he had an important appointment in Cheyenne. A miner laughed and said he did, too, in Deadwood. Neither the marshal nor the Pinkerton agent responded; they were too surprised by the audacity of the question.

Stepping next to Lockhart, Hogan explained the situation. "We've been tracking Dr. Milens, or whatever his name is, since Kansas City. He called himself Dr. Woodsmeier there. Gets information about bank deliveries—by mesmerizing a bank president. Like your mayor. Or a stage-line manager. Then his gang hits the coach when there's a valuable shipment on board. Agent Buenstahl is from Pinkerton's home office—in Chicago—and I'm from the Kansas U. S. Marshal's district. Didn't figure anyone around here would know us. We didn't tell anyone. Not even the mayor. Looks like our mesmerist friend managed to get the news of the gold without much trouble."

Stunned by the suddenness of it all, Norborg walked over to Marshal Hogan, finally working up the nerve to declare, "Roberts *und* Dusty, dey should've been the ones to *ge* out the new horses. If they killed dem, I think vee should hang dem right here. *Ja*, I do."

Lockhart's eyes flashed angrily. "What about Beezah? Has anyone checked?"

Norborg's expression was first fearful, then annoyed. "Reckon he is dead. Dey put *fyra* or *fem* slugs in him. Ah, four or five, *ja*."

Lockhart broke away, headed for the coach. His words trailed him. "Warriors like Beezah are hard to kill. The stones sing to them."

Slightly amused, Hogan watched him for a moment, then returned his attention to the Swede driver who was rattled once more. "Should I go with . . . him? Should I look for

Roberts *und* Dusty? Should I hitch up new horses? *Vad* are vee doing?"

"Go look for them. See if you can find some rope, too. We're going to need it," Marshal Hogan said. "You can hitch up the new team, but we're not pulling out until I say so."

A few feet away, Solak groaned, "I-I need a d-doctor."

Marshal Hogan motioned with his head toward Dr. Milens.

"Not that kinda doctor. I need a real one. I'm gut-shot. Right here, dammit."

"Well, if he can't help you, no one can. Or will," Hogan replied.

His eyes narrowed into slits, Dr. Milens snarled, "Shut up, you fool."

"Shut up yourself, Jefferson," Gleason snorted. "You said this was gonna be easy."

Marshal Hogan grinned. "Jefferson, huh? That's a third name."

The mesmerist looked up at Hogan, then at Lockhart who was disappearing around the front of the coach. "You're quite mistaken, sir. I am a law-abiding citizen. I will be talking to the governor about this treatment. You are in for serious misfortune, I guarantee it."

"And I guarantee you're going to prison, Milens, Woodsmeier, Jefferson, or whatever your name is."

The gray-haired outlaw looked at Dr. Milens, then at the two wounded outlaws and Gleason. "This was my first job with 'em, Marshal. Honest. I didn't know anybody was gonna get hurt. I'm ... jes' an old man. Grinshaw's my name. Of the Kansas Grinshaws."

The auburn-haired assistant named Geraldine straightened her glasses. "I understand why you have these men under arrest, but why us? Elsie and I were forced to do what this awful man made us do." She motioned toward Dr. Milens.

Marshal Hogan's smile was a sarcastic one. "Anyone else just strolling by?"

Buenstahl snorted and motioned with the shotgun for someone else to speak.

In response, Solak knelt in obvious pain, but none of the gang spoke or tried to help him. Dr. Milens acted like he didn't know him. Solak wheezed and was quiet.

After shoving the dead Billy Joe Thornton aside, Lockhart knelt beside Beezah and turned the black man slowly over on his back. His coat and shirt were blood-soaked. Why hadn't the two lawmen acted quicker? Or the driver? The thought angered Lockhart, even as he realized they didn't know when or where an attack might come or who on the stage might be involved. Even Beezah. Even himself.

One of Beezah's revolvers lay on the ground; the other remained in his right fist. A few feet away was his bowler. Next to the black man was a small derringer that had evidently fallen from his pocket.

A soft groan.

Lockhart's energy level jumped. "He's alive," he said with more confidence than he felt. He straightened Beezah's legs, then removed the man's bloody coat and vest. The guard's shirt was mostly glistening crimson and its buttons quickly surrendered to Lockhart's pressure.

In spite of the softening nightfall, he could see four bullet holes in the man. Slugs were imbedded in his lower back. Another piece of lead was in his upper left bicep. His right leg was bleeding badly, but it looked like the bullet had cut through the fat side of his thigh and not penetrated.

"You will live, Beezah. They do not know how to kill a strong man," Lockhart said. "I will be right back."

Beezah's eyes fluttered open. "Where is *Mawhu*? Is she . . ."

Lockhart frowned. "I will look for her. Later. I promise."

"She is my . . ."

"Be quiet now." Lockhart retreated to the rear boot, climbed up and pulled free his canteens and a folded shirt from his bag. The water was tepid, but it would do. He looked over at Hogan, Buenstahl, and the two groups watching him.

"Beezah's alive," Lockhart said. "He's hurt bad, though. I'm going to need help."

He returned to Beezah, who had passed out. Methodically, he tore apart the shirt and began cleaning the wounds with wet rags.

From the building, Norborg reappeared, holding two fat coils of rope. Walking beside him were two men, rubbing and stretching their arms.

"I found dem. *Ja,* tied up inside dey were. Not hurt none, though," Norborg announced proudly. "Got some *rep,* too." He held up the coiled lariats.

Marshal Hogan held up a hand to stop them. "Quick. Start a fire. We need hot water. Bandages. The guard's alive."

The taller stockman, Roberts, turned in midstride and headed back; the shorter man was a step behind.

"Get a lantern, too. Two, if you've got them," Hogan added, "so we can see what we're dealing with. Going to need a sharp knife. Clean it in the hot water."

From the front of the coach, Lockhart yelled, "Bring the can of kerosene, too. I'm going to want it."

"*Vad? Fotogen? Du* aren't going to burn my coach, are *du?*"

Lockhart shook his head. "I'm going to put it in the wounds. Sterilize them. Help them heal."

"Oh. Never heard of dat." Norborg shrugged his shoulders and hurried after the two stockmen, catching up with the shorter Dusty.

"What's this all about?" Dusty asked, his big ears poking out from his woolen cap. "All this worry about a colored man?"

The round-bellied Swede frowned and walked faster, motioning for Dusty to do the same. "Jean-Jacques Beezah is from Orleans."

"But he's a nigra, ain't he?"

"*Ja*, that he is. He is also a friend of Vin Lockhart's. Keep walking. I will tell *du* later."

Lying on the ground now, Solak groaned again, "What 'bout me? My gut's all ripped up and you're worried about some nigger."

Glancing at him, then in Lockhart's direction, Marshal Hogan said, "I wouldn't say that real loud, mister. If Lockhart hears, I doubt the lot of you will see the sunrise. Including you, Doc Whatever-your-name-is."

The gray-haired outlaw folded his arms. "Who is that hombre anyway?"

"Lockhart. Vin Lockhart. From Denver."

His eyes widening, the old man began to cackle. "Ain't you somethin', Jefferson. Dun led us into a trap with a federal marshal, a Pinkerton agent—an' Vin Lockhart to boot. You're a damn fool." He spat for emphasis.

Dr. Milens stared at his feet, but said nothing.

The auburn-haired assistant pushed her glasses on her nose, looked at Dr. Milens and said, "It could've been worse. I hear Wild Bill Hickok's coming back to Cheyenne. He could've been on the stage, too." Her laugh was trilled.

Marshal Hogan turned away and headed toward the front of the coach. "Lockhart, do you want to move him? Inside?"

Without looking up, Lockhart responded, "Not yet. He's lost a lot of blood. I'm afraid moving him would just make it worse."

"How much lead's still in him?"

"Three slugs." Lockhart placed a folded wet cloth on Beezah's forehead.

"Can you get to them?"

"I think so. Come morning."

With a look of exasperation, the plantation-hatted businessman stepped forward. "Now see here, Marshal. We must get moving." He straightened his back. "I demand you get those new horses hitched up and let's get moving."

Hogan cocked his head to the side. "There are saddled horses out back. Take one and leave."

"What?"

"You heard me. Ride out or shut up. The stage leaves when I decide it does," Hogan growled. "If you want to help, you can put those gold pouches back into the strongbox. Then two of you can hold the lanterns for us while we work on Mr. Beezah."

The businessman's expression flashed from surprise to annoyance to fear and he stepped back with the other passengers, not daring to meet any of their eyes. Two miners offered to help with repacking the money. Another said he would hold a lantern. A businessman volunteered to take a lantern as well.

Moving Beezah's discarded coat to give him more room, Lockhart remembered the black stone the shootist had shown him earlier. Reaching into Beezah's coat pocket, he retrieved the stone. From his watch chain, he yanked free the small red pebble. Carefully, he placed both in Beezah's left hand and closed his fingers around them. He left the revolver in the guard's tightly gripped right fist and slipped the derringer back into Beezah's wet coat pocket.

"May the stone songs find you and make you strong."

CHAPTER SEVENTEEN

Cheyenne was bustling when the stage finally pulled up next to the stage-line office. Jean-Jacques Beezah lay on top, sleeping and covered with a blanket. His revolver remained tightly grasped in his right hand and the small stones were gripped in his left. Both rested on his chest. Beside him sat three miners; none had made any attempt to comfort him during the trip.

Trailing the stage was Pinkerton Field Agent Roger Buenstahl riding one of the outlaw horses and guarding Nolan Gleason, Frank Diede and Old Man Grinshaw on three other mounts, with their hands tied behind them. The bodies of Thornton and Solak were draped and lashed over two other horses, led by the lawman. Inside the coach were Marshal John Hogan, a tied Dr. Milens and both women, neither bound, as well as the remaining miners and other passengers.

Sitting in the driver's box, next to Big Nose Anton Norborg, was Lockhart holding Beezah's Henry carbine. In his lap lay Beezah's black cat. Like its master, the cat was injured, but alive. Lockhart had splinted its broken leg and wrapped the bruised body with torn pieces of a station bedsheet, then with a blanket for warmth. Bound within the splint were Morning Bird's cardinal feathers from his gear. He thought Morning Bird's nuturing ways might sink into *Mawhu's* broken leg and help heal it.

An occasional petting of the quiet animal assured Lockhart of the cat's continued survival. "Little panther," he called it. He was rewarded with a soft licking of his hand.

The sight of the coach, outriders and dead bodies drew a curious crowd, which Norborg was glad to oblige with a loud report of the attempted holdup, laced with Swedish words and exclamations. If he was tired from his all-night driving, his enthusiasm covered it well.

Marshal Hogan shoved open the door and stepped out, brandishing his revolver. "Move on, folks. This is federal business. We've got prisoners. Go on now." He looked up at Lockhart. "We'll help you get Beezah to some place comfortable as soon as we have this bunch behind bars."

"That's fine. He's resting easy." Lockhart studied the sleeping guard, then patted the cat's head.

A well-dressed businessman in a herringbone suit and

boiled shirt with a crisp collar pushed his way through the gathering, yanked the cigar from his mouth and said, "Marshal, I'm Jonathon Crispin, president of the Cheyenne Cattlemen's Bank. The strongbox, is it . . ."

"It's right up there," Hogan assured. "It will be turned over to the stage office manager. You can deal with him. Standard procedure. Got it?"

"Oh, of course. Of course. Thank you, marshals," the banker said and realized Beezah was lying on the coach roof. "You have wounded?"

"Yes." Hogan took another step away from the coach and motioned for the mounted prisoners to dismount. "The guard was shot up. Bad. Thanks to him—and Mr. Lockhart up there—we caught the whole gang." He glanced in Buenstahl's direction. "Oh, and, of course, the great Pinkerton agency played a crucial role in their capture."

Buenstahl nodded his thanks. Founder Allan Pinkerton always insisted his field agents secure proper credit for the national detective agency whenever news was good.

The banker's eyebrows arched in appreciation. "That is good news, sir. Indeed. Indeed. My thanks to all of you for your courageous actions." He rubbed his hands together and his smile was a controlled response. Acknowledging several customers in the crowd, he folded his arms to wait.

All of the prisoners were led away by the marshal and the detective to the Cheyenne sheriff's office and jail. Buenstahl mentioned to Hogan that he should also stop by the newspaper office and make sure the capture was "properly recorded." Eagerly, the passengers exited the coach from inside and on top; those staying in Cheyenne retrieved their luggage with help from Norborg and the replacement driver, a lanky man with a curled mustache, a long coat and pushed-up-front brim on his hat.

Lockhart got his gear, left it on the sidewalk and returned to the driver's box to help with the strongbox, which was tied shut with rope. The coach was going on to

Deadwood, but he intended to buy horses and supplies, and head in that direction by himself. He had experienced enough of riding in a stagecoach to last a long time. Besides, he didn't intend to go east; his intentions were to the north. His planned destination was the Rosebud, possibly his tribe's last encampment; he would scout from there until he found his friends. A strong part of him hoped they weren't in that area.

The stage-line district manager came out to take control of the strongbox. Beside him were two larger men with shotguns who would have rather been elsewhere, judging by their expressions. A suit coat that needed considerable shortening at the sleeves accentuated the manager's lack of height. His string tie wasn't quite centered at his neck and his right eye wandered free of its relationship with his left. Hatless, his dark hair was parted in the middle and slicked down on both sides.

"*God middag, Herr* Ellison," Norborg said and hurried to the front of the coach where Lockhart handed him the strongbox. "I am behind schedule, but the gold is safe—and so are my passengers. *Ja?*"

"Under the circumstances, it is well. It is well," Noah B. Ellison said, adjusting his tie, and offering his customary repetition of key phrases, "but our company is built on being on time. Being on time. Regardless." He frowned and glanced at the armed men next to him, then at the waiting fresh driver. "I want you pulling out of here in fifty minutes. Fifty minutes. No later. Pulling out of here."

Before the new driver could respond, the manager told the two guards to take the strongbox from Norborg and carry it to the bank. The banker stepped forward again, thanked Ellison and left with the guards lugging the locked trunk.

As they left, Ellison spotted Lockhart. "You, sir, I'd like to offer you a job as a stage guard. Stage guard, it is. I'll pay a hundred a week. A hundred a week, sir."

Lockhart tried to hold back a grin. Norborg whispered something to Ellison and the manager's face turned crimson; his right eye danced to the side and back. The Swedish driver moved to his horses and began unhitching them and the new driver slid over to help.

"Oh, Mr. Lockhart, forgive me. Forgive me, sir. Oh, I-I didn't know who . . ."

"I'm not interested, but your offer was generous," Lockhart interrupted. "You must believe in taking care of your guards."

"Our guards. Our drivers. Everybody who works for us. Yes sir, everybody who works for us," Ellison chirped, waving his arms to make a circle. "Our people have made us successful. Successful. Yes, they have. Our people."

Lockhart pushed his hat back from his forehead. "I thought so. You'll be paying for your wounded guard's stay in a hotel, I take it. Until he's well. Again." His right hand motioned toward the top of the coach.

"What? But . . . he's a colored man! A colored man. Surely, surely, you don't expect me. You don't expect me to do that. Not that. Surely."

Lockhart's eyes cut into Ellison's face. The manager licked his lower lip, shuffled his feet, examined them, then looked up again. Lockhart hadn't moved; his stare was hot.

"I can't do that. Can't. Can't do that."

"Mr. Ellison, when Marshal Hogan returns, we're taking Beezah to that hotel across the street," Lockhart said. "You're going to help us. So's Anton."

"B-But the hotel won't let him stay. Won't let him. No, they won't."

Lockhart put his forefinger to his mouth to quiet the man.

Ellison glanced around as if expecting someone to suddenly appear to assist in this discussion with a dangerous man. His eyes glimmered with an idea.

"Ah, we have bunks. Inside. Bunks inside. In the back. In the back, yes. They're for employees. Employees." Ellison motioned toward the office and wished his hand would stop shaking. "How about there . . . instead? How about there . . . instead, Mr. Lockhart? Sir."

Lockhart nodded. "That will do just fine. Better even. Beezah will be there for several months, I imagine. So will his cat. It was hurt, too, by the men trying to hold up your stage."

Ellison looked like he was going to vomit.

Lockhart stepped closer. "If you—and some of your workers—want to help, we can bring Beezah inside now. So you can have room for more passengers up there."

Ellison gulped and stuttered an affirmation, then started for the office. Lockhart's continued response stopped him.

"Beezah's going to need care. Soup for now. Water. A little whiskey," Lockhart explained. "Same with his cat. No whiskey, though. Some cream would be nice." He smiled briefly. "I'll get the doctor to come over."

"I don't think Dr. Ainspeace will, uh, see Negroes. No sir, Dr. Ainspeace, not Negroes. He won't see them."

"I think he will."

"But . . ."

"Understand this, Ellison." Lockhart's voice had an ominous edge to it. "You're going to take care of him—and his cat. I'm leaving Cheyenne for a few weeks, but I'll be back." He tugged on his hat brim to return it to its regular position, letting shadow cover his narrowed eyes. "I'll hold you responsible if anything happens to either of them. You understand?"

"Y-Yes. Y-Yes, I do. I do understand. Yes." Ellison blinked back tears forming at the corners of his eyes and continued heading inside, ignoring the growing wet stain in the middle of his trousers.

A half hour later, Beezah was resting comfortably in the farthest bunk and *Mawhu* was sleeping on a pillow, lying on the floor beside the bed. A saucer of cream waited nearby. In spite of Ellison's dislike of the idea, Lockhart left the gun in Beezah's hand. Beezah's hat, gunbelt, with the holstered second revolver, and rifle, and other gear were shoved under the bunk. So was the derringer removed from his coat pocket. His bloody clothes were folded; Lockhart thought he would try to find a laundry and see if they were cleanable. He doubted it, but it was worth trying.

Satisfied, Lockhart stepped outside. His own things waited on the sidewalk. A team of fresh mules was harnessed and ready.

"*Du* need help, *Herr* Lockhart?" Norborg came from the front of the coach, where he had been talking with the new driver.

"No thanks, Anton. Take care of yourself." Lockhart held out his hand.

"*Ja.* The same to *du.*" Norborg shook his hand eagerly and said he would return Dr. Milens's envelope with the money to the Wilcoxes on his return trip to Denver.

After thanking him, Lockhart slipped the shotgun-holding quiver onto his shoulder over his suit coat, followed by his filled saddlebags. Taking his rifle and two canteens in his left hand, he started across the street. Dr. Ainspeace's drugstore and office was a half block away, according to Ellison.

Like most once-an-end-of-the-track towns, Cheyenne had survived its overnight tent-city status and become a mixture of structures, many shabby and unpainted, some of adobe and logs, a few of brick and fine appointments, some of packing boxes and building paper and flattened tin cans for roofing, and a few more of finely trimmed gables and white fences. Besides two hotels, two churches, two newspapers and twenty or so saloons, there were three banks and a one-story, white-framed house for the territorial governor. No capitol building, however; the state legislature rented several rooms for their meeting purposes. Cows and hogs meandered along the streets, as well as dogs. Vacant lots were gathering places for empty bottles, rusting cans and rotten lumber. Yet the railroad had brought new profits and the year-old military bridge over the North Platte at Fort Laramie made the town a major jumping point for the gold in the Black Hills, vying with Sidney, Sioux City and Yankton for the honor.

"Mr. Lockhart! Mr. Lockhart!"

The Denver businessman with the gunfighter reputation looked toward the salutation. Hurrying toward him was a young clerk holding a folded piece of paper. Lockhart completed his crossing, stepped up onto the planked sidewalk and waited.

The pimply-faced youngster with a dirty white shirt and green armbands swallowed his haste and said, "Telegram for you, sir. Marshal Hogan told me you would be at the stage office."

"Thank you, son." Lockhart laid his rifle and canteens on the sidewalk and handed the clerk a coin.

Happy with himself, the young man excused himself and trotted away, retracing his earlier path.

Unfolding the message, Lockhart noted it was from his partner and smiled. So like Crawfish.

"ALL IS WELL HERE STOP SEAN WANTS YOU TO KNOW MAGIC LIKES THE MARES STOP KOLA IS DOING FINE STOP DR MILENS GOT A THOUSAND DOLLARS FROM MRS WILCOX STOP HE WILL BE ARRESTED IN CHEYENNE AND HELD STOP WIRE WHEN YOU CAN STOP CHANDELIER ARRIVED STOP YOUR FRIEND CRAWFISH P S NEWTON SAYS HI"

He looked up as a freight wagon rumbled past in the street, followed by a man on a bicycle. His mind raced to watching the Irish lad riding the big war horse, then wandered onto Touches-Horses, Stone-Dreamer and Morning

Bird. Would he find them? Safe? His gaze took in the retreating messenger and he called after him.

"Where is the telegraph office, son?"

"Around the corner, sir." The boy stopped and pointed. "Big sign out front. Telegraph office. It's in McGinnis's store there. You know, lumber and coal. Building material. His sign's there, too."

"Thanks."

He watched the boy run ahead, guessing the youngster would make a stop at the general store to use some of his just-acquired money for a stick of candy. Shoving the refolded note into his pocket, he picked up his rifle and canteens and headed in the indicated direction. Falling Leaf came to his thoughts and he wondered if she was doing well. Crawfish hadn't mentioned her. Was that a good sign or a bad one?

His telegram to Crawfish and Sean covered several subjects quickly: his safe arrival; the arrest of Dr. Milens and his holdup gang; the guard Beezah being shot, the U. S. Marshal and Pinkerton agent being onboard and making the arrests; the coming return of the Wilcox money; and asking about Falling Leaf. Satisfied, he set out on his original task to bring a doctor to Beezah. An argument was expected from the physician and he kept reminding himself that getting angry wouldn't help matters.

There wasn't much this Dr. Ainspeace could do, or at least he didn't think there was. Marshal Hogan and he had managed to remove the embedded bullets without complications. Yet, Beezah deserved the attention of a real doctor. He stepped off the end of the sidewalk into the alley opening between the resuming sidewalk. Halfway back in the shadows, a magpie was pecking on something red and raw. Lockhart stopped.

The black-and-white bird stared at him, flapped its iridescent wings and flew away crying its annoyance. Chug. Chug. Chug. Chug. As it passed, the dark color seemed to change from a greenish bronze to a purplish hue and back again.

A magpie in town was not that common, he thought. Perhaps it had come to bring a message from *Yata*, the North Wind. From the north. Probably where Crazy Horse was camped now. Were his friends with him? He followed the flight of the dark bird, wishing it would return. How silly, he thought to himself and glanced down at his watch chain with its missing red pebble charm.

His mind returned to the devastated camp after the Shoshoni war party attacked while he and his fellow warriors were away hunting. His adoptive father had told him prior to their leaving that the *tunkan* had whispered something bad was coming from the north. Yes, it had been the stones that told him, not the sometimes irresponsible magpie.

The whispering had come when he poured sacred water on the stones as part of his daily ritual. The holy man had misread the warning as an alert about an early winter storm, not an attack on the village. Misinterpreting messages from the spirit world happened.

Or sometimes, the messenger got it wrong. Like the magpie. Or the meadowlark from *Okaga*, the South Wind. They could get things mixed up. It was rarer, though, with the sacred stones. It was the listener who misunderstood, not the *tunkan*. They were the first people and had sung to knowing men since they created Mother Earth and the mysterious power, *Taku Skan Skan*, that flows unseen through everything in this world. However, their songs could be misunderstood. Even by the greatest of holy men. And had. His thoughts turned to the question: When the Indians were forced to the reservations, would the stones stop singing? Or would there simply be no one to listen?

He suddenly realized that he was kneeling in the alley, examining the many small pebbles strewn about in the dirt. His rifle and canteens lay beside him. His mind slid once more to an earlier time when he told Touches-Horses of his frustration at not hearing the stones sing, and his concern about disappointing Stone-Dreamer.

"But I do not hear the stones song. They did not come to my vision. They do not come to me in my lodge or in my dreams. I bring special stones into my lodge, but they do not speak to me as I prepare for war or ready myself for the hunt. I call out to them, but they do not answer. I know it has to hurt his soul. I know he has fasted and dreamed to receive understanding from the spirits."

Touches-Horses responded evenly, "Few hear the stone songs, my brother. The panther is your spirit helper instead. That is a strong life-guide, and your deeds in war show it."

"But I am . . . the son of Stone-Dreamer."

"Did you lose something, mister?" The question from behind him snapped Lockhart from his daydream.

Still on his knees, he turned toward the tall questioner. Another man with a dark goatee, wearing a broad-brimmed hat and fringed leggings, was with him. He had never met either, but it was obvious who the tall questioner was, dressed in a black Prince Albert coat, brocaded vest, salt-and-pepper trousers, long boots with half-moon designed tops and a wide, flat-crowned hat over shoulder-length hair.

James Butler Hickok. Wild Bill. The two engraved, ivory-handled .38 Colt revolvers, butt-forward in a scarlet, embroidered silk sash.

Both men seemed genuinely interested in Lockhart's behavior.

"Can we be of assistance?" Hickok asked. His voice soft.

Lockhart stood and brushed off his pants. His mind raced for a possible excuse to share. The truth would be difficult to explain. And sound silly. Yet, nothing in him was comfortable with a lie. His father, Stone-Dreamer, would never allow it. Lying was simply not the Oglala way.

"Well, thanks for asking," Lockhart said. "It'll sound strange, but I was looking for a special stone."

"Gold?" The shorter man asked.

Nattily dressed in linen pants and a fringed buckskin coat to match his leggings, his outfit was completed with beaded moccasins, a huge belt buckle and two pearl-handled revolvers with gold-and-silver plating.

Lockhart shook his head, thinking the man was either a dandy desiring to look like a frontiersman—or one of the flashiest plainsmen he had ever met. He explained that a special pebble had been given to him by an Indian holy man and he, in turn, had given it away to a wounded friend. He was hoping to find one similar to replace it and held up his watch chain to show where it had hung.

"Oh, a good luck charm." Hickok's friend immediately knelt and began combing the loose rock with his fingers.

"That's all right. It wasn't important," Lockhart said, embarrassed by the attention.

"Nonsense. All of us could use a little luck," the shorter, handsome man said, his blue eyes studying a smallish black pebble. "How'd you come by this Indian rock?"

"That's getting personal, Charlie," Hickok said, holding his arms and smiling as he watched his friend scratch among the pebbles.

The stranger held up the pebble for Lockhart to examine and the Denver businessman accepted it. Should he try to explain that his rock was powerful because Stone-Dreamer had placed the *sicum* of Eyes-of-the-Wind, an ancient medicine man, within it? Should he say something about stones speaking to a fortunate few? That the stone had saved his life, protecting him during his great battle with the Shoshoni war party?

"Here, Bill. Here's one for you." The stranger handed a similar pebble to the tall gunfighter. "Sure not as lucky as one blessed by a medicine man, but it can't hurt."

"No thanks, Charlie. My luck's just fine."

"Suit yourself. Wonder if it'll help bring the cards my way?" Charlie chuckled and shoved the pebble into his coat pocket and stood, brushing off his leggings.

"My names's Hickok. Some folks call me Wild Bill. And worse. I answer to a lot of things." Hickok held out his hand. "And my rock-searching friend here is Colorado Charlie Utter. He's in the freighting business—and the pony express business—and anything else he can make money on."

Lockhart shook Hickok's hand, then Utter's. "I'm Vin Lockhart from Denver."

"Vin Lockhart from Denver. May I call you Vin?"

"I would like that."

"Thanks. Say, Vin, did you just come in on the stage?" Utter asked. "That story true about a gang being caught?"

"Depends on the story, but a holdup gang was arrested and brought in for trial."

"Got a feeling you were part of the reason for that," Hickok said with a smile. "Say, Charlie and me are heading to Rowan's. See if we can stir up a game. Want to join us?"

"Better count me out. Right now, I've got to find the doctor. For a friend." Lockhart motioned in the direction he had been going. "He's the one I gave the pebble to. Then a steak and a nice bed sound pretty good."

Immediately, both men wanted to know about what had happened. Lockhart explained about Jean-Jacques Beezah, the two marshals, Dr. Milens and his gang's attempted holdup.

"Nothing takes it out of you more than a stagecoach," Hickok said. "Unless it's a gunfight," he surmised. "Well, we'll probably be there tomorrow, too. Who knows? I might get rich right here in Cheyenne and not need to go to Deadwood. Got a fine new wife waiting in Cincinnati. Figure she needs a nice house, you know."

"Sounds like you are a lucky man," Lockhart said.

"Thank you, Vin. I am. Yes, I really am." Hickok nodded. "If you have any problem with the doc, come an' get us." Hickok grinned slowly. "Charlie here can be very persuasive."

CHAPTER EIGHTEEN

The stage was gone when Lockhart returned with the reluctant doctor. Only a lone miner leaned against the building, drunk and mumbling to himself. He saw the two men approach and waved at them as if they were long-lost friends. He started to move toward them, stumbled and decided it was safer against the building.

Lockhart returned his greeting; the doctor did not. The miner nodded and returned to his mumbling as they passed.

Already in a bad mood, Dr. Ainspeace didn't want to come, but there was something about this man beside him that disturbed him enough to come along. It wasn't Lockhart's words; they had been polite, yet compelling. Rather formal, as if the stranger had been educated in the East. A gentleman for certain. Yet there was something the doctor sensed about this man that warned him to be careful.

Maybe it was the unusual weapon carried by the stranger that signaled this was not a man to deny casually. The sawed-off shotgun in its quiver lay over Lockhart's saddlebags on his shoulder. Maybe it was the way he carried himself. Strong. Athletic. Wary. A rifle and two canteens were in his left hand, leaving his right hand free. A man used to trouble and trouble, to him.

Still, it annoyed him greatly to be asked to tend to a Negro, even if he was a stage-line employee. A hero of sorts, according to this stranger. What would the townspeople think if they knew? At least this stranger didn't seem like the type who would go around talking about it. Dr. Ainspeace decided he would make an appearance, dispense some medicine and get out of there as quickly as possible.

"Did Mr. Ellison, the manager, approve this colored fella being here?" Dr. Ainspeace asked without glancing at Lockhart as they stepped onto the sidewalk.

"Why wouldn't he? Jean-Jacques is an employee. He was wounded, protecting the stage, its passengers and its entrusted valuables." Lockhart's explanation was straightforward.

The doctor, however, wasn't certain what to think of the comment or the man beside him. Was the stranger goading him?

"Come on, man, he's colored," Dr. Ainspeace countered. "That's not the same as white Christian employees—and you know it."

Lockhart studied the physician without speaking as he neared the stage-line office door.

Wiping his brow with his fingertips, Dr. Ainspeace let his voice soften, almost purr. "Of course, I have no problem with that personally. Others do. Not me. I am a doctor of medicine."

"Figured that," Lockhart said and opened the door to let him enter.

Inside, the main room was split roughly into two equal sections by a low railing. Half was a small waiting area with five chairs, a scratched table with a soot-covered lamp, a black stove with an empty coal scuttle resting on top, and a posted schedule controlling the south wall. The other half of the room was a cramped ticket-purchasing section. A high-backed, rolltop desk was the only furniture in this area and the only thing that would fit there. Another lamp rested on its flat ridge-top and the writing portion itself was cluttered with stacks of papers. No one was in either part of the main room.

Motioning toward a rear door, Lockhart laid down his gear, sawed-off shotgun and rifle, and led Ainspeace through to a second room of six bunks and a lone washbasin with a cracked mirror precariously attached to the wall above it. In the far corner, a larger stove was quietly belching heat. Beside it, on the floor, were a coal scuttle and a tin shovel.

Only two beds were occupied. Anton Norborg was in the closest, snoring. The magnificent sounds befitting his enlarged nostrils. In the far corner, Beezah lay on another. A gray silhouette hovered over his bed. The silhouette looked up as Lockhart and Ainspeace entered. In his hands were a cup and a spoon.

"Oh, it's you, Mr. Lockhart. It's you. Good. Good," Ellison said eagerly. "Just finished giving him a little broth. A little broth. Got it from Wagner's. Across the street. Just across the street. Wagner's."

Walking closer, Lockhart asked, "How did he do?"

Repeating himself frequently, Ellison explained the wounded guard had taken about half of it, but was sleeping again now. The manager planned to give him some more after letting him rest. He was proud of his effort, hoping it would be enough to satisfy this unusual stranger. Norborg had told him enough to know Lockhart was not a man to trifle with.

"How about *Mawhu*? Has she?" Lockhart said.

Pleased with himself and the question, Ellison said, "Yes. Yes. Half of the cream is gone. See? Half is gone."

"Good."

Ellison turned toward the doctor and greeted him eagerly, "Evening, Dr. Ainspeace. Evening to you. Came to see *our* patient? Came to see him, right? *Our* patient."

The doctor's answer was to step closer, carefully avoiding the sleeping cat next to the bed. He saw Beezah's folded coat, pistol belt with one holstered revolver, and his Henry rifle laying beside it. He opened his heavy leather satchel and withdrew a stethoscope. Settling himself on the side of the bed, he noticed Beezah had a revolver in his hand.

"Does he need this?" Dr. Ainspeace pointed at the gun with his stethoscope.

"Yes, he does. It makes him comfortable," Lockhart said.

"I can think of a lot of better things for comfort."

"Probably so. But you didn't face a gang of armed highwaymen trying to kill you, did you, Doctor?"

Hesitantly, the doctor resumed his examination. As he touched the end of the listening device to Beezah's bare chest, the stagecoach guard sat up with the revolver pointed straight ahead.

"What the . . . ?" Dr. Ainspeace exclaimed, jumping off the bed.

"It's all right, Jean-Jacques," Lockhart said calmly. "It's me, Vin Lockhart. It's all right. You are safe. It's all right." He eased past the frightened physician, next to the head of the bed, and put his hand on Beezah's left shoulder. "Beezah, *Mawhu* is right here, too. She is asleep. She has a broken leg and bruised ribs. Like you, she has been treated. Like you, she will be well again."

"Do you want some more broth? Some more broth?" Ellison asked, his right eye straying toward the wall.

Beezah's ebony face was drawn and pale as it slowly took on a smile. He looked down at his gun hand, chuckled and lowered the weapon until it rested against the bed's blankets. He stared at Lockhart and said, "Well, Governor, did you stop them? I wasn't much help. Where am I?"

"You got two of them—and the rest surrendered pretty fast after that," Lockhart explained and told about the incognito marshal and Pinkerton agent, and the fact that Beezah was resting in the stage-line station's back room in Cheyenne, being cared for by the manager, and repeated that his cat was resting beside his cot.

"I should've listened to you, Governor, and checked out those miners more carefully," Beezah said. "Did you say I was in the stage office? The bunk room?" He glanced down at the blanket around him. "I've got to get out of here, Governor. I can't be in here, you know that."

Lockhart's gentle hand on Beezah's shoulder stopped his attempted rise. "No, Beezah, you're supposed to be here. Isn't that right, Mr. Ellison?"

"Oh, yes. Yes. Supposed to be here. Supposed to be here."

"Lie down now, Beezah. Relax. The doctor's here to check out your wounds." Lockhart motioned for Dr. Ainspeace to resume his examination.

As the annoyed physician stepped forward, Beezah held up his left fist and opened it to reveal the two stones. "Plenty of healing spirit I already have. Right here. They sing to me, songs of healing."

Looking from the stones to Lockhart to Ellison, the physician said, "Ah yes, of course. That's . . . ah, real good."

Beezah's smile widened. "Governor, I don't think he believes in our stone songs."

After the examination was completed, Dr. Ainspeace gave Ellison an amber-colored bottle of dark liquid and told him to give Beezah a spoonful twice a day until the medicine was gone. It was a stimulant for the entire body, he said. The doctor seemed impressed by the treatment of the man's wounds, and especially, the removal of the bullets.

"Smells like cod-liver oil. Cod-liver oil. Yes, it does," Ellison said, sniffing the uncorked bottle.

"It is. That will be seventy-five cents," Dr. Ainspeace announced. "Twenty-five cents for the medicine. Fifty for the . . . examination."

Ellison fished in his vest pocket, retrieved some coins and handed them to the doctor. Ainspeace's demeanor was changing, from mere annoyance to full disgust.

"Where are the rest of your employees, Ellison?" The question carried an understanding of the answer.

The slick-haired manager looked like he had swallowed something rotten. Using his good left eye, he glanced at Lockhart who was saying good-bye to a reclining Beezah.

"Ah, eating supper. Eating supper. Or sleeping. No stage in 'til morning. Not 'til morning."

"Thought they slept here when they're on duty," Dr. Ainspeace challenged.

"Well, yes. Yes. Drivers. Ah, drivers." He pointed toward the sleeping Norborg while watching Lockhart out of the corner of his eye. "Billy Taws is over at the hotel now. Billy Taws. He'll take the reins in the morning. In the morning. To Salt Lake. Salt Lake is where he's headed. Anton Norborg takes the reins back to Denver this afternoon. Denver, it is."

"Didn't want to sleep here, did they?" the physician fumed. "No wonder. What about your stock tenders? Where are they? In the hotel, too, I imagine. Did you make them pay for their rooms? Or did the company pay? Costly move." He straightened his back like a snake about to strike. "Who are you going to bring in here next? An Irishman? A Chinese pagan? A painted redskin?"

Lockhart patted Beezah on the shoulder and joined them. His face was unreadable.

"I think he'll be up and around in no time. Up and around in no time. Don't you, Mr. Lockhart?" Ellison said, hoping the fearsome stranger hadn't heard the doctor's comments.

Finding courage, Dr. Ainspeace turned toward Lockhart. "Sir, I find your manner most distressing. You have forced this good man—and his employees—into an untenable and costly position by insisting on housing . . . a Negro of all things. My God, man, don't you know the way of civilized society? A black man sleeping in a white man's bed! They don't belong there, even if the whites are mucking out stables." He folded his arms and his eyebrows pinched together in a hateful frown.

Cocking his head to the side, Lockhart imitated the folded arms motion. "Doctor, you scurry on, back to your drugstore. You aren't worth my anger—and I don't want your kind smelling up this place of honor any longer than necessary."

His glare was more than the physician could handle and Dr. Ainspeace lowered his eyes to wipe at his trousers.

Ellison put his hand over his mouth to hold in the gasp that wanted out, lowered it and added, "I've got cod-liver oil. You can take this with you." He held out the amber bottle.

Dr. Ainspeace grabbed it and reached into his pocket for Ellison's repayment.

"Keep it. Yes, keep it. I don't want your money. Your money," Ellison said, raising his chin defiantly. "Beezah is an upstanding employee of our stage line. A hero. I agree you need to leave."

With an exaggerated harrumph, Dr. Ainspeace spun around and walked toward the door. As he passed Norborg's bed, the big Swede grunted and raised his head off the pillow.

"*God afton*, Doc. *Du* not be *komma* here no more. We vill take care of our own." Norborg's sleep-heavy eyes burned with fury.

Dr. Ainspeace paused momentarily, snorted his disgust, and continued out the door. Norborg watched him leave, patted his pillow into a more favorable shape, laid his head down again and was snoring loudly within thirty seconds.

As Lockhart turned to express his gratitude to Ellison for his strong response to the doctor, U. S. Deputy Marshal John Hogan came into the sleeping room, carrying a double-barreled shotgun.

"What did you boys do to that fella with the satchel?" Marshal Hogan asked with a wry smile. "He looked like someone had made him eat a cow pie."

Lockhart explained and Hogan said, "We thank you, Mr. Ellison, for your courtesy to Beezah. He saved lives—and valuable property. Put his own life on the line. Color doesn't have anything to do with courage."

With the shotgun at his side, held casually in his right fist, he turned back to Lockhart. "I see you didn't wait for our help. Somehow, I didn't think you would. Left Agent

Buenstahl standing guard at the jail. Didn't think he would be needed—and the local law was a bit overwhelmed with our load of prisoners."

"Well, Mr. Ellison insisted on taking care of his brave employee in the bunk room," Lockhart said. "So he and Anton and I moved Beezah here."

"How's he doing?" Hogan asked, looking past them to Beezah's bed and cradling the shotgun in his arms.

Lockhart smiled. "He'll be back, good as ever."

"You bet. Good as ever," Ellison supported. "You bet. Good as ever. In a little while. Just a little while." He wiped his forehead quickly with his fingers, hoping no one saw the sweat beads building. "Beezah is a hero. A hero, yes." He said it like he believed it, even more forcefully than before.

"There's a reward for bringing the gang to justice," Hogan said, nodding agreement. "From your own company, Mr. Ellison, and the bank. A thousand dollars. We figured to split it between Mr. Lockhart and Beezah. Even though he is an employee of the stage line."

Lockhart stared at Hogan, then pulled on his hat brim. Tiredness was creeping into his body. "There's going to be extra expense for Noah . . . Mr. Ellison . . . in caring for him, give my half to Ellison—to take care of that. Or if that's awkward for the company, give it to me and I'll give it to him."

Ellison beamed and, for once, was silent.

Hogan invited them to have some supper and celebrate the day's victory. Lockhart liked the idea; Ellison was pleased to be included.

"Looks like I'm going to be here in Cheyenne for awhile," Marshal Hogan explained as they headed for the door. "My boss wants me here for the trial. Got orders an hour ago. Just as soon as we wired the results." He paused and added, "Roger's supposed to return to Chicago. By train. Tomorrow or the next day. Soon as possible, anyway."

He opened the door, stepped out into the front room, stopped and looked back. "Come to think of it, we're going to need your testimony, too, Lockhart." He smiled. "Since you're still legally a deputy, I was hoping to talk you into helping stand guard, too." He pointed toward Lockhart's gear against the wall. "These your things out here, Lockhart?"

"Yeah, haven't had time to check into a hotel. I'll do that after we eat," Lockhart said. "I also need to take Beezah's clothes to the laundry. Maybe they can get the bloodstains out."

"Leave them here, Mr. Lockhart," Ellison asserted. "I will talk with Chou Wung about them. Tomorrow." He paused, feeling quite proud. "He does our company laundry. Down the street."

"That's great. Proably won't come clean, though."

"Chou Wung is quite good at getting out things like that. He is a real magician," Ellison said.

"We can eat and get you registered at the hotel at the same time. Roger and I are staying at the Rollins House. If it sounds okay to you, you can check-in there. Got a huge restaurant there." Hogan stepped over to Lockhart's gear, shifted his own shotgun to his left hand and held up the quiver holding the sawed-off shotgun with his right. "This looks like it would be mighty handy—in case of a jail break." His smile cut across his face.

Standing in the doorway, Lockhart asked, "How long— until the judge gets here?"

"Oh, the circuit judge should be here in a week. Maybe sooner."

"I'll stand guard some tomorrow, got to buy supplies and horses; then I'm riding north. Got friends to catch up with," Lockhart suggested. "How about I write my testimony."

"That's fine. Roger's writing his. That much hurry sounds like gold," Marshal Hogan said with a smile. "Didn't take you for a prospector."

"I'm not. Already did that," Lockhart said. "This is about

horses. That reminds me. Hey, Anton, we're going to get some supper. You want to join us?"

Norborg's snore stopped in mid-snort. In one motion, the big Swede raised his head, threw back the blanket and jumped out of bed.

Everybody laughed.

"My goodness. My goodness sake!" Ellison exclaimed. "I've never seen Anton move so fast. So fast." He chuckled and shook his head. It felt good to be in the company of men like Vin Lockhart and Marshal John Hogan. The lawman added that they had received signed testimonies from most of the passengers; those who couldn't write had placed their marks The plantation-hatted businessman had included a comment about the delay costing him considerable loss of time and money.

As Hogan grabbed Lockhart's saddlebags along with the quivered weapon, he said, "Almost forgot. The mesmerist— Woodsmeier, Jefferson, Milens, whatever his name is—asked to see you. Said it was something about a young Indian woman. Said she wanted to talk with you." He stood up straight, cradling the bags and quiver along with his own shotgun. "Mean anything to you?"

CHAPTER NINETEEN

Early morning found Vin Lockhart sitting in the Cheyenne sheriff's chair behind a wobbly desk laden with papers and posters. Everything was quiet in the cramped office and jail, except for the snoring of the cells' occupants and the gurgling of the coffeepot on the grumpy potbellied stove.

Sipping hot, strong coffee in a chipped mug, he shifted the sawed-off shotgun in his lap with his free hand and left it resting on the trigger guard. He had relieved Marshal

Hogan before seven and agreed to stand watch until noon. Gone were his business clothes, replaced by the attire of a plainsman. His gray trousers were tucked into knee-length boots with a beaded trim. A herringbone vest was unbuttoned, holding his watch in one of the pockets. At his neck was the choker necklace of white elk-bone and sky blue stones his late Indian wife had presented him as a wedding gift. He had left it at the Ghost-Keeping Lodge of Young Evening when he rode away from the tribe. Four chosen warriors had presented it, along with other tributes, when they sought his help a year ago.

His Smith & Wesson revolver was now carried in an open-top holster and gunbelt at his waist. Handle forward. Left side. From the other side of his gunbelt hung a war knife in a beaded sheath. A gift from Touches-Horses last year. Across his right shoulder lay the shotgun's empty quiver; the strap ammunition loops were filled with fresh shotgun shells. The weapon could be drawn with either hand.

He pushed back the brim of his sweat-tested Stetson and continued to savor the coffee. It was freshly brewed, thanks to Hogan. Breakfast had been swift at the hotel restaurant; some ham, fried potatoes, biscuits and coffee. Sleep, though, had been mostly good with only a brief, fitful nightmare. His unconscious mind had twisted his days as an Oglala warrior into a strange concoction of memory, fantasy and distress, then into a repeat of his dream about Young Evening, Morning Bird and the Ghost Road, induced by Dr. Milens at his house seance. Awakening in a full sweat, he had immediately arose, then washed and dressed. A weary Hogan was glad to see him come early; they talked for a few minutes and the marshal left.

Four of the six cells, strung along the back side of the small, dreary building, were occupied by Dr. Milens, Nolan Gleason, Frank Diede and Old Man Grinshaw. The two remaining cells were empty because the women assistants had been moved to a locked hotel room, guarded by local deputies. A move recommended by Sheriff Crandall to accommodate the women's special needs. Marshal Hogan didn't think the court would be hard on them; he planned on charging them with conspiracy to defraud, but not involvement in the holdups. Actually, the deputies were already suggesting the women were innocent of any wrongdoing, asserting they believed the women didn't realize Dr. Milens was a crook. Hogan didn't buy that, but was willing to be lenient, if the assistants testified against their boss.

"Well, well, good morning, Mr. Lockhart. I almost didn't recognize you in that outfit. Are you going to war?" The voice was throaty with a forced cheerful manner.

Dr. Milens stood in his cell; hands wrapped around the bars comprising the door. His suit coat was badly wrinkled and his shirt was streaked with dirt from his abrupt exit from the stagecoach. His bowler lay on his cot; a dent on the crown's left side. Next to it was his untied cravat.

Lockhart looked up. "Good morning. Breakfast will be along shortly."

A smirk rushed across the mesmerist's face and vanished, but not before Lockhart noticed.

"How come you're here?" Dr. Milens asked.

Lockhart didn't answer, sipping his coffee. The other gang members were slowly awakening. The wounded Diede groaned and cursed; Old Man Grinshaw told him to shut up; Gleason chuckled. Dr. Milens frowned at the disruption and squeezed the bars with his hands as if they might crumble if he did it hard enough. His voice belied his concern.

"Where's Marshal Hogan? And that Pinkerton agent? How come they aren't here?"

"Getting some sleep."

Lockhart stood and walked toward the stove; his nearly empty cup in his left hand; his sawed-off shotgun in his right hand at his side. At the groaning stove, he placed the gun under his left upper arm to hold it against his chest, freeing his right. He poured the steaming liquid into the cup, placed the pot back and retrieved his gun.

Dr. Milens watched him without speaking. Old Man Grinshaw had found an old newspaper left by the previous cell occupant and was reading it while sitting on his cot. Gleason was standing and looking out of the tiny, barred window at the back of his cell. Diede had laid back on his cot.

"Hey, it says here that Will Bill Hickok's in town. How 'bout that," Grinshaw said, looking up from *The Leader*, getting no response. He added, "An' Calamity Jane's been arrested for grand larceny. Wonder why she's not in here—with us?"

Turning in the older man's direction, Gleason declared, "You dumb ass, that's a June eighth paper. She was let go awhile back. When I was in town last week, I heard she'd left for Fort Laramie." His voice softened. "But I heard Hickok's still in town. Him an' Colorado Charley."

From his bed, Diede said, "Thought Hickok an' Cody—and Texas Jack—were in some stage play back East."

Grinshaw rustled his paper authoritatively. "Talk about me bein' behind. That was three years ago, Frank. Damn."

"Wonder if Hickok's gonna join up with them army boys goin' after all them Injuns. Up north," Gleason said and motioned in that direction. "Heard Cody's with 'em."

Lockhart listened without commenting. He was pretty certain the conversation wasn't for his benefit. He sipped coffee and watched Milens without appearing to do so. There was more to the mesmerist's questioning than mere curiosity, Lockhart guessed. The edge to Dr. Milens's voice indicated worry and that could only mean one thing: a breakout was planned and scheduled to happen soon. It was easy to see Dr. Milens liked being in complete control, knowing all the angles, and right now he was troubled by Lockhart's unexpected presence. Did it mean the plan was known and marshals were waiting outside? Or was it just happenstance?

Lockhart was alert, but decided to act like he was relaxed. He kept his eyes on Milens's hands. If they left the bars, he would expect a hidden gun.

"Heard you wanted to see me, Milens," Lockhart said. "What's up? Got some ghosts with no place to visit?"

Deciding the Denver businessman's appearance was merely coincidental, Milens was almost jovial in his response. "Spiritualism is not a laughing matter, in spite of what you may think. My skills are beyond reproach and are sought by many believers across the land," he declared. "I shall be found innocent of this awful mistake." He pointed with his finger, then returned his hand to the bars.

Knock! Knock!

"Breakfast!"

The cheery female voice from the other side of the sheriff's office door was not familiar.

Yet something about it was. What? The answer slid into his mind as he watched Milens trying to act nonchalant. The voice was the same as the one pretending to be Mrs. Wilcox's departed sister. During the séance. Of course. One of the mesmerist's assistants, or both, were at the door.

It made sense, he thought. The women had probably seduced and overcome the deputies, then managed to alert Dr. Milens through the tiny window at the back of his cell. Most likely a passed note, something Hogan wouldn't have noticed. A gun could have been passed at the same time, if care was taken. Lockhart now had to assume that Milens was armed.

The knocking came again. Louder and more persistent.

"Open up, please. We've got breakfast for the prisoners. It's hot."

Putting down the cup on the desk as he passed, Lockhart turned toward Dr. Milens. "If you say anything, anything at all, Milens, you get both barrels. Same with the rest of you."

Dr. Milens's icy blue eyes widened and a curse neared his

lips, but died there, unreleased. The look on the faces of the gang members was genuine surprise; Lockhart realized they didn't know of the breakout plan.

"Coming," Lockhart yelled. "Hold your horses."

Diede sat up on the cot, his movements stiff, his face a question mark; Gleason mumbled he was hungry without turning from the window in his cell; Grinshaw kept reading, mouthing the words as he did.

"Gleason, get away from the window. I want you on your cot—where I can see your hands." Both triggers of his short shotgun were cocked; an ominous sound in the quiet room.

The outlaw turned slowly, saw Lockhart's double-barreled gun pointing at him, and complied.

"I'm coming. I'm coming. You're early," Lockhart yelled, guessing this was the case. He took two swift steps and stood with his gun inches from Milens's terrified face. "I want the gun, Milens."

"Gun? What gun? I don't . . ."

"I don't have time for this," Lockhart snapped. "Hand me the gun by the barrel—or I'll shoot you now and get it myself." Over his shoulder, he yelled, "I hope you brought plenty. I'm starving."

Gulping back his fear, Dr. Milens stepped away from the cell bars. Slowly.

"Keep facing me."

The mesmerist gingerly lifted his bowler, removed a pearl-handled, gold-plated derringer and held it out to Lockhart.

Moving swiftly to the door, Lockhart shoved the small gun in his waistband and laid the shotgun at his feet. With ease, he lifted the heavy plank, set across the door to provide additional security, from its iron hooks and placed it against the wall beside the hinges.

The key rested in the lock where it was usually kept for convenience.

"Just a minute, I forgot the key," he yelled as he retrieved the shotgun and silently stepped next to the opposite wall.

Glancing at the unmoving prisoners, Lockhart laid down, placing his drawn revolver beside him. Somewhat awkwardly, he stretched out and turned the key with his left hand. Quickly, he slid back another foot, grabbing his revolver as he moved.

"Door's unlocked. Come on in. I'm going to fix some coffee."

The door sprung open and both women bounded inside, brandishing big revolvers. Their intense gaze was focused on the desk and beyond. Elsie's revolver belched fire and jumped in her hand; the bullet struck the forlorn wall near the ceiling.

For an instant, neither woman realized that Lockhart was on the floor a few feet away from them.

"Drop the guns, ladies." His shotgun was pointed at Geraldine; his revolver, at the Southern Elsie.

Both women froze.

Elsie's eyes slid to the side to glimpse Lockhart below and almost behind them. Geraldine glanced at the mute Dr. Milens for guidance. None came. Her mind was a fury; why didn't he use the gun they had given him? To shoot, she would have to swing to the right and back some. A move that would take longer than she would have. If Lockhart fired.

"You wouldn't be the first woman I've shot." His words were a growl. It was a lie, but it might save bloodshed. "Drop the guns—or try to use them. By the way, I've got Milens's gun. He didn't want it."

Gleason leaped across his bunk and yelled, "Shoot 'im! He won't shoot a lady. Come on!"

Lowering his newspaper, Old Man Grinshaw snarled, "You're dead if you try, ladies. That's Vin Lockhart." Almost as quickly, he returned to his reading.

Dr. Milens nodded his agreement and turned away from

the cell door and sat on his cot with his head down. The bowler jiggled at the impact.

Geraldine's gun clanked on the floor, followed by Elsie's.

"Good decision," Lockhart said, standing and silently thanking the old outlaw. "Move against the cells. Now." He kicked both guns toward the wall and holstered the revolver with a reverse move.

Minutes later, both women occupied the two remaining open cells and Lockhart was drinking coffee again as if nothing had happened. Dr. Milens hadn't moved from his cot; Gleason was asking Elsie why they hadn't slipped him a gun; Diede lay with his hands behind his head; and Grinshaw was well into his month-old newspaper.

From the street, Marshal Hogan's command broke the silence. "Lockhart, it's me—and Buenstahl. We've got trouble. Those two assistants have escaped."

"They're in here, Marshal," Lockhart said casually and got up to open the door.

He smiled as he heard Agent Buenstahl laugh and tell Hogan that they should've expected that.

After the door was unbolted and unlocked, the two men entered, both carrying their shotguns. Hogan was sleepy-faced and tense; Buenstahl looked rested and his expression changed from worry to wonder. Lockhart explained what had taken place and showed them the derringer. Hogan said he recalled Dr. Milens getting up a few minutes before Lockhart arrived and guessed that was the timing of the note and gun exchange. He admitted to being drowsy at the time and not wanting to watch what he thought was a man peeing. Lockhart's arrival kept them from pulling the stunt on him. Buenstahl said the two deputies were unharmed, just bound and embarrassed. Sheriff Crandall was with them now.

The bespectacled Pinkerton detective, ever looking like a professor, walked to the cells, then along the row, inspecting the quiet prisoners. Beside Grinshaw's cell, he paused. "You boys realize your boss didn't trust you enough to have guns slipped to you, don't you? Who do you think was going to be left behind—if the jailbreak worked? Want a hint? Which one of you had a gun?"

He walked on. At the last cell containing Geraldine, he turned toward Lockhart and Hogan. With a slight smile, he said, "Looks like we add assault of an officer, attempted jail-break and . . ."

"Attempted murder of a federal lawman," Hogan blurted. "Lockhart is a duly authorized federal deputy."

"What?" Geraldine screamed, spinning toward the front of the cell. "That can't be. We didn't—"

"Yes, you did." Buenstahl ended her response, pointing to the bullet hole in the wall. "And you're going to pay for it. Cheyenne will enjoy a good hanging. Especially of two women."

The conversation between Lockhart, Hogan and Buen-stahl was easy and filled with coffee. They expected the women to eagerly exchange lesser charges in exchange for testimony against Milens. Finally, Hogan said he planned to return and try to get some sleep. Buenstahl said he was ready to resume the jail watch, that he had wired the home office and said he had received approval to stay here for a few days, and that Lockhart could get on with his business. Lockhart wrote out his account of the attempted holdup, as requested. Hogan asked Lockhart if he would consider join-ing him as a federal marshal, that he was certain an ap-pointment could be arranged. Lockhart thanked him, but declined. Hogan told him to keep the pearl-handled der-ringer as a reminder of the past two days.

After leaving the sheriff's office, Lockhart headed to the livery to see what kind of mounts might be available for sale or, if not available there, where they might be found. Yes-terday, he had noticed a string of horses in the accompany-ing corral and hoped they were for sale, perhaps on consignment from one of the area ranches. That would save him a trip and time. He was pleased to discover they were available. Mostly young and all green-broke, according to the livery operator. They came from the ZBar2 where the owner was in desperate need of cash.

After some friendly haggling, Lockhart bought a sturdy bay and a long-legged, line-back dun from the string, along with a saddle and blanket, rifle sheath, two head stalls, and a pack rig. Leading the saddled dun and the bay with the empty pack rig strapped to its back, his next stop would be the general store for supplies and ammunition.

From a distance, he saw two men heading toward the stable. It was Hickok and Utter. He waved and the greeting was returned immediately by Utter, then by Hickok after Utter told him who it was. Stopping outside the front doors of the livery, Lockhart waited for their advance, stroking the muzzle of the dun. He was pleased with both horses.

"Vin, where are you headed? Looks like you're preparing for a long trip," Utter said. "Deadwood, by chance? We're putting together some men and wagons for the Black Hills. You'd be welcome."

Without waiting for Lockhart's response, he explained further that his brother, Steve, was joining them and so was a friend, "White-Eye Jack" Anderson. They were planning on leaving for Fort Laramie on June twenty-seventh to meet up with a larger train of thirty or so wagons at the fort, then head to Deadwood.

Grinning, he added, "Gonna be a bunch of whores joining us there, too. Lots of ways to find gold in Deadwood, you know." He chuckled.

"Vin Lockhart, I barely recognized you out of your city clothes," Hickok declared. "My eyesight's not what it was, I guess." He studied Lockhart for a moment. "Heard you stopped a jailbreak this morning. Without a shot. You're a busy man. You sure you're not a lawman? Your name's familiar to me. I just can't place it. Denver, right?"

"Denver, it is, Wild Bill." Lockhart smiled. "No, I'm not a lawman. Just a businessman. If you and Charlie get down that way, please look me up—at the Silver Queen Saloon or the Black Horse Hotel. My partner and I own them." He rubbed his chin. "How'd you hear about the trouble at the jail? News must travel fast in this town."

The tall pistol-fighter nodded. "Yeah, it does. Of course, it helps to run into a U. S. deputy marshal on his way to the hotel." Hickok crossed his arms. "Hogan told us about it. Asked if I'd help stand watch. Said I would." He glanced around, out of habit. "So you're a saloon keeper. Do you run an honest game? Of course, you do," Hickok laughed. "What are you doing here? Pardon me, that's mighty personal."

Lockhart said he was headed north to join with some friends on a horse hunt, that he and his partner in Denver had just started a horse ranch and wanted to secure additional animals along with a good trainer. Hickok's eyes showed he was not entirely convinced of Lockhart's travel purposes. Utter moved to examine the horses Lockhart was leading and asked if he knew if any mules were for sale at the livery. Lockhart said he had seen none, but it was worth checking with Noah Ellison at the stage-line office in case he had mules he didn't need.

Utter's expression indicated he had already checked. "Well, you're welcome to join us—and leave whenever you want."

"Thanks, but I'm in a hurry. Hadn't planned on helping with guard duty at the jail."

"Sounds like it was a good thing you were there. Say, you know you're headed into some bad Indian country. Sioux and Cheyenne refusing to go to the reservation. And horses mean Indians, for certain," Hickok said. "Of course, the Black Hills isn't exactly a tea party, come to think of it." He motioned toward Lockhart's quivered shotgun. "Would you mind letting me look at that? Quite a weapon."

"Sure." Lockhart drew the sawed-off shotgun with his left hand, grabbed it by the barrels with his right and handed it to Hickok, shortened stock first.

"Look at this, Charlie. A real street howitzer. Haven't seen one in a long time. No offense, but I reckon this was part of the reason you handled the problem at the jail without shooting. Who would want to face this from close range?" Hickok ran his long, slender fingers along the shortened barrels, cracked open the gun, then closed it and returned the weapon to Lockhart, holding the barrels. "I'm guessing you're handy with a six-gun, Lockhart, why the hand scattergun?"

Lockhart returned the weapon to its quiver. "My partner gave it to me. It's his. From our prospecting days. Comforting, though, especially where I'm headed."

"Prospecting? You?" Utter blurted. "Well, I'll be. I should've guessed."

Hickok's expression indicated he thought it was, indeed, the real reason for Lockhart's departure.

Shaking his head, Lockhart explained that his prospecting days were quite a few years ago, that he and his partner had done very well and were successful businessmen, but he had a strong desire to create a horse ranch. He added that his friend had a desire to open a bank and was probably doing so.

Hickok frowned at his friend and said, "Wish you had been here a few weeks ago. Our friend, Will Cody . . . Buffalo Bill . . . would have enjoyed meeting you. He left town with the Fifth Cavalry. General Carr's in command. Cody's chief of scouts. Might've been in that fight on the Rosebud. Haven't heard." He folded his arms and continued. "When he's through gallivanting around, I figure he'll head back East and start up another one of his melodramas. Made himself a pretty penny on that stuff. Hard to believe what some people will pay to see." He cocked his head to the side. "I think ol' Cody would be interested in having you join him. Yes sir, I'll bet he would." Both thumbs settled themselves inside his scarlet sash, letting his fingers rest on the two revolver handles. "Of course, I've got a feeling you wouldn't like it any more than I did."

Lockhart laughed; he had heard the stories of Hickok not liking the theater. "I think I'll stick to horses."

"If you see Cody, tell him I said he was full of it," Hickok chortled.

After politely answering another question about gold from Utter, Lockhart said, "Wild Bill, it's been an honor meeting you. You, too, Charlie. I wish you much luck. If you come back through Denver, I look forward to your staying at the Black Horse and enjoying a drink at the Silver Queen. On me."

"Mighty generous of you, Lockhart," Hickok said, shaking hands. "But I've got a hunch Deadwood's going to be my last stop—an' then I'll hurry back to Cincinnati."

Utter joined in the farewell, shaking Lockhart's hand firmly. "Hey, I almost forgot. That rock didn't help any. Couldn't draw a pair to beat hell. Ol' Wild Bill's the lucky one."

Lockhart nodded and swung into the saddle, leading the bay by its lead rope. He heard Utter tell Hickok that he thought Lockhart was really going hunting for gold. After leaving the livery, Lockhart stopped at the general store and purchased what he needed for the trail: salt pork and jerked beef, a coffeepot, tin plate, cup, and utensils, a small sack of salt, a large one of beans, another of coffee and one of sugar, cans of peaches, matches, a bottle of whiskey and a dozen cigars, some apples and potatoes, three boxes of cartridges and another of shotgun shells, and packed them on the bay. Two filled canteens were added. A third was strapped to his saddle horn.

He was pleased with the way the horse was handling the load and couldn't help wondering how Sean and Harry Rhymer were doing with the new horses, especially Magic. It seemed like another world. He shook his head to remove the thoughts; it would be a long time before he could turn them into reality. Telling Hickok and Utter about hunting for horses made him decide, if things went right, that he and Touches-Horses just might round up some mustangs for the return trip.

His stop at the telegraph office found a message waiting for him. It had just arrived, the lanky operator said without looking at him. Silently, he read the wire from Crawfish:

TOLD FALLING LEAF WHAT YOU ARE DOING SHE CRIED STOP ALL RIGHT OTHERWISE STOP MATTIE BACON CAME BY MY HOUSE SURPRISED YOU WERE GONE STOP BE CAREFUL NEWS UP NORTH IS NOT GOOD STOP RESTAURANT WILL BE OPEN WHEN YOU RETURN STOP WITH AN ORCHESTRA STOP HORSES DOING GOOD STOP WILL KEEP YOU IN OUR PRAYERS CRAWFISH

Lockhart wrote a return message, telling his friend and partner that he was leaving Cheyenne today and would wire if he could, but not to expect it. He congratulated Crawfish on his progress with the restaurant and the horse ranch, then added that Falling Leaf might be helpful with the horses. In a one sentence recap, he said Jean-Jacques Beezah, the stage guard, had been wounded in the attempted stage holdup, but would recover. He said that they had become friends. He told about meeting Hickok and Utter and their intention to go to Deadwood. He stopped short of stating that he missed everyone back home; what good would that do, except make them feel bad?

A quick checkout at the hotel produced his packed saddlebags, long coat and rifle; all were added to the dun's saddle. His last stop before leaving town was the stage office and a visit with Beezah. Ellison greeted him warmly in between handling ticket requests from waiting passengers and waved for him to go on back. As he entered the small sleeping quarters, he was surprised to see the black gunfighter sitting up in his bunk, petting his cat. Its leg splint was fresh; the feathers were gone.

"Good day, Governor, happy to see you I am," Jean-Jacques Beezah said, looking up. His bare chest and shoulders were wrapped in bandages. One of his shiny revolvers lay on his bed. Beside them were the two stones.

Mawhu saw Lockhart advance and slipped from Beezah's lap to greet him, carrying its right-front, splinted leg away from the floor and moving on three.

"Didn't figure to see you up, my friend," Lockhart said, walking toward the bed. At the stove in the back, a stock tender was fixing coffee. He was glad to see Beezah's presence wasn't totally keeping the other employees away. Beezah's bloody clothes were gone.

"Looks like you're heading out." Beezah held out his hand. "Thanks for all you've done for me. Deep in your debt I am."

"You would've done the same for me."

"Not the same. I am a black man."

"Hadn't noticed." Lockhart grinned.

At his feet, *Mawhu* curled around his leg, seeking attention. Lockhart leaned over and scratched the cat behind her ears. She licked his hand.

"Thank you, little panther."

Beezah returned the smile and reached down to grasp the red pebble Lockhart had given him. "Here. You should have this with you. I have a feeling it will be good to have it close to you. Headed north, are you not?"

"I gave it to you."

"I know you did. And it brought me strong medicine." Beezah took Lockhart's hand and placed the stone in it. "And now, I give it back." He frowned and looked at Lockhart. "If I could, I would ride with you, Governor."

"I know you would—and I'd be happy for the company,"

Lockhart said, placing the stone in his vest pocket with his watch. "I'll see you on my return."

"If I am not here, I will leave word. Beezah's body heals fast. I will be riding guard again. Soon."

With that, Lockhart patted him on the shoulder, scratched the cat again between its ears and left.

Beezah looked down at his cot, remembering something. He searched beneath the turned-back blanket and held up the two cardinal feathers. "I almost forgot. *Mawhu* wants to return these. They gave her strength when she needed it most." He paused and cocked his head to the side. "She and I think they are something you should have—for your journey. Someone will ask for them, I think."

Lockhart accepted the small feathers and placed them carefully into his shirt pocket. He wanted to ask why Beezah thought someone might ask about them, but didn't. He nodded and left.

Beezah's words followed him. "May the stone songs find you and make you strong."

CHAPTER TWENTY

In the Little Bighorn valley, a massive encampment of a thousand lodges and eight thousand Indians were settled in the shade of cottonwoods. Along the gentle river, women and children swam and played, while older boys searched for grasshoppers to use for fishing bait. Around shady lodges, other women gathered to gossip and share news. Some older women dug for turnips. Young men played a vigorous game of hoop and pole. Warriors worked on weapons and some were driving the great horse herd to water.

It was the largest assembly of Sioux and Cheyenne warriors ever known. Even the oldest men and women could not recall such a gathering. Hunkpapa, Miniconjou, Oglala, Sans Arc, Brule, and Northern Cheyenne waited and wondered if Sitting Bull's prophecy would really happen, if their victory at the Rosebud would prove decisive or merely prolong the *wasicun* advance. War leaders Crazy Horse and Gall seemed to be in constant motion, like two mountain lions expecting a storm.

Camped within the honored Oglala circle, Black Fire's tribe was close to splitting apart. Very close. The fiery warrior Painted Badger and many men with war coups wanted to stay with Crazy Horse, while the tribe's leader, Black Fire, was counseling the wisdom of moving to the reservation and its sad safety.

Returning to his lodge after another frustrating tribal council meeting, Stone-Dreamer grabbed his chest in shock. He cried aloud, bringing warriors running from all directions of the camp to aid their spiritual leader. Thanking his friends for their prompt response, he assured them he was well, but shocked them with his news.

"My son, you call his name Rides-With-Spirits, just came to me and my heart embraced him. He believes the blue chargers are coming. To find us. He is worried about our safety."

His face showing the strain of the tribe's arguing, Black Fire was the only one to find words. "Stone-Dreamer, does this mean he is coming back? What does he think we should do? Does he bring word from the Grandfathers? Are we safe here?"

"I must wait for the stones to tell me. I must build a *wanagi glepi*. There is much I must prepare." Stone-Dreamer waved his arms in nervous anticipation.

"But, holy one, is not your son protected by the spirits of our ancestors? Would they not help us?" Black Fire asked. "Would they not guide us to a place where the blue chargers could not find us—if our gathering here is not safe? What are the stones saying to you? Should we take our lodges to the *wasicun's* agency as they tell us?"

This time, the response came from Touches-Horses, placing his fist over his heart. "I believe *Wanagi Yanka* will return to help us. To guide us. We have done nothing wrong. We have fought the blue chargers only when they attacked us. I think we should move our camp now and wait for my brother's arrival."

Slamming the tomahawk in his hand high into the air, Painted Badger stood in front of Stone-Dreamer's lodge and shouted, "I do not believe *Wanagi Yanka* is coming. I do not believe he is talking to you. He is not coming. He lives in a lodge of lightning and thunder. He cares not for us anymore. He is *wasicun* once more." He swung the club again, slashing downward. "We have no choice, except to stay with Crazy Horse—and fight if the blue chargers come. This is our land. Our land! Together with other brave warriors, we can drive the *wasicun* from here."

Walking over to him, Black Fire stood a few feet away with his arms outstretched as if in preparation for prayer. "You know this is not so, Painted Badger. The Grandfathers have told Stone-Dreamer the *wasicun* will stay here. They will grow in number. Stronger each day. They will build stone houses and cut up Mother Earth into small pieces. To grow corn. To cut down trees for their lodges. To find yellow rock. You know this. You have heard. You have seen."

"I am not a coyote to run yelping into the night, afraid of the great wolf. I am an Oglala warrior. I believe in Crazy Horse. *Hoka hey!* It is a good day to die!"

Black Fire shook his head and looked around at the gathered tribesmen, "Better that we take care of our women and children. Our worthy elders. Better that we have real courage. The courage to change. The courage to go where they want us to go."

Stone-Dreamer nodded, but did not say anything. Painted Badger gathered his warriors and left, snarling insults as he left. Black Fire watched them in silence.

After a few minutes in his lodge, the old shaman left the

village and did not return until the following day. He immediately erected a *wanagi glepi*, a spirit post, to represent Vin Lockhart. It was placed outside the camp's circle, to the south. Tied to the carved pole were eagle and owl feathers, panther claws, sacred stones and the magical purring circle of gold, Lockhart's gift to him, one only a *wankan* warrior could give. He began chanting a song strange to the tribesmen's ears; it was repeated seven times in the direction of each wind. Last, to the South Wind—and the direction of death.

"Father, I remember your promise to me this day. I wear the morning star on my head. Mother Earth is wrapped about my waist.

"I am coming into your sight. I bring *tunyan* and wear white elk that you may know me. I will circle the earth wearing the long wing feathers as I fly. The panther, the bear, the wolf, the eagle and the buffalo have brought me to your light. I have heard the words of the chickadee. Together, we ask for guidance. Help us to understand the Winds and their words of warning."

He paused, lowered his head and then thrust up his arms in tribute. "Yes, he is coming. Rides-With-Spirits is coming. A sacred stone is singing the news. Grandfathers ride with him. He seeks their help. *Tunkan* sing the news. Grandfathers ride with him. He is coming. Rides-With-Spirits is coming. *Wakatanhewi kin heyau welo E ya ye yo.*" The weary holy man finished by hanging small tribute bundles of tobacco on nearby trees.

As they watched, the warriors with Painted Badger challenged him, saying that the magic of the white man had grown superior to Stone-Dreamer's. That the *wasicun's* yellow rock was more powerful than any singing pebble of his. That the real power of the stone was worn by Crazy Horse himself. That the small rock he wore into battle turned into a power that kept away all bullets, all arrows, all lances. That he could never be killed. That the weight of the stone was why the war leader's horses often went down in battle.

If the holy man even heard them as he completed his ritual, he didn't show it.

With swelling arrogance, Painted Badger proclaimed their Oglala Grandfathers had left Lockhart's side forever because he no longer lived among the tribe. He said Stone-Dreamer was an old man who no longer saw what really was there. He was feeble-minded and only saw yesterday's memories.

Even Black Fire appeared bothered by their assessment.

The impact of their message created not the arousal to fight among the rest of the tribe, but greater fear. Talk of returning to the reservation grew in hushed exchanges throughout their small circle of lodges. Some added their concern that it was time to choose a new leader, that Black Fire was no longer the right man to lead them. Everyone in the camp sneaked fearful looks at the busy holy man's efforts as they went about their daily tasks, trying to make everything seem normal. Painted Badger and his warriors gathered at his lodge and talked of war, of honors, of driving the *wasicun* from Lakota lands.

Only Black Fire watched Stone-Dreamer openly; the savvy leader knew his leadership was being tested, but he realized, in his heart, that they could only be safe if they left the great circle of lodges now and from their new camp, planned their journey to the *wasicun's* agency.

It was that simple. That hard.

The old man completed his ritual and gave strict instructions to the shirtwearers, the rest of the small tribe's selected leadership group. They should break camp and head north. The post would be taken with them and placed in the center of the new camp. Each day the women of the camp, except those menstruating, were to hug the post and tend to the fire of sweetgrass, setting at its base. This sacred fire must be kept burning at all times. A new bowl of cherry juice was to be daily set at the foot of the post; the old bowl—from the previous day—must be purified with sage before used again. The leaders saw the agonizing stress

Stone-Dreamer felt and reluctantly agreed to consider his orders; most without believing in their value.

Immediately, four shirtwearers relinquished their responsibilities, siding with Painted Badger and the need to stay and fight. That left only three agreeing with Black Fire. Most of the tribe, however, clung to the holy man's wishes as their last hope for survival.

Stone-Dreamer advised they should move to a new camp immediately and there, they were to be vigilant for signs from the Winds about the coming of Rides-With-Spirits. An unexpected breeze from the south would be a favorable one. Such a breeze, soft and gentle, from any direction would be a good indication. Except from the north. Any kind of activity from there would not be favorable. He asked that anyone sensing such a sign come to him.

"Even the Winds have left us, old man," Painted Badger said sarcastically. "The only thing left is the wind of our weapons." He made a swooshing motion with his tomahawk.

As if the interruption hadn't occurred, Stone-Dreamer continued his directions. He knew Painted Badger was growing stronger. Yet there was reluctance by many to join him. There was still a chance the tribe would hold together and leave the Little Bighorn valley to wait for Lockhart in a safer place. The old man knew he would come and would advise them well.

To the tribesmen assembled, he gave further counsel. After they were encamped safely elsewhere, they must watch the night sky. On any given night, the *wanagi tacanku*, the Ghost Road, could dim. If it does, more ghost warriors were coming to Lockhart's aid and that was good. But like all warriors' deaths, the sight of a falling star—particularly a very bright one—would mean he had been killed coming to their aid. If this should happen, they should expect the Thunder-Beings to protest loudly.

If there was any positive sign, he would give them a new song to sing while he hung seven additional tobacco bundles.

If the symbols were bad, each warrior should look immediately to his own spirit helper for guidance, Stone-Dreamer solemnly advised. At all times, men should avoid strange women in the woods; they may be deer women, taking advantage of the camp's distractions. Sexual contact would be fatal to the warriors involved.

Turning back from his conversation with the other warriors, Painted Badger spat, "I thought the Grandfathers were supposed to take care of him."

From the gathered tribesmen around him came polite, but pointed, questions: "Won't the Grandfathers take care of Rides-With-Spirits?" "He is protected by spirits so he needs no help, isn't that right?" "If the Grandfathers can't save him, how can he save us?" "How do you know where *Wanagi Yanka* is?" "When will he come? How will he find us if we move from here?" "How do you know what he is thinking?" "Aren't you afraid of the *wasicun* magic?" "Will the *wasicun* come for us next?" "Should we go to the *wasicun's* fenced-in land?" "Aren't we safe here with Crazy Horse and Sitting Bull?" "How could there be more *wasicun* than this gathering?"

A few warriors dared to challenge his words directly: "*Wanagi Yanka* is a *wasicun* again, why should he care about us?" "What difference does it make to us if he lives or dies?" "What if we don't do the things you ask us to do?" "What if the spirits get mad at him for interfering? Will they be angry with us, too?" "We must fight. If *Wanagi Yanka* wants to help us, let him fight at our side. Let him join with Crazy Horse and fight the blue chargers." "Maybe the spirits have decided to let *Wanagi Yanka* be just a warrior again, like us, and he will die. Maybe he will even lead the blue chargers to us. He is a *wasicun* and they may promise him much yellow stone."

Gritting his teeth to hold back the frustration, Stone-Dreamer told his fellow tribesmen the spirits of long-dead warriors, Red Horse, Counts Rain and Grizzly Head, and the ancient medicine man, Eyes-of-the-Wind, had found him in the night and told him Lockhart was coming to help. Tears nudged their way into the corners of his old eyes.

"Your questions to me I understand, even though they hurt my heart." The old shaman spoke carefully, staring only at the pole he had built for Lockhart.

From the shadows came Morning Bird. She broke away from her distraught mother and ran to stand near the old shaman. "Listen to Stone-Dreamer! This is not the time for counting coup. This is the time for protecting our children, our weak. We must leave now. We must wait for Rides-With-Spirits."

Shrill laughter was the only response from Painted Badger and his warriors.

Waving his men into silence, Painted Badger declared, "Are the Oglala reduced now to listening to a mere woman weep? Is that who we are?"

Her eyes burning brightly, she turned away and walked slowly to Stone-Dreamer. "We need you to help us, oh great one who sees things we cannot. There are things we do not understand. There are concerns we cannot let pass."

Nodding, Stone-Dreamer's voice gained new strength from her support. "Listen—and listen well. I ask you to do these things out of respect for me. From the caring within you for me. Do this one time. For me, if not for yourselves. Do not doubt Rides-With-Spirits is one of us." He paused and looked around at the intense faces. "Remember he went to free his marriage brother, Touches-Horses, last summer. Where were you then, Painted Badger? Never forget it. Never doubt it. Many things I am given to see that you cannot see. That is the wish of *Wakantanka*. It is not my wish. It carries a heavy responsibility. The stones have told me he is coming. The stones have told me we must leave the greasy grass and wait for him." He inhaled and crossed his arms. "Know this, I do not expect to be asked more. Know this, I do not expect to be doubted. Know this, my words are truth."

"*Aiiee!* The old man does not understand what he is hearing. Singing rocks bring only the sounds of war," Painted Badger snorted and ran two fingers across the bridge of his nose to indicate war paint. "There has been enough talk. I stand with Crazy Horse. He is *Inyan*, the Rock. All true warriors will ride with him. We cannot wait any longer for *Wanagi Yanka*. We are warriors, not sheep to go into the *wasicun's* pasture."

As he turned to walk away, a well-known figure came riding hard toward them. It was Crazy Horse on his yellow pinto, painted with hailstone marks on its chest and a lone hawk feather in its mane. He was waving his Winchester over his head and yelling that the blue chargers were coming. Scouts had seen them. They were nearing the Hunkpapa circle beside the river. Behind him, warriors were scrambling for weapons or racing for the horse herd. Terrified women and children were running for their lodges.

Clothed only in breechclout and moccasins, his face and body were painted yellow and accented with white dots of hail. A white lightning streak down the side of his face. His stone *wotawe* medicine amulet was secured under his left arm; the red-backed hawk body on his head, its stiff head and wings fluttering in his unbound hair. Around his neck bounced his familiar eagle-wing-bone whistle hanging from a leather thong. At his waist was a cartridge belt holding a stone-headed war club.

He reined up and his horse reared its own challenge. "Come! Die with me! It is a good day to die! Cowards to the rear! *Hokayhe!*"

Painted Badger yelled his support, but added they had few bullets.

"Be strong, my friends!" Crazy Horse replied with magical confidence. "Make them shoot three times fast, so their guns will stick and you can knock them down with your clubs!"

With that, he raced for the river and the advancing troopers. Joining him was another great Oglala warrior, Big Road, his face and body painted with his war medicine. The warriors in Black Fire's camp—including Black Fire himself and all shirtwearers, save one, an old man—dispersed to ready themselves for battle; women began packing to move their lodges to safety.

Stone-Dreamer turned away so none could see the tears in the corners of his eyes. He remembered Sitting Bull's prophecy that soldiers would fall into their camp. If only his son, Vin Lockhart, had been here to talk sense to his friends before this. Now it was too late; he stared at the *wanagi glepi*.

Not running in fear or to hurriedly pack, a determined Morning Bird stepped beside him. Her eyes were laden with worry, but she had made her decision to stand with the old holy man. Along with her shawl clutched at her waist, she held a tomahawk. In her other hand were two tiny cardinal feathers.

CHAPTER TWENTY-ONE

More than five weeks had passed since Vin Lockhart left Cheyenne and its relative comfort and safety. Like the days preceeding, he rode silently across the changing land with an early summer sun seeking command of the day. Ahead were the black shapes of timber cutting across a dark green ridge. Sunlight glistened from a meandering stream as he passed. In an adjacent meadow, three old buffalo bulls plotted the return to their herd.

His plan was simple: ride to the Rosebud, learn what he could and make another decision as to the direction he should ride. Northwest, if he saw no signs indicating another way. In spite of himself, he couldn't help but consider the folly of his journey. He had no idea where Black Fire's band might be, except his memory of their past summer camps and the newspaper stories of Crazy Horse and his warriors. He expected his friends were with the wild, charismatic leader.

He knew that's where he would have been. Yet he was beginning to feel that Crawfish was right. The Indians had no choice but to go to the reservations. What purpose did it serve to stand and be destroyed? What was served in this action? For there could be no victory, no lasting one. The *wasicun* way of life left no room for the Indian's ways, right or wrong. Better to go to the offered island of peace and teach their children things of the spirit that could never be changed. Better to live on an island than to die needlessly.

Would Crazy Horse allow him to enter their camp if he even found it? Would Crazy Horse allow him and his friends to leave? Would Crazy Horse let him speak what was beginning to form in his heart?

For days, he had observed the tracks of unshod ponies crisscrossing the earth. Sure signs of war parties on the move. In response, he carried his Winchester across his saddle. Soon he would switch to riding at night and hiding during the day to make him less visible to roaming eyes. To a knowing man, the land offered places where he could sleep safely and his horses would not be seen. Even before he had discovered the ominous tracks, he had kept a cold camp. A fire, even one without smoke, was too risky.

Glancing up at the sun, he saw it was well past noon; his stomach had been telling him that for an hour. When he reached the shade of the shadowed ridge ahead, he would stop and let his horses rest and graze while he ate something. He rolled his tired shoulders and shifted his weight in the saddle. It would be good to get down.

From the far side of the same welcoming ridge came an

electrifying screech and eighteen painted and feathered warriors cleared the outcropping at a mad gallop.

"Heya! Heya!"

Their bold war cries supported the shaking of rifles, bows, lances and war clubs. The Cheyenne dog soldiers were spread out and coming at him in a reckless charge they were known for. All were painted for war and their long hair braided; some wore trooper jackets and slouch hats with their breechclouts and moccasins.

His rifle jumped into his hands and a war pony ran without a rider as he whirled the dun and kicked it into a gallop. His canteen bounced wildly, but was firmly attached to his saddle horn. The pack horse jerked itself into a matching run. He turned in the saddle, firing as fast as he could level new rounds and aim. A warrior wearing a wolf's head and long pelt screamed and fell.

A lone arrow whizzed by, then another. Six bullets sang past him; one clipped his upper arm and another tore away a piece of his saddle cantle. They weren't firing as much as he was; he guessed bullets were at a premium.

Methodically, he shoved new cartridges into his gun and turned to fire again. Several of the warriors were gaining on him. The closest was dressed in a blue cavalry jacket and kepi hat with an eagle feather stuck in its band. Lockhart aimed at the Indian's chest and fired. Twice, missing both times.

As he levered the gun, he saw the pack horse stumble, lumbering from bullet wounds. An arrow bounced from its flank; another, from the pack itself. The animal tried valiantly to continue, but its rapidly decreasing strength was already slowing the dun and allowing the closest warriors to gain ground. He had no choice. Holding his rifle in his right hand and the reins in his teeth, he yanked free his big knife and severed the lead rope from his saddle horn with one swift slice. Maybe they would stop to explore the contents of the pack as the dying animal staggered and fell.

He returned the knife to its sheath, the reins to his hand and his attention to the closest three warriors. One had half his body vertically painted in red, carried a feather-tailed shield on his right arm and a revolver in his right fist. The middle warrior, waving a feathered lance, was the one in a cavalry jacket and feathered kepi hat he had fired at before. The warrior's pockmarked face was streaked in black-and-white bands. The third warrior wore a full war bonnet and aimed a Henry carbine.

As Lockhart turned to fire, the jolt of a bullet nearly made him drop the rifle. His lower right leg flamed with pain and began to bleed. He gathered himself, fired a wild shot and slapped the reins across the dun's flank to make him run harder. The courageous mount complied and increased the distance between them and the war party.

In the near distance was an isolated rocky incline, as if a giant wedge of earthen pie had been centered within an open valley that itself was half-surrounded by cottonwoods and a small pond. The incline widened into a long, low ridge of buffalo grass. He remembered it from passing earlier. At the crest of the incline was a huge dead tree struck by lightning years before, a silent testament to the power of nature.

Aiming the hard-charging dun up the incline, he tried to ignore the numbing pain and gripped the animal's side with his wounded leg as best he could. He shoved the rifle back into its sheath, shifted the reins to his right hand and pulled free his hand-shotgun with his left. As they galloped past the tree, he reined the horse hard to the left and looped around the dead obstacle. The dun raggedly adjusted, maintaining its balance, in spite of the abrupt change of direction. Suddenly Lockhart was headed back toward the three surprised warriors. Wrapping the reins around the saddle horn, he drew his revolver and cocked both weapons.

At point-blank range, he blasted the red-painted warrior in the face with the first barrel of his shotgun and the

Indian's shield flew in the air with its feathered tail acting like a whip. The freed revolver spun to the ground. The second barrel tore at the cavalry-jacketed warrior's neck and shoulder. His revolver barked three times at the third warrior as he cocked his rifle. The war-bonnet-wearing dog soldier cried out as his face disappeared in crimson. His rifle bounced off the horse's back and fired a bullet toward the horizon.

The next group of warriors were startled by their intended victim suddenly becoming the attacker. Lockhart pushed the empty shotgun into his waistband and shoved new cartridges into the revolver and kicked the dun to keep it running. The long-legged mount was breathing heavily and white foam spewed from its mouth. When the revolver was reloaded, he repeated the process with the hand-shotgun, switching the guns in his waistband.

Bullets flew at him and one burned his left cheek, drawing hot pain. He held his fire until almost in front of the warriors. Both of his guns roared simultaneously and he was past them. One warrior was down and one was unable to raise his right arm. Shoving the empty shotgun into his waistband, he emptied the pistol at the remaining warriors who had stopped to examine his dead pack horse. They screamed and jumped for their ponies, strewing food sacks and tin utensils as they clamored to escape. One Cheyenne spun around and fell on top of the sack of beans.

A dog soldier slid to the far side of his war pony and fired at Lockhart from beneath the horse's neck with a long-barreled pistol. Lockhart's return shots dropped the horse, but the unseated warrior was helped onto another warrior's horse and both galloped away.

Lockhart reined in the heaving dun, knowing he had asked more than he should have, shoved the pistol next to the hand-shotgun, and yanked free the rifle once more. He emptied it at the fleeing warriors. One warrior slumped against his horse's neck. Then they were out of range and becoming mere sticks against a hot sky.

As suddenly as it had begun, it was over.

The silence of the land swarmed to fill the emptiness once more. He slid from the saddle and fell to his knees as the pain in his leg exploded throughout his body. From a sitting position, he wiped blood and sweat from his face with his shirtsleeve, then remembered his guns were empty.

His hands trembled as he attempted to reload. First, the rifle. Three cartridges fled his fingers and slithered to the ground, then another. Finally, he completed the Winchester's reloading and the revolver's, returning it to his holster, added new shells to the sawed-off weapon and slipped it back into the quiver. Attempting to stand once more, he became dizzy and decided against it. For the first time, he realized the reins were laying free on the ground; the dun's head was down and its legs apart. White foam and sweat lathered its body. Along its wet and heaving chest was a bleeding cut; his flank was burned by bullets. Many horses wouldn't survive the exhaustion; much less the injuries. His gaze took in the open land in search of an Indian pony left behind. There were none. All had run with the escaping dog soldiers.

Without much thought, he turned to his own wounds. A look at his right leg revealed the bullet had cut along his calf. Painful but not serious, unless it got infected. However, he had lost a lot of blood, judging by his reddened pant leg. The same with his arm. His cheek was crusted over, merely a burn.

He had been very lucky and couldn't help thinking of the *tunkan* in his vest pocket. Patting his pocket, the hardness of the small stone was, somehow, reassuring. He peeked at the feathers in his shirt pocket and was reassured they had not been bent or torn. From his sitting position, he looked around. The land was flat and open, except for a sometime creek and several trees, behind him about twenty yards. The shallow ditch contained water when rainfall was sufficient. Right now, it was a long streak of mud. Three cottonwoods that had remained to watch were stout and tall; another had fallen. Pieces of a fifth tree were close by.

His concentration slid into a world of nothingness, guided there by pain and shock. He wasn't certain how long he sat without knowing. It was late afternoon when he realized his situation was precarious. The dun was down and lying on its side, probably dying. His clouded mind tried to contemplate his options. They were few. He had no horse and his leg wouldn't allow extensive walking. Fort Fetterman was, maybe, a week's ride to the south. No settlement of any kind was nearer. Unless it was an Indian camp.

Obviously, the Indians had been victorious in some kind of fight with soldiers, hence the wearing of trophies by some in the war party. The Cheyenne were also better armed than he expected. A few Winchesters and Henrys were mixed with Springfields, bows and arrows, several revolvers, and lances. He had been fortunate that they were short on bullets and shooting ability. Not on boldness, however.

A soft whinny broke his concentration. The dun raised its head, shivered and attempted to stand, but couldn't.

Forgetting himself, Lockhart limped to the horse, stroked its nose and told it to stay down. It surprised him that his words were Lakotan. Soft. Soothing. Like Touches-Horses would have done. He yanked free one of his canteens from the saddle, untied his kerchief and soaked it with the water. Slowly he began wiping away the blood, sweat and foam from the animal's chest, neck and head. Another whinny thanked him. From his saddlebags, he secured a jar of salve, one of Crawfish's discoveries, and lathered it on the horse's wounds.

Out of the corner of his eye, he caught movement by one of the nearest downed warriors. It was the dog soldier who had fallen against the sack of beans. Lockhart's revolver jumped into his hands and he fired six times into him. Farther away, the warrior with the broken arm fired at him. The bullet hissed several feet from his shoulder. Lockhart grabbed his rifle and fired into the wounded Indian and the other body a few feet away. He reloaded both weapons, more surely this time, and returned to treating the dun. Focusing on caring for his horse kept him from anxious feelings about his situation. He returned his sawed-off shotgun to its quiver; his pistol, to its holster and held his rifle.

Pain jumped through his arm and he realized it was bleeding again. For an instant, he was back with his Indian friends, dying from the wounds suffered in his lone attack on the Shoshoni war party that had killed his wife and others in their camp.

In his heart, he knew his decision was made. He must remain close to the dun for it to have any chance of recovery. The horse's regained strength was his only real chance for survival. How long would that take? Two days? A week? Two weeks? Never? It depended, of course, on the individual animal.

During the night, wolves or coyotes would seek fresh meat. The Cheyenne would likely return. First, to get their dead. Second, to get revenge. If they returned, it might be with additional tribesmen. If so, he would deal with it. They could find him if he tried to hide. They might be worried that he didn't, that he remained where they left him.

Yes. He would stay right here. Right here. Right where the Cheyenne could find him easily. He had plenty of food and water. The pond where he had filled all three canteens and watered his horses wasn't far away either. Too far to attempt walking the dun. At least for a day or two. The animal couldn't stand. His saddle would give him some cover to shoot behind, if necessary. So could some of the fallen timber. And even sacks of food. A long drink from his canteen helped; one thing he couldn't afford now was to let his wounds sap his resolve. To do that was to die.

He wasn't going to die. Neither was the dun.

Remembering the returned sacred *tunkan* once more, he reached into his pocket and withdrew the small pebble. A memory oozed into his mind. It was a story told to him by his brother-in-law as Lockhart was being tended by tribesmen after the great remembered fight. Touches-Horses said that Stone-Dreamer made a proclamation before the assembled warriors. The holy man's voice grew louder, his shoulders thrust backward in an authoritative pose.

"Around us, always something moves. Always. It only takes to listen. The most ancient of living things, stone, is always moving—but most men cannot see this moving. It is the will of the Grandfathers. The most ancient of living things, stone, is always singing—but most men cannot hear this singing. It is the will of the Grandfathers. The most ancient of things, stone, is always powerful—but most men cannot use this power. It is the will of the Grandfathers."

Touches-Horses said that the many-couped warrior Bear-Heart nudged his pony alongside Black Fire's horse. Neither spoke, only exchanging eye words. From behind them, Stone-Dreamer continued his pronouncements.

"Today, into battle, Panther-Strikes carried a sacred *tunkan*. The stone of Eyes-of-the-Wind," he had proclaimed in a trembling voice. "Eyes-of-the-Wind was pleased to be called into battle by my son. It had been too long. He brought many of our ancestors to ride with Panther-Strikes."

The memory wisp disappeared and Lockhart studied the small stone in his opened hand. The stone was credited with curing people, finding lost things, and giving counsel to scouts through the holy man. Had it been part of his victory years before? Had it kept him from being seriously wounded now? Or had Morning Bird's feathers been a factor? Mumbling a prayer of sorts, he placed the stone gently on the dun's neck. Since the horse was breathing a little easier Lockhart decided to remove the saddle and complete wiping down the animal's body with his wet scarf. He positioned the saddle on its side where he would shoot from, then gave the horse a few drops of water to drink. The horse was too hot for much; it would only bring on colic. From his saddlebags, he took a shirt, tore it into sections, soaked them with water and wrapped the horse's legs as best he could, tying them on with rawhide thong, also from his gear.

After satisfying himself that the dun was resting as well as possible, he forced himself to stand and began his preparations for the night. He took his time, but kept his stiffened leg and arm moving. First, he went to the area where the three fleeing warriors had been shot, including the one lying against the bean sack, and dragged each dead warrior to a spot fifty yards away, leaving them in a circle. Their arms were outstretched so their hands touched, creating a visual interlocking. The fourth escaping Indian was too far away for him to go after and drag back. To make certain of his state, Lockhart fired four times into the unmoving shape.

A lance was jammed into the ground in the center of the human circle. He stripped the bodies of guns—a Springfield, a Winchester, and a long-barreled Colt—and bullets and returned them to his camp. He wouldn't worry about the two warriors killed early in their attack; they were farther away. Too far to walk and drag.

As he started to check on the downed warriors in his initial counterattack, a thought hit him. Taking scalps was something they would respect. Especially if he hung them from a lance in the middle of his camp. A challenge that might make them tentative, make them wonder what sort of man would do something like that, maybe even wonder if he was really a man after all. He returned to the circle, ripped off the scalps and tied them to the lance with ribbons hanging from it. The task was gruesome. Bloody. Nauseating. But he knew it was the smart thing to do. Most Indians were superstitious. His sawed-off shotgun would have been a weapon they most likely hadn't seen. For once, he wished the story of spirits riding with him had been told in wider circles than just his small band.

Pulling the lance from the ground, he left a large rock in its place and carried the weapon with him to the earlier battles near the incline. The rock was a powerful symbol. Powerful. So was a circle. As an afterthought, he picked up a bow and pulled a quiver of arrows free from the body of one of the downed warriors. He slipped the quiver over his shoulder, alongside the quivered hand-shotgun, held the lance and bow in his right hand; they were lighter than the rifle in his left and, thus, easier on his wounded arm.

His eyes ever-checked the horizon where the Indians had fled, but he didn't expect their return. Not yet. They would need to talk it over, decide if their medicine was powerful enough today. Or if it needed time to return. Still, it was always wise to assume Indian behavior was unpredictable. They might not listen to their medicine man.

After dropping the lance, bow and arrows inside his camp, he headed for the next group of dead warriors, the ones he had attacked at the incline. Two were dead, but the cavalry-jacketed warrior had dragged himself a few hundred feet away and was attempting to stand. Lockhart hated to do it, but to leave him alive was foolhardy. Rifle shots ended the warrior's struggle. Their bodies were far enough away that he chose to leave them there, dragging them into a circle like the other and adding their scalps to his lance. He used thong from their moccasins to hold the wet chunks of hair in place. A rock was placed in the center of the circle like the first.

As before, he secured the guns and ammunition from both sets of downed warriors and returned to his camp, cradling the lance, his own rifle, a Henry and a Springfield in his arms. A Merwin open-top revolver was shoved into his waistband. He also brought the war bonnet, piling it on top of his carried guns.

Back at his makeshift camp, he began work on a breastwork

of sorts, or what he could create. His propped-up saddle would be the foremost point, aimed at the horizon where the war party had fled. Next, he moved the sacks of beans, coffee, salt, and sugar to provide a second short wall to his left; the dead pack horse would serve as the wall to his right. The dun lay to the back of his protection at the moment. That left the worn-out horse vulnerable to stray bullets; he didn't think the Indians would deliberately shoot the animal as long as it looked dead.

A quick review of what he had constructed stopped him. If the Cheyenne came at him from all directions—and that was likely—they could be almost on top of him before he would be able to see them and respond.

He needed a position of height, a way to look down upon their movements and then fire. His gaze took in the cottonwoods behind him.

Yes, he must wait for them there. It would give him an excellent field of fire. Even if they tried to hide at the base of the trees themselves. Could he climb a tree with his weakened leg and arm? He must, if he wanted to live.

First, he must move his "walls" away from the dun—and the dead pack horse. That would reduce the likelihood of stray bullets hitting the dun. He expected the Cheyenne to come at him; this time, with silent weapons—knives and clubs. Get close before showing themselves. After moving his saddle and sacks farther away from the animals, he dragged one large, fallen branch into place as a rear protection. The camp must look right, must look protected.

After drinking more water and resting, he resumed his task and finally pushed and shoved a log alongside the dun's prone legs. That would provide some protection from the outside. A second log was added close to the animal's back. Satisfied with the protection the logs would provide, he returned to readying the camp.

CHAPTER TWENTY-TWO

Twenty feet north of his saddle, he placed the lance with its bounty of fresh scalps and placed the war bonnet on top of the shaft. It gave an eerie appearance of an invitation to the Cheyenne to advance if they dared. He didn't expect it to stop them, but if he could hold them off once, it might be enough. If not, he would die and no one would know it for a long time. Next came the appearance of a man lying down. His rolled blanket became the body and legs. His hat propped on a stick would look like a head in the darkness. After breaking the firing pins of the Springfields, he placed one as if it were ready to fire, on top of his saddle. The second gun was laid next to the fake body.

Preparation of a special surprise for attackers was next. In the center of his camp, he began separating bullets from shells and pouring the gunpowder into a pile. First, he used the Indian cartridges, then a full box of his own. On top of the mound of explosive powder, he placed a small rock. It would help him see the target. Within the pile, he pushed all of the separated slugs. He loaded the two Indian carbines and the two pistols from a second box. To each rifle, including his own, he tied a piece of rope to act as a shoulder sling; the pistols would be returned to his waistband when he was ready to climb.

It was time to decide on food. Added to his store purchases were foods from trail scavenging. An old habit resumed. They were composed of a handful of Indian potato roots, cattails for food and medicine, and a few bee plants to eat. He selected all of the jerky, two apples, and a can of peaches and tied them into his sole remaining packed shirt, along with the boxes of ammunition, and left the rest. One of his cigars was shoved into his shirt pocket, next to the cardinal feathers. After applying ample smears of Crawfish's medicine on his leg and arm, he placed the jar inside the shirt as well.

Some jerky, an apple and water gave him a renewed strength and he refused to give in to the dizziness and pain. Before eating, he presented pieces of jerky and apple to the land in thanks. He opened all of his cans of food, emptying them onto a tin plate. They might not keep but he needed the cans themselves. Sunlight was fading when he finished stretching the remaining lead rope two yards from the log protecting the dun's belly and parallel to it. Tied in clusters to the ropes were the tin cans, utensils, coffeepot, cup, and his spurs. Anything that would make a noise if disturbed. It would warn him if a wolf or coyote got close and he hadn't seen the advance.

He returned to one of the unmoved logs near the creek and sat to rest a few minutes and catch his breath; his shirt was sweated through. For several minutes, he stood looking at his surroundings without comprehending what was there. Lockhart didn't remember falling asleep. His white father put his hand on Lockhart's shoulder and said he was proud of him. From the doorway of their sod hut, his mother smiled and waved, then held her hand to her mouth to hold back tears. Crawfish joined them outside the house, then Stone-Dreamer and Young Evening. Now they were standing by the tepee with his own warrior's markings decorating its sides. His white father and mother joined the others. Lockhart yelled at them to come and help him, but they didn't hear his plea.

Crawfish shook him awake and he came around, gradually understanding it was just a dream. A shiver shot through him when the realization reached him that he had fallen asleep, sitting on the log. Night had taken over the world. All around him were comforting night sounds, except for a wolf howling somewhere. He made his way to the dun. The horse was cooler, so he poured water from one of the canteens slowly along its body, then placed a small amount of water in its half-opened mouth. The dun shivered and Lockhart wiped him down with handfuls of dry grass, then unfolded his remaining blanket and covered the animal with it.

It was doubtful the dun would try to stand for awhile, but Lockhart didn't want a standing horse to become a target, so he removed the sleeves of his shirt and cut them into strips. The one was quite bloody, but that didn't matter. He told the dun what he was doing and the importance of lying still as he tied the front legs together, then the back. This time it was in English. His knife became a peg in the ground and he wrapped the reins around it. Tightly. If the animal did try to stand, the tied reins, combined with his bound legs, would act as a restraint.

For the first time, he noticed the sacred stone had slid from the horse's neck to the ground. He picked it up and held the pebble above his head with his good left arm and began to chant. A chant he had heard Stone-Dreamer use, or what he could recall of it, adapting it to his situation.

"*Wakantanhewi kin heyau welo E ya ye yo.*

Tunkan sing to me. Sacred stone sing to me. I am listening.

Tunkasila ride to me. Grandfathers ride to me. I am calling.

Wakantanhewi kin heyau welo E ya ye yo.

Tunkan sing to me. Sacred stone sing to me. I am listening.

Tunkasila ride to me. Grandfathers ride to me. I am calling.

I need your help. Send someone to this fight; let him hear the stone singing.

His name, Eyes-of-the-Wind. His name, Eyes-of-the-Wind.

Someone waits for this one coming. Panther-Strikes. Panther-Strikes.

I need your help. Send someone to this fight; let him hear the stone singing.

His name, Eyes-of-the-Wind. His name, Eyes-of-the-Wind.

Someone waits for this one coming. Panther-Strikes. Panther-Strikes.

A stone singing. A spirit coming. A man waiting.

A stone singing. A spirit coming. A man waiting."

He took the cigar from his pocket, tore it into shreds and tossed tobacco tributes to the four winds, the sky, the earth, and the eagle, the sacred messenger, replaced the stone on the dun's neck, clasped his hands together and prayed, this time, to the white man's God.

It was time. A stop at the creek bed gave him mud, which he applied to his face, neck, arms and hands. The darkened skin would make it even more difficult to see him. Laying down the rifles, he gathered the bow and filled quiver, his canteens, the pack of supplies and shoved the two pistols into his waistband. He selected the middle tree and prepared to climb it. With his good left arm, he flung the knotted end of his rope upward toward a thick branch fifteen feet above him. He missed and it slithered back to the ground. On the third try, the rope looped over the branch and he encouraged its descent by flipping the rope until he could reach the balled end.

To the rope, he secured the straps of two canteens, the slings of the two Indian rifles, the bow and quiver, and the pack of supplies. Around his shoulder, he placed his own rifle sling and the third canteen strap. He figured his strength wouldn't hold for a second try at climbing and, if something went wrong, he would at least have some water and one long gun. As an afterthought, he pulled open the corner of the shirt pack, withdrew two pieces of jerky, rolled and placed them in his vest pocket. After rebinding the torn shirt, he grabbed both ends of the rope with his hands to begin his climb, ignoring the jolting pain in his right arm.

He stopped. Not because of the pain. He looked back at the dun.

Moving away from the horse now was a greater worry than the Cheyenne returning. Predators could get close so quickly, so silently, that they could be upon the defenseless animal before he could react from the tree.

If the Indians returned, it would be with the dawn. He was certain they wouldn't attack while it was dark. To die at night meant the warrior's soul would wander helplessly forever, unable to find the path to the Ghost Road. As Stone-Dreamer had told him, darkness is ignorance and light is knowledge; a reminder of this truth is sent every morning by *Wakantanka* with the arrival of *Anpo wicahpi*, Morning Star. Of course, like everything else spiritual, not all Indians believed the same things.

Indeed, he wasn't certain that the Cheyenne wouldn't attack at night. Or at least most of them. Still, waiting beside the dun through the night made sense. His presence would keep away wolves and coyotes. An hour before any sign of dawn, he would move to the tree. It was risky, but leaving was more so. If warriors came during the blackness, he would probably die.

He found himself talking to his vision guide, the panther, asking for it to come and help him, to warn him of trouble coming. He shook his head. It had been years since he had sought such supernatural help. It wasn't that he came to feel it was foolish, rather that he thought the spirit guide wouldn't appreciate his becoming a *wasicun* businessman. Or was it that he didn't think of those times? Until now.

With that, he returned to the dun and sat down beside the horse. He patted its head and neck, and spoke quietly. The horse's soft whinny was all he could ask for; the animal might not make it, regardless of what he did. Only time would tell. Like a symphony, the night sounds continued to reassure him of their relative safety. Being in a raw land alone—and in the darkness—did not scare him. There was something about the openness that brought renewed energy. He was tired, but not sleepy. The pain in his wounds had subsided as well. Only a throbbing continued. His eyes were accustomed to the darkness now and he scanned the land often for shadows that shouldn't be there.

He reached into his shirt pocket. His fingers felt the tips of the cardinal feathers and, for an instant, he thought about placing them on the dun. But he liked having Morning Bird so close to him and rationalized that the stone would be all the spiritual medicine needed. Then he took out a piece of jerky and began to chew on it. After a few minutes, he gave the dun a little more water. It made no attempt to rise, either understanding what the restraints meant or not having the strength to do so.

A pair of glowing yellow eyes appeared ten feet away. Then another pair. The dun squealed and tried to stand. Lockhart patted the horse to reassure it of his presence.

"Not tonight, *kola*," Lockhart said, using the Lakotan word for brother. "You will not harm my horse. Come closer and you die. Tonight, you must find dinner elsewhere."

His Winchester cocking was thunder in the night. He waited. Just as quickly, the yellow eyes vanished.

Of course, they might return. Later. It was enough to keep him vigilant. He was hopeful they would also stay away from the dead pack horse as well. At least until the dun could walk and they could move to a new location, probably by the pond. It didn't really matter if they tore into the dead horse; he just didn't want to see it; the animal had served him well.

The hours passed slowly. One star was joined by a cluster of timid ones; a moon fingernail rested just above the horizon. A breeze tried to sneak through the trees, but rustling leaves gave it away. He forced himself to stand and walk around every fifteen minutes or so to keep his body limber and his mind from deciding on sleep. Rest would have to wait. To sleep now was to lose.

He chuckled and muttered to himself that a cup of coffee would taste good. The Cheyenne already knew where he was, so a small fire made no difference. It might even bother them, wondering why this strange fighter would signal his presence. A quick gathering of sticks and twigs soon produced an almost smokeless fire a few feet from the log protecting the dun's belly and legs. The fire would also serve as an added deterrent to four-legged predators. After removing the pot and cup from his noise-rope, the coffee was soon boiling over a circle of red and orange coals. He avoided staring at the comforting heat, knowing it would take away his night vision momentarily.

Sugar made the hot brew taste even better. Sipping the coffee brought thoughts of Crawfish and Sean. They would be sleeping right now. Snug and safe. Would he see them again? Would his dream of building a horse ranch become theirs? Crawfish was an excellent mentor for the Irish boy, if only the lad was smart enough to realize it. He thought he was; he hoped he was. A short prayer spilled from his parched lips about Sean becoming a good man. Thoughts of the horse ranch brought images of Touches-Horses, Stone-Dreamer and, lastly, Morning Bird. Was this the way his journey would end? In the middle of some nameless land facing Cheyenne? Even if he survived, there was no assurance he would find his friends. Ever. What did he expect to see at the Rosebud?

Shaking off the negative thoughts, he drank the rest of his coffee and swore not to let them return. Mattie Bacon tried to enter his mind instead, but he wouldn't let her either. Lockhart was certain, even in this time of melancholy and reflection, that she was not the woman he wanted to spend his life with, assuming there would be one. Was Morning Bird? He touched his shirt pocket and the cardinal feathers there. They brought him comfort; they brought him Morning Bird. She came easily to his mind and stayed there.

After savoring the coffee and images of Morning Bird, he pulled the pot from the coals and emptied the black remainder. The cup was returned to his noise-rope, right next to a fork. He gathered all of the just-emptied cartridge shells and placed them in the cooled coffeepot. The rattle was perfect. The noise-rope was looped through the pot handle and returned to its position across the ground.

Two short branches were added to the coals to keep it going without creating large flames. He wasn't worried about the glow being seen; it would be. Rather, he didn't want flames to get out of hand and create another problem. His mind went dark and he tried to concentrate on his preparations. Had he done everything he could?

No. He hadn't tried his hand with a bow and arrow. Years had passed since he used the weapon, but its silence could be an important advantage. Pulling three arrows from the quiver, he faced the trees behind him and placed an arrow into firing position, with the other two held vertically against the bow. His right arm screamed when he pulled the bow string and its attached arrow toward his face. He took a deep breath and eased the string back to its static position, waited for a few seconds and tried it again. The pain was acceptable and he aimed and fired. The arrow hissed past the base of the targeted tree. He grimaced and tried again. This time the arrow struck. So did the third.

Satisfied, he retrieved the two arrows that hit the tree, and returned to the dun to check on the animal. The horse was sleeping and its body temperature was normal, he thought.

Finally, the sky told him it was nearing false dawn. Stars had disappeared and the moon was losing its shine. Even the sounds of the land were changing. It might mean the Cheyenne had returned and were working their way toward him. It was safer to assume that as he returned to the tree. The dun seemed to be resting now; he hoped that was a good sign.

He grabbed his rifle and canteen and headed toward the trees. A vigorous start got him to the lowest major branch of the previously selected tree and he managed to pull himself into place on top of it. His shirt was again soaked with sweat and he was weak all over. A glance toward the fake camp told him he must get higher. At least another ten feet. Probably where his rope hung.

Using the closest branches as steps, he worked higher. As he tried to put his left boot on a slightly higher branch, his right leg buckled. Only a fierce grab at a branch kept him from falling. He stood in place, heaving for breath that wouldn't come fast enough. Should he make do with where he was? It was certainly much better than his original plan to wait on the ground.

Someone told him to climb again and he did. A dark shape swooped down at him. He jerked instinctively, but held on. Flapping its wings, the owl disappeared into the blackness. Some of his tribesmen thought the owl was the soul of a dead warrior and was to be avoided; Stone-Dreamer didn't believe that. The holy man told him that this special bird always joined his friends from the other world during the night. Together they would rule the land until the morning bird brought the sun.

Finally, he rested on top of the roped branch and looked down. He could see almost to the first ridge. It was perfect. The branches provided a clear opening, with no low hanging leaves to bother an arrow. Looking down, he was pleased to find that he would be able to see someone even if he were standing next to the tree itself. After a few minutes to resecure his breath and assure him that the dun was still safe, he began pulling on the end of the rope holding his things.

It took longer than he expected to lift the attached weapons, canteens and supply sack around and through the maze of branches, but gradually he had them again in his control. He tied the supply sack to a close branch, then the canteens to another. The rifles were laid out across several branches with the bow and quiver on top of them. Slowly, he cocked his Winchester, letting the guttural "click-click" sputter through the trees, and placed it next to the other guns. His legs straddled a sturdy limb; fingers of pain danced along his right leg and his right arm, but he ignored them.

Looping the recoiled rope over a thigh-thick limb behind him, he let the ends drop and dangle against the trunk about eight feet from the ground. If the Indians began shooting from his camp, the tree position would quickly be untenable. He would use the rope to slide down the tree from the back side and, hopefully, find new cover. Hopefully. Finally, he checked his shirt pocket and decided the feathers had made it through the climb in good condition.

Next, his gaze took in the rocks resting in the dry stream bed and they brought the wise shaman, Stone-Dreamer, easily to his mind. If they were together now, he would be telling Lockhart to feel the spirit song coming from these *Inyan*, the true Grandfathers, the only life-forces to endure through the ages. *Inyan*, the Rock, was one of the *Wankan akanta*—superior *wankan*—along with *Wi*, the Sun; *Skan*, the Sky; and *Maka*, the Earth.

There, the old holy man would say, *hear their singing? It is all around us. It is a song without beginning or end. It is a song of forever. It is the force of creation. I will sing the stone songs and let them know we understand.* He would begin singing some stone song that only he knew. Lockhart gazed at the harsh rock ridges below. He smiled. He could see the conversation. It was like many they had, but that was years ago. Now Lockhart was a *wasicun*—and rocks were simply something to ride around or over. Or worry that enemies hid behind.

In the distance, he heard the unmistakable cry of a mountain lion. The distinctive roar sounded as distant as the haze of the mountain range in the skyline. Yet as close as his heart. A strange sensation followed. Was his long-forgotten vision guide telling him that he was still with him, that he was responding to his plea? Was he warning of the Cheyenne coming? He took the bow in his hand and withdrew six arrows from the quiver; one was quickly readied.

Shadows near his fake camp were the answer to the last question. Warriors were crawling toward it, ever careful, ever quiet. He counted four. No, six. They were spread out and coming from the front and both sides. He squinted to study the far hillside. There on a painted horse was a lone tribesman. He guessed it was the war party's leader. His gaze shifted to the base of the trees and the stream bed. Another three warriors were slipping across the shallow ditch toward his camp from the rear. Lockhart examined the trees below and near him one last time to assure no warriors remained there. He thought there were eighteen in the original war party, but he wanted to be certain they hadn't picked up some additional help from their camp, if there was one.

He shifted his weight and brought the bow to a firing position. Firing accurately was more important than swiftness. That was the advantage of a soundless arrow. No telltale boom or flame. He aimed at the closest warrior, a war club in his hand, ascending the stream bed. Reminding himself to aim low because of his higher position, Lockhart drew the bow string and arrow to a familiar place against his right cheek, took a breath and held it, aimed and released.

A groan snapped from the warrior's mouth as the arrow drove deeply into his lower back. The two closest tribesmen glanced in his direction, angered that he had made a noise. Lockhart's second arrow was already on its way, catching the second warrior half-turned toward the first. A wordless cry came as he went to his knees, grabbing at the shaft protruding from his stomach. None of the warriors coming from the other directions were aware of their fellow warriors' distress.

Holding his tomahawk in a readied position in front of him, the remaining warrior looked anxiously around for a sign of their attacker. He moved to his left just as Lockhart's arrow was released and it struck the side of the stream bed where the dog soldier had been. The warrior, his face cut in diagonal stripes of dark and light color, saw Lockhart as his next arrow was on the way. The shaft tore into the Indian's throat and he fell back into the stream bed, gurgling.

At the fake camp, a warrior with a fully painted face accented with a white circle on each cheek jumped over the short wall of food sacks and slammed his tomahawk into Lockhart's hat. Another warrior in a kepi hat with an eagle feather drove his knife into the rolled-up blanket. The first warrior shot with an arrow staggered into the camp, intent on getting revenge. He shoved the kepi-hatted warrior away and struck savagely with his war club. The pushed-aside warrior stepped away, puzzled by the shaft protruding from the other warrior's back and turned to the others waiting around the encampment. All looked worried in the grayness. One had discovered the two downed warriors in the creek bed. Downed with arrows! Cheyenne arrows!

Where had the mysterious *wasicun* with the strange gun gone? Where had the arrows come from? Was this strange evil medicine at work?

Only one of the standing warriors carried a rifle; another held a bow. The rest were armed with hand weapons. Lockhart could see a pistol butt protruding from the breechclout of a tall warrior wearing a sleeveless army jacket and a rumpled cavalry, broad-brimmed hat on his head.

Lockhart's right arm was numb and his wounded leg was throbbing and bleeding again. He ignored both and decided to keep firing arrows. His silent projectile took down one more standing beside the camp wall; second and third arrows missed altogether.

When the painted-face warrior turned to look up the trees, Lockhart switched to his Winchester and fired at the unnoticed pile of gunpower and slugs.

The explosion rocked the small encampment, sending lead a short distance in all directions. Warriors yelled and dove for cover on the outside of the low walls. The painted-face warrior staggered and fell across the sacks. The arrow-wounded warrior lay still; his face, a crimson mess.

Lockhart emptied his Winchester at the scattering Indians, laid it across the branches in front of him and grabbed the second long gun. Three warriors were running toward their waiting war-party leader. His trailing shots clipped the slowest runner's feet. A fresh morning was creeping across the land, chasing their retreat with light. It was also making his position more visible, he thought, and decided to move.

Pistol shots roared through the trees, tearing through leaves and ripping branches. The tall warrior in a sleeveless army jacket and cavalry hat was firing at him from behind his own saddle.

Hurrying, Lockhart turned to fire back. A bullet slammed into his lower right leg. Jerking in reaction to the pain, he lost his balance and fell backward, past the tree trunk and between the branches behind him.

Chapter Twenty-three

His rifle flew from his hands as he toppled into the air. His empty Winchester, the other Indian rifle and the bow and quiver crashed through the branches toward the ground. Vin Lockhart grabbed for the nearest branch and it broke off in his left hand.

Thick foliage jabbed at his face and body as he fell through the leafy maze. An upright branch cut his back. One of his pistols was pulled from his waistband by the rush of entangling leaves and branches and he couldn't do anything about it as he fell six feet in a breath.

His outstretched hands grabbed again for anything that would stop his fall and caught hold of branches on either side of his body. Immediate cracking told him his hold was tenuous. His feet could feel no limb immediately beneath him. The straps of his canteen and shotgun quiver were hung up on a twisted branch just above his right shoulder; he ignored their pinning for the moment. His greater concerns were the remaining Indians and the need for a strong limb.

Two warriors were shooting at him now; one was limping toward the trees, firing as he advanced. The limping dog soldier's leg was cut by bullets sprayed from the powder explosion. Another bullet snapped through the tree where Lockhart had been shooting. The two Indians were unsure of where he was, but that would change as soon as the advancing warrior reached the tree. At the creek bed, a warrior managed to get to his feet and was hobbling away, holding both hands against his bleeding stomach.

Lockhart reached for the escape rope with his left hand, continuing to hold onto a breaking branch with his right. A piercing ache flushed through his right arm and he let go of the branch as his left arm took control of the two hanging cords. His right leg was throbbing from the fresh wound. The double-thick lariat burned in his fist as his weight pulled him slowly downward, but he wasn't falling. The canteen and quiver straps popped free and returned to his shoulder, but stopping his downward slide was his only concern as his legs sought firmness below and found none. Gritting his teeth and continuing to slide, he grasped the rope with his trembling right hand as well. It had little strength, but enough to end his descent for the moment. Long enough to study what was beneath him.

A trio of limbs offered safe haven a few feet more and his descent stopped when his feet found them. His raw hands were nearing the ends of the rope. The sloping land was only eight feet away. His mind was whirling with the adrenaline of pain, fear and lack of sleep. Yet deep within him a cold fire continued to burn. He must attack to live.

Below, the Indian with the leg wound reached the base of the tree and fired wildly into a cluster of branches on the opposite side of where the plainsman now stood. Lockhart's right hand reached for his holstered revolver, but the pounding ache in his arm and hand wouldn't allow him to grip the weapon. He switched hands on the rope, hoping the limb at his feet would hold and his right hand would, at least, help him maintain his balance. He kept most of his weight on his left leg, not trusting his right to hold him.

With his freed left hand, he yanked the sawed-off shotgun from its quiver on his right shoulder, cocked the hammers and fired both barrels as the Indian's face and gun hand appeared eight feet below him. A scream preceeded the warrior's disappearance.

Silence. A soft groan, then a throaty gasp. Silence once more.

Another bullet slammed into the tree trunk. From the tall warrior behind his saddle, Lockhart thought. Would fleeing warriors find enough courage to return? He had to assume so. Looking around, he decided his position wasn't a bad one. His feet were solidly positioned on two of the three sizable tree arms at this level. They would hold him.

He wiped blood from his eyes with the back of his left sleeve. A scratch along his forehead had produced the bleeding. He shoved the empty hand-shotgun into his waistband and drew his revolver with his left hand.

Throbbing in his right leg—from both wounds—forced him to stand completely on his left leg for a few minutes, leaning against the tree itself for balance. His canteen, hanging from his shoulder next to the shotgun quiver, clanked against the trunk and surprised him. He patted the container out of reflex. Breath came in heaves and not nearly as fast as his body demanded. Slowly, he eased his head to the left side of the trunk, enough to look out with his left eye. There had been no more shots at him.

Nothing was moving near his fake camp. In the distance, two silhouettes bobbed toward the horizon. A shadow changed direction on the far side of the camp, near one of the logs. He leaned farther forward to get a better view. It was an Indian crawling beside the log, headed for the dun; Lockhart guessed it was the one who had fired at him, then saw the hawk shape on his head. Yes. A gleam in the warrior's hand told Lockhart what he feared. The warrior had realized the dun was not dead and intended to change that into reality with his war knife. Possibly he thought the horse, tied down, was a part of the deadly *wasicun's* medicine.

Using an eye-level branch to steady his gun, Lockhart thumbed back the hammer and fired. Three times. The warrior stood and staggered, but didn't drop the knife. Lockhart emptied the handgun, holstered it and drew the remaining Indian revolver from his waistband. It wasn't necessary as the Indian crumpled and fell against the log. The war knife slid from his hand. Lockhart fired anyway, twice more.

Silence came again, then a faint roar echoed from the same faraway mountains. Was it the panther again? Was his vision guide signaling victory? Or was his imagination just playing tricks with his weary mind?

This time Lockhart saw no movement, no shadows changing shape.

Still he waited. Patience in such situations was his greatest asset. Besides, his mind and body needed time to recover. He leaned against the tree once more; this time to reload the pistols using both hands. His right hand was less numb, but still shaking. Holding each gun against his stomach with his right hand, he managed to shove new cartridges into place with his left. Returning the warrior gun to his waistband and his own to his left fist, his gaze revisited the hillside; the horseback leader was gone.

It was midmorning when he finally decided to leave the tree. He lowered himself using mostly his left hand, hung from a smaller branch and let go. The pain in his right leg as he hit the ground was excruciating and he lay for minutes unable to think or move. Finally, he retrieved his fallen Winchester and reloaded it, leaving the other weapons where they fell. The Indian with the cut-up leg was dead, lying next to the tree; most of his face was gone. He yanked free the rope, coiled it and placed it over his left shoulder.

Working his way around the encampment, he assured himself that none of the downed warriors was still alive. Four bodies remained; the others had managed to escape. He retrieved his bashed-in hat, placed it on his head without pushing out the crown, and noticed his rolled-up blanket was seared by the powder blast. Returning to the dun, he laid the lariat on the ground, removed the leg bindings and released the reins from his knife hilt. Immediately, the horse rolled onto its stomach and whinnied. A good sign. He didn't notice the medicine pebble fall to the ground, roll a few inches and be still. Lockhart reached the canteen hanging from his shoulder and poured the remaining contents into his hat. Water streamed from a slice in its top where the tomahawk had struck.

He pinched the slice together with his fingers to contain as much liquid as possible. Gratefully, the horse accepted the cool drink and wanted more. Lockhart looked around for his other canteens, angered that the Indians had stolen them. His tired mind finally reminded him they were tied in the tree. It took three shots from his rifle to break the retaining branches and send the two canteens and supply sack flying downward. When he returned to the dun, the animal was standing. He gave the horse more water from his leaky hat and a handful of grain from a sack found with his other supplies.

Battle adrenaline seeped from his body and will, accelerating the lack of sleep and loss of blood, but he wanted to make certain of the dun's safety before resting. Limping badly from his stiffening leg, he managed to lead the horse around the camp twice. The dun walked easily and seemingly without pain. Although a check of its legs revealed strained ligaments with the horse wincing when he touched the sore areas. He suspected as much. His horse was weak, but had recovered well. And fast. However, riding the animal was days away, he knew.

Returning to the same spot, he looped the retrieved tree rope around the horse's neck and staked the lariat to his grounded knife, leaving a good amount still coiled. The horse could graze, but not too far. He noticed the fallen pebble for the first time and returned it to his pants pocket.

With caring for the horse completed, Lockhart thought about making some coffee. He unfastened the coffeepot and cup from the noise-rope and gathered some sticks to add to his cold fire. He sat on the log beside the struggling flames. His fingers sought the tips of the cardinal feathers, only slightly ruffled, in his shirt pocket.

Then he was asleep.

CHAPTER TWENTY-FOUR

From his comfortable living-room chair, eccentric Denver entrepreneur Desmond T. Crawford heard noises outside in the street. Loud agitated voices. What could be the problem so early in the morning? He lowered his July 20, 1876, *Rocky Mountain News* to his lap and clicked open his pocket watch. Six thirty-five. Awfully early for a disturbance.

A clatter of footsteps preceded young Sean Kavanagh coming from the kitchen where he was preparing breakfast for them and the sleeping Falling Leaf. Crawfish tried to step around the array of newspapers, booklets and magazines laying about the living room, but managed to step in the middle of two newspapers, a periodical and a medical pamphlet. A new book had arrived a few days ago and was already marked with a fork where he had stopped in his reading of *Eight Cousins* by Louisa May Alcott. The energetic businessman had read about it in a newspaper and ordered it from the general store.

"What be goin' on outside, Crawfish? 'Tis the wee hours yet," the Irish lad asked, motioning toward the front door.

"Hop-a-bunny, I don't know, Sean. Was just going to see," the businessman said in his usual quick-as-a-hiccup manner of talking. He reached for his silver-topped walking stick leaning next to the chair.

"I'll go." Sean was already hurrying across the room.

Nodding his approval, Crawfish returned to his newspaper, scanning the headlines for any sign of troop movement—or Indian activity—that would give him a sense of where his friend might be. It was silly, he knew, and sillier still to worry about Vin Lockhart. If any man could take care of himself, it was him. Yet Crawfish knew he would continue to worry until he was home again. With or without his Indian friends. He had already read a story about Buffalo Bill Cody claiming the "first scalp for Custer" in a duel with a Cheyenne chief named Yellow Hand at Hat Creek a few days ago.

Lockhart's folded telegram lay on the floor, partially covered by a New York banking journal. The wire was the only communication to them since leaving more than a month ago. The big Swede stagecoach driver had filled him in about the trouble on the stage, including the return of money to the Wilcoxes. Crawfish knew they wouldn't receive any more wires until Lockhart happened upon a telegraph office. Most likely, where he was going, that would have to be a fort. And just as likely, Lockhart would avoid such a gathering of soldiers unless he thought they could tell him something useful. That, too, was unlikely.

Ever since the Custer massacre at the Little Bighorn, the newspapers had been filled with stories and claims by U. S.

Army commanders in the field as well as promises of retribution by politicians at every level. The first, unbelievable news had come from General Terry's report telegraphed all over the nation.

The outcome was even more devastating as most people were following the daily dispatches, sent over the wire to major newspapers, from *Bismark Tribune* correspondent Mark Kellogg who had accompanied Custer. The Seventh Cavalry advance had been documented by Kellogg up to the day of the massacre and his own death there.

Custer's demise had laid upon Denver's Fourth of July celebration like a smelly blanket with many residents fearing the Indians would actually come south and attack cities. From what Crawfish had read, it appeared the Indians had split up after the great battle, but there was no documented indication of where they might be heading. According to the newspapers and telegraph updates, the Indians separated near the foot of the Bighorn Mountains, but their whereabouts were unknown at this time. Various reports had them at the Tongue River or along Lodge Grass Creek or at the foot of the Bighorn Mountains. Even returning to Rosebud Creek.

On July seventh, Crawfish and Denver learned the *Far West* steamboat, accompanying the army expedition, had docked at Fort Abraham Lincoln near Bismark, North Dakota, bringing fifty-four wounded soldiers. The swiftness of the boat's return was credited with saving lives. The steamboat—draped in black and with its flag at half-mast—arrived at 11:00 P.M. on July fifth.

Warriors under Crazy Horse had attacked Crook's base camp on July tenth; it read like harassment to Crawfish, not a serious tactic. Like thumbing one's nose. The Indians had quickly vanished. The last three battles had been won by the Indians: Reynolds at the Powder; Crook at the Rosebud; and Custer at the Little Bighorn. How long would that last? Men and supplies were on the U.S. Army's side. And time.

Western newspapers had greatly criticized Crook's handling of his forces both during and after the battle of the Rosebud. Many blamed him for Custer's defeat, noting that if Crook had stayed in the field, the combined forces would have probably taken the day at the Little Bighorn. Many also called for the government to gather an army of volunteer frontiersmen to eliminate the Indian menace. Sheridan ordered a dozen more companies of infantry to join Terry in tracking down the warring Indians. Responding to Sheridan's pressure, the Interior Department assigned temporary control of the Sioux reservations to the army. The great Sioux leader Red Cloud, already on a reservation, became outraged at the move and led his tribesmen away from the Chadron Creek agency.

It was clear, though, that Crook was in great need of supplies and ammunition. But, if he had returned to the field after being resupplied, the newspaper editorials claimed, he could have still been a factor in the Little Bighorn fight with his 1,300 men.

Crawfish had read, somewhere, how Major Carr was responsible for destroying the core of the Cheyenne dog soldiers along the upper Republican and Smoky Hill rivers. That was 1869 and his efforts brought safety to settlers in the area and, especially, to the freighting routes across there. That was part of Sheridan's strategy to locate Indian villages and destroy them, removing havens for returning warriors on the warpath against whites. He had read recently that Brevet Major General Wesley Merritt had taken over command of the Fifth Cavalry from the retiring Carr. With Buffalo Bill Cody serving as chief of scouts, Merritt's ten cavalry companies had been ordered to join Crook's refitted command at Goose Creek and now the combined force was on a hard march to join up with General Terry at the Yellowstone.

"Hang the red bastard! He killed General Custer!"

The yell brought Crawfish from his newspaper again, and a twitch to his cheek, as Sean opened the door allowing the unfiltered voices inside. Sean stood in the doorway startled to see four men pushing and shoving an Indian in a torn and muddied gray shirt and white man's trousers, ripped at the knees. The terrified Indian had his hands tied behind him and a rope around his neck that was yanked periodically by a fat man with bouncing jowls, a slouch hat cocked to one side of his head, and a habit of puffing out his cheeks when he was out of breath.

A litany of claims, curses and threats became a loud clamor: "There's a good hanging tree. Right over there." "I'm gonna scalp the sonvabitch. Just like they did Custer's boys." "You no-good red nigger!" "We'll teach the heathen not to butcher our soldiers." Hate snarled from the mouths of the four men; a bottle passed among them heightening their courage and resolve.

Sean stepped away from the doorway, unsure of what to do. He turned toward Crawfish; his eyes wide with fright.

The redheaded businessman had disappeared.

Sean hurried into the living room to determine what had happened to his mentor. Crawfish reappeared, limping without his walking stick and holding the long-barreled Colt that the Irish thugs had carried, and Lockhart had cleaned and reloaded.

"Stay inside, Sean," Crawfish barked and headed for the door.

"What ye gonna be doin'? There be four o' 'em."

"I'm going to stop this madness right now." Crawfish strode onto his front porch, trying to hide his stiffened leg as best he could. "What's going on, gentlemen?" he demanded, forcing his voice to sound deeper than its usual birdlike level.

"Well, good mornin'! Gonna help us git rid o' one of them red bastards that killed General Custer?" A sunburned farmer with long, wiry side whiskers and a bald head yelled back and waved the whiskey bottle. "We caught 'im tryin' to sneak into town."

In the farmer's other hand was a Bowie knife. His faded overalls were unbuttoned at the sides revealing he wasn't wearing underwear.

"I were the one who saw him." A short clerk with a huge handlebar mustache that dwarfed his face, wearing a soiled apron and a tan bowler, pounded his chest. A Henry rifle was in his other hand at his side.

"Yeah, he's probably a scout for the rest of them redskins," a lanky freighter said. He was dressed in a wide-brimmed hat, a checkered waistcoat and mule-eared boots with his britches tucked in them. In his waistband was the handle of a revolver.

Crawfish stepped off the porch and headed toward them. "Gentlemen, that is a Ute Indian you are abusing. They're peaceful, you know. They didn't have anything to do with the Custer fight. He probably hasn't even heard about it." He paused and added, "Let him go."

The fat man yanked on the rope around the Ute's neck and hollered, "What did ya say? Are ya some kinda Injun lover?"

"Say, I know you. You're the saloon keeper that had an Injun woman livin' with him for awhile, aren't ya?" the short clerk asked, thought about raising his rifle and decided against it.

All four men laughed and the tall freight driver asked, "How is that red pussy?"

Crawfish raised the Colt and aimed it at the farmer. "I said let him go. Take the rope from his neck. Do so now."

"Hell, there's only one o' you—an' you only got six shots, mister," the freighter declared, narrowing his bloodshot eyes. "Then what ya gonna do?"

"Then I be shootin' at ye—'til he be reloadin' an' we both be shootin'." Sean's clear retort came from the doorway.

Attention by the four would-be lynchers was drawn to the front of the house. The Irish boy stood with the other Irish thug's gun, the Merwin & Hulbert open-top revolver, in both hands. It was cocked and moving slowly from one to the next.

"It's just a kid," the fat man whispered.

"That gun says he's a big man," the farmer grunted.

Crawfish didn't turn; a wry smile found his mouth. Leave it to the Irish boy to be there when it counted.

"My first shot will take your stomach," Crawfish said, continuing to point his gun at the stunned farmer, almost like he was teaching a class. "My second will do the same to you." He motioned in the direction of the freighter. "Or maybe you, instead." He waved the gun at the stocky clerk.

"Me be leanin' toward shootin' ye first," Sean said, pointing with his left hand at the fat man.

A moment of hesitation passed. Crawfish hoped they didn't notice the bead of sweat running down the side of his face. He also hoped Falling Leaf stayed asleep; he didn't need the added agitation of their discovering the Indian woman was still at his house. He had deliberately let it drop in conversation in the saloon that the woman had left to join her tribe. It was safer that way for her—and for them. He knew Lockhart would understand. Shortly after that, on her own, Falling Leaf had begun carrying the pipe bag with her old revolver in it, whenever she went outside. He wondered if the weapon had ever been cleaned or if the cartridges in it would even fire. She wouldn't let him even look at it.

"Oh hell, he isn't worth gettin' gun-shot for," the farmer said and began removing the neck rope from the Ute. The Indian glanced at Crawfish, not understanding what was happening. His fearful eyes, however, flashed hope.

"Yeah, let the sonvabitch go." The freighter waved his arms and glanced downward at the gun in his waistband.

"You go right ahead and try it," Crawfish challenged in a soft voice. "It'll be interesting to see if I can pull this trigger before you can skin that pistol."

The freighter's hands jerked upward and his eyebrows followed suit. A whisper came from the shortest would-be lyncher. "He's Vin Lockhart's partner."

"Oh crap!" the farmer gulped.

"Heard Lockhart was dead," the fat man said, shaking his head and causing his jowls to bounce even more. His statement was punctuated with puffed-out cheeks and a rush of whiskey-laden breath.

"George, you're always hearin' dumb shit stuff. I'm leavin'." The red-faced farmer walked away.

"Me, too." The short clerk followed, trying to decide if he should leave his rifle or not. Without daring to look at anyone, he decided it was all right to keep the weapon as long as it was at his side.

Minutes later, the quartet of upset avengers had vanished. The only indication they had been there was the discarded rope in the street.

Crawfish laid the Colt down on his yard and walked to the Ute. He tried to recall the Ute words he had memorized years before when he was a struggling prospector.

"*Mique wush tagooven,*" he said and hoped it was the correct greeting.

The Ute smiled weakly at hearing "Hello, my friend" in his own language.

After untying the Indian's hands, Crawfish patted him on the shoulder and invited him inside, using Ute words he recalled, "Welcome to my camp." He motioned toward his front door where Sean stood.

Continuing to smile, the Ute rejected the offer politely and said he just wanted to return to his people. Crawfish didn't get all of the words, but enough to understand. He turned toward the house and yelled, "Sean, bring a glass of water. Put some of that bacon you were frying on a slice of that fresh bread. Bring that jar of salve, too, will you? The one with the blue lid. Thanks, son."

"*Tograyock.*" The Ute thanked Sean for the glass of water and thick slices of bread, one layered with six slices of just-fried bacon and the other with a mound of gooseberry jam. As the Ute devoured both, Crawfish applied some of the salve to the Indian's raw neck, explaining it was "*tuhaye*." Good. It was the only appropriate word he could recall. The Ute nodded and stood quietly.

Soon, the Indian was on his way, walking briskly; then he stopped, turned and yelled back, "God . . . bless . . . you" in English and resumed trotting down the street. Crawfish and Sean repeated the blessing to him and watched until he was no longer in sight.

"Well, I'm hungry," Crawfish said, picking up his gun. "Or did you use all the bacon?"

"Aye," Sean said, walking toward the house again. "A wee bit o' time 'twill be—before more bacon be ready. I be giving all to hisself, the Indian."

"Good for you, my boy. That's what I would've done. He was badly mistreated."

"Why do men hate men they do not know?" Sean's gaze sought Crawfish's face for the answer.

Crawfish shoved the gun into his waistband, thinking of how to respond.

"Fear, mostly, I think," he finally said. "Fear of somebody different than you. Negroes. Mexicans. Indians. Irish. It's easier to go along with others than to try to understand somebody different. Or help him."

"Aye, I be thinking they would've killed him if ye hadn't stepped in." Sean looked again at Crawfish.

"And you," Crawfish said. "Bad things happen when good men just stand by and let them happen. Remember that." He glanced down at the resting gun. "That's what Vin is doing. Trying to save some friends from something bad. From white man's fear. And greed, I reckon."

"Is he going to be all right? We haven't—"

"Vin Lockhart is going to be all right. He is a plainsman with few matching his skills," Crawfish interrupted with more confidence in his voice than he felt.

"What be the first thing ye said to hisself, the Indian? Was it . . . '*Mique wush tagooven*'?"

"Very good, Sean. Very good."

"What be its meaning?" Sean reached the front door first, opened and held it for Crawfish to enter.

"Well, thank you, my boy. I said, 'Hello my friend.' The Ute language is a Shoshonian dialect. Ah, it's similar to the Shoshoni language. Maybe others are, too. I understand the Comanche language is also." Crawfish stepped inside the house. "You know they originally came from around here. Live mostly in the region of Texas now, however."

"How ye be knowin' such?"

"Well, back when I was prospecting—in the hills," Crawfish said, pursing his lips and frowning to help his recollection. "That was before Vin joined me. Once in a while, a Ute or two would visit. I learned some words to make them feel welcome. It was nice having company."

"How ye be knowin' about the Comanche? Did they visit, too?" Sean closed the door behind them.

Crawfish chuckled as he pulled the gun from his waistband and laid it on the big chair. "No. Glad they didn't. Those boys are something fierce, I hear. I heard it from a Texican in the Silver Queen. You can learn a lot in a saloon—if you just listen."

As he passed his mentor, Sean announced proudly, "Me be knowin' some Irish. Words from the old country." He swallowed and said, "*Dia duit*. That means 'hello.' And *Sean is ainmdom*. 'Sean is my name.' And . . and '*Go raibh maith agat*.' Thank you." He licked his lips. "Me know more. Just canna be bringin' them to me mind ri't now."

"Webster-and-whistles, that's terrific, Sean. You have an ear for words. That will take you far." Crawfish studied the gun carried casually in the boy's hand at his side.

"Thanks to ye, teachin' me their meanin'."

"You're most welcome. It's my pleasure. You're a good student. Like Vin was." The red-haired businessman held out his hand. "Why don't you give me that gun and I'll put them back."

"Aye. 'Tis as if Vin hisself were with us, him seeing that these guns be ready an' all." Sean handed over the gun and headed directly to the kitchen.

Crawfish thought about that for a moment, then laid the open-top revolver next to the Colt. He would put them away later. Having them close at hand might be best right now.

When Crawfish caught up with him, Sean asked if the older man was worried about the four men coming back. Crawfish indicated he was not, but decided to himself that he would start carrying a pistol and be more careful about his comings and goings. They both began working on breakfast.

The subject of Falling Leaf's safety came as Sean laid fresh bacon slices into the frying pan. "Falling Leaf, be herself safe, Crawfish? Here, I mean."

"I won't lie to you, Sean. It is troubling. The Custer tragedy has a lot of folks just plain scared. You saw what some people will try to do." Crawfish studied the two eggs in his hand, selected from the basket on the counter, and laid them aside. Sean had gathered them earlier from the small chicken coop in the backyard. "But she wouldn't last a day riding. Draw-a-deuce, who knows where her tribe even is? Or what agency?"

"Should we be takin' herself to the ranch? Vin said she be good with horses."

Settling on two more eggs, Crawfish reminded the boy of why he had told the lie about her leaving. Sean nodded, keeping his attention on the popping meat. They had been careful about keeping her hidden since then. When she went outside, mostly in the backyard, she was dressed in white woman's clothes and wearing a scarf around her head, carrying her pipe bag. If asked, Sean was to say they had hired a cook. He hadn't been asked. It had occurred to Crawfish that she could stay out at the ranch, but that seemed quite unfair to the Rhymers; they were excited about the new venture and their involvement in it, but having an Indian live with them was a stretch. For anyone. Except Lockhart—and now, them.

"Do ye think she be able to fire that old wheelgun? The one she be carryin' in her bag?" Sean asked.

"I don't know, Sean. It probably wouldn't fire. Who knows how long those cartridges have been in there," Crawfish said.

"Aye. Those French guns be used in the great War between the States, me hear." Sean returned the frying pan, filled with fresh bacon, to the stove.

"Yes. I think so," Crawfish said. "There were different kinds of center-fire revolvers from Europe. Britain. Belgium. Spain even. Many mountain men carried them; many travelers west, too. That Le Faucheux revolver was first made back some twenty, twenty-five years ago. The gun was ahead of its time."

"Where do ye think she be getting such a gun?" The young boy studied the popping meat and pushed two slices apart with a long fork.

Leaving the eggs for later, Crawfish explained what Lockhart had told him about her escape as he spooned fresh coffee grounds into the coffeepot.

In the middle of turning over the sizzling bacon with the fork, Sean declared, "*Fir*. That's 'men' in Irish. Canna be recallin' what 'women' be." He smiled and added, "Oh, and *Le do thoil*, that be 'please.'"

Crawfish muttered his approval, but his mind was on Vin Lockhart. It never got too far from worry. Men were dying where Lockhart was riding. Men of white and red. He turned to see the Irish lad lift a piece of hot bacon from the pan with his fork and lay it aside. The businessman smiled again. He knew what that was to become. A tribute to the Great Spirit. Before every meal, they had taken a small morsel outside, given it to the earth and said a quiet prayer. The tribute was really to Vin Lockhart, but it was important to both of them. It was Crawfish's idea for each to say a silent prayer that their friend be safe. Sean had embraced the idea with relish.

Over a breakfast of fresh bacon, fried eggs, hot steaming coffee and thick slices of bread covered with jam, they discussed plans for the coming day. Sean was eager to share yesterday's horse-ranch events once more. He had told Crawfish about them last night. Twice. He and Harry had worked four geldings and two mares so all of their horses now had at least three "saddles." Actually, Sean had done all the riding, but Harry had helped with the saddling. Harry thought the geldings would be prime for selling in groups of ten each. They planned on starting another round of training today. Sean was especially eager to ride Magic and was excited that four of the mares were now carrying his foals.

After complimenting him on the work done, Crawfish asked about progress on the house being constructed at the ranch for Lockhart and his friends to live in. He had hired some men to begin work on it two weeks ago. Almost on a whim. But he had been too busy with the grand opening of the finished hotel to get out to the ranch since then. The Black Horse Hotel was fully transformed as planned and customers were talking about the restaurant in glowing terms, expecially the fine cuisine. And the orchestra.

Sean's face showed his concern before he stated it. "W-What if he not be finding them, Crawfish? W-What if the soldiers be findin' them first? Didn't yourself be readin' much about how angry the soldiers be . . . because of General Custer? An' the great American president hisself? W-What if . . ."

Crawfish's face was controlled emotion, but he was fast losing the battle to contain his worry. He took a drink of coffee and nearly choked. He understood the boy's emotion; Sean had gone from thinking he must kill Lockhart to avenge his Irish friends to seeing the man as almost a father. Crawfish guessed that made him an uncle, sort of. A visit to the cemetery hadn't come up for almost a month. The last time Sean had done so, the boy had commented afterward how little he knew of the Irishmen, not even their full names. Headstones with "Lightning Murphy" and "Big Mike" and the dates of their deaths had reinforced that fact. It was interesting that the boy hadn't even commented on the two revolvers once belonging to his Irish mentors.

"All we can do, Sean, is keep praying," he finally concluded. "Just keep praying."

Sean stared at his plate and tried to eat a last piece of fried egg, but it wouldn't go down.

Falling Leaf entered the room without a word. Both turned toward her, meeting her sudden appearance with forced greeting.

"*Hau*," both said, having learned from Lockhart that the simple expression covered everything from hello to good morning to good evening.

She was dressed in a white woman's dress Crawfish had purchased for her. At her neck was the fine choker she had worn when Lockhart found her. Barefoot, her gray hair hung about her shoulders. She had gained weight staying with them and had even learned some English—and taught them some Lakotan. This morning her face was taut; her eyes, bright with fear. At her side, the Le Faucheux revolver was held in her right hand.

Crawfish was puzzled at the sight of the gun. He knew she had been carrying it with her when she went outside, but he had never seen it out of the buckskin bag. Why had she felt the need to have it now? Did she hear the commotion outside earlier? Was this her way of preparing to help?

In a mixture of broken English and Lakotan, she told about having a nightmare and asked about Lockhart. "*Hanble sica mitawa.* Bad dream . . . Lok-hart. *Kociapi metanka.* Big fight. He hurt. *Tookiyaya hwo?* . . . where he . . . Lok-hart?" She held up the gun as if this was an explanation of its appearance.

A tear found its way down Sean's cheek and he looked away.

Crawfish didn't know what to say. A few days before the Custer massacre she had told them about a dream she had of blue riders being killed by a great many Indian warriors. He thought it was just that, a bad dream. Now this.

"*Tookiyaya hwo?* . . . where he . . . Lok-hart? Where *Wanagi Yanka?*" she asked again, staring at both.

The corner of his mouth twitching, Crawfish reminded her that she knew Lockhart was going to be gone for many days—trying to say it in her language took much longer than his usual quick expression. She studied him without changing her expression.

A knock at the front door surprised all of them.

"Me get it." Sean jumped from his chair.

"Let me, son. It might be them. Again," Crawfish cautioned and rose, but Sean had already gone to the front window and peeked outside. He turned back and proclaimed, "It's Ms. Bacon."

"Mattie? Hop-a-bunny!" Crawfish said as he limped toward the door. "You know what she wants."

"Aye. Herself be wantin' Vin Lockhart." Sean's grin swept across this face.

Crawfish nodded and frowned. "Yeah, guess so—and he doesn't want her. I've got no news about him either." He shook his head. "Wish she would get the hint."

CHAPTER TWENTY-FIVE

A dream brought smells of sweetgrass, juniper needles and ground cedar gently to Vin Lockhart's exhausted mind. In the otherworld of sleep, the anger of his wounds was gone. A warmth spread through him like a peaceful song. A small fire built from the materials he smelled was a few feet away. Above his head was a sacred circle made of curved branches and rawhide strings, with both the tail and breast feathers of the great eagle dangling freely. The large circle was suspended by a leather strip from a long stick jammed into the ground. Tied to the base of the circle was a killed badger; his slit belly emptied of its entrails revealing only congealed blood.

Now, through the dreamworld, Lockhart could see his face in the reflection from the blood's hard surface. The reflected image was that of Lockhart as an old man. A good sign, he remembered. He would live a long time, according to Stone-Dreamer. Surely, his adopted father was near.

In his dream, the Denver businessman's wounds were tightly bound with white soft bandages. A scent of medicine underneath the wrappings wafted into his awareness. Not sweet like cedar or mapled syrup; more like the smell of just-cut hay. The muscles in his right arm tingled; he had moved it without pain. Near his head was a tin bowl of crushed willow bark, a special medicine to be taken for pain. He recognized the bowl; it had been on his pack. He recognized the potion, too; Stone-Dreamer had used its curing powders on others.

On a spit over the fire was a roasting grouse. The delightful aroma danced over the odors of the kindling. A sack of roots for cooking was a few feet away. Around him were four slender sticks, stuck into the ground. Tied to each stick were buckskin bags of tobacco and willow bark, offerings to *Wakantanka*.

He felt his face; it was fully painted. From somewhere a mirror appeared in his hand and he saw the paint was red for good luck, with sacred white stripes over the darker crimson. His body was painted with light blue hailstone markings for protection. None of them touched the prideful chest scars of his long-ago Sun Dance ordeal; the sign of a great warrior.

A spotted robe of a young mountain lion skin lay across his legs and stomach. Red porcupine quillwork, a symbol of magic power, decorated the robe. Attached to the tiny doeskin medicine bag he wore around his neck was a stuffed chickadee, a hunk of shed buffalo hair dyed red, and four panther claws. Instinctively, his fingers felt for Young Evening's choker necklace at his throat. It was gone. In its place was his old warrior choker. His sawed-off shotgun quiver was gone and, instead, hung a small parfleche holding precious bullets, a mixture of brass cartridges, copper, paper, linen and skin cartridges, and a pouch of powder and loose caps and balls. Just like he wore when he was an Oglala warrior. At his side was the decorated Henry carbine he had carried then, not his Winchester. His war belt carried a tomahawk and knife, not pistols.

He sat up, looked around and saw Touches-Horses. "Is that you, *kola?*"

"*Aiiee*, you were not easy to find. Took all of us to track you here. A strange place, a sacred place I think."

"Well, it wasn't anything I did. That horse you trained carried me here. I don't even know where I am."

Nearby, his dun was transformed into a fiery black horse, adorned with the markings of battle medicine; his own shield was encased and hanging against the horse's flank. Feathers were tied to its mane and tail. Behind the fine mount was his dead pack horse, only it was alive and grazing.

Touches-Horses smiled and Lockhart looked around at the other Indians. All were from his old tribe; Thunder Lance, Bear-Heart, Spotted Horse and Sings-With-Stones, the four who had come to ask him to find his former brother-in-law a year ago. Even Black Fire was there, looking worried. He didn't see Stone-Dreamer, but a growing fog had probably hidden him from his view. Now he sensed someone moving within the thick mist, coming toward him. He was certain it was Crazy Horse and not his adopted father. Where was Stone-Dreamer? Where was Morning Bird?

"None would leave without finding you, *kola*," the Lakotan horse trainer said. "I told them to go on, but they would not. They wanted to find you."

"I came for you. And Stone-Dreamer. And Morning Bird, if she wants to come."

"She waits for you, my brother."

With an explosion of pent-up emotion, they grasped each other's forearm in the traditional warrior's salute, then hugged each other heartily. Within the fog, Lockhart saw the tips of Oglala lodges and the shape of a man still advancing. The shape was that of Stone-Dreamer.

"I will wait for you at the horses," Touches-Horses said. "The others want you to lead them against the evil *wasicun*."

"Is that why you are painted for war?" Lockhart saw, for the first time, that his former brother-in-law—and all of the warriors—were adorned with their war-medicine markings.

"Yes, *kola*. We are ready for you to lead us."

Lockhart looked into the mirror and saw that his face and body paint had changed into the war medicine he wore as Panther-Strikes. White paw marks, red claw lines and yellow lightning bolts. Across his nose and cheeks was a single line of dried blood, Young Evening's blood. He had placed it there before going after the Shoshoni war party that had killed her. When his finger felt the mark, it became moist and dripping.

"I-I-I don't know if I can, Touches-Horses, I-I-I am so weak. I thought I was going to die."

The fog grew ever thicker; its fingers wrapped around Crazy Horse and pushed away. In his place was Stone-Dreamer. The holy man was wounded. In the same places Lockhart had been wounded against the Cheyenne. Stone-Dreamer held out his hand and vanished.

In the same moment, Touches-Horses transformed into a vague shape, then into a rail-thin white man wearing a woolen jacket with filled pockets, a worn slouch hat and smoking a pipe.

"He's alive, Bill. Sure nuff. Got some lead in him, I reckon. Lost a lot o' blood," the white man said without removing his pipe.

All of the dreamworld Indians—and the Oglala medicine, paint, weapons, clothing, and sacred objects—disappeared as well. Lockhart's wounds were as they had been, angry and crusted with dried blood. The glorious smells of roasting grouse and sweetgrass were overtaken by the acrid odor of sweat, horse and tobaccoed breath.

Lockhart stirred from a sleep that wouldn't leave quickly, shedding the world of dreams as his mind fought to locate reality. Instinctively, he reached for the rifle in his lap as his left boot clanged against the dropped coffeepot.

"Whoa, mister. You're safe." The voice was gruff, but reassuring.

The thick-whiskered scout put a hand on Lockhart's shoulder. "Yur with friends. We're with the Fifth Cavalry." He smelled of leather thick with camp smoke, stale sweat and horse; his hot breath was laced with pipe tobacco.

Struggling to fully awaken, Lockhart thought he heard a command to restart his fire and wondered why Crawfish hadn't already done that. The gruff voice walked away and another took its place. He felt something cool and wet on his face and looked into the piercing blue eyes of a tall, handsome man with a light brown goatee, long flowing hair and a confident, easy way about him.

"Good day to you, sir. Name's Cody. Bill Cody," the lead scout said, kneeling next to him and wiping Lockhart's face with a wet bandana. "That sorry-talkin' fella is Bull Sedrick. Better scout than he looks. Appears you've been through it. I count four down close by—and I reckon that lance of scalps is yours, too, and they relate to those two circles of dead Indians." He shook his head and grinned. "There's a few more strewn about. You flat tore those dog soldiers apart. Like something we did in the theater. With ol' Colonel Judson. Ah, Ned Buntline."

Cody pointed toward Lockhart's worn-out fire. "Sell, give Bull a hand and get that fire going—and get some coffee on. Find me something for bandages."

A young-looking scout, named Sell Morgan, leaned forward on his horse. "How come I have to do that? I made the fire last night."

"You'll do it 'til you get it right, boy," Cody barked. "Sammy's riding back to Merritt to tell him what's going on."

"Lemme go—an' Sammy kin make the fire."

Without another word to the young smart-aleck scout, Cody turned to the second mounted scout wearing a shapeless hat with a stampede tie-down under his stubble-bearded chin. Cody pointed toward the south. "Sammy, ride to General Merritt. Tell him about this. Tell him there are no hostiles left in the area. Make sure he understands that. A real fightin' man has already seen to that, got it? We're clear to those hills and to come at his own speed." He motioned dramatically toward the far ridge. "Merritt will tell Crook. God knows what Crook'll want to do." He glanced at Lockhart. "The man's choking on guilt. Should've been at the Little Bighorn."

Without a word, the scout yanked his horse toward the south and kicked it into a run.

Not understanding the comment, Lockhart noted to himself that it was the place where the dog-soldier war party had descended upon him the day before.

The sassy Morgan muttered something as he dismounted and handed his reins to DuBois, the tall Frenchman holding Cody's horse, his own and Bull Sedrick's.

DuBois bowed deeply. "*Oui.*"

Morgan frowned and the Frenchman added, "*Je vous en prie.*"

Cody snorted, "He said you're welcome, Sell."

"Why doesn't he say it in American, then," Morgan snapped and moved reluctantly to obey the chief scout's orders.

Cody walked over to a third rider, a long-faced man wearing Cheyenne leggings over his pants and boots and beaded cuffs with long fringe at his wrists. Quietly, he told him to find Major Frank North and his Pawnee battalion, indicating they should be somewhere west of Lockhart's camp. His orders were to tell the famed Pawnee commander what had happened here and that they would meet up about three miles north of the closest ridge and decide their future course at that time. Or rather the generals would decide for them. He added to keep a watch out for a few Cheyenne hightailing it, probably north.

"After you catch up with North, see if you can find Grouard, tell him what we've got," Cody continued, waving toward the northwest. "He's out there somewhere." He turned to Lockhart. "Frank Grouard is the chief of scouts for Crook, you know. Guess he's the boss over us all."

"What about Little Bat?" the scout asked, shifting in his saddle. "Should I look for him, too?"

"Naw, you'd never find him." Cody waved his hand in a negative motion. "Baptiste Garner. Little Bat. He's our best tracker. I'll let him find us." He winked.

The scout muttered his understanding and headed west, kicking his horse into a gallop.

Meanwhile, the other four white scouts were in various stages of inspecting Lockhart's camp and the dead Cheyenne bodies strewn about the area. At the first circle of dead bodies, five Indian scouts, three Pawnees, a Crow, and a Shoshoni, were studying their placement, talking rapidly to each other, and pointing to the second circle of bodies with another big rock centered in it. Another Crow scout was leading three riderless ponies; their paint markings indicated they had belonged to the attacking Cheyenne.

Lockhart tried to stand and his stiffened right leg betrayed him. He staggered and dropped his rifle as he sprawled face forward.

"Get him! He's hurt," Cody yelled and reached for him unsuccessfully.

Bull Sedrick dropped his gathered sticks and hurried to the downed Lockhart.

Coming behind him, Sell Morgan stopped, holding a small gathering of sticks. "What's the matter with him? Is he dead? Can I have his Winchester?"

Bull flashed the young scout a fierce scowl and leaned over to check on the downed plainsman. "Hold on, podnah. Thar's no reason fur traipsin' about. Rest easy."

"I-I'm all right. It's just stiff," Lockhart said, shifting his weight onto his left leg. He pushed the shotgun quiver back on his shoulder, grabbed his rifle, and carefully stood.

"Good Lord, man. Looks like you've been in a one-man war," the gruff-talking scout said. "These hyar are dawg soldjurs, ya know. They be the meanest o' the mean. Looks like they dun were with Crazy Horse, Gall an' Sittin' Bull at the Little Bighorn by the looks o' thar outfits—an' shootin' irons."

"They didn't introduce themselves," Lockhart said, shaking off the remaining vestiges of his dream. It had been so real. He couldn't help but look around the camp to assure his awakened self that none of his Indian friends were there. Seeing his recovering dun, he limped toward the grazing horse.

Cody laughed heartily. "Looks like you did the introducing. With bullets for calling cards. What's your name, mister—an' if you don't mind my asking, what are you doing out here?" His hand went to his Vandyke beard and rubbed it.

Patting the horse's back, Lockhart looked back at him. "Lockhart. Vin Lockhart. Of Denver." He started to say "Denver City," but caught himself, remembering Crawfish constantly reminding him the town wasn't called that anymore. "I'm looking for some friends. Should be north of here."

"Denver? Shoot, I was in Denver. A few years ago it was," Cody said. "Sixty-nine, I think. Some boys stole Fifth Cavalry stock. Seven horses and four mules." He shook his head. "Worst thing, they got General Carr's fine thoroughbred. Yessir, that was real dumb." He pushed back the hat from his forehead. "Caught 'em trying to auction 'em all off at the Elephant Corral. You know it?" He pulled his hat back in place to reinforce the statement. "Denver was a right busy place back then. Not like St. Louis or one of them Eastern cities, but plenty busy anyway."

"Yes, it is a growing town. Freight wagons coming and going night and day."

"What do you do there?"

"Oh, my friend and I own a saloon and a hotel."

"Sonvabitch."

Interrupting their conversation, a Pawnee scout in a cavalry shirt and leggings galloped over to Cody and began briefing him with a mixture of excited Pawnee and supporting sign. When finished, the Indian pulled back his horse and rode toward the other Indian scouts. After watching him ride away, Cody walked over to Lockhart. The tall chief scout's manner could just as easily have been a stroll along the streets of Cheyenne, instead of moving through the site of a Indian attack on a lone man.

From under a pushed-up-brimmed hat, his light brown hair eased down along his shoulders. The chief of scouts for the Fifth Cavalry was dressed in a fringed buckskin jacket with beaver trimming, over-the-knee-length black boots, black trousers and a dark-red bib shirt with a now wet, pink bandana retied loosely at his neck. Around his waist were two pistols in formed holsters with exposed barrels and a war knife. His self-assured smile was contagious and the men around him obviously saw him as their leader, with or without any title.

He stopped beside Lockhart who was leaning over to check the dun's legs, using the butt of his rifle for balance.

"Doesn't look hurt. Can you ride him?" Cody avoided asking about the man's health, judging Lockhart to be stronger than he first appeared.

"Not sure. I'm not going to push it, though. A few days, I suppose," Lockhart said, looking up. In a few sentences, he explained what had happened.

Cody listened quietly, then observed that the dead Indians were, indeed, dog soldiers, an elite band of experienced, cruel fighters. He said they were a fierce fighting unit that had vowed to die fighting the white man or drive him from their land forever. They were *hotamintanio*, one of the select warrior societies with their own secret ways, ceremonies, and songs. Songs of daring and honor. He said the Fifth Cavalry had defeated them at the battle of Summit Springs seven years ago and that many of the remaining Cheyenne under Tall Bull had surrendered at Fort Sill, but the rest had ridden with White Horse to keep fighting.

Lockhart ran his hand along the dun's back-left leg, nodding silently at the absence of flinching. Without looking up, he said simply, "I know about dog soldiers."

"Figured as much. Didn't mean any disrespect." Cody frowned and pushed his hat brim once more from his forehead.

"You didn't give any."

"Well, let me try again." He grinned. "Did you know about General Custer and his men bein' wiped out at the Little Bighorn? By three or four thousand Sioux and Cheyenne," Cody said, tilting his head to the side. "Him and some two hundred and sixty men. He was supposed to wait for Gibbons coming up the Bighorn. Instead, he sent Reno's three troops toward the south end of this big village. About one hundred and twenty men. Benteen and his three troops stayed with the packs. In reserve. Custer took five troops to the other end. Too many redskins. They rammed Reno up the river bluffs and into a defensive position. An' flat run over Custer's boys. Every last man. Reno, he lost a bunch of men, too."

"How long ago?"

"June twenty-fifth."

"What day is it now?" Lockhart asked and stood, adjusting the rifle to hold it one-handed at his side.

Cody grinned again. "I know that feeling. Must be a few days into August. I think." He wiped his hand across his mouth to remove the thin smile. "Scouting for the Fifth. We're part of General Crook's army. Headed north to join up with Terry. Looks like we're going Indian hunting." He rubbed his bearded chin. "I don't think there's much prospect of any more fighting, though. Crook wants it bad. After screwing up at the Rosebud. Some of his own men blame him for what happened to Custer. Not to his face, of course. Who knows?" He placed his hands on the butts of his revolvers. "But it won't happen. All the Sioux and Cheyenne are down to small parties and moving fast. Every which way. Like the one you messed with." He grinned again. "Me. I'll probably be running dispatch for Terry—an' then I'm going to organize a new dramatic combination, have a new drama written for me, based upon these Sioux wars." He folded his arms in satisfaction. "Say, I could use a good man, like you. Quite a story, this fight of yours here. People in the East would eat it up." He lifted his right hand to scratch his nose. "Fact is, I could probably get ol' Buntline to write it up in one of his romance magazines. Make you a real western hero."

Lockhart frowned and moved his right arm, testing its weakness from the gunshot. The sleeve was torn in several places and streaked red. "You're sure Custer went down with all his men—at the Little Bighorn?"

"Yeah. You're probably the only white man who doesn't know about it." Cody shook his head. "That's three in a row for the red man. Reynolds at the Powder. Crook at the Rosebud. And now, Custer at the Little Bighorn."

Lockhart shook his head. "Probably so. I knew about the first two. I've been on the trail—from Cheyenne—since late June. Guess I missed the Custer news by a few days."

Cody hitched the heavy gunbelt. "Yeah. The whole country is wound up about it. Washington wants all the Indians dead or on the reservation. Preferably dead, I reckon. Army's taken charge of the Sioux reservations. For awhile. Heard tell ol' Red Cloud got so pissed, he took his tribe out of the reservation. A real mess."

"Yeah, I suppose it is."

"Everything's changing. Everything. Some of those Indians we're after, they were friends of mine. An' Bull's," Cody said and brought up a different subject to avoid staying on one that was distasteful to him. "Say, did you happen to see my old friend Hickok when you were there—in Cheyenne?" Cody's smile returned.

"I sure did. He was with . . . ah, Charlie Utter. Said you had been in Cheyenne, but left a few days before I got there." Lockhart slowly returned the smile.

"Yeah, I had to report. For this."

"They were headed for Deadwood. Said they were hoping to find gold."

"Hell, the only thing Hickok'll find is a poker game. Unless his luck's changed, he won't win much either. Maybe he'll get lucky this time an' win some gold for that sweet new wife of his back in Cincinnati."

They walked together back to where Lockhart's old fire was now blazing and his coffeepot was boiling. Morgan met them and presented a folded white cloth for use as bandages.

"Did you get the salve?" Cody asked, receiving the material.

"You didn't ask for salve," Morgan said, sneaking a glance at Lockhart.

"You're dumber'n a brick, Sell." Cody shook his head. "Go and get the salve."

Lockhart held out a hand. "That's all right, Bill. I'm not hurt bad. Probably hurt myself more falling from that tree branch than from their lead."

"Well, you're not lookin' at yourself," Cody said, waving his arm up and down. "Better let DuBois have a look at you. We don't call him 'Medicine Man' for nothin'."

"Sure. That's mighty nice of you."

Cody told Morgan to take charge of the horses the Frenchman was holding and send him over. He motioned for Lockhart to sit down on one of the logs. Bull brought him a cup of coffee and a piece of jerky.

"I didn't see the salve," Morgan spouted.

"You didn't see it? It's right with the bandages," Cody said, accepting a cup of coffee from the big, whiskered scout. "You've been spending too much time with those corset-model drawings in that Sears and Roebucks in your saddle-bag. It'll make you go blind, you know."

Morgan blushed a deep crimson and turned away.

The chief scout watched the young rider walk over to DuBois, then returned his attention to the sitting Lockhart. "My own Pawnee scouts are on edge—about you, Mr. Lockhart." Cody finally brought up the subject, studying the fire as they approached.

"Vin. It's Vin."

"Thank you. Please call me Bill," Cody said. "As I was saying, my Indian friends are puzzled by your circles of dead dog soldiers with the rocks in the middle." He paused and wiped his mouth for time. "They also can't figure out the Cheyenne arrows stickin' in some of those boys." He stopped, but clearly wanted to add more.

"That's easy enough. I wanted those dog soldiers to judge me strange. Make them wonder what kind of white man I really was," Lockhart said. "They'd already seen this sawed-off shotgun in action. Hoped they hadn't seen one before an' it would bother them." He patted the quivered gun on his shoulder. "Guess I was hoping those circles would be enough to keep them from coming back. Didn't work, though." He explained the dummy and the gunpowder, and his position in the tree with a bow and arrows.

Cody shook his head. "That's really somethin', Vin. I'm sure we could use that in our theater act. Even that blaster. The money's awfully good, Vin. Awfully good."

"Thanks, Bill, but I've got things in Denver waiting for me."

"Sure. But if you change your mind . . ." Cody finally returned to the subject of Pawnee interest. "I suppose you saw the panther tracks around your camp. And the tracks of wolves that came and went." He sipped the coffee and studied Lockhart. "Nothin's touched your dead pack horse, ya know."

"Hadn't noticed. Lucky, I guess."

The offhand comment brought surprise to Sell Morgan's face as he studied the tracks surrounding the fake camp. In spite of himself, he shivered.

"My Indian scouts, they think you're a witch who can change shapes," Cody said, licking his lower lip. "A panther. A wolf. Even a Cheyenne dog soldier." He tried to smile, but couldn't.

"*Bonjour, Monsieur,*" DuBois said, bowing. "*Pardonnez-moi, ca va?*" In his hands were a large jar of brownish salve, a canteen and a tightly folded white rag.

Cody introduced the Frenchman to Lockhart and DuBois began methodically cleaning and treating his arm and face. His assessment of Lockhart's condition came in spurts of French and English. After his arm was wrapped, Lockhart sipped his coffee and chewed on the jerky and let DuBois determine the extent of his leg wounds. The second was worse than the first; neither had hit bone and he didn't think any lead remained. Carefully and smoothly, the Frenchman completed the bandaging, noting Lockhart had lost blood, but was not seriously injured. Lockhart thanked him and agreed with his diagnosis. With a cock of his head, he added that he was steady, and swallowed the rest of the jerky and washed it down with coffee.

Mumbling to himself, Sell Morgan stood holding the

reins of the quiet horses, counting the dead Indians there and beyond. He looked over at Cody with an ornery gleam in his eyes. "Hey, Bill, this sur nuff beats your first scalp for Custer, don't it?"

Cody didn't like the interruption or the observation, but it was Bull who responded. "Bill did his hand-to-hand a'in a Cheyenne war chief. Yellow Hand."

"Yellow Hair. *Hayowei*," Cody corrected.

"Ya should'a seen it. Really somethin'. We was at Hat Creek. 'Bout two, three weeks back. Yessir," Bull said from his position at the far end of the same log Lockhart sat on. "Ya know'd ol' Buffalo Bill hyar dun got the Congressional Medal o' Honor. Four years back, it were."

"That's enough, Bull," Cody said. "But I thank you for the kind words."

Shifting his worn boots away from the fire's advancing warmth, Bull studied the wounded Lockhart as if assessing an old, hard-to-read map. He removed his pipe from his teeth, licked his parched lips and lowered his gaze to take in the pipe bowl in his hand, seeking the courage to tell what was churning in his mind.

"Years back, I was a'trappin' in the hills. Ever' now an' then, I'd visit me a Injun village. Sioux, usually. Sometimes Shoshoni. Always treated fine I were." He glanced at Cody, then back to his held pipe. "One village I visited three times. No, it were four. Black Fire was the headman. Oglala Sioux, like Crazy Horse. In this hyar village there were a young white fella among 'em. A full warrior, mind ya. Lots o' coups. Bin a Sun Dancer ev'n." He made a slicing motion across his chest with the stem of his pipe and returned it to his mouth. "The panther were this hyar white warrior's spirit guide, they tolt me." He started to point to the panther tracks around the camp and decided against it. "Wal, this hyar feller spoke some 'Merican, so he always sat with the tribe's headmen and white men who came a'vis-itin'. Kinda like a middleman, I reckon." He saw his coffee

cup beside the log where he sat, picked it up and stuck a
finger in the remaining brew to check its warmth. "Sure
don't wanna insult ya none, Mistah Lockhart, but ya remind me some o' that white warrior fella."

Lockhart stepped toward the thick-chested man, stopped
and crossed his arms. "Yes, I remember you, too." A smile
broke across his tired, tanned face.

Bull's expression jerked like a whip into a matching
smile. "Wal, I'll be damned!"

Lockhart answered in Lakotan that he was glad to see the
man again, *"Ake iyuskinyan wancinyankelo."*

Cody's eyebrows rose.

Buoyed by Lockhart's acknowledgement of his past, Bull
said his last visit to the tribe brought a dramatic discovery.
Tribesmen told him the white warrior had left to return to
the white man's world. They said he had fought alone
against a Shoshoni war party and killed most of them.
They believed he was protected by ghosts during this fight.
Some thought he was a spirit himself. The scout said
Lockhart had supposedly stopped breathing once, according to the stories. Stopped breathing! Stone dead, he said,
and a holy man had brought him back to life. With relish,
the grizzled man related that the Indians believed the
white warrior was blessed so he couldn't be killed unless
their ancestors decided so. When Bull finished, he withdrew
a pouch of tobacco and began refilling his pipe, mostly to
have something to do.

Without responding, Lockhart walked to the fire, leaned
over and picked up the coffeepot and refilled his own cup.
He looked around to offer more coffee to Bull, then to
Cody. Both nodded agreement and Lockhart refilled their
cups. Casually, he explained the reason for his journey was
to find his old tribe, and see that they were safe and help
them to the reservation. He made no attempt to explain the
ghost stories or his reason for leaving the village.

Cody's eyebrows arched again in suspicion of Lockhart's

reason, but the chief scout said nothing. Bull looked relieved and gulped his fresh coffee.

The French-speaking scout came to Cody and apologized in French for interrupting. They exchanged words and the Frenchman hurried away.

"DuBois says we've got blue coats coming our way," Cody said. "We're going to have to mount up. You're welcome to come with us, Vin."

"Thanks, but I'd better stay." Lockhart motioned toward the dun.

Cody's response was to offer Lockhart the captured war horses; one for him to ride, one to carry his supplies and the third as a spare. Within minutes, Lockhart's saddle and supplies were in place on the Cheyenne ponies. He rode out, leading the replacement pack horse who was not particularly happy about his load, the third unsaddled war horse—and his dun, moving easily.

Cody rode beside him, talking about his wife and three children.

As they left the area, Lockhart looked back and noticed the Pawnee scouts were gathered tightly around one of the circles of dead Cheyenne. He couldn't make out what they were doing. Several were waving freshly cut cedar branches over the area.

Bull rode up beside Lockhart, looked around to make sure no one was close enough to hear. "Did ya ev'r cross o'vr to the oth'r side? The spirit world? Go thar wi' them Grandfathers?" He looked around again and his voice was barely a whisper. "I did. Onc't. Found a special place high up in the mountains. Walked ri't thru. Easy as can be. Yessuh."

Lockhart smiled and touched the stone in his pants pocket, then the feathers in his shirt pocket.

CHAPTER TWENTY-SIX

Young Sean Kavanagh placed his boot into the stirrup one more time. The dark brown gelding he called "Chocolate" had reared when he tried moments before. And again a few minutes earlier. The green horse was one of a small herd they had just purchased with Crawfish's approval—and money.

Swinging up and over, he retook his position in the middle of the gelding's saddle. The horse reared. Again. Wide-eyed, Sean yanked on the reins and the animal stutter-stepped on its hind legs, froze in the air momentarily, flailing its front legs, and finally returned to the ground.

From the corral, Harry Rhymer watched, ran his fingers through his thick, white hair and said, "Sean, halfway between saddle and earth is a dangerous place to be, if'n a hoss rears up. Ain't no place good that's fer sure." He made a falling motion with his hand.

"Ye can be jerkin' the reins, Harry, so he be knowin' it's wrong." Sean pulled on imaginary reins.

"Yeah, an'you'll be havin' a hoss on top o' ya, boy."

Jumping from the saddle, Sean frowned. "Well, if me be kickin' him now, he won't be knowin' what the punishment be for."

"Right, son. An' after you're in the saddle, he'll settle down," Harry said. "Kin I show you somethin' that always worked fer me—when I was a'breakin' 'em."

Sean frowned again and stepped back, making an exaggerated bow.

"Be ri't back. Gotta git somethin'." Harry hurried away toward the barn. A fresh coat of red paint—along with some well-placed boards—had given the structure a new life. Just like the repairs had done on the two corrals. A rebirth of the ranch of sorts. Much like the renewed enthusiasm and purpose Harry and Martha Rhymer had found in their "partnership" with Lockhart and Crawfish.

Sean watched him; then his gaze caught the magnificent Magic in the nearby second corral. Morning sun wrestled to clear the other outbuildings and windmill and then rested across the proud bay stallion's back, turning it into a brown diamond. In the wide green field, 200 horses and a dozen milk cows met the new day and the plentiful grass. With Crawfish's blessing, Sean had taken to staying at the ranch for days at a time. It allowed him to get to work earlier in the morning and the Rhymers seemed to enjoy the company.

The Irish lad couldn't help thinking of Lockhart and wishing for his return soon. Would he be pleased with what they had accomplished? Would he be excited to see how the colt *Kola* had grown? What if he didn't come back? News about wild Indians was in the newspapers all the time. What if he was attacked and killed? Sean shook his head to push away the awful thought. He missed Lockhart a great deal; Crawfish and the Rhymers had been very nice to him, very nice, indeed. Still, he missed the man who had changed his life.

Harry returned, holding up a small steel ring, two rawhide strings and a leather strap.

"Found 'em!" he declared.

The white-haired man grabbed a coiled lariat from the closest corral post and slipped between the poles into the enclosed area. He laid out the rope on the ground next to the horse with one end just beyond the horse's head and the rest of the coiled rope a foot beyond its tail. He took a pocketknife from his pocket, opened its blade and cut the rope at the point.

"Here, you kin put the rest back on the pole. Hold on to the t'other—'til I tell ya different."

"Aye."

Without further comment, he walked over to the brown horse and said something quietly to it. He leaned over next to the horse and tied the metal ring in the middle of the tightened cinch with one of the strings. Then he tied the leather strap tightly to the animal's right hind ankle, making sure it lay between the joint and the hoof.

He stood and looked at Sean. "Now, you tie that rope—good an' tight—to the noseband. All right?"

"Aye."

As soon as that was done, Harry told him to run the rope between the horse's front legs and through the ring and then tie it to the strap on its rear foot.

"Use that slip hitch I taught ya," Harry advised. "Ya wanna be able to yank it free in a hurry, if needs be."

Sean finished making the knot with a big loop for a quick untie. "Now what?"

"Now you can try mountin' up." Harry folded his arms. "When that brown outlaw rears up, he'll flat pull his own hind leg out from under himself. That'll teach 'im real quick-like. Yessuh."

"Won't he be hurtin' hisself?"

"Naw. He'll do it twice. Three times at the most. Then he'll figger it ain't the savvy thing to do." Harry pointed at the horse. "Best thing is, he's gittin' the hurt ri't when he's a'rearin'. So he'll know it's the reason fer it. Nev'r seed it not work, Sean."

"Aye." Sean moved to the horse and regathered the reins.

"Nice 'n easy, Sean," the old man cautioned. "He'll be feelin' ya quick—an' ya don't wanna be in the saddle if'n he yanks his ass to the ground." He chuckled.

Sean glanced in his direction, shrugged and lifted his boot to the stirrup.

From the nearly finished house being built for Lockhart and his friends, Crawfish watched the young lad jump away as the wild horse jerked his head and staggered in response to its own doing. Shaking his head, Crawfish turned away and saw the head carpenter appear in the doorway of the new house.

"Morning, Adrian," he yelled. "May I have a word?" He began walking toward the house without waiting for a response.

"'Course. What's up?" Adrian Ominis smiled as Crawfish neared.

"We're gettin' close," the stocky carpenter said, pointing to the finished roof of the long house and adding that most of the interior work was finished as well.

Crawfish was pleased with the response and eager to get a definitive date. He wanted to have it furnished before Lockhart returned. Having an important project kept him happy now that the hotel was running well. This one was especially stimulating. He couldn't wait to see the expression on Lockhart's face when he saw it. That brought the worry that was never far from his thoughts. Was his friend all right? Would Lockhart find his old tribe in time? Would they be safe? Soon the region would be feeling the bite of early winter. Would he return before the cold settled in? Would he return? He swallowed the last question as Ominis held out his hand.

As they shook hands, the jovial carpenter began telling about the status of the house. Ominis was one of those rather excitable men who was always working, always with too many things going on. Crawfish liked him, but knew the man needed the discipline of asking questions and demanding specific deadlines. Rather than resenting it, Ominis seemed to find relief in the specificity.

"Mr. Crawford . . . there's a man in front . . . he wants to see you."

The announcement came from Martha Rhymer, coming from the back door of the low-roofed Rhymer home. With her walked Falling Leaf. Both Crawfish and the Indian woman had come out in his carriage this morning. Crawfish had been eager to check on the house. It wasn't the first time Falling Leaf had visited the ranch and Martha Rhymer had welcomed her graciously. So had Harry.

"Have him come around." Crawfish returned to Ominis's assessment.

Swallowing, Martha said, "H-He's a black man. I asked him in, but he said he preferred not to." Crow's-feet jumped around her eyes in reinforcement of her declaration.

Crawfish looked up again, more puzzled than annoyed. The gap between his front teeth was visible as he spoke. "A black man?"

Nervously, she explained the man worked for the stage line, and that he had a dispatch letter from Vin Lockhart.

"Mail-and-money! Why didn't you say so in the first place?" Crawfish rushed toward the front of the house, leaving Ominis in midsentence.

Outside, a thin Jean-Jacques Beezah waited, holding an envelope in both hands. His cutaway navy blue coat and vest were sprinkled with dust. As Crawfish approached, he removed his matching bowler hat. A quiet horse stood at the hitching rack; in its saddle sat a black cat, half-asleep.

"Mr. Crawford, I have a postal letter for you. From Vin Lockhart," Beezah announced, presenting the communication. "A dispatch rider from Fort Laramie brought it to the stage office. In Cheyenne. He came, bringing all the army mail like usual. Only he brought this, too. It came from William F. Cody himself. Buffalo Bill. From General Merritt's camp. Up north. Near the Yellowstone. That's what he told me anyway."

"Oh, thank you, sir. Thank you." Crawfish took the envelope, noticed the official dispatch order from Cody, ripped it open and began reading aloud without realizing it.

A few feet away, Martha and Falling Leaf watched him read aloud. Martha's mouth moved along with every word he pronounced.

Crawfish, I am well and headed for the Bighorn Mountains. I expect to find Black Fire's people there unless the army arrives first. Bill Cody advised me on their possible whereabouts. A Pawnee scout told him of a small band of Oglala headed that way. It appears the Indians spread out after the Little Bighorn. I did not hear about Custer's great defeat until a week ago. I heard it from Cody himself.

I had a run-in with a Cheyenne dog-soldier war party two weeks ago, but I was only slightly injured. It is nothing to worry about. Tell Sean and Harry that I have three Cheyenne war ponies now. Two are geldings. The other is a stallion. I also have a dun that has proven a fine, strong horse. None are as good as Magic. Or what I think Kola will be. I will bring them when I return.

I rode for a week with Bill Cody and his scouts as part of General Crook's army. He is chief scout of the Fifth Cavalry. They are camped on the Rosebud with General Terry. This makes a huge army of over 3,500 men. It is the greatest force ever to enter Indian country. It sounds like they intend to stay the winter, if it is necessary. I am leaving them now and Bill has generously taken the responsibility for seeing that this letter gets to you. I don't think Bill will stay with the army much longer. He is interested in doing a stage act again.

It has been a long time since I left Denver and I am sorry to have left so much for you to do. I hope the hotel and restaurant are going well. I hope the ranch has not been too big a burden. Harry and Sean will do well I am certain. Is Falling Leaf well? I hope she has not been trouble for you. Have you taken her to the ranch? Sean can learn much from Harry who is a good horseman. I think Falling Leaf can help if Harry and Martha do not mind her presence.

Keep praying that I find my friends in time. You are right. They must go to the reservation. It is very sad.

Vin

Crawfish looked up and mumbled that he wished the letter was longer.

Nodding agreement, Martha glanced at Falling Leaf, then back to Crawfish, then again to the Indian woman who was staring at the open land from where Beezah had come. Martha wondered if the older woman was thinking Lockhart himself would be coming. Falling Leaf's dress was one Crawfish had bought for her, a soft blue trimmed in white with long sleeves that were puffed out at the cuffs. Around her neck, however, was her tribal choker and in her hand was the pipe bag holding her old gun. Over her dress, she wore a pale yellow apron that Martha had given her.

Beezah's smile was wide as Crawfish peered over the top of the handwritten page. The black shootist explained his relationship with Lockhart and it being the reason he wanted to deliver the letter personally. He said this was his first trip riding shotgun after the attempted holdup and his wounds.

For the first time, Crawfish noticed the black man was well armed, wearing a holstered, black-handled .44 Remington revolver on a silver-appointed gunbelt strapped over his navy blue vest. A second matching gun was shoved into his belt in the middle of his stomach.

"Of course! Of course!" Crawfish waved the letter. "I should have guessed. Lockhart told us about you. In a wire. Seems a long time ago now." He lowered the sheet and frowned. "How are you?"

Beezah raised his right arm to demonstrate his fitness. "I am well, Governor. Beezah's body heals fast."

"I heard Dr. Milens broke out of the Cheyenne jail. A week ago, I think," Crawfish said. "What happened?"

Shaking his head, Beezah said, "I am not certain. It came while the town constable and his deputies were on guard." The black man's eyebrows arched in disbelief. "From what I heard, the spiritualist talked them into doing a séance, hypnotized them and got ahold of the keys."

"Did his gang escape, too?"

"Yes. All of them, except the two women assistants. They had been transferred to a hotel room—and kept under guard," Beezah said. "That's why I am riding shotgun now. I'm a little weak, but I felt I owed it to the company. They were good to me."

"They're lucky to have you."

Beezah laughed. "I now check everyone riding on the stage roof—for guns." He frowned and added that U. S. Marshal John Hogan said Dr. Milens was furious at Vin Lockhart, blaming him for the arrest and the subsequent stopping of his first jailbreak attempt.

"Do they know where that bunch was headed?" Crawfish asked.

"Well, the last I heard, Marshal Hogan was leading a posse. Headed west. But that was two weeks ago. At least. I suppose Dr. Milens and his bunch could be anywhere. When I got to Denver, there was a report the gang had been seen just outside of town. Who knows? All I really know is they didn't try to rob the stage." He nodded to emphasize the point.

Crawfish's thin eyebrows jumped in response to the last bit of news. The corner of his mouth twitched in rhythm with the movement. He listened intently as Beezah told him of the initial arrest and Lockhart's role in it, and his stopping the gang's first attempt to escape. All of it had come to the black guard secondhand from Marshal Hogan.

"Well, I'm sure the authorities will catch them soon enough."

"Let us hope so. The Sioux and Cheyenne are enough worry, running wild all around up there. Some fear Crazy Horse himself is going to attack Deadwood," Beezah said. "It doesn't seem to me that the army moves very fast."

"No, it doesn't," Crawfish replied.

Beezah nodded. "Ah, did you hear Wild Bill Hickok has been murdered?" He continued without waiting for an answer. "He was shot in the back of the head. By a fellow named McCall."

"Really? Oh my gosh, how awful! Vin told us in a wire about meeting him—and you." Crawfish glanced at the sun, which was nearing its zenith in the sky. "Do you have time to eat? I'd enjoy hearing more. About Vin. About you."

"I go out again tomorrow morning, Governor," Beezah said. "I would like to talk with you. Perhaps we should do it out here. Black men are not exactly welcome in most places."

"You're welcome here." Martha motioned toward the house. Her eyes sparkled with defiance.

Both Beezah and Crawfish glanced at her, as if not realizing she and Falling Leaf had been standing there all this time. Beezah looked surprised and pleased. So did Crawfish. He hadn't talked about blacks with the Rhymers, but both had welcomed Falling Leaf like she was a long-lost aunt.

"That is most gracious of you, madam," Beezah said, "but I would not want to cause you any trouble."

Martha completed the welcome, wiping her hands against a wrinkled apron at her waist. "Mr. Crawford, you and Mr. Beezah go on back and tell Harry and Sean that dinner will be ready in fifteen minutes." Her attention returned to Falling Leaf who was still studying the open land. "Falling Leaf . . . Vin Lockhart . . . will come . . . later . . . ah, many . . . suns . . . from now." Her words were deliberately slow, hoping they would be understood.

Falling Leaf nodded her head to indicate she understood. Without waiting for further response, Martha took Falling Leaf's hand and turned toward the house. As they retreated, Falling Leaf peeked over her shoulder at the vacant hillside, then at the cat sitting on Beezah's saddle, then at Beezah himself, and back to the door. She halted, pulled her hand free and went to Beezah's horse to retrieve the cat. Her smile was broad as she carried it to the house, along with her pipe bag. Martha had already disappeared inside.

Watching her, Beezah smiled his approval.

"Well, Jean-Jacques, we have an assignment." Crawfish waved toward the corral. "Please call me Crawfish. Everyone does."

"I thank you for the kindness. All of your kindnesses. It is easy to see why you and Vin Lockhart are friends. He saved my life."

From his pocket, Beezah withdrew the small black stone he carried and told about its significance, and Lockhart giving him a small pebble to hold, one that was also magical, and Lockhart's efforts to help him heal.

As they walked, Crawfish explained the development of the horse ranch. He pointed out Magic, the bay stallion in the second corral and said they were expecting some good colts next spring and summer. Beezah asked if they were interested in selling horses to the stage line, indicating he would arrange a meeting with the manager. Crawfish thanked him for the offer but that the operation would be under Lockhart's direction when he returned.

They stopped beside the under-construction house. Ominis wasn't in sight. Hammering inside indicated where he was. Crawfish explained what the construction was all about and Beezah seemed impressed.

"Did you grow up in New Orleans?" Crawfish asked, then realized such a question might be misunderstood. "Forgive me. I wasn't riding your back trail as some like to say around here. But your manner of speaking isn't . . . Cajun."

"I did not take it that way. I was born in Haiti. Grew up there. Mostly in Port-au-Prince. Came to New Orleans as a man. A young man." He patted his guns. "My skill was rewarded well. It was not so in Haiti."

"You know I read a fascinating book about the Caribbean—and Haiti," Crawfish said, ignoring the comment about gunfighting and resuming his walk toward the corral.

They began an energetic conversation about Haiti with the red-haired businessman eager to share his new knowledge of the small country.

Returning his derby to his head, Beezah raised his chin proudly and announced, "I am named for Jean-Jacques Dessalines, the father of the republic."

"Names-and-glories, that's great," Crawfish said and resumed bubbling forth what he knew about the region, sounding very much like the teacher he had once been.

As they walked, Crawfish waved at Sean in the corral without pausing in his dissertation. From atop the brown gelding, Sean waved back, then patted the horse's neck and resumed working the horse. Leaning against a corral pole, Harry turned, waved his own greeting and shouted encouragement to the boy.

"Are you a follower of voodoo, then?" Crawfish asked, stepping around an unused saddle propped on its side ten feet from the corral gate. A folded saddle blanket lay across its mantle. He noted to himself that Harry encouraged switching saddles often; the older man thought it helped keep back sores from occurring on the green horses. Crawfish guessed it had to do with keeping the leather and saddle blankets dry.

"Yes, I am." Beezah stepped to the other side of the saddle and continued to the corral itself. "Vin and I decided voodoo and the Oglala religion had . . . ah, things in common." He smiled widely. "Maybe something in common with Dr. Milens, too. We believe in communicating with the spirits. They work between man and the all-powerful God, *Nana Buluku*."

"I'm not sure how much communicating with the spirits Milens did." Crawfish reached the corral and waved both his arms to get the attention of Sean and Harry. "Martha says dinner's ready—and I want you to meet a friend of Vin's. He just brought us a letter from him!"

Sean's face lit up and he reined the horse to a stop. "When's he coming home?"

"Soon, I hope," Crawfish said and explained the content of the letter.

Harry wobbled toward Beezah and Crawfish, and Crawfish introduced the two men. Discussion ensued about Lockhart and the letter. Crawfish reached into his coat pocket to retrieve it, but Harry told him to wait because his glasses were in the house.

"Let's wash up. Don't want to keep Martha waiting," Harry said cheerfully.

"You're in for a treat, Jean-Jacques," Crawfish said. "Martha is one fine cook."

"I look forward to the meal—and the friendship."

CHAPTER TWENTY-SEVEN

After washing up and leaving their hats outside on the back porch, the men entered the house and walked past the rolltop desk with the framed hand-drawn map of the ranch above it. Beezah noticed a well-used Bible lying on its top. He glanced at Crawfish, but the businessman was talking with Sean about Lockhart.

Smells from the kitchen were tantalizing. The house was small and tidy, swept clean just this morning. On the north wall of the dining area, set off from the kitchen, was a framed Currier & Ives print of a mountain scene. It was one of Harry's proudest possessions, in spite of the inexpensive framing. The table was set with care and a bouquet of flowers, the last of the year, in a green glass container, decorated the center of the table.

Harry pointed at a chair for Beezah and sat. The others followed quickly. Martha brought a large, steaming bowl of stew, then a platter of biscuits, and filled the white cups with boiling coffee. A bowl of jam and another of butter was added to the table.

Falling Leaf was not in sight; she was feeding the cat, the

"little panther" she called it. She joined them as they prepared for grace, carrying her heavy pipe bag. After their dinner prayer, Martha said that the Indian woman had been outside, paying tribute to her God, as Mr. Lockhart does.

Sitting between Sean and Crawfish, Falling Leaf laid the pipe bag in her lap and stared at Beezah. Finally she asked Crawfish if the black man was a medicine man, then if he knew about Lockhart. The words came in a mixture of Lakotan and English. Crawfish explained the situation and shared the essence of Lockhart's letter, trying to find the right words in her native tongue.

She asked another question that he didn't understand, something he thought had to do with why someone was following Beezah and if they were spirits. He realized his knowledge of the Lakotan language and hers of English created many pockets of misunderstanding and decided not to pursue the matter.

"When do you think Vin will be home?" Sean blurted, interrupting the exchange.

"Wish I knew, Sean." Crawfish sipped his coffee, understanding the boy's eagerness.

"Ye be thinkin' hisself'll be likin' the way Magic be doin? An' the others?" Sean shoved a big spoonful of chunks of meat, potato, carrot and broth into his mouth, followed by a bite of a biscuit lathered with jam and butter.

"Of course he will."

Sean shook his head. "Me not so sure. He be soundin' strong on that dun, he be."

Crawfish smiled and asked Beezah if he had seen the horses Lockhart mentioned in his letter. Beezah started to answer when they heard a thud at both the front and back doors, followed by heavy boots. Before anyone could rise from their chairs, Dr. Milens entered from the back door. His clothes were filthy and his face indicated he hadn't shaved or washed in a long time. His normally placid face was sunburned; his hair, disheveled; and his piercing green eyes, narrowed into slits. At his side was Nolan Gleason. A step behind came Frank Diede and Old Man Grinshaw from the front door. All brandished revolvers; Gleason held two.

"How nice, just sitting down to eat. Quite a cozy little place you have here, Mr. Crawford. Where's that bastard Vin Lockhart?" Dr. Milens snarled.

Crawfish pushed on his wire-rimmed glasses and tried to think. He wasn't armed, having decided it wasn't necessary any longer.

"Oh no! This is my fault!" Beezah moaned. "They followed me here."

Dr. Milens sneered at the black guard. "You egotistical darkie, we didn't even know you were alive." He waved his gun in Old Man Grinshaw's direction. "Check out the house to make sure he's not hiding somewhere."

The gray-haired outlaw snorted and spun around. He bumped against the end table next to the worn settee and sent the purple-and-gold vase crashing to the floor. Martha let out a whimper. Grinshaw hesitated momentarily and headed into the bedroom.

Gleason stared at the broken vase and giggled. "Oh-ho. Old man Grinshaw was a naughty boy."

Dr. Milens frowned at Gleason, then turned his gun—and stare—back to Crawfish. "Nolan here went into your fancy hotel and asked where you were. Your clerk was most helpful, gave us directions. Easy as can be."

"Aaron Whitaker told you Vin was here?" Crawfish asked; the corner of his mouth twitched. "Vin is up north. Has been for months."

"If that's your clerk's name, no, he didn't. He said you were here. He didn't know where Lockhart was." Walking over to the seated Crawfish, he jammed the barrel of his gun against the businessman's temple. "Where is your meddling friend? Tell me or I'll put your brains—what there is of them—against that wall."

"I just got a letter from him. That is why Mr. Beezah is

here. He brought it," Crawfish said, motioning toward Beezah. "Vin Lockhart is, ah, up north. With the Fifth Cavalry. Just left General Merritt's camp to find some friends of ours."

"Bullshit!" Dr. Milens said. "Try again. There won't be a third."

"Please," Crawfish said without moving. "The letter is in my pocket. I'll show it to you."

"Let's see it." Dr. Milens lowered the gun and motioned toward Crawfish's coat.

Crawfish handed over the folded paper from his coat pocket and Dr. Milens said, "Watch 'em, while I read this."

"Sure, Jefferson. Say, this chow looks awfully good. Can we eat before we leave?" the square-faced Gleason said, motioning toward the food with one of his two handguns.

Crawfish frowned and wondered why he called the mesmerist that and just as quickly decided it didn't matter. He glanced at Beezah, but the black shootist was sitting with his hands folded on the table as if praying.

"Of course," Dr. Milens muttered, then looked up. "Well, the fool was telling the truth. Lockhart is long gone. He's headed for the Bighorn Mountains."

"We're not waiting for him, are we?" Frank Diede asked, tugging on the bent brim of his bell-crown hat with dirt-covered fingers and scratched his stomach where the earlier gunshot wound had not yet healed.

"Of course not, you fool," Dr. Milens snarled. "If I can't have his head, I'm going to do the next best thing. I'm going to give him hell." Dr. Milens licked his lower lip. He looked thoroughly insane. "He'll come riding in here and find his ranch burned to the ground, his horses gone—and his friends hanging from trees. Rotted. Should be quite a sight."

Martha whimpered and began to sob. With her hands in her lap, Falling Leaf said something comforting in Lakotan.

Returning to the dining area, Grinshaw announced, "Lockhart ain't around."

"I already know that." Dr. Milens waved the letter. "What do you figure we can get for that herd of horses?"

"At least fifty a head. That bay stud, he'll go for a lot more," the gray-headed outlaw replied, grinning savagely. "We'll have to drive 'em south, though. Safer than robbin' a bank, Jefferson. Might be more profitable, too."

"Of course."

Sean jumped from the seat. "Ye be leavin' Magic alone!"

"Shut up, kid." Gleason pointed his gun at the Irish boy. "An' sit your Irish ass down—or I'll sit it for you."

Crawfish reached over and touched the boy's arm. "Sit down, Sean. Please."

Sean's face was hot. There was no fear in his eyes, only anger. But he obeyed. Reluctantly.

"Hey, what's with the redskin?" Grinshaw said, his weathered face crinkling even more into disgust. "Can you beat that? A redskin—an' a darkie. You people are really somethin' . . . to spit at."

"Stand up, darkie." Dr. Milens remembered Beezah and aimed his gun at him. "Didn't think you would make it."

Pushing back his chair, Beezah rose slowly. "I was cured by a magic stone. It has cured others. It comes from Haiti. A sorcerer made it for me. It is special."

"What?" Nolan said. "Whaddya mean?"

Dr. Milens smiled, a vicious smile. "Let's see this magic stone, darkie. I might want to use it in my next séance. When we get to California."

"Certainly. It is in my pocket." Beezah raised his hands toward his vest.

"No, first you take those guns out—and put them on the table. Real easy like," Dr. Milens commanded. "Make the wrong move and I'll find that stone myself—over your dead-ass black body."

Without a word, Beezah withdrew the two revolvers, one in each hand with his fingers barely grasping the handles, and placed them on the table. Dr. Milens nodded approval and motioned with his gun for him to resume his search for the stone.

Almost ceremoniously, Beezah's left hand went to the right-hand vest pocket first, followed by his right. His left hand held open the pocket's lip as he reached inside with his other hand to withdraw the stone.

He paused with his hands at the pocket and stared at Crawfish. "It's like you were telling me earlier, Crawfish," Beezah said, straight-faced; his hands, frozen in place at his vest pocket. "Not everyone should touch this stone. Isn't that what you said?"

Crawfish was puzzled. He hadn't said anything like that. What was Beezah doing? What did he want?

"You should tell the spiritualist," Beezah urged, "what you said."

Crawfish's cheek twitched. "Ah . . . sure." He turned toward Dr. Milens. If he was right, Beezah wanted the evil mesmerist distracted for a moment. "Dr. Milens, I have seen healing stones. Like this. It is sacred. It is voodoo," Crawfish said, holding his hands out toward him and wiggling them to represent power. "It must not be used for evil. It is too powerful. You must promise."

Dr. Milens threw back his head and guffawed loudly, then glanced at Frank Diede. "You can count on that. Right, Frank?"

"Right." Diede joined the laughter.

Still chuckling, Dr. Milens spun to face Beezah as the black man's derringer cleared his vest pocket and fired. Twice. Dr. Milens's gun exploded and the bullet shattered the stew bowl, spraying food in every direction. The gun slid from his hand and Dr. Milens crumpled to the floor, crying in pain.

Frank Diede stopped scratching his stomach and looked like a man who didn't believe what had just happened.

From her lap, Falling Leaf lifted her Le Faucheux revolver, firing at Nolan Gleason to her right as it cleared the table. Martha screamed and hid her face in her hands. The first bullet struck the outlaw in his right shoulder, punching him sideways and forcing the revolver from his hand; the second, misfired.

Beezah dropped the empty derringer and reached his guns on the table, tossing one in Crawfish's direction as he brought the other into firing position in his right hand. All in one blurred motion. His silver revolver roared three times, once at each standing outlaw.

Frank Diede shivered, dropped his gun and grabbed his right arm in pain. "God dammit, I'm shot. Again! Damn. Oh-h-h-h-h." He went to his knees, groaning.

Harry stood in front of his chair and grabbed Gleason's pistol.

Beezah's second shot spun Gleason around again and the outlaw reached out for Grinshaw as he stumbled. His third shot hit Grinshaw high in the chest. He stutter-stepped backward and Falling Leaf fired at him, hitting him in the left forearm. Her fourth shot misfired. Adjusting to the impact of the two bullets, Grinshaw fired quickly at Beezah, missing; then at the Indian woman just as Sean took a step and dove at him, forcing the gun to shoot high. Grinshaw clubbed Sean's head with the barrel of his gun and cocked it and then stopped.

Facing him were Beezah, Falling Leaf, Harry and Crawfish with their revolvers pointed at him.

"Looks like I'm staring at a stacked deck," Grinshaw growled. "Mama didn't raise no fools. I'm too old for this crap—an' these boys couldn't shoot their way out of an outhouse." He let his gun drop from his hand and raised his hand. A small hole in his chest was turning red, as was the lower part of his left shirtsleeve.

"Watch him, Jean-Jacques—and Harry," Crawfish said and moved beside the unconscious Irish boy, studying the bloody cut in his head.

From the far side of the table, Harry snorted. "If that boy's hurt bad, mister, I'm gonna skin your goddamn hide."

He glanced at the crying Martha and the worried Falling Leaf, now both on the floor beside Crawfish. "Sorry, dear."

She nodded her understanding and rose. "I'll get some hot water and a cloth."

"Thanks, Martha," Crawfish said.

Harry's face was crimson as he rambled toward them from the far side of the table. Beezah watched him pass, then returned his attention to the outlaws. Harry walked around the table and kicked Milens's side to check his status.

Groaning, Milens drew up his legs like a child.

Bounding up to the gray-haired outlaw, Harry stopped. "You no-good piece of horse dung. You hurt a fine boy." Before anyone realized what he was doing, the old horseman clubbed Grinshaw along the side of the head with his gun barrel. Grinshaw's hands withered to his sides and his body completed the descent.

Harry stared at the fallen outlaw, thrust out his chin and quietly returned to his chair, keeping his revolver on the outlaws.

"Harry . . . Sean's coming around." Crawfish half-yelled his enthusiasm.

"What?"

"Sean's coming around."

Harry jumped up from his chair and returned to the downed boy. Beezah resumed the chore of guarding the outlaws without being asked.

"W-What h-happened? D-Did I?" Sean stared at the four adults close to him. Martha wiped the moistness from her eyes; Falling Leaf muttered something in Lakotan; Harry mumbled a combination of joy and concern; and Crawfish patted the boy's shoulder and told him to rest easy, that all was well.

Standing to let Martha and Falling Leaf tend to him, Crawfish turned to Beezah. "You've saved our lives, my friend. We are in your debt."

"Nay, the debt is only even. Vin Lockhart saved mine first," Beezah said. "The spirits deemed it so."

A half hour later, Sean was resting in the Rhymers' bed with a wrap around his head and both older women tending to him. Harry had hitched up a team to his buckboard and was waiting out front for the outlaws, wounded and tied, to be brought for a ride to Denver.

Crawfish kept a gun on Diede, Grinshaw and Gleason while Beezah half-carried, half-dragged Dr. Milens outside to the waiting vehicle.

As they cleared the door, Dr. Milens mumbled, "T-There never was . . . a magic stone, was t-there?"

Beezah smiled. "Of course there was." He patted his vest pocket. "But you forgot to ask the spirits' permission to see it."

"W-What spirits?"

"Ah, Governor, if you really could communicate with them, you'd know."

Chapter Twenty-eight

A hot August sun lay across his shoulders, forcing Vin Lockhart's mind to race ahead to Morning Bird. For days now, the closer he got to where he thought the tribe was hiding, the more he was afraid of the reaction he might get from her. It had been more than a year since they had been together. Long enough to have forgotten him.

Why did he think she would wait? Because he said he would return? She was probably married now. Maybe with child even. The thought made him nauseated and he vomited on the side of the trail. Riding on, he tried to focus on finding the small village. Follow his instincts, like Stone-Dreamer had taught him. Was this another way of saying listen to the stones talk to you? He wondered and patted his shirt pocket where the cardinal feathers were kept. They felt warm to his touch.

If he was right, Black Fire's band would be camping within a thickly timbered creek line where they had often gone when Lockhart was with them. It was more than a day's ride, more like two, and almost due north. The location had proved an excellent natural protection for the tribe. A twisted wall of underbrush and saplings, butted up against huge shadow caves of dense greasewood, cottonwood and willow trees, and flanked by towering pines that made it impossible to see through—or think there was an opening large enough just on the other side for Black Fire's lodges. In his mind, he was already there.

He reined up to read the trail ahead of him. Wiping the sweat from his neck, he brushed against the Eyes-of-the-Wind pebble hanging from his ear. A rawhide string was looped over it and tied to the small stone. He had been wearing it since leaving Cody and the Fifth Cavalry. He eased his legs from the stirrups and straightened them. Both his leg and arm were healing, but stiff, from the Cheyenne fight and long days in the saddle. He could endure the pain for as long as it took, he told himself.

In spite of his desire to get to the tribe as quickly as possible, he had taken good care that his horses, especially the dun, did not get worn down. Several times, he had switched to one of the three Cheyenne war ponies on a lead rope behind him. One carried a pack of supplies as if it had been trained to do so since it was a yearling.

He had cut across a cavalry column headed northeast. A full column with at least twenty outriders. Scouts, he assumed. They were almost a day ahead of him, judging by the softening of the edges of the tracks. He hadn't seen riders of any kind since he left Cody. And these were the first tracks.

When he left Cody, Crook and his force of 1,800 troopers, including the Fifth Cavalry, and 250 Shoshonis and 200 civilian guides and packers, had joined Terry and his force of 1,700 troops at his new camp near the mouth of the Rosebud. They were behind somewhere. Quite a ways, he thought. However, Terry had several cavalry units out on serious probes of the region. This was obviously one of them.

There were fresh rumors that the Cheyenne were headed north to settle into a winter camp and withdraw from further fighting. Many of the Hunkpapas were moving toward the invisible medicine line and Grandmother's Land for safety. Sitting Bull was supposedly leading them, but it wasn't clear.

Jokingly, Cody had said the army thought the main Indian camp, led by Crazy Horse, was either at the Little Missouri, or the Killdeer Mountains, or Slim Buttes, or maybe the Short Pine Hills, or Powder River. Or even the Black Hills. A winter campaign, if decided upon, would be hard on everyone involved. Especially the Indians. The army badly wanted Crazy Horse, but they would attack any and all encampments found.

That fear drove Lockhart.

Before leaving the camp, Cody saw to it that Lockhart had fresh provisions and ammunition. Cody had wished him well and reminded Lockhart that he was still welcome in his theater group if he should ever change his mind. In turn, Lockhart had reminded Cody that he was always welcome as his guest at the Black Horse and the Silver Queen. Just in case it was needed, Cody gave him a letter indicating Lockhart was riding scout for the Fifth. It was even signed by General Merritt; Cody didn't say how he obtained the signature.

Lockhart eased the dun forward and the string of war ponies behind him reacted appropriately. This time his mind slipped to a happy moment last summer when he had returned to his old village with Touches-Horses after securing his escape from Farrell and his outlaws. The sweet intoxication of Morning Bird. Her eyes caressing his. Inviting him close. Their parting had been difficult, but he had to return; he did not belong with the tribe any longer. Most of them thought of him as a spirit.

He had promised to return for her. Now he was keeping that promise. Would she even remember it? Few times in his life could he recall ever being so uncertain, so anxious. He tried to prepare himself for the worst, the rejection. Polite, of course. But nonetheless, a rejection. Clearing the ridge, Vin Lockhart's attention was drawn to a sight almost a half mile away. He knew what it was immediately and the nausea climbed back into this throat.

Bodies were strewn about the open plains. Black shapes against Mother Earth's robe of brown and green. Either the cavalry he was following had been ambushed—or they had found and attacked a band of hostiles. A lone feather, then another, dark spindles against the sun, fluttered in the air from where they were attached to an inert shape and Lockhart had his answer even from this distance.

As he rode closer, his gaze took in the full impact of the horrible sight. Indians lay where they had died, fighting without cover or the chance for escape. Caught in the open by an overwhelming number of mounted soldiers. Were they headed to the reservation? He had a hunch they were. If so, they might have thought the advancing cavalry was coming to escort them there. Until it was too late.

He stopped twenty feet from the first downed casualty and dismounted near a lone cluster of scrub oak trees; one barely four feet tall. They were the only trees for two hundred yards in any direction. None of his horses, including his dun, wanted to go closer to the stench of death. He unlooped the lead rope from his saddle horn and tied it to a sturdy branch, then did the same with the dun's reins.

Although there didn't appear to be any need for it, he yanked his Winchester free of its scabbard anyway, cocked it and started toward the small massacre. The heavy metallic readying gave a sense of purpose that belied what was before him. The worry that was climbing within him turned into reality as he recognized the closest dead warrior.

Black Fire!

The steady leader lay with oozing black holes on his warshirt and leggings and one in his head. He had been scalped. Scalped! His body lay across his dead wife—and two children. He had tried to shield them from the rain of bullets that killed them. Lifeless shapes. The attack had come this morning, he guessed. It was over quickly.

Lockhart stopped, not believing his eyes. The bodies were a mix of men, but mostly of women and children. Where were all the warriors? He fought his mind to keep it from telling them his friends would be here. He walked among the dead, hoping he wouldn't find the bodies of those he cared most about. His old friend, Bear-Heart, was sprawled on the earth, killed in fierce battle. The ground beneath had turned black from his blood. He, too, had been scalped; his head, now a mass of dried blood and skin. The wing of a magpie, the messenger of the North Wind, dangled from what remained of his hair. The massive necklace of bear claws he had always worn had been yanked away.

Not far from him was the lifeless body of another old friend, Thunder Lance. His death grip held a familiar lance, decorated with eagle feathers, strips of otter fur and special beads to represent the Thunder-Beings. A small pouch of war medicine was bound to the lance just above his hands.

Sings-With-Stones lay beneath a dead horse. Lockhart had once been jealous of the young warrior. Stone-Dreamer had become a second father to him because the warrior had received a stone-vision and he hoped to learn from the holy man's teachings and become a shaman. Lockhart wondered why the stones hadn't alerted him to this danger.

He walked slowly through the death circle. Several women cradling small children were frozen shapes. Strewn about the area of death were lodgepoles and travoises, signs of a moving village. Only a few horses were dead.

Either the cavalry had run them off—or most of the tribe was walking.

His head was swimming with fear, anger and remorse. He had not found Stone-Dreamer. Or Touches-Horses. Or Morning Bird. For that, he tried to be thankful. But it didn't mean they were alive. What if the soldiers had taken her to . . .

He screamed into the still air and fell to his knees. No words came. Only a scream that sounded more like the panther of his vision than that of a human.

How long he knelt there he wasn't sure, but the sun was pushing against the horizon when he finally stood again. His shoulders rose and fell, and he tried to study the scene objectively. Clearly, many warriors were not there. Only those who had families. He was certain Black Fire was leading them to the reservation. It was the only thing that made sense. The cavalry had seen them and charged. The few warriors with the tribe had fought bravely. It looked to him that the soldiers had taken away weapons for trophies as well as scalps. One woman had been scalped; he turned away from the sight. She was Blue Sky, the mother of Sings-With-Stones. He hadn't seen the young warrior's father, but he guessed that body was there, too mangled to identify.

Everything in him wanted to follow after the cavalry and take revenge. Their trail led to the east. Revenge. Hot, black revenge filled his soul and he stood shaking with anger. How could the *wasicun* be so evil? How could they despise people they didn't even know? In spite of himself, he looked again at the scalped woman.

He swung the rifle to his shoulder as if to begin a march and knocked the stone from his ear. It fell to the earth and he stood, looking at the small shape. A thought washed over him, if Stone-Dreamer, Touches-Horses and Morning Bird weren't here, where were they? Had they stayed behind in the camp—with the missing warriors? Seeking revenge only meant death; finding them meant a great deal more. He leaned over to retrieve the earpiece. Had it spoken to him?

In minutes he was riding again. There was no time to bury the dead; he would have to leave that to Mother Earth. Ahead of him, twisting toward the one-time camp, were conflicting sets of tracks. Faint trails, coming and going, consisted of unshod horses, moccasin prints and long lines of lodgepoles being dragged. A small village moving their lodges, their women, their children, then moving again. He rode steadily into the settling dusk.

Early the next morning, his weary eyes studied the timbered land looking for a crease where the Indians had slipped through. As he slipped between two lodgepole pines and headed northeast, he began to yell loudly, "*Hokay!* It is a good day to die. I am Oglala. Only the earth and sky live forever. It is a good day to die." The Oglala battle cry was followed by the Kit Fox song, "I am a Fox . . . I am supposed to die . . ." He ended with the loud statement, "I am Panther-Strikes. I am an Oglala warrior who rode with Black Fire. I am the son of Stone-Dreamer. I am a brother to Touches-Horses."

Clearing the natural tree walls that encircled the small village, he came to a stop. Nothing was in sight, except two upright tepees. The rest had been there and had gone.

"*Kola.* Brother, I knew you would come," came an invisible, but familiar, voice in Lakotan.

Coming around the closest lodge was Touches-Horses, thinner than Lockhart last saw him, but smiling broadly. Jumping from his horse, Lockhart grasped Touches-Horses's forearm in the traditional warrior's salute; then they hugged each other heartily. Stepping back from the emotional reunion, the warrior explained the tribe had split. Painted Badger had taken all of the young warriors with him to join Crazy Horse; Black Fire had taken the rest of the village to go to the *wasicun's* agency two days ago. Touches-Horses had stayed behind, as had Morning Bird, to be with Stone-Dreamer who was dying.

Hearing that Morning Bird was here caused Lockhart to look around. She must be in Stone-Dreamer's lodge, he decided. His nerves were on edge and he tried to calm himself. In halting Lakotan, he said, "I came for you and for my father . . . and for Morning Bird. If she wants to come." He swallowed back the anxiety of what response his statement might bring, then told his former brother-in-law of the massacre.

Touches-Horses dropped his eyes to the ground and groaned as the significance of the destruction of Black Fire's group reached his soul. He staggered and Lockhart held the warrior's arm to keep him from falling.

"It is as Stone-Dreamer said. Our days are over."

"Not if you come with me." Lockhart told him about the horse ranch and that they could live there, but added that they needed to go before the soldiers found them. He hadn't used the Lakotan language so much in years. Some of the words came hard.

The idea of the ranch reached Touches-Horses's eyes for the first time and he blinked away the tension. Such a choice had never occurred to him. Never.

With a long inhalation, Touches-Horses stared into Lockhart's eyes. "My sister, Morning Bird, she waits for you. In Stone-Dreamer's lodge. He told her that you would come. He told her that you wanted her. She cried." With a deep sigh, he led the way, walking the few steps to Stone-Dreamer's painted lodge.

Speaking softly, Touches-Horses said, "Your father has not been well since the fight at the greasy grass." He swallowed and added, "He was rejected when he tried to counsel the tribe to leave that area and wait for you. After that, the Grandfathers told him to come home."

An eight-inch clay figure rested upon a skin of white ermine in front of the lodge's opening. Lockhart knew this was the image of the Great Spirit from Stone-Dreamer's medicine bundle. He hadn't actually seen the totem before; it was rarely displayed—but he knew what it was, from years-ago descriptions of others. Next to the *wankan* piece was a smaller deerskin cutout in the shape of a man; buffalo wool was attached to represent the man's hair. Encircling both shapes was the gold chain and watch he had given to Stone-Dreamer as a present.

The piece was a representation of him. He winced at the thought. More surprising was to see his own medicine shield on display next to the tepee, the shield he carried as a warrior. Around it were four slender sticks, placed upright in the ground. Tied to each stick was a buckskin bag of tobacco and willow bark, an offering to *Wakantanka*. Laying beneath the shield was a red-painted buffalo skull. Three stones in a row, also painted red, lay a few inches from the top of the head, as if a crown.

Standing outside the lodge, Lockhart choked and said, "Father, it is Panther-Strikes. It is your son. I have come to take you with me."

There was a rustling inside the tepee, then several mumbled phrases that sounded like pieces of prayer, and a weak invitation to enter. Lockhart went inside the lodge to see a pale Stone-Dreamer lying on a painted buffalo robe. His usual white buckskin shirt and leggings were filthy. Entering behind Lockhart, Touches-Horses said quietly that the streaks of blood along the holy man's right sleeve and shoulder belonged to Spotted Horse, who had died after the great battle at the greasy grass. Stone-Dreamer had tried to save him, but couldn't.

Kneeling at the old holy man's side was Morning Bird. She watched Lockhart enter. Her face was tense. Without words, her eyes sought Lockhart's directly, and held them seeking an answer, then glanced away.

"I have come for you, Morning Bird," Lockhart said, his voice billowing with emotion as he lifted the feathers from his pocket and displayed them. His Lakotan flowed as if he had never stopped speaking it. "I want you to be my wife—and to go with me to my home. To become as one as your birds of the morning have done. I have asked Touches-Horses to go as well. And now I ask Stone-Dreamer."

Morning Bird rose in one motion, tears washed across her tan cheeks and her whole body trembled. She half-fell, half-ran to Lockhart and wrapped her arms around him. The cardinal feathers in her fist brushed against his neck.

They embraced and the world was only them.

She whispered in Lakotan, "My heart ached for you. I think you not come back. I think you care for me then only because of my sister." Her voice lay across his fevered face like a gentle spring breeze. Holding up two cardinal feathers like his, she said, in hesitant English, "I . . . Morning . . . Bird, I . . . love . . . you."

"When I first saw you, that is so. But you are very different than your sister." Lockhart choked, glancing at the feathers in his hand. "I love the difference." In English, he added, "I love you. You, Morning Bird. I want us to have many children together."

"To raise them as *wasicun*?" she asked gently in Lakotan.

"To raise them to be free and strong—and caring."

"I want the same. With all my heart, I am yours." She laid her feathers in his hand with his two.

Stone-Dreamer's feeble words broke into their reverie. "M-My son! M-My son! I knew you would come. T-The *tunkan* sang to me. T-They told me you were coming." He pushed back from Lockhart. "T-They told me you were hurt. You were in a fight. Darkness surrounds Black Fire I am told. Where are the others?"

Kneeling by his father's side, Lockhart returned the small feathers to his pocket and said he had been attacked by a Cheyenne war party, but that his wounds were slight, then told of Black Fire's massacre and said again what he wished to do, take the three of them with him.

Stone-Dreamer held out a shaking hand for Lockhart to take. "T-The Grandfathers are with you, I see," Stone-Dreamer whispered. "I prayed to *Wakantanka* . . . that I might live long enough . . . to see you once more, my son. They have honored . . . my wish." He stopped talking, fought to breathe, then continued, "I-I know you did not . . . I-like my t-telling . . . about the G-Grandfathers . . . being with you. I-I k-know you did not. But t-they are, m-my son. They are."

Lockhart started to respond, but the dying holy man kept talking.

"I-It was they . . . who brought you h-here," Stone-Dreamer said. "A-A cave is n-near. R-Remember it? You and I went there . . . w-when you were a boy." He pointed a feeble finger toward the east, shut his eyes. "T-The stones there, they wait for me. Bury me there, my son. Do not have concern about a Ghost-Keeping Lodge. The Grandfathers will care for me." He rose slightly, using his arms for balance. "D-Do you wear the stone of Eyes-of-the-Wind?"

"Yes, my father." Lockhart touched his ear.

"You . . . and C-Crazy Horse . . . sacred stones . . ."

Lockhart whispered, "My father . . . I came back to tell you . . . the stones sang to me. They told me where you were. Eyes-of-the-Wind will guide you to the spirit land. He told me so."

Morning Bird reached up and touched the old man's face. "He is gone, my love."

It was raining the next morning when Lockhart, Morning Bird and Touches-Horses completed the burial scaffold in the cave and held the funeral ritual itself. They killed his fine white horse and laid its body near the four upright poles so Stone-Dreamer would have a good mount in the Other-Side-Land. His medicine bundle, medicine pipe and the watch and chain were laid beside the wrapped-in-buffalo-skin body. Stone-Dreamer's red shield was hung from a post on the west. Lockhart's shield was carried on his pack horse. The old holy man's lodge was ceremonially burned.

As they were preparing to ride away, Lockhart reined up, dismounted and removed his warrior shield from the pack. With Touches-Horses and Morning Bird silently watching, he laid it at the covered entrance to the cave.

Lockhart looked at Touches-Horses, then into Morning Bird's beaming face. At the corner of his eye, a tear was finding its way out. "The Grandfathers know you well. But the shield of your son, Panther-Strikes, will protect you on your way to the Ghost Road." He took a deep breath. "And I will be listening to the stones. Always."

GET 4 FREE BOOKS!

You can have the best Westerns delivered to your door for less than what you'd pay in a bookstore or online. Sign up for one of our book clubs today, and we'll send you 4 FREE* BOOKS, worth $23.96, just for trying it out...**with no obligation to buy, ever!**

Authors include classic writers such as **LOUIS L'AMOUR, MAX BRAND, ZANE GREY** and more; plus new authors such as **COTTON SMITH, JOHNNY D. BOGGS, DAVID THOMPSON** and others.

As a book club member you also receive the following special benefits:
- **30% off all orders!**
- **Exclusive access to special discounts!**
- **Convenient home delivery and 10 days to return any books you don't want to keep.**

Visit **www.dorchesterpub.com**
or call
1-800-481-9191

There is no minimum number of books to buy, and you may cancel membership at any time.
*Please include $2.00 for shipping and handling.